THORN IN MY SIDE

C. J. SKUSE

ONE PLACE. MANY STORIES

This novel is entirely a work of fiction. The names, characters and incidents portrayed in it are the work of the author's imagination. Any resemblance to actual persons, living or dead, events or localities is entirely coincidental.

HQ
An imprint of HarperCollins*Publishers* Ltd
1 London Bridge Street
London SE1 9GF

www.harpercollins.co.uk

HarperCollins*Publishers*
Macken House, 39/40 Mayor Street Upper,
Dublin 1, D01 C9W8, Ireland

This edition 2024

4

First published in Great Britain by
HQ, an imprint of HarperCollins*Publishers* Ltd 2023

ISBN: 9780008608347

This book contains FSC™ certified paper and other controlled sources to ensure responsible forest management.

For more information visit: www.harpercollins.co.uk/green

This book is set in 10.7/15.5 pt. Sabon by Type-it AS, Norway

Printed and Bound in the UK using 100% Renewable Electricity at CPI Group (UK) Ltd, Croydon, CR0 4YY

CJ Skuse was born in 1980 in Weston-super-Mare. She has two First Class degrees in Creative Writing and Writing for Young People, and aside from being a novelist works as a Senior Lecturer at Bath Spa University.

For the female geniuses I grew up watching on TV who moulded my funny bone – Caroline Aherne, Dawn French, Pauline Quirke, Jennifer Saunders and Victoria Wood.

He who dares not grasp the thorn
should never crave the rose.

ANNE BRONTË

January 2020

Friday, 24 January, 11.30 p.m. – John F. Kennedy International Airport, Queens, New York City

1. *People who hog airport seats for hours and when they finally vacate, you have to sit in the ghost of their arse warmth*
2. *People who crowd the baggage carousel*
3. *People who aren't ready when they're next in the security line. GET YOUR FUCKING SKECHERS OFF, KAREN.*
4. *Everyone involved with the movie version of* Cats *– also, Idris Elba as Macavity is off-the-charts hot in this but he's a cat. How am I meant to feel?! Like I want to shag a cat? I don't get it.*
5. *Mitch Silverton – the convicted sex offender currently living under the same roof as my daughter*

Don't look. Just don't look.

I march down endless walkways thronging with families studying leaflets for the Statue of Liberty and Empire State. I'm not looking at them. I'm not looking at their kids. I'm not looking at the other departure boards either because I am not going to London. I'm going to Gate C61 to get my connecting flight – Delta 762 to San Diego.

But there are so many children about. So many tiny reminders. Small, wriggling guilt trips everywhere I look. My throat constricts with every laugh; my stomach churns with every shriek or scream. Every single one of them sends my thoughts straight back to Ivy in my mind. Straight back to England, where I should be headed now. I should go to her. She needs me.

A ginger kid dances across my path, toy monkey wrapped around her waist. A small boy kicks his legs in his pushchair – he wants his cake *now*. A girl rides a blue Trunki; another sits on a luggage cart, pretending she's on a gondola. One noms on a colossal tit. In slings, on shoulders, running in shops, along travellators, walking a toy bunny along the back of her dad's seat.

Get out of my way. Get away from me.

I pass gate after gate seeing 'London – Boarding Soon' on the screen. 'London – Now Boarding'. London. London. London.

The place where Ivy is. My baby who needs me. My baby who is in danger.

I don't stop for the sandwich I've promised my grumbling stomach since Seren's house – instead I keep walking. Only six more hours and I'll be home, in my fiancé's arms. Raf will talk me back to sense. I just have to turn off my brain until I get to him. I doom-scroll the latest apocalypse trend, see what Flag Twitter's losing its shit about today. Someone's chopping coleslaw. Someone else is cancelling some singer for a tweet they sent eleven years ago. Someone's collapsed in the street in China and there's a video of it doing the rounds.

Ivy needs you. Your baby needs you.

No, she doesn't. Claudia won't let anything happen to Ivy. And Seren promised to keep a close eye on things. I'm allowed to call her once a month for updates. It'll be OK. Ivy doesn't need me, she's better off without me, that's what I try to tell myself. There's always another voice in my head though – the one that never leaves.

She needs her real mum. Ivy's living with a convicted sex offender.

I go into a shop and scan the mags. All the celebs are having babies. Smiling kids. Crying kids. Little shoes, little socks. Little girls.

Claudia married a sex offender. My baby lives with a sex offender.

I make a sharp U-turn and scan the books. It's all auto-biographies of gammony politicians and self-help books by middle-aged women who think you can be cured of anything by shoving a crystal up your backside.

The girl was thirteen. Mitch isn't a threat to Ivy. Seren said she would keep an eye on them.

Seren lives thousands of miles away from them. She can't do anything. Remember, she's lied to you before, hasn't she?

I arrive at the gate and present my boarding pass, trying to drown my inner thoughts with the conversations of others in the queue and the smell of freshly cooked churros at the Cinnabon concession.

You can save Ivy. You must kill Mitch. It's the only way to be sure.

Pretty sure I'm just quoting lines from *Aliens* now.

A baby is crying in the queue behind me. Far away, but not far enough.

I shove my earphones in. Beyoncé, 'Save the Hero'. It starts off soft and slow and pianoey. Not loud enough to mask the kid's wailing.

I haven't done my ten minutes of meditation today. I've been doing it since Mexico. Tenoch taught me how. I focus on my breaths – try to clear a space in all the mess. Hold for seven, out for four. Release them slowly. I am here. I am breathing. I am loved.

The universe loves you, Ophelia. The sun, the animals, your flowers, they love you. That's what Tenoch had told me. He wanted me to be better. Both he *and* Beyoncé were telling me how great I was, how loved I was, how they want me to be strong because I'm a hero; a hero who saved the world.

But what do YOU want? You want to kill Mitch. That's what you want.

I breathe away the time it takes for us to board the plane and take our seats. Once I'm ensconced by the window in Row 19, I feel somewhat at peace. Doing the right thing never feels right to me but that's why I gave her up in the first place, let's face it. To do the 'right' thing. Nobody needs a serial killer for a mother. Nobody needs *me*.

'Good evening, everyone, this is your captain speaking,' crackles the announcement. 'Welcome to your Delta Flight 762 to San Diego . . .'

The cabin doors close. They move the staircase away. The engines start up. There's no way back. There's nothing more I can do.

I'm going home.

My chest and head ache with short, stabbing pains, which could be the stirrings of a menstrual migraine but are more likely to be all the uncried tears screaming to get out. It feels like a heavy stone is sitting on my lungs. I turn off my music and open my Duolingo app to continue my Spanish tuition – twenty minutes a day for the past year. But I can't concentrate. Everything's annoying. Everything's fractious.

The kid next to me starts grizzling the second the plane begins its ascent. It *would* be a little girl – a tiny, chubby-legged toddling reminder of the girl I did not go to. Like the girl I have left at the mercy of a sex offender in England. Because I am a bad, bad mother. That's why I left her in the first place. Why I dumped her. The pain tightens.

'She'll settle down in a second.' The girl's mother nervous-laughs, flapping about like a fart in a colander, not knowing which hole to go out of, begging the kid to be quiet, squeaking her elephant toy, flicking through a lift-the-flap book about shapes, but the child is restless and nothing settles her.

Very much like myself.

Damn woman. Why bring a kid on a plane at this time of night? I try to breathe in a lungful of decent air but there's no such thing on an airplane – it's all farts, feet and Fenty perfume. An air stewardess who's all pinched and pouty, and as thin as my patience, minces along to check we're belted up.

Just bring the fucking drinks trolley already, Beverley! I think but I don't say it out loud; instead, I breathe the fart air and flick through the channels. It's a roll call of every programme and film I loathe. Unfunny animals. Unfunny comedians. Non-disabled actors in wheelchairs careening through pigeons on their way to their next Oscar. And an episode of *The Chase* where the stupid bitch takes the minus offer and STILL loses. Ugh.

7

The same thought whirls around my head and won't go away: I should have gone to Ivy. The airplane walls close in. Everything's so small, confined, like I'm a tin can in a garbage crusher.

But soon, we are airborne. What's done is done. And I have to live with being the worst mother in the universe.

Apart from the one next to me cos the kid is still screaming.

Once the seatbelt signs have gone off, the drinks trolley appears up ahead. I resolve to drink it dry. There's a touch on my left arm and I snap my head round to see the toddler standing on the middle seat, all shining eyes and biscuit drool. Tiny pudge arms. She smiles at me. And I do what I don't want to do, what every fibre in my body is telling me not to do: I melt.

'She's a good flier, apart from take-off,' Useless Mom tells me.

I lean forward and take Richard E. Grunt out of my bag, my little Sylvanians pig in his blue dungarees which I sprayed with Raf's cologne before I left home. I can't smell it anymore – I've sniffed him dry. Me and the kid play peekaboo with Dicky for a bit. She reaches for him when he disappears.

'Pig gone!' she cries.

I magic Richard up from my sleeve and her eyes widen and she makes a grab for him again. And it's the arrow straight to my heart. It's not so scary after all, engaging with a kid.

The girl looks at me, expressionless, reaching. 'Want pig! Want pig!'

No way, kid. This pig dies with me.

'Do you have kids yourself?' asks Useless Mom.

'Yes,' I say, as the snooty flight attendant with the severe Posh Spice haircut and hips like blades hands me my vodka and orange in my weak hand and my grip ain't great so I almost drop it all over the kid. Thank God for old Righty. Anyway, I knock it back in one. I ask for another and Bev gives the up-and-down eyes to judge me but pours it out regardless.

'I have a daughter. But she doesn't live with me.'

'I'm Kim,' says Useless Mom.

'Ophelia,' I say, breaking out my bestest all-American gal accent that I use on strangers. I show Kim the picture of Ivy that Seren let me keep.

Kim smiles. 'Oh, she's beautiful. What's her name?'

I don't want to lie. 'Ivy.'

'She looks just like you. This is Imani. I'm Kim.'

'She looks like her *dad*,' I say, staring at the picture. 'Curly caramel hair, a smile that could make the sun rise. That's all him, not me.'

'Would you watch her for me?' says Kim. 'I need the bathroom.'

'Yeah, OK.' She gets up and Imani gladly sits on my lap and plays with my phone, which is an old iPhone of Raf's with some games on it that I never play; shooting games that I find too loud and *Crash Bandicoot*, which gives me motion sickness. Imani's still asking for the pig every moment but I pop my earbuds in her ears so she can discover the delights of Queen Bey. I play 'Run the World' for her and she teaches me some fire baby moves.

'Again! Again!'

We read the in-flight magazine and it's all about Japan. There's an article about kintsugi – the Japanese art of mending broken crockery with gold to highlight its brokenness and make it even more beautiful.

9

'God the Japanese are bloody brilliant. Seriously. You can get like roast dinners from vending machines there and robot prostitutes. And they are actually growing melons with Hello Kitty already *on* them. They're *amazing*.' I order another voddy from Bitch Spice.

Imani smashes her way through the mag but she's getting bored so I take a pen out of my bag and hand it to her so she can draw all over Tom Cruise's pearly whites at some premiere.

'Did I do the right thing?' I ask her. 'I know I did – that's why I did it – but why does it feel so wrong? Maybe if I was on the London plane now, *that* would feel wrong. Everything's . . . wrong. I can't make myself feel better. And the vodka measures they give on this flight are a joke.'

As Imani's bent over the magazine, I tell myself not to but I do it anyway: I smell her hair. Milk and peaches. I get lost in it.

The girl looks back up, having completely scribbled out Cruise from existence. 'Want pig.'

'No, he's asleep.' I sniff her head again. 'What shampoo do you use?'

'Poo,' she replies.

I swear if I caught someone smelling my kid, I'd be wrapping their veins and arteries around me as an extra seatbelt, but I can't help myself. There's so much heaven on that one teeny head. I can't help but cuddle her in. I imagine she's Ivy. Within moments her head is heavy on my chest. I stroke her tiny eyebrows, aka kiddy catnip. Soon her eyes close altogether.

Kim returns from the toilet and goes to take her from me. I don't want to give her back but it's clear from the way she is extricating Imani that she is the one who gets the privilege of lollopy cuddles like this, not me.

I feel cold without Imani so I put Raf's North Face on and inhale what's left of his cologne in the collar, trying to get comfortable against the wall.

Kim picks up the *New York Post* when Imani's bundled in her blankets between us, fast asleep. She tries to make conversation about the coronavirus – 'It's already reached France' – and the *Seinfeld* repeat – 'God that Kramer is so funny' – but I ain't biting cos a) I don't care and b) no, he's not. Her clanging arm bracelets when she's yanking open her nuts have already pinned her in my mind as someone I'll never be friends with anyway and I'm too tired to pretend. We exchange moans about the turbulence over Tennessee and I catch her looking at the scars on my wrist.

I usually tell people it fell off from all the wanking, just to see the reaction on their faces, but today I wasn't in the mood for jollity. Mind you, the truth wasn't exactly an option either. There is no polite way of telling a stranger, *Oh, I hacked it off myself with a machete when I was handcuffed to a fender at the house of an ex-cartel hitman as his lieutenant ransacked the place for hidden money and he threatened to kill three children if I didn't tell him where it was. It was either that or watch them all die, one by one.*

I therefore resorted to some kind of bullshit in between the two.

'Caught it on a circular saw at the paper mill where I work. Came clean off, right before my eyes.'

I can tell Kim's shooketh; she's doing the hand-on-mouth thing. I've done that when I'm supposed to be shocked, like whenever I hear some relative has bitten the dust or see someone getting mugged.

'I've got some motor skills back. I can toss a baseball a fair distance now. And wrap birthday presents.'

'Does it hurt?'

'It aches sometimes. And I get a bit of numbness. I should be wearing my brace but it's at the bottom of my bag and I can't be bothered to fish it out. It hurt like a motherfucker when it first happened, before I passed out.'

Kim is left speechless and stops talking to me soon after. I don't know what I've said. Maybe I've sniffed my pig too much, I dunno. We were enthusing about our kids like two mums at the school gates hours before. A brief taste of normalcy, but those never last long. Not with me.

By the time we land at San Diego International, Imani doesn't give me a second look. I was once Superstar Plane Woman with Magical Defacing Pen and Talking Toy Pig. Now I'm the Stranger It Takes One Sleep to Forget.

I make it through security – always dicey – and walk through the maze of blazing white corridors. Everyone from my flight has scattered – gone to baggage claim or to be greeted by family. The California sky is dark through the windows towards Arrivals. There's a breeze as warm air gushes in through sliding doors. Kids scamper to relatives. Overtired babies grizzle on shoulders. I see Imani in the arms of a big, bald king-of-the-grill type in a checked shirt who cuddles her like she's the jewel he's crossed continents to find.

The thought returns – *I should have gone to England. I should have gone to Ivy and saved her. He could be hurting her right now. She's so far away.*

I head towards 'Exit' and 'Taxis' but I'm so tired I run out of steam before I get to the doors. I go to check the time on my phone but it's out of charge. It's been such a long day. My eyes sting. My feet throb. I can't face another journey. I can't face making small talk with another stranger. More bullshit burgers with a side order of lies.

I should have gone to my child. It's all my fault.

I sit on a vacant seat; sit and stare, like Tom Hanks in that movie where he's stuck in the airport with a bad accent for two hours. Neither here nor there. I don't know what to do. I'm in the plotline that God forgot all about. I've forgotten what our town is called. The number for Rafael's parents' place. My name is Ophelia now, not Rhiannon. I can't be Rhiannon here.

I thought once I got back here, I would feel different but if anything I feel worse. This has fucked me up more than my conscious self can understand, especially when it's this tired. I can't see straight. I can't do this anymore, pretend everything's OK when it's not. My head's still pounding. I've got to let some tears out, but I don't know how. I can't cry for myself. I need something else to break the dam.

But then the crowd parts and an angel appears – a brown angel with shining eyes and thick black hair curling up at his neck, and he's wearing the Ninja Turtle T-shirt I got him for Christmas which clings to his pecs like it was tailored just for him. He strides towards me with the biggest smile on his face – the David Guetta Face. I can't believe it. And it feels like that first moment I saw him in Mexico, at the airport. When I was alone and unsure and so tired and then I saw his face: the most beautiful face I'd ever seen. A face that made the bustle and heat of a crowded airport suddenly the only place on earth I wanted to be. And of all the airports, in all the San Diegos, in all the worlds, he is in mine. And his arms are outstretched.

He gathers me up like I'm a wilting plant, all my petals and leaves dangling, enveloping me in a hug I didn't know how much I needed.

'I thought I'd surprise you but I didn't think I'd get this reaction.' He laughs as I grab him and breathe in the smell of his warm neck – the scent was all him, mixed with some Hugo Boss. But I can't stop crying.

'Hey, what's up? You're not mad I came to get you, are you? Me and the guys were at home playing FIFA and Nico was winning as always so I thought I'd . . .' He's not laughing now – his face is different. 'Baby, what's wrong? You're worrying me.'

He thinks I've been in New York seeing a publisher about *The Alibi Clock,* aka my unpublishable novel. I can't tell him the real reason – that I've been to see my sister in Vermont to ask her why she 'killed' me and lied to the police about it. I can't tell Raf what she told me about Ivy – I won't be able to keep my cool. What if I lash out at him? I can't say a fucking word. And I hate that – it was OK before I went to New York. I'd parked Ivy in a back bedroom in my mind. But now I'm back there, with her, and she's trapped under all these boxes and only I can get her out. But I didn't. I walked away from her. Left her to God-knows-what fate. I know she's in danger, and it hurts in my heart. I can't lie to him about this – he always sees it when I'm in pain.

To him I'm just Ophelia Jane White, a runaway from the English care system. Ophelia who moved to New York in her twenties to study. Ophelia who met him in 2019 in Mexico. Ophelia who was groomed by Tenoch Espinoza, an ex-cartel hitman who pimped her out to his mates.

Ophelia the whore, until he galloped up on his white

horse and saved her. He knows nothing about Ivy or Seren or Rhiannon. Because Rhiannon's the avalanche that'll bring this whole mountain full of snow crashing down around our ears.

Tears stream down my cheeks and he wipes them away, his smile dwindling. 'Has someone hurt you?' I shake my head. 'Are you in pain?' I shake again. He cups my cheeks like I'm a priceless bowl he dares not break. '*Tranquila, mi amor,* I got you; I've got you.'

I grip onto him again and cry it out. *He's got me.* He's the gold in my broken fragments, piecing me together and making me feel more beautiful than I've ever been. This was the right decision. Thank God I came home.

He strokes my hair back from my face, kissing my scar. 'Come on, let's go. You look exhausted.'

As soon as he's put on my belt and his, he settles in the driver's seat and takes my hand in his. He doesn't let go until we pull up at the lights on El Cajon Boulevard.

'How's your wrist? You're not wearing your brace.'

'No. Had to take it off at security in New York. Forgot to put it back on.'

'Where is it?'

'In my bag.'

'Have you been doing your exercises?'

'Yeah.'

'Liar.'

'I'm sure this arm is shorter than the other one,' I say, bending my hand back and forth to stretch it out. 'I think that hospital nicked some of it when they sewed it back on.'

'Your muscles are weak in that wrist. Dr Zweig said that

would happen if you didn't do your exercises. You gotta keep it moving.'

I have almost full function now. I can do up buttons and turn taps on and off. OK, so I'm not going to win any awards for Best Handjob but I can do most stuff. Dr Zweig said I've 'surpassed expectations' which is medical speak for *we thought we'd have to take the fucker off again*. But at that moment I don't want to talk about my hand. I don't want to talk at all. Everything I say is lies anyway – lies that grow like tumours and spread until there's no hope left. Lies that metastasise.

'You said on the phone they're publishing your book? That's amazing.'

'I lied,' I say. 'It's rubbish; it'll never get published. You know why? Because *I* wrote it. And everything about me is rubbish.' I let go of his hand.

Without warning, he swings into the car park of a Denny's. He switches off the engine. 'You gonna tell me what's happened? When you get like this, we gotta talk it out of your head. Come on, lay it on me.'

At that moment in time, staring at his handsome face, I want to tell him the lot: the killings, the real reason I was at the Hacienda, the necrophilia and all. I want to save him from myself because nobody deserves that. But I know the second I do, the avalanche will fall and I'll lose him. I'll lose those brown eyes forever. And that smile. And that hug. And his skin against mine when we're in bed. And the hum of his voice against my neck when we're spooning. And our morning cuddles. And our pillow chats last thing at night. I need him. I'm selfish like that. He smells so good – Tom

Ford Noir and the last Red Vines from the glove box. It's hard to be truthful when he's looking at me, looking like he does and smelling like that.

'I'm hungry. Let's get some breakfast.' And I'm out of the car before he can argue, striding past a hobo with his head in a bin.

A way-too-smiley-for-the-early-hours waitress called Berenice greets us at the door. She's in her mid-sixties and she looks every damn year of it; all thick cankles and tits like sacks. But if she's tired, it doesn't show.

'Good morning, guys. Table for two?' she chirps, grabbing two menus and sitting us in a booth by the window. There are only two other tables with people at them right over the other side of the restaurant. 'Can I get you any coffee or juice?'

'Decaf, please,' says Raf, not taking his menu.

'Ma'am?' she says, looking at me.

I take my time, scanning my menu like I'm choosing my burial shroud. 'Bourbon bacon burger, two patties, extra bacon, Swiss cheese, double seasoned fries, wedges, wings, Salsa Huichol and large Sprite. Thanks.'

Berenice doesn't even blink.

'Oh and a side order of nugs,' I add.

'Chicken tenders?' she says.

'Yeah, supersize. Thank you.'

If Berenice judges me for being greedy, she's not showing it. 'OK, guys, I'll be right back with your order,' she says, bustling off.

'She's good. We should tip her,' I say to nobody in particular. 'She's probably pulled an all-nighter. That's not right, a woman of her age. She probably has kids. Or grandkids. Little girls . . .'

Raf looks at me. 'You don't even want all that food, do you?'

'No. I'm trying to disgust you. Is it working?'

'No. It isn't.' He reaches across the table for my hand – the weak one – and squeezes it. 'What's wrong?'

I rip my hand away. 'Why do you love me? What is it? Why doesn't this disgust you?'

'Why do you want to disgust me? What happened in New York?'

'What *would* disgust you? What could I do?' I look outside. 'Shall I go and offer that hobo a blowy, would that do it? The sight of me taking that crusty cock into my face. How about that?'

He pulls my hand back and stares at me, not blinking. 'What is it?'

I want to save him – that's all I want. To save him from a life spent with me, who will only drag him down, burn him out, torture him and probably, eventually, kill him. I love him too much for any of that.

He stares at me. 'Ophelia? Tell me . . .'

'"Ophelia",' I snort. 'What a stupid name choice *that* was. There are no good words with the suffix Ophelia. I looked it up. Basophilia is a blood disorder. Zoophilia is sex with animals. Necrophilia is sex with corpses. Coprophilia is an obsession with shit. Ophelia is a ridiculous name.'

I try to size up his reaction – there is none. *Leave me*, I think. *Get up and leave. Never look back. Go home and bag up my stuff and leave it on the kerb. You don't deserve what I am. And I definitely don't deserve you.*

'Baby, cálmate, come on.'

'Why should I calm down?' I pick at the frayed edge of the Formica table. 'I'm sick of myself. I'm sick of being in this head and this waste-of-space body. Can't even get to grips with my fucking level on Duolingo. I keep forgetting that *pollo* is chicken and *polla* is cock. How stupid is that?'

'You're not stupid.'

'Yes, I am – I'm as stupid as a sloth. You know how stupid a sloth is? They grab their own arm thinking it's a branch and fall to their deaths. I'm like that. Stupid. Grabbing-my-arm-thinking-it's-a-branch stupid.'

'Why are you so mad?' His voice hasn't raised once, even though mine has gone up and up. He's just asking me. And I'm still blazing like a blowtorch with all the propane in the world.

I stare through the parking lot window at the hobo talking to a woman at the bin. The hobo looks like Steven Tyler – the woman looks like Steven Tyler's dead mum, walking. They're fighting over some tin foil. *Calm, calm, calm,* I think. *Focus on the breaths. I am here. I am loved. But Ivy's not safe, is she? And I am so far from her. Damned if I do or don't; damned forever.*

I remove the picture of Ivy from my pocket and slide it across the table.

'Who's this?'

I risk it and tell him her real name. 'My daughter. Ivy.'

He picks up the photo. I don't know what's going through his mind but he doesn't speak again for the longest time.

'I gave her up the day she was born.'

He breathes out. 'Have you been to see her?'

'No. And I didn't go to New York to see a publisher either. I used that as an excuse. I did write a book once but . . . anyway, I went to see my sister.'

I don't spill the tea that Seren actually lives in Vermont or that Seren shot dead a woman *pretending* to be me on her own doorstep earlier this month – lies sandwiched between truths, remember. But I do tell him about my and Seren's fractured relationship and how her being in touch with Ivy in the UK was the one golden thread keeping us connected.

'My sister is in touch with the woman who adopted Ivy – Claudia. She's an old work colleague. I never liked Claudia much but she'd always wanted kids and I knew Ivy would be taken care of. She's loaded. Just bought a big house in the Cotswolds. They've become quite close, Claudia and Seren. And my sister promised me that she would keep in touch, let me know how Ivy is. A once-a-month phone call, nothing more.'

'That's a good thing, isn't it?'

'No. Because I thought I'd left Ivy in good hands. But, as it turns out, I couldn't have left her in *worse* hands. I should have taken her to the zoo and dropped her in with the fucking tigers.'

'What do you mean?'

'Seren told me that Claudia has married a man who has done time for sexual offences with a child. A thirteen-year-old girl. When he was a teacher. And now he's living with *my* kid. He's kissing her goodnight, he's cuddling her, changing her nappy. She's calling a sex offender *Daddy*. And there's *nothing* I can do about it.'

Raf slides out of his seat and comes round to my side of the table to hold me. I'm shaking with pure rage. I'm dripping with it; it's riddling through me like a fever. He rubs my back up and down. 'Sshhh, it's all right.'

'I nearly went to her, Raf. I so nearly got on a different flight and went to Heathrow instead. I know where they live – I saw the address on Seren's fridge. I'd have gone. I'd have gone to that house and . . . ripped his fucking head off.'

'But you came back to *me*.' He holds my still-shaking hands and looks into my eyes, dazed and unblinking.

'I still want to go. I have to, I *have* to—'

'—you did the right thing. You came home. You will see that in time. Sometimes we have to adapt to what's not right and be OK with it.'

'Where did you get that crap from?'

'It's not crap. I learned it in therapy.'

Raf was getting help for his mental health issues – his army PTSD and his tendency to bottle his emotions. The same emotions that got him kicked out of the army. He strokes my cheek as Berenice brings his coffee. I'm trying to hide my face by looking through the window. Steven Tyler Hobo tries the handle of the Altima.

Berenice sets down my feast and slips a scrap of paper onto my lap. *Blink twice if you want me to call the cops*, it says and there's an *x* after her name.

When she's gone, the kindness she's left in her wake sort of mellows me. The burner's on simmer now, rather than boil. I show Raf the note.

'She's a good person.' He smiles. 'Like you.' He kisses my forehead and wipes the tears from my cheeks before I even know they're coming.

'I don't know *how* to be good.'

'I wouldn't be marrying a *bad* person, would I?'

'You don't know the half of it. You don't know what I've done—'

He lowers his voice. 'You've killed people.' I stop dead in

my tracks, barely breathing. 'Baby, you were living with an ex-cartel hitman when I met you. It'd be kinda stupid to think you were just there to "clean house". I know you only told Mom that so she wouldn't think less of you.'

'I killed . . . a lot. I had to.'

He nods, strokes my cheek again. 'It's OK.'

'Is it?'

'Yes.'

I search his eyes, trying to find the lie, but it's not there. He means this. And it's such a fucking relief. Like taking that heavy stone off my lungs, or at least jemmying it up. I try unloading another weight.

'It's kind of why I left the UK too. I wasn't in care – that's another story I made up. I killed . . . someone there. A man. A . . . paedophile.'

Raf sips his coffee, but the cup makes no sound when it hits the saucer. 'I suspected it was something like that.' He looks at Ivy's photo. 'He hurt her, didn't he? Or he was gonna. It's OK, you don't have to say it, I get it.'

'No, you don't, Raf, you have no idea—'

'—I do,' he interrupts. 'Ivy's dad, right? You killed him.'

I should tell him everything right there. I should say, *No, AJ was a good guy and I tipped a full kettle of boiling water over him, then stabbed him twenty-four times on my kitchen lino because he shouted at me.*

But it doesn't feel right to tell him all that. I could offload some of the heaviness, but that was one big fat boulder I still have to carry myself. I can't dress that one up in a valiant robe – it was what it was. I *had* killed an innocent nineteen-year-old – the father of my child – all because he had shouted

22

at me. All because he was rightfully angry with me. Nothing more. So I revert to type and I lie.

'I killed a paedophile. *One* paedophile. And it *wasn't* Ivy's dad.'

'You got nothing to be ashamed of. I'm only sad that your life's been ruined by it. That's what they do – ruin lives without taking them.' And he sips his coffee one more time and this time, the cup does make a clink as he says: 'I was molested by a paedophile. When I was eight.'

That pulls me up short. 'What?'

'This guy who worked at the pool. A lifeguard. Dragged me into the locker room when I'd gone in for a piss. He didn't get far cos Nico came looking for me, thank God. When the guy heard Nico calling, he ran out. Years later, I found out he raped a boy the same age, few blocks away from our house. Abducted him from a trailer park about a week after. They caught him, put him through a programme then let him out. I don't know what happened to him after that. Hopefully he went to prison for ever. Or he's dead.'

Raf looks at me. I expect his eyes to be wet but they're not. They're steely brown as always. I wish I could read his thoughts.

'The army helped me put my anger somewhere useful.'

'What was his name?' I ask.

'The guy at the pool? Elliot . . . Manning? Mancini? Don't recall. I try not to think about it. He was this lizard-lookin' fuck with dirty fingernails and a scorpion tattoo on his neck. And he smelled of weed. I've never told anyone that before, not even Nico. I told you because I want you to know that the depth of feeling you have – that hatred – I get it.'

'You do?' I say hopefully. In one way it was pure comfort

23

to know I'd found someone who felt the same – in another way, it was terrifying. Because I didn't want him to be like me. I needed him to be the exact opposite.

Raf nods. 'It's *his* face I see in my head every time I'm punching the bag at the gym. I'll never lose that hate.'

'What would you do now, if you saw him?' I ask.

'Elliot?' He shrugs. 'I don't know.'

'You'd kill him, wouldn't you? You would do that, for little eight-year-old Raf. And that other kid.'

He doesn't answer, just picks up the photo of Ivy, a couple of his fingernails still glitter-pink and black from where I'd painted them a few weeks before. He looks better in make-up than I do. 'Your sister would go get Ivy if she was in danger, wouldn't she?'

'Yeah, probably.'

'And this guy's done time for abusing a *teenager*, right? Not a baby?'

'The girl was *thirteen*, Raf. That *is* a kid. It was when he was a teacher, twenty years ago. And he's been married before. What if his ex-wife knew—'

'—it doesn't mean he's attracted to kids in general, does it? I know what he did was bad – *real* bad – but if it was a one-off—'

'—you don't know it was a one-off.'

'Do *you*?'

'No, but—'

'Maybe it was one mistake. You were sure about this Claudia woman who adopted Ivy, right? Else you wouldn't have left her in the woman's care.'

'No, but—'

'—no buts. You can't go back there or you'll be arrested, right?'

'Yeah.'

'So there's nothing you can do about it. You have to learn to be OK with not being OK. OK?'

I don't answer for a long time. I still don't understand this 'being OK with not being OK' thing but I am getting there. 'My sister did say I could call her once a month for an update.'

'Good. Keep in touch with her and trust this Claudia to bring Ivy up safely. And even if this guy is on the scene—'

'—he *shouldn't* be on the scene though. And Claudia's had cancer. What if she gets it again? He'll adopt her and then he'll—'

'—you don't know that. And even if you did, you can't fix it. And if you can't fix it, you gotta trust someone else will.' He taps Ivy's photo. 'She's safe. She's got good people around her who will protect her. And we got a wedding to plan.'

I hug him and he kisses my hair. His decency overwhelms me. I want to be with him so badly but simultaneously, nowhere near him at all. I find myself doing that sometimes – like a yoyo – pushing him away only to claw him back. Ugh. Humans are so complicated! I wish I *were* a fucking sloth.

'Is our first dance still "Mi Gente"?' he asks. 'I've been practising.'

I smile. 'No, "Bonnie and Clyde". Or something from the *True Romance* soundtrack.'

'Whatever you say.' He'd poured the gold in and mended my fragments and made it all beautiful again. This was why I came back. My world made sense with him.

'You really don't care that I killed people?' I say, tugging on the little sticky-out bit of hair at the nape of his neck.

'You had to. Like I had to kill in the army. It was my job.'

'Yeah, but . . . sometimes I enjoyed it. If the men were bad men.'

'So did I.'

'You did?'

'Yeah. You shoot an enemy, it feels good. It's kill or be killed.'

That would have to do. He knew I'd killed some people and that was as much as he *could* know. I was still amazed he was OK with that.

'You're so cool,' I tell him, closing my eyes as he wraps his arms around me. 'Whenever I'm being a cow, please know that I love you.' He laughs. 'No, I really do. That doesn't change. You have to understand that. I know I'm an endless bitch but—'

'—you're not a bitch. You're my queen.'

I nuzzle into him again. 'Say more things about home. What's been happening? You been watering my pots?'

'Every morning, as requested. Garden looks awesome. The kids came over yesterday – Mateo and Dad were out pitching baseballs for three hours.'

'Is Matty as good as me now?'

'Nearly. Elijah's in time-out cos he ordered a ton of toys from Amazon on his mom's account.'

'Oh dear,' I say. 'Wonder how he got her password.'

'She left her phone unlocked. Mom liked your designs for the beds. She said you can start planting them out. Go heavy on roses. She loves roses.'

'Yeah, so did my mum. So do I.'

26

Berenice reappears and asks us if we need refills.

'Actually, can we take all of this to go, please?'

'Sure, no problem.' And again, if she's pissed, she doesn't show it. If she were a Brit, she'd definitely be spitting on my nuggets. Maybe she will when she's bagging them up.

'Let's go home. I want to see your mum, and Nico and the kids and Liv. Oh, is Liv OK? You said on the phone she fell over?'

'Yeah,' he says, checking his Apple Watch absent-mindedly. 'I think we both know she didn't fall over.'

The acid in my chest that had been quelled by hearing his voice returns to burn me once more. The pall of Edo – Raf's abusive brother-in-law – still hangs over this family, making them all miserable, namely his estranged wife.

'That bastard. We have to go—'

'I'm not letting you anywhere near him.'

'I'll be OK.'

'I know *you'll* be OK – it's him I worry about.' He winks at me – another knicker-melter – and produces his wallet from his jeans.

'No, I'll get this,' I tell him, holding my hand over his wallet and kissing his cheek as we slide out of the booth. 'Go start the car.' Which, to his credit, he does.

Berenice brings over the payment machine as I remove one of the $10k stacks from my bra. 'That's better. Been sticking in my tit since we landed.'

She looks at me, eyes wide. 'Y'all done a bank robbery or somethin'?'

'Close relative died. We just got back from his will reading.' I hand her the stack. 'Go on, I'm in a good mood.'

'Oh, stop this madness!' She chuckles, trying to give it back. 'Honey, I can't take all this.'

'You did a nice thing for me. I want to do a nice thing back. Take it.'

'I don't know what—'

'Quick, take it. These moments never last long.'

She hugs me with tears in her eyes. 'Thank you so much! What a wonderful person you are! I hope you have a <u>really</u> great day!'

I think she meant that and I walk out the door with every one of my bad feelings now rolled in honey and praise. So shines a good deed in a weary world. I *am* a good person. I *can* be better than I want to be. If I can keep this up – doing good stuff and making people happy and keeping the anger and fear at bay – maybe I can do this. Maybe I can live this life and not kill. Maybe I will deserve good things. With Raf here to love me, maybe I can wipe the slate clean. It's dangerous to pin so much on one person, I know it is, but you've got to pin it on something. And he is all I've got.

In the parking lot, I give the doggy bag of food to the Steven Tyler hobo – everything except the nugs – and head back to the Altima. Engine's running, air-con's on. The sun's poking its head up at the far end of the street. Hope is on the horizon again. Hope with a dash of acid.

'How much did you tip?'

'Ten grand,' I say, removing another stack from my bra and then the ones tied to my waist and both shins. I chuck it all down into the footwell and he stares at it.

'What the—'

'Have a nug,' I say, shoving one into his open mouth.

28

September 2021

Daily Mirror

Garden of Evil

John Cambridge

01 September 2021, 15:28

A WAR HERO has revealed his horror after police dig up two dead bodies, linked to Sweetpea Killer Rhiannon Lewis, in his back garden.

Bob Stanbury, 94, was horrified when detectives turned up at his door, following a tip-off that murder victims were buried in his flower beds.

Officers turned up searching for the corpses of two lawyers thought murdered by Tommy Lewis, father of serial killer Rhiannon, and unearthed a 5ft-deep grave. Bob told the *Mirror*: 'I couldn't believe it. To think these bits and pieces being carried out in bags were people. I was so upset.' Bob, who bought the house eighteen months ago, had planned to use it as a holiday cottage but moved in when his previous home was struck by lightning, added: 'I've tried to grow things in those beds but nothing. Now I know why. I can't stay here now. I'll have to sell up.'

The bodies of defence lawyers Nick Philbin-Franks, 56,

and Carl Frewins, 43, are thought to have been buried by notorious vigilante Tommy Lewis, around 1999. The property then belonged to Lewis's father-in-law, Dennis Kelly, father of Rhiannon's mother, Joedi. The search continues at Honey Cottage and other properties Tommy worked on, for the remains of a third lawyer, David Micah Robinson.

Tommy, who died in 2015, served four years for vigilante attacks on paedophiles and their lawyers, along with several other men, in the early 2000s. Rhiannon, sole survivor of the Priory Gardens Massacre, went on to become the worst female serial killer in modern history, fleeing the UK in 2019, but was herself killed by her sister during a break-in last year.

Meanwhile, the former detective on the Sweetpea case has hit out this week at colleagues for failing to follow up leads suggesting Rhiannon Lewis is alive. Nnedi Géricault, 55, who was taken off the case just after Lewis absconded, has described the Met's handling of it as 'incomplete'. 'There is compelling evidence Lewis is not dead. The world has been led to believe Rhiannon was shot by her sister in a botched burglary in Vermont, USA, last year. I believe Rhiannon is still at large. I would stake my life on it.'

Sunday, 5 September 2021

1. *Nnedi fucking Géricault*
2. *My sister-in-law Ariela*
3. *Elliot from the pool*
4. *Edo*
5. *Shops that give you vouchers for money off when you've just bought the only thing you want*

The old Panny D has been a boon for a serial killer in hiding. Stay-at-home orders. Forced distancing. No meaningless conversations on dog walks. Face masks. Little did I know when I had facial reconstruction surgery that I'd spend the next year and a half behind a fucking mask but there you go.

It seemed like my criminal ass was blasted off the front pages all over the world in favour of the Rona, which initially bummed me out but I knew it was all to the good. The more the death toll rose, the more toilet roll thievery, price gouging, lockdown haircuts, people wearing buckets or fanny rags as masks, 5G conspiracy theorists, 'quarantinis', insensitive celebs whining about boredom and all the endless stick-bleach-in-your-veins debates there were, the more my star faded into the background.

Prince Harry helped a little bit too.

And I slowly learned to be OK with not being OK. The routine the pandemic forced on me was a game-changer. I started to relax. I slept more – every night, a full eight to ten hours sometimes. Unheard of when I lived with Craig. But lying next to Rafael, I don't know, sleep came easier.

You wouldn't recognise me anymore. Rhiannon 4.0 is an all-improved model. Better shapeshifting abilities. Improved self-awareness. Emotionally, a lot more stable.

Well, all right, I'm not *entirely* emotionally stable. But I'm much better than I was. Granted, I do still flirt with the idea of stalking pervs down the odd dark alley like the good old days, but America is a bit more gun-ho than I'm used to and I can't afford to take the chance here. I only ever did that when I could be sure of a win – that's where the thrill comes from.

We sleep with knives under the mattress and grilles on our doors as it is and there's a metal baseball bat in our wardrobe which Raf says he's used before 'more than once'. People carry holstered guns into drug stores, museums, even the zoo. So I have to play it safer here for my own sake and my family's. But I do keep eye and ear out for anything I can assist with – my form of community service.

I only write when I need to bleed out the daily frustrations life as a serial killer affords me and I haven't needed to, see?

Until now.

Because last weekend, a Google alert came through on my phone and I haven't been able to stop thinking about it:

KESTON HOYLE, FORMER-DETECTIVE-
TURNED-VIGILANTE, CAPTURED IN CANADA
AFTER THREE YEARS ON THE RUN.

And the past opened up to me again like a rancid flower, assaulting me with its stench.

Keston was in Dad's gang. He'd helped me too when I had a certain corpse in a certain hole that I couldn't get rid of. And this has got me worried – why have they found him and not me? How did they find him in Canada? Do they know I'm in the US? Are they biding their time, tying up loose ends, catching all the minnows before landing themselves the big fat trout?

All of this would be fine and I could have brushed it off but then this morning, I received another alert:

TWO BODIES FOUND AT SERIAL KILLER'S FORMER HOME

One old fart's petunias won't grow, he digs a bit too deep to check for tree roots and hits a femur. And suddenly my name is everywhere again. There are debates about me on morning TV. Sales of Rhiannon T-shirts spike again. Overly woke TikTokkers with no discernible qualifications perform monologues telling 'the kids' not to obsess about murderers and to *always* choose kindness.

But a very tiny part of me – the Rhiannon part – is thrilled. Because that's the part of me that won't die. Like that little red light in the Terminator's eye. It's still there – it always will be. An addict will always want the thing they are addicted to, no matter how long it's been since they last partook. And a serial killer will always want to kill.

So these two dead dudes might not have been my kills – they were my dad's and Keston's – but with them two being dead and in prison, respectively, they are very much my problem.

Because my face being back in the news in the UK means increased paranoia about who's seeing me. About where I go. About what Rafael might find out about his soon-to-be wife.

I haven't had this feeling for a while and I don't like it. Everything feels uncertain again. Unsafe. Like I'm about to be uprooted.

The longer I've gone without killing (824 days) the easier it has become *not* to, which has surprised me because when I lived in England, I could barely go a day without thinking about it or planning the next one. But while I've been focusing on the good stuff, it's been a breeze not to sweat the bad. Good stuff like family meals and walks in the park with the dogs and barrio art crawls and fire-pit philosophising and having my face slammed into a birthday cake made just for me. Great stuff like dancing with Raf around the kitchen and watching *Ted Lasso* with the family and laughing at all the same bits and eating fish tacos and birria from real Mexican food trucks and the *endless* enthusiasm. Even the bullshit smells better here. I find myself being genuinely pleasant to store clerks and delivery drivers, and sometimes even putting up a cheery hand of greeting to neighbours while out mowing our lawn or weeding.

Not all of them though, obviously. Not our racist snitch of a neighbour across the street, Marji Blumkin – aka Have Fabletics Will Karen. But more about her later.

Re: the dogs: I have *six* Tinks to walk most days. Six little doughnut beds, all named, lined up against the kitchen wall. Six little chihuahua face-licks in the morning. Six little mouths barking so shrilly, the sounds echo off the marble floors and grate my brain like cheese wire every time the doorbell goes. Chonk, Giblet, Diablo, Pandora, Tigre and Traumatised Bob (he's the newest adoptee in Bianca's posse – rescued from an overcrowding situation, and his face looks constantly like he's having 'Nam flashbacks). I think he's my favourite.

Some things do still get me down – I am insane, after all. The mailbox being at the end of the drive is one of them. Marji Blumkin is another. Sales tax. Not having an electric kettle. The obsession with fucking *Tiger King*. The way people over here say *'erb*. And I <u>hate</u> tipping every five minutes. Oh and the whole faith-is-better-than-science malarkey. And the gun laws. And the healthcare. Seven hundred dollars for an ambulance. Seven. Hundred. Dollars.

And then there's Eduardo, my sister-in-law's husband. We'll come to him later. Put a pin in him, preferably a six-foot one with a sharpened point . . .

But for the most part, I am happy. I kind of like myself these days, probably because people like me and I don't have to pretend to like them, I just do. I can be the me I am when I'm not killing. Confident. Fun. Because I'm surrounded by confident, fun people. I'm helpful here too. I babysit Raf's niece and nephews sometimes and I even volunteer down at the vax hub with Raf's mum. Well, I did that once until some old bat decided to shit her pants in the chair and I had to clean it up. I helped plant some trees at the community orchard. I baked cakes for elderly people in the neighbourhood and sang Beyoncé through their windows when they couldn't get out.

I don't know how many of them appreciated that but I did it anyway.

And when Raf's dad, Michael, took a turn for the worse last summer, I was the wonder wall my family could lean on.

37

I googled 'How to be supportive when a family member dies' and ticked off the list, one by one, every day:

- Baked cookies to make the house smell of cookies ✓
- Memorised how they all liked their coffee and made sure it was on the go, all the time ✓
- Created a photo montage of Michael in happier times and got it framed for Bianca's birthday ✓
- Entertained the kids and became Cool Aunt Ophelia, taking them to the park or baseball games or picking them up from school ✓
- Hugged everyone, even Nico's wife Ariela, even though she stinks of cigarettes and her neck mole went in my mouth ✓
- Didn't tell anyone how ugly they looked when they cried ✓
- Bought some organic pampering products for Bianca, drew her baths and replanted the whole back garden *and* maintained it for her ✓

I did think I'd made a boo-boo at one point when I told Bianca that at least she could starfish in bed now and wouldn't have to put up with Michael's morning farts again but she actually laughed. Apparently, my humour works in this family. Thank fuck.

The sun shines all the time here and all sweet peas need sunshine to grow. Sunshine and warmth. And the Arroyo-Carranzas are my sunshine *and* my warmth *and* my water. I need them. I hope I don't mess things up, like I normally do. It has been known.

Monday, 6 September 2021

1. *People who don't mute their mics on Zoom calls*
2. *People who don't know how to UN-mute their mics on Zoom calls*
3. *People who Reply All to emails – Gill, you grossly over-estimate the size of the shit I give about the successful removal of your mole cluster. Let alone anyone else in the office.*
4. *Woman with her mask beneath her chin behind me in the queue for coffee, pull it up. I ain't dying on FaceTime.*
5. *Marion Hicks – can eat a bag of dicks*

Back to work today after the weekend and get this: I actually *like* my job! I'm a receptionist for a realtor in town so I'm still firmly ensconced in admin, but it's OK as jobs go. They let me have a go at the real estate side of things but on my first showing I let a manic cocker spaniel out and all hell broke loose so they put me back on office-based tasks. The pay is good and since Covid hit, I'm the only one who's chosen to go into the office so there's no other sod around to annoy me. No colleagues, no banter, no coffee breath and a distinct lack of WhatsApp *pings* from home-schooled teens who don't know how to switch on a fucking microwave.

As office jobs go, I've hit the jackpot.

My desk is next to the fish tank and it's one of my duties to keep them fed and clean. And get this – there were twelve fish when the first stay-at-home order was announced and there are twelve now. I've kept twelve whole-assed fish *alive*. See, I'm not *all* about the killing.

Another great thing about working there is the coffee. My snooty old snack of a boss Wilmer insists on stocking up on it but he's never here to drink it, so it's all mine. Just me, the De'Longhi and the fish, making sweet full-caffeine music, all the live long day. Occasionally though, I do have to Zoom in for a team meeting.

As I strap on my wrist brace, my black screen separates into six images – Wilmer (Boss Man), 'Peppermint' Patty Filbert, Marion 'Bag of Dicks' Hicks, Kortnie (yes, that's K-O-R-T-N-I-E, which is reason enough to hate her), Gill the Pill Popper and me, Suki Serial Killer. Together we are: The Wilmer Pinchot Real Estate team. Tagline: *Where there's a Wilmer, there's a way!*

Ugh.

'Good morning, everybody!' says Wil.

Each member gurns into their webcams with various backdrops – floral wallpaper, heaving bookshelves, fridge art juvenilia and piles of paper to show that yes, they are indeed working in between yoga sessions (Kortnie), church (Patty) and/or hard-core cunnyling-dings with one's mistress (Wilmer). I know all their antics – it started when I saw Porn Hub tabbed on Wilmer's computer when he shared-screen for a presentation and I followed his filth trail to a load of saucy email backs and forths. They all trust me with their passwords when they need a document printed off or sent over.

'How y'all doing this morning, everyone good?' says Wilmer.

I can't always tell what people's facial expressions mean but I can always tell when my boss has nutted recently. It's in the pink of his cheek, the sheen of sweat on his brow, how happy he is with himself having been up herself, whoever 'herself' is this month.

'Morning, Wil,' I say fake-cheerily, opening my minutes document. There follows several 'how are yous' and comparisons of vax site soreness, then we all go around the class with our news. Gill (who is always ill) enters into some everlasting diatribe about her long Covid which makes me want to drive a car through a wall. I usually practise my Duolingo during these bits or scroll the internet, maybe do a couple of BuzzFeed quizzes – 'Work Out How You Will Die Based on What's on Your Fridge's Top Shelf' (cancer) and 'Shag, Marry, Kill: The Hemsworth Brothers'. I'd do all three to all three so that was a big fat waste of time, but then, so's work.

'So our numbers still look great,' Wil begins, 'prices continue to climb and low mortgage rates and inventory mean demand is still strong. We've gone over asking price on every property in our portfolio this month. Truly, we are in a buyers' *and* sellers' market right now, guys, so we need to keep it up. Obviously, safety still comes first but overall, we're doing real good.'

Patty butts in, mid-mint. 'I helped that lovely family, the Bettners, secure their dream house in La Jolla.' She beams. 'They'd been looking to rent then they saw this place and I negotiated the price to a reasonable one based off comparable sales. They've even invited me to their housewarming!'

In Normal Times, sixty-four-year-old Patty sits at the desk to the right of me and she's one of the Heck and Darn mob, into God and cardigans, knew Adam before Eve did – and as dull as a rice cake. I learned early on that you don't ask Patty *anything* – how she is, weekend plans, ailments, because you always get the Snyder cut version. No wonder her husband stays in his coma.

Kortnie 'Fucknugget' Muggett is next up to bat – she's worked for the company for six years, four of which have been spent on maternity leave. Her organisational skills are about as efficient as the pilot of that boat that got stuck in the Suez and her teeth are so yellow, they shouldn't be near a webcam. She's not well liked – understandable when she keeps taking year-long baby holidays, then getting knocked back up again upon her return.

Having been out of the job game a while before I got this one, it took a while to get into the swing of the professional pleasantries you have to throw out – *Your tan looks great! Any plans for the weekend? That new hair really suits you. No, you don't look at all like the Yorkshire Ripper . . .*

I've not changed *completely*. Richard E. Grunt sits atop my computer, so I can do the look offscreen to someone whenever the bullshit drops. Which is *a lot*.

'How are your wedding preparations coming along, Phee Phee?' Kortnie asks. I don't know why she's so interested in my wedding – we're not friends. It's probably because she hasn't made a sale this week and she's trying to throw Wilmer off the scent of her ineptitude. I ain't helping her.

'Fine thanks,' I say, offering no more.

'Oh you haven't cancelled then?' says Marion, a forgettable wisp of a woman with an arched eyebrow climbing up her huge forehead. I am everything Marion hates – young, happy and not keen on licking her arsehole. She enjoys causing people pain so it's useful that I don't show any.

'No, we're still on for July third. It would've been Raf's dad's fifty-seventh birthday so we thought it would be a nice way to honour him.'

'You might have to think again, Ophelia . . .'

'Uh, why's that?'

'Haven't you seen the news this morning? There's over a thousand cases of the Delta variant now in San Diego County. They're advising people to call off all large gatherings. *Including* weddings . . .'

I momentarily mute my mic and camera so they don't witness the stream of curses from my filthy gob.

'No, no, no, not again, not the fourth fucking time,' I'm muttering as I'm opening tabs, trying to prove Marion is lying. Turns out: she's not.

San Diego County public health officials today reported 1,500 new cases of COVID-19, seven deaths and 210 new hospitalizations—discouraging news as the Delta variant continues to surge
. . .

'FUCK IT!' I yell, making the fish jump. I scroll down the article until I reach a section that catches my eye and throws my stomach into turmoil.

The CDC recommends people minimize risk and avoid large gatherings. Weddings are risky business. Lots of people packed into one area, dancing and hugging, creates an ideal

environment for Delta to thrive. Couples are again being
asked to postpone . . .

'You could still get married, Ophelia,' says Patty, her brown
cardigan clearly taking some lockdown strain. 'Perhaps you
and Ralph could elope?'

I unmute. 'His name's *Rafael*, and we don't want to elope.
We want everyone to be there. All the family.'

Patty offers me a meek, sympathetic smile; Gill sizes up
a stain on a pair of football shorts; and Wil scrolls his phone,
probably begging for another pegging from Mistress Gigi and
her robo-schlong.

'Rafael's family is enormous.' Marion laughs, mindlessly
raking a hand through her frizzy, over-furloughed bonce. 'Can't
seem to *stop* breeding.'

'Whereas you can't seem to start,' I clap back. Mute.

'I think this wedding is cursed,' she says, continuing to
press her fuckery pedal. 'It's one thing after another. First the
stay-at-home orders, then your father-in-law's death, then your
brother-in-law's breakdown—'

'Nico *didn't* have a breakdown,' I tell her.

'He threw a chair through a Hodad's window.'

'He pulled his chair out a bit quickly,' I correct. 'And it was
The Waffle Café, not Hodad's. And his father had just *died*.'

Marion smiles, one tooth twinkling in her cavernous gob.

'Can we get to this week's agenda?' says Gill, pursing her
vinegary pout as she scrolls her phone calendar. 'I've got an open
house this weekend for the duplex at Emerald Cove. Escrow is
closed on the beach casita on Barber, the Pearl Street diner guys

still haven't decided whether to accept the lower offer. The great news is the Temecula Heights property is now officially sold . . .'

That house has been on the market six times because nobody can afford to keep hold of it. It's enormous; the kind of place that would charge you to walk around. There are twenty-seven bathrooms. I've seen a homeless guy in the street taking a crap in an egg box. This world is so messed up.

'Ophelia – do we have any new listings this morning that you want to pass on?' asks Wilmer with resting douche face. He caught me skiving once and now he gives me these pop quizzes every so often to keep me on my toes.

I unmute. 'Er yes,' I say, rifling through the one-sheets. 'We have a couple of apartments on University Avenue, and a lovely multi-family residential that's come through from Mr Oxlong. Mike Oxlong.'

None of them smile. None of them get my humour. It was the same at the *Gazette*. The number of phone calls I'd take from people called Munchma Quchi or Jenny Tulls or Wilma Fingerdoo (who then mysteriously rang off). Barely a raised eyebrow. I am wasted here. Still, Raf laughed when I told him. He always laughs at my jokes. I really have to marry him soon.

I click the tab on my *Hello Magazine UK* bookmark:

Sweetpea Killer's ex Craig Wilkins and wife Sophie show off her blossoming baby bump

There's a picture of them both gurning; him stood behind with his big chipolata-fingers clutching her belly, so there's no mistaking where the baby is, like in case we thought she was carrying it in her ear.

'Craig's made a start on the nursery already,' says Sophie in the article, 'and we've bought lots of accessories from Ikea which we both love doing.'

That's a lie for a start. Craig *hates* Ikea. The only thing he ever liked about Ikea when *we* went was the free wood in the car park.

The interviewer keeps congratulating them, like it's a big achievement. She lay on her back and opened her trap, she's hardly Malala.

'Craig will be an amazing daddy,' says Sophie.

He looks at your stomach the same way he looks at a Ginsters, love, so I wouldn't get your hopes too high.

They have to mention moi in the article, obvs, but Craig clearly doesn't want to go there. The most he says is 'I never loved her the way I love Sophie. How could anyone truly love a woman like *that*?'

That's not what he said the night of the carnival when I sucked him off at the back of Budgens.

I've read that sentence over and over again. Clicking in and out of the article all week. Like visual self-harm.

How could anyone truly love a woman like that? I ask myself this question every day. Raf loves me. All the Arroyo-Carranzas do. Well, they love Ophelia. Craig's right about that – nobody could ever truly love Rhiannon.

I stare at Sophie's bump and I remember Ivy being mine. All big and safe. Talking to me, even though in my head she sounded like Ray Winstone and told me off all the time for wanting to kill. Did I want to be pregnant again or did I just miss *her*? Maybe that was it – I missed that bitchy little bump.

Raf's sister Liv had a baby eight months ago and though I love her, I'm so jealous. I'm not jealous of the abusive bumpkin she married, mind you.

See, this is what I do to myself. Whenever life is good, I start to dismantle my self-worth until there's nothing left and then I resort to killing to make me feel better. Ugh, why do I do it? Round and round we go again.

Inhale. Exhale. Deep inhale for three, hold it for two, exhale for four. Clear away the bad thoughts. Think about Mexico. Me and Raf on the beach. Fish tacos. Baby turtles in the sand. Ocean water splashing up my shins . . .

I'm mid-mindfulness when a text comes through from 'Tortuga' – aka my beloved. He who makes all the aching go away. It's a meme of a kid being hit in the face by a swinging door, set to the 'Eye of the Tiger' music.

I smile. I love that he sends me stuff he knows I'll laugh at. If I wasn't so on-the-run, I have a fantasy that we could be two loved-up TikTokkers like the Italian husband who can't pronounce words and his American wife who can't cook for shit. That'd be cute.

LOL, I text back, sending him one of Michael Myers dancing to Fleetwood Mac. *Me psyching myself up for work*. He sends me a cry-laughing emoji.

How's work? I ask.

Thrillsville – Luiz got me stackin garbanzo beans all the live long day hbu. He sends a tortoise emoji with a heart, like always.

Did you see the latest? I text. *Delta cases through the roof*

47

Was hopin you hadnt seen that. We could push it back into spring?

I send back a sad face emoji. And not because he never punctuates his texts which make them all the harder to read, but because yet again, our wedding may have to be cancelled. For the fourth time.

Gill's finished up her monologue and Wilmer unmutes to launch into another verbal wank-a-thon.

'Can I say, Gill, you've been incredible this month. What with your father's diagnosis [Parkinson's] and your own housing problems [roaches] and all the other stuff you got going on right now [glue-sniffing son, shoplifting daughter, irregular smear test], you've been a real Trojan . . .'

I try to do the same face as everyone else – eyebrows, a bite of the lip. A nod, a rictus grin. It's all about the grin. My mic's muted so I can sneak out 'What a load of crap' under my breath as I perform.

Gill smiles and wanks back over Wilmer in response. 'And you're such a great boss, Wil. Honestly, the support you've given us all throughout this whole time has been incredible. You care about the company so much . . .'

Dickens, Gill's husband, enters the room behind her as we're clapping. That's not his name but I call him Dickens because he's always writing some novel and because his dick is rarely out of his wife. They've got seven kids. Quite the pipe too if the sag in his sweatpants is anything to go by.

'Ophelia, could you dig out the portfolio for 30665 Roadrunner Ridge for me? I got a couple who are interested in a tour—'

Patty's question interrupts my bollock-gazing trance. 'Huh?'

'The duplex at 30665 Roadrunner Ridge? I have a couple

who'd like to take a look at it. They want the views, and they *love* the idea of a recording studio. He's a musician so the soundproofing would work well for them.'

'Lilac Hills . . .' I say, scrolling through the database. 'Yeah, I got it. 30665 Roadrunner Ridge. Wow, it's been empty for years.'

'Yeah, it's always been too remote for some viewers but my clients say that's the appeal of this one.'

'Professionally soundproofed basement?'

'That's the one. The gentleman is a drummer and he has a couple kits he wants to put down there.'

Be a perfect house for a serial killer too, or a serial killer who specialises in drummers. I scroll the photos – remote, basement, soundproofing. Such a waste. I could brutally fillet Travis Barker down there after an intense drum-off and no one could hear a bloody thing.

Before I can think any more on it, a Google alert for 'Sweetpea Killer' comes through:

FORMER DETECTIVE SAYS 'SWEETPEA KILLER' IS ALIVE AND LIVING IN THE USA

'Oh you bitch!' I shout at the sanctimonious Nnedi Géricault photo in the corner of the article. 'I'm dead, I'm fucking *dead*!' It's not for a good ten seconds that I realise my mic's unmuted and they're all staring at me. Even Dickens.

'Erm, Phee, is everything OK there?' asks Wilmer.

'Oh,' I say spryly. 'Sorry, it's . . . one of the fish . . . it's dead. I've just noticed. It's fucking . . . *dead*.'

Tuesday, 7 September 2021

1. *People who say 'It's got the wow factor' when they're looking at houses*
2. *Edo*
3. *Elliot from the pool*
4. *Nnedi Géricault*
5. *The tall guy at the open house on Rosebud Lane this morning. If I cut your legs off you'll have a better view of the mountains, how bow dah?*

First Keston, then the bodies at Honey Cottage and now, Géricault popping up on a viral podcast to reaffirm her view that I am, in fact, still alive and killing. Well, one out of two you got right, Neds. I've cleaned up my act. No dead heads now for 826 days. Go new, improved me!

Bloodiest Crimes Monthly may sound like a rundown of the world's worst periods but it's one of America's most popular true-crime podcasts. The YouTube videos regularly get between five and six million hits. And today, funnily enough, he's talking about Sweetpea. Aka, me-pea.

'He' being the testical with teeth that is Kyle Kuric – the host; an over-excited basketball-vest-wearing ex-snowboarder from Colorado whose interest in true crime began when he found a dead girl by the roadside and took a selfie with her before calling the police.

I mean, he's lauded as a hero *now* but he still took the picture before sounding the alarm. He's still one of *those* guys. The Joe Rogan of serial murder YouTubing. And he's totally bubbly in the gusset for moi.

As is the delightful Nnedi Géricault; the ex-detective unceremoniously jettisoned from the Met for letting yours truly slip through her eight fingers.

'So on today's show, our guest has first-hand experience with the Sweetpea Killer, Rhianna Lewis . . .'

'Rhiannon,' she corrects, to her credit. She sits opposite him, stony-faced as usual.

'Detective Inspector Nnedi Géricault joins me to talk about Sweetpea Killer RhiannON Lewis and her belief that she is still alive. So Nnedi, you retired from the police last year but before that, you were spearheading the Sweetpea investigation.'

'Yes. I was the senior detective when we were looking into the various murders supposedly committed by Craig Wilkins but our focus switched to Rhiannon Lewis when we learned she had framed him.'

'And how did you learn that?'

'Through her written confession, same as everyone else. But prior to that, we discovered she'd fled the UK on a Mediterranean cruise.'

'So I have it down here that you were brought before the Independent Police Complaints Commission who directly blamed you for the failure to arrest Rhiannon Lewis before she fled.'

'She is a very difficult suspect to apprehend. She is manipulative and ruthless. She also has friends in high places who almost certainly helped her skip the country. Her father had been a Freemason. It helps.'

'And now she has the Bad Seeds and their vow—'

'—ugh,' she groans. 'This stupid vow.'

'The Bad Seeds are Rhiannon's diehards, and they've made a vow . . .'

'. . . that if they see her in public, they will turn the other way, yes. They don't approach her but they don't report her either. They protect her identity. There haven't been any confirmed sightings anyway and all the fake ones are quite ropey but yes, she has legions of people out there protecting her.'

sobs Gawd bless 'em.

'And in your view this is not helping matters at all, is it?' asks Kuric.

'No. Rhiannon's dangerous.'

'All the interviews I've seen, as a kid when the Priory Gardens thing blew up and more recently on TV, she seems quite sweet and innocent. A girl-next-door type. Would you say she is a Jekyll-and-Hyde kinda character?'

'There is no Jekyll. Only Hyde.'

'You were accused of misconduct and taken off the case, weren't you?'

'The case was dropped, eventually. But yes, I was taken off the case.'

'And this was because you hounded Lewis prior to her fleeing the UK and she was pregnant at the time?'

'I paid her a few visits to ascertain her whereabouts at

the time of key events. It was routine questioning as part of an ongoing police investigation.'

Nnedi looks pissed. I've been on the receiving end of that face myself.

'You've written a book about your experiences with Rhiannon Lewis which comes out in two months – I have a proof copy here . . .'

Oh good, someone else has written a book about me.

Kuric holds it up to the camera. *'My Struggle to Root Out the Sweetpea Killer: A Detective's Story.* In the book, we get an insight into your long career.'

'Yes, I talk about rising through the ranks of the UK police force from the age of twenty-three, starting as a constable and then on to sergeant and detective inspector. I'm now working on cold cases.'

'And I guess the main theme of the book is your theory that Rhiannon Lewis is still alive, so that's one of the leads you are following up, is that right?'

'Yes, absolutely.'

You're the only one who thinks that, Neds. I am, to all intents and purposes, as dead as your police career.

'Well, there are people who still think Elvis is alive so I guess this isn't a unique case.' Kuric snickers. Nnedi doesn't. 'Seren Gibson shot her sister dead at her home in Vermont on January eighth, 2020. Rhiannon had broken in. Seren identified the body as being Rhiannon's. She then held a funeral for her. But in your view, the woman she buried was *not* her sister? This was a ruse?'

'That's what I believe, yes. Seren Gibson shot *a* woman. She identified *a* body. She shot *an* intruder. And she buried *someone* – most likely a doppelgänger of Lewis who had been stalking the family for months. Most likely Kacey Carmichael, who had been reported as a missing person three weeks prior to the shooting.'

Nnedi must eat, sleep and breathe my case. Bloody woman.

'She was a junkie who went a little . . . woo hoo, this Kacey Carmichael chick, right?' asks Kuric.

'She was a woman with some mental health issues relating to depression and recreational drug use, yes. She became obsessed with the Sweetpea case because it gave her a strange sense of belonging.'

'She was a drifter though. So it's perfectly possible that she could turn up at her family's house any day now?'

'No,' Nnedi says emphatically. 'It's been over eighteen months. However long she's drifted before, it's never been this long. Three months tops.'

'So you definitely think Seren shot *Kacey*, not Rhiannon?'

'I'm sure of it, yes.'

'But how are you gonna prove it?'

'Well, I can't do much as I'm not directly involved with the case anymore but I've been advising Kacey's family on next steps and they've been liaising with the district attorney's office in Vermont and have petitioned to get the grave exhumed. It's their belief, as it is mine, that it is Kacey in that grave, *not* Rhiannon.'

Bollocks. She's probably got shovels in the boot of her car right now, knowing her. She's probably been up to the gravesite, sized up the plot.

Kuric continues. 'So why do you think Rhiannon's still alive?'

'Well one reason is her sister, Seren. I have spoken to her on a few occasions since the killing at her house, and each time, I knew she was lying.'

Blimey, she's stalking *Seren* now? How long's this been happening? If she's not involved with the case anymore, why's she nipping over to Vermont on the regular? Does she have some big kink for Ben and Jerry's? Or is it just purely for tea and interrogation with my big sister?

'How did you know she was lying?'

'Liars give themselves away and once you know what the tells are, it becomes obvious. She's not as good a liar as Rhiannon and doesn't cope well with stress. I believe her shooting this intruder was a ruse to protect Rhiannon and it allowed her to go deeper underground.'

'But Seren was the one who originally called the cops in the UK to tell you guys what Rhiannon had done, right?'

'Maybe she felt bad for doing that. In any case, I believe they have reconnected over the past two years. Perhaps Rhiannon has calmed down somewhat – if she wanted Seren dead, she would be. Seren originally called the police because she panicked about Craig Wilkins's false incarceration and felt she had to help him. She's a good person. Unlike Rhiannon.'

There's a knot in my chest – a knot that hasn't been there for over eight hundred days. And today it's back. Géricault put the knot back. And I can feel it tightening.

'But why is Rhiannon hiding at all?' says Kuric. 'She left the UK and disappeared but she left behind a whole host of evidence and a full confession, all of which has been followed up and painstakingly sifted through and proven, so does she wanna hide or does she wanna be found?'

'My theory is she wants both. She wants to fit in as much as she wants to stand out and that's her problem. In order to carry on killing, she has to be plain. Blank. Ordinary. That goes against her baser instincts to be adored. She will be loving the fact I'm talking to you now. And every time she trends on Twitter when some film or documentary comes out, she'll be scrolling those tweets. She craves love and attention but finds it in all the wrong places.'

She looks directly at the camera, as though she's addressing me personally. Even though I'm DEAD, Nnedi. I'm DEAD.

'So what are "the right places" for someone like Rhiannon?'

'The right place is a decent human relationship – one of love and trust and understanding. She needs someone to rein her in as much as she needs them to let her be herself. And she's not going to find anyone in their right mind who will give her that so she will continue to kill. Killing fills the void.'

'I guess the publication of her confession also gives Rhiannon control over her own legacy, doesn't it?'

'Absolutely. It's her own words, for the most part, although Litton-Cheney changes a few names in the book. I think, on some level, she wants to be caught. Even if it's someone like me who wants to imprison her, it's that feeling of being wanted. Fundamentally, that's what she's after.'

A look washes over Kuric's face – it's either lust or admiration, I can't tell. 'So OK, Imma play devil's advocate: Rhiannon has become a legend since her "death" because she killed people whom society would say were pretty nasty-ass. The Bad Seeds and their mutuals keep the legend alive.'

Nnedi fumes, even I can see it. She HATES that word *legend*. When Guy Majors used it on *Up at the Crack*, she baulked.

If she wasn't trying to find me so badly, she'd have Eternal-Sunshined all fangirl mention of me from her thoughts. She *hates* the Bad Seeds – my legion of fans who flood social media with hashtags and love declarations and selfies at the deposition sites. They wouldn't *let* her arrest me, even if she *could* prove I wasn't dead.

'Let's look at some of the victims mentioned in her confession and later backed up by the investigation – we got pederasts, serial rapists, opportunistic attackers, her school bully, an animal abuser, a domestic abuser . . .'

'—we also have an innocent nineteen-year-old man who was the father of her child. A taxi driver, working two jobs to support three children. An elderly fortune teller looking forward to retirement with her grandchildren.'

'Guess she didn't see *that* coming . . .' Kuric smirks.

Nnedi doesn't. 'I don't think that's very funny. Gavin White, yes, he was an opportunistic sexual predator and Derek Scudd had priors for underage molestation. But he was also an old man living quietly, and we had systems in place that were keeping a close eye on him . . .'

Kuric checks his notes. 'Well, according to several British news outlets, Scudd got off with a three-year suspended sentence, a two-month rehab order and a place on the Sex Offenders' Register for life.'

'He was being dealt with by the system.'

pauses for hollow laughter

'Are you expecting us to feel sorry for these people, Nnedi? To want justice for the poor ickle rapists of this world, because I don't know about the listeners but I don't have an awful lot of forgiveness for these "victims" of hers.'

'It doesn't mean we can allow any member of our society to mete out the kind of "justice" which Rhiannon takes it upon herself to dispense. She is also a necrophile, let's not forget. A necrophile who took that young man's body and defiled it before cutting it to pieces in a bathtub. She sexually assaulted a woman *postmortem* to plant Craig Wilkins's DNA inside her.'

Yeah, I did that. But I'm not proud of it. I was going through a lot. They shouldn't keep bringing that up. Serial killers can get triggered too, you know.

'This was her school bully, Julia Kidner, right?'

'Julia Kidner was a mother of three. A wife. A good person. And there were others – Lana Rowntree. She drove this poor girl to suicide. She did these things for her own gratification, not out of community spirit.'

'Ugh,' I say to the screen, 'how well you know me, Nnedward . . .'

Kuric smiles. 'Lana was fooling around with Rhiannon's fiancé, right?'

'Craig Wilkins, yes.' Nnedi sighs. 'Now if any of these women or men had committed crimes prior to their deaths, there is a process by which we investigate and incarcerate: we make them *pay*. It's a system that works.'

'It's also a system that's *failing*,' counters Kuric, at which point I leap out of my chair and fling a fist into the air. 'You mean our taxes prop them up and then they get released early and reoffend?'

Woot woot, go, Irritating Joe Rogan Wannabe!

He continues. 'We have in this country alone nearly a million sex offenders who are out free as a bird, eyeing up our kids right now. Is that right, Nnedi? Is that a system that works better? Do you have kids?'

'I don't see that that is relevant.'

'I think it's hella relevant. I've got four kids, all under ten. And if one of them was hurt by a creep, and Rhiannon Lewis took it upon herself to destroy that person . . . I don't have a big problem with her, I gotta say. I ain't gonna cry cos some kiddy fiddler got theirs.'

'It's not only, as you put it "kiddy fiddlers", Kyle. This woman is given to kill whomsoever she does not agree with. You hunt, don't you? Deer, bears.'

'Sometimes.'

'See Rhiannon doesn't approve of that. And if you're on her "list" as being an exponent of an act she doesn't like, in this instance hunting, you're fair game. This is what made her so difficult to catch – killers who don't have an obvious pattern of victims are notoriously hard to apprehend because they've made connections in their own minds.'

Have to agree with her there – Kuric, consider yourself now on The List.

'Wait a minute, so you're saying that if someone like me, someone who's never abused a kid or hurt a woman, shoots a deer for its meat, then Rhiannon could make me one of her victims?'

'Yes. See her victim Patrick Edward Fenton never molested a child – but because he had abused animals, Rhiannon lured him to a disused well and left him to die. He'd been trying to get his life together – he was getting treatment for depression, and he'd had a troubled life—'

'What does this have to do with anything?'

'Because his life ended in unimaginable pain and fear. She then, allegedly with the help of one of her father's old acquaintances, Keston Hoyle, dissolved his remains in lye. Without her confession, Patrick's family would never have known what happened to him.'

'Her confession actually helped them out?'

Nnedi ignores that. 'There is collateral damage to every murder Rhiannon commits, Kyle. While you see "kiddy fiddlers", I see troubled men and women and family members who don't know how to help them: who must live on and grieve their loss.'

Kuric is quiet – a man with the wind ripped from his over-protein-powdered sails. 'You think Sweetpea is still out there killing, don't you?'

'Undoubtedly. She has not stopped. She can't. Serial killers are either killing, thinking about killing or planning to kill. They never, ever stop.'

'So she could be looking for her next victim right now?'

'Chances are, she's already found one.'

Wednesday, 8 September 2021

1. *Nnedi Géricault*
2. *Those Facebookers sending around the screenshot of a DM from a 'nurse they know', claiming the Panny D is a hoax and the wards are all empty*
3. *Edo*
4. *Elliot from the pool*
5. *The 'All Lives Matter' crowd. Take it from me, no, they fucking don't.*

I can feel my grip on my 827-day killing sobriety slipping with each minute. Each Google alert. Each Nnedi Géricault interview. With each numb-fuck who doesn't hold open a door for me or mispronounces *aluminium*.

The last guy had been in self-defence anyway so technically he didn't count – he'd broken into the Hacienda to kill Tenoch. It wasn't premeditated and I didn't enjoy it. I've done *sooooo* well. In my head, the slate is almost clean if I can make it to a thousand days. Almost.

But Géricault is on the case again and, possibly, on my tail. I'm back to looking over my shoulder. Jumping at the sound of a text alert. Back to short-changing the dogs on their walks if I suspect I'm being followed. Back to snipping at Raf and pushing him away.

UGGGHGHGHGHGHGHGH. I don't like this. Feels like I'm being pulled back down into a place I've tried so hard to dig myself out of. Even my shit-ass wrist aches at the thought of holding a knife again and plunging it into someone who deserves it. Bloody woman!

What does Géricault know? Where *is* she? What's Keston telling the police about Bobby Fairly and Tenoch? What if they track the money he left me? What if they're somehow marked bills?

Raf had booked an impromptu day off today without telling me as a surprise – 'quality time' and all that. We were going to do wedding stuff and choose our flowers *again* but with all the new hospitalisations, we'd cancelled it then spent the rest of the morning in bed. I should have been sailing away on a wave of bliss and jizz but unfortunately, my mind was in overdrive.

'Ahh yeah baby, you feel so good . . .'

What if we went ahead with the wedding this time and right at the last minute Géricault strides into my mother-in-law's garden, assisted by the entire San Diego PD, and announces in front of my entire new family who I really am? Case cracked. Medal incoming. Yours truly heading for the slammer. I'm spiralling. I need to calm down. It's all fixable.

'Ahhh God baby, I'm close now . . .'

Keston's going to spill his guts and somehow that'll lead to Bobby and that in turn to Tenoch and Mexico and Raf and San Diego and then she'll find me here. Why else would he have been found? They're tying up the loose ends. First the bodies, then Keston, now Géricault's pestering Seren and talking to any podcaster who'll listen to get her story out that I'm not dead.

'Are you close, baby? I'm close . . . Ahhhh God, I'm cumming . . .'

Raf had been edging for about five minutes and the framed Padres shirt on the wall had been rattling for a lot longer. Don't get me wrong – I love our sex life. We are hot to trot in a boiling pot, most days, and I haven't even watched porn since I met him. I am attracted to him in ways I've never been attracted to a man before. His jawline. His nipples. His tiny paunch when he hasn't been to the gym in a week. I want to bite him all over. Suckle him. I want him everywhere – on me, in me. Maybe that's how we end up – I eventually just damn it all and cannibalise him altogether. Fry him up with some fava beans and a nice stack of Pop Tarts.

But on days like today when my mind is tied up in knots like Christmas lights, I can't focus. I'm all, *Oh cum already so I can carry on being paranoid about this Brit detective sniffing around my very much not-dead arse.*

'Uggghh yess . . . gnnnnnngh,' he groans, his pipes finally flushed through. He slumps against me, hot breath in my ear. 'Jeeez, I came so hard . . .' Two chihuahuas run in, yipping in alarm as always, then run out again.

I didn't cum at all. I'm still in a brainal tailspin. The two lawyers found at Honey Cottage were nothing to do with me or Seren – Dad and his boys were responsible for them, so why ask her about them?

'Huh? Did you cum?'

She's so certain I'm still alive – like that guy who gets on

TV sometimes, claiming everyone's a lizard person in disguise. He's so convinced, most people think he's gone off his rocker but what does he know that we don't? What does *Géricault* know that *I* don't? Maybe she's found the trail – the trail that leads from Bobby Fairly to Tenoch to Raf to me. She can't do – she just *can't*.

'Did you?' Raf huffs into my ear again. 'Baby?'

'Hmm?'

Seren's right. Ophelia *is* just a skin – Rhiannon is only ever one layer away. Rhiannon is the clench in Ophelia's gut, the rapid heartbeat in her chest, the second look at a knife block whenever I see a new bruise on my sister-in-law's arm.

Maybe there's been a photo of me uploaded on some site? Twitter. TikTok. It's possible – there are always 'sightings' – like Elvis and that toff who bludgeoned the nanny. People are always seeing them around the place. There was that video of Michael Jackson supposedly leaping out of the ambulance and going in a back door. Someone's seen me. Someone will find me.

Raf looks at me face-on, upper lip all sweaty. 'I said did you cum?'

'Oh yeah, yeah, that was great, thanks.'

'What?'

'What?'

'You thanked me liked I'd served you an iced tea.'

'Sorry. I was thinking about . . . wedding stuff.'

'I can go again,' he puffs, nuzzling my neck. 'I want to make you moan.'

'Leave your shoes in the middle of the floor. That usually does the trick.'

His cock springs out of me as he rolls off and twitches to a slow death against his thigh. 'What is it? Come on, talk it out.'

I rustle up a quick excuse: the wedding.

He hugs me and kisses the top of my head. 'It's all good – this time, baby, this time. You and me, Raf and Phee, K.I.S.S.I.N.G.'

I smile, despite myself, and cuddle against him. 'It's costing a lot of money though, isn't it? All those nonrefundable deposits. Every time we think it's finally going to happen, it's snatched away again.'

'We're all right,' he assures me, stroking my arm. 'We're good. We both got jobs. And we can stay here with Mom as long as we want.'

Raf used to work at his parents' restaurant but they lost it due to bad debts and the Panny D. His friend Luiz gave him a job at the Food 'n' Home a few blocks from our house – it's like a giant Target but with a bigger organic section and they were the first store in the area to sell printed-out meat. If you go to the other end of the warehouse, you'll find bathrooms and bedroom sets – Food and Home, see? Except the sign out front's been broken for ages so when it lights up it says 'Food 'n' ome'. I call it the Food Gnome.

'Bianca's living on what was left from the restaurant sale and a bit of mobile hairdressing,' I remind him. 'She can't afford to put us up forever.'

A car door slams out front, setting off the dogs. Raf leaps out of bed and goes to the window. 'Fuck! I thought she was vaxxing all day?'

'She switched – half day today. We're going to Alfonso's this afternoon.'

'What's on today?'

'*Young Victoria.*'

'What's that about?'

'No idea. Some young tart called Victoria, one presumes.'

'Make sure you wear your brace.'

'Sir, yes sir.'

Raf's uncle Alfonso has a small movie theatre in town closed during the lockdowns but he would open it for us, on certain Wednesday afternoons when he went in to do paperwork. And what started as a bonding exercise between me and Bianca had become a regular date on the calendar.

'I thought *we* were spending the day together?' says Raf.

'You can come if you like but normally Wednesday afternoons are for me and Bianca. Mami and English dort-in-law bonding time, remember?'

'OK, I don't wanna get in your way.' He crawls back into bed as his Apple Watch pings with a message. 'She's talking to the neighbour.'

'Which one, Bitchbag or The Accountants?'

'The guy who has the dogs when we're away. Mows-a-Lot Guy.'

'Why don't you come with us today? Alfonso gave it five stars. It'll be better than that subtitled bollocks you make me watch. And that one we saw where all those people went to the beach and got old.'

'You said you liked the last one – the French one.'

'Only cos you wouldn't stop banging on about the cinematography and that scene where the old woman wanks herself off in the field.'

He chuckles. 'She wasn't wanking, it was a spiritual epiphany.'

'Same diff.'

'Awesome!' he cries, scrolling a message on his phone. 'Billy's coming to the wedding.'

'Who's Billy?'

'Billy O'Shea, my old army buddy from your neck of the woods, London. Well, he's originally from Ireland so—'

'—neither London *nor* Ireland is "my neck of the woods", Raf. Ireland is about three hundred miles to the left of my woods.'

'Whatever. Point is he's coming and he's gonna stay here for a few weeks. Help Nico out in the gym. Do some travelling around. Awesome.'

'Bit late letting us know, isn't it? I ain't tour-guiding for him.'

'You don't have to. Billy's pretty happy-go-lucky, he'll go wherever, do whatever. He's a bit of an enigma. Nobody knows quite where he lives, or when he's gonna text or turn up. A bit like Bill Murray.'

'Without the allegations.'

'He said he's had to jump through a few hoops and get all kinds of certificates from the Irish police but as long as he behaves himself and he's back home within three weeks, he can come. Awesome.'

'What do you mean, "as long as he behaves himself"?'

'He got a few minor convictions in Ireland after he came out of the army. Went off the rails for a while.'

'Convictions for what?'

'I don't know. Bit of anti-social behaviour stuff. He was injured out about two months after they kicked me out. He used to drink a lot but he's better now.'

'How old is he?'

'Same as me, thirty-three.' He continues to scroll. 'Tony and José are still out on deployment. Max can't make it this time.'

'That the guy in Thailand who owns the beach bar?'

'Yeah. Amongst other things. Actually he's pretty good with fake IDs. Passports and stuff. He has a stock of stolen blank ones he got from a corrupt Slovakian official when he left the army. Got his Iranian girlfriend into the UK on one to visit her family. Passed the biometrics at Manchester *and* Glasgow.'

He leaves the sentence dangling.

'Why are you telling me all this?'

Raf shrugs. 'Just, you know, if we ever needed new passports. Max would be able to get them. Quickly. We have the option, that's all.'

He won't look at me. But I don't have time to dwell on it because it then dawns on me about Billy: the one army friend Raf has who *is* coming to our wedding. Billy was Irish, therefore European, therefore the one person at the ceremony who could feasibly recognise me. I'd spent the last two years dodging Brits and Europeans who would have lived on a diet of my face in between their booster jabs or protests *against* booster jabs, and Billy the Irish Lag might be the first to see me up close and personal. He'd been injured out of the army around the time my story hit the headlines. I had to hope that the new hair, face and brown contact lenses did their thing and tried to put it out of my mind for now. I had enough to worry about, what with Keston and Géricault and not being dead.

'Is Liv going with you and Mom this afternoon?'

'Nope. And she still hasn't answered my last three texts so I'm not in the best mood with your sister as it goes.'

'It's not a good sign when she's quiet,' says Raf. 'Maybe

I'll go see her this afternoon. See if she wants to go out for a walk. I feel bad – haven't done any art for weeks.'

'Life's what happens when you're busy making money, baby boy.'

'Ain't *that* the truth. I don't feel like it much these days.'

Rafael used to paint all the time when he'd been kicked out the army and a lot when his dad was in hospital. Now when he goes out to the garage, it's once in a blue moon and even then, he says he often can't find inspiration to paint anything. I feel like that's a bad thing.

His art's pretty mediocre at best. Seriously. It's all headachy and messy and weird and filled with hidden meaning. There's a pig on YouTube who creates better paintings with his own shit than Raf does. I wouldn't tell him that though. I don't like the way his face looks when I'm that honest.

'Play with my ear,' he says, as my arm reaches across him. But it is my left arm – the weak one – and after a few seconds of ear-play, I start to lose feeling and have to stop. 'It's cos of you, you know. I only paint when I'm unhappy.' He gently manipulates my fingers to bring the feeling back. 'Better?'

'Yeah.' I stare at his arm tattoo – the blue diamond in the bird's beak is supposed to represent him. Mi joya, Bianca calls him – *my jewel*. But he is everyone's jewel. Everyone loves Raf. And someone got to him before I did. And I hate that.

'Did you paint a lot when you were with Tina?'

Le sigh. 'Not this again.'

'I haven't mentioned her for weeks. Three weeks, actually. I want to know how we compare.'

'You don't,' he says. 'None of the family liked Tina. They all adore you.'

I smile, despite myself. 'Really?'

'Except Ariela. She got on well with her.'

'Figures,' I mutter. Here I go pushing him away again. As soon as things start to get testy, he's back on his string. 'In fact, if you're thinking of having an affair can you give me a heads-up? That'd be great.' He's giving me one of his vacant expressions – mind you, most people look vacant to me.

'Yet again with the affair thing, huh?'

'San Diego is swarming with beautiful, curvaceous hose beasts dying to get their lip fillers around you. I wouldn't blame you if you did succumb. I'd make you wish you were never born but still, men cheat, Rafael.'

'So do women, *Ophelia*.'

'Yeah, but men get kinkier as they get older. I read about it in one of your mum's magazines. This dude from Chula Vista started fucking his wife's shoes. He was a perfectly normal guy for, like, thirty years of marriage and then one day she sets foot inside her high heels and *wallop*, jizz toes.'

Raf traces the lines on my palm. 'I can assure you that I am not interested in fucking my ex-wife, your shoes or anything else but you for the rest of my life, OK? Are we good now or do I gotta write that in my vows?'

I smile at him and we melt into each other, his kiss breaking through the looming doubt in my mind, smashing it to pieces. As much as I try to push him away, thank *God* he pulls me back in. As much as I try to set fire to this relationship before it sets fire to me, he douses it dry.

'I love you, Ophelia White,' he murmurs.

It's bittersweet when he says that because I know he means it – but he means it to Ophelia not Rhiannon. I can't think about that for too long because if I tell him about her, he'll leave. I've never had someone who stayed before like Raf wants to. Someone who wants to be around me forever. I am ready to mount him properly when Bianca calls up the stairs.

'¡Hola mis angelitos!'

'Hey, Mom!' we call back, springing out of bed in unison.

Bianca's an old-school disciplinarian. She doesn't approve of being in bed during the day, at least not until we've torn the arse out of our chores, which we haven't cos we've been shagging since her car left the driveway.

Raf hurries around the room, picking our clothes up from the floor and chucking over my brace. 'She's gonna be pissed. We haven't done a thing.'

I laugh, strapping the brace onto my wrist. 'At ease, soldier, she's not your sergeant major.'

'You ain't seen her mad. Even the dogs clean up their own toys. She grounded Diablo this morning for back-talk.'

'She has a sixth sense when it comes to us having sex,' I tell him. 'She always appears after we've done it, like a genie. You rub my crotch and she pops up with a stack of washing.'

He comes back to the bed, a towel around his waist and lies down beside me.

'Things might be different if we had our own place,' I say, immediately knowing that I've picked the wrong moment to bring this up again.

'No.' He shrugs.

'No more sudden appearances. No more waiting for her to walk the dogs so we can grab a quickie up against the wardrobe. No more sojourns indoors from the family barbecue to fuck me against the washer when it's on spin.'

'Nobody knew.'

'They so knew. You were sweating, I was panting and we *both* had afterglow.' My eyes flick to our wardrobe – the mirrored door is open and the Nike shoebox sits innocently on the top shelf, like it just contains shoes.

'I am not putting a red cent of that money towards a house. Small spends – gas or food – fine. Wedding spends, OK. But we smack down ten thousand dollars or more against anything, we'll have the IRS on our asses like *that*. They find out you were given a hundred thousand dollars from an ex-cartel hitman, they'll close all of it down – Liv's salon, Nico's gym—' He gets up and goes to turn on the shower in the en suite.

'This is the man who only five minutes ago was telling me about his mate who can get us fake passports stolen from the Slovakian government.'

'That's different.'

'No, it's not. You're talking about fake passports – I'm just talking about money – *clean* money. Tenoch wanted me to live a good life.'

He drops his towel as he comes back into the doorway. 'Blood money. Death money.' He walks over to me and lifts my wrist into the air. 'You almost died for that money, or had you forgotten?'

'Well, let's burn it all then.'

I snatch back my wrist and wave it in front of his face. 'This is all we argue about, you know that?'

He sits next to me on the bed. I roll over and ignore him. He pulls me back and blows a raspberry into my neck which gets me laughing. 'You know I'm right. I'm *always* right.'

He tickles me until I fold over, laughing. 'Little Always-Right shit . . . with an ass that won't quit.'

He snuffles against my ear and bites my lobe. I can never resist that and he knows it. That and when he does jump rope in the garage in his grey sweatpants. He knows his audience, my man.

'I love you, you Maniac,' he tells me.

Maniac – always the pet name or the fake name, Ophelia. Never my real name. Never Rhiannon. Because how could anyone truly love *her*?

Americans are, in the main, relentlessly positive which chafes against my relentless negativity. I miss someone saying, 'Yeah I know, it's a pain in the arse innit?' I miss British accents, people losing their shit over rain or the clocks changing or who went out on *Bake Off*. I miss using *bollocks* in a sentence and have people fully understand it. I only started watching James Corden to hear an English voice but I couldn't keep that up for long.

Bianca and I got stuck in a tailback on our way to Alfonso's but we did our usual thing of eating all our pre-made snacks in the car and singing along to her Wings CD. Singing with her in the car reminded me of singing with my dad to Fleetwood Mac. For once in my life, the traffic didn't bother me.

I live in the ninth most visited county in the USA with the best zoo and the worst traffic. And there are no seasons, just heat, so I always have swamp ass. My tan is awesome though. On the neg, there are earthquakes and wildfires that take out whole counties, so they don't get weather here, they get *weather*. Bush fires. Spontaneous human combustion. Melting cars. Any excuse to sit in an air-conditioned cinema for hours.

We made it in time for the trailers and free popcorn.

'So beautiful,' said Bianca, staring up dreamily at Emily Blunt. We weren't the only ones in the auditorium – there was a woman sitting a few rows back on the other side, but we could still speak freely without a kick to the seat or bullet to the head. I read the leaflet. 'What's on next week?'

'That Julie Andrews one where she's a flapper and it gets a bit racist.'

She grimaced. 'I'll volunteer at the centre that day.'

I have a few things on my Notes app to ask Bianca about herself, cos I really wanted her to like me and small talk never comes easy to me but it seems to be what people want. Life at the vaccination hub was one such note.

'Is it still really busy down there?'

'We get a steady stream. You should come down again. See if you can stand to be around human beings for longer than two days.' I grimaced harder and she laughed. 'You are not that way inclined, are you, niña?'

It wasn't a spiteful comment – just honest. That's the way they are as a family and I love it. At first, when Raf's aunties said things like 'That dress makes you look fat, niña' or 'You're too white for that neckline, OJ' I envisaged them skewered like spit-roasted chickens, but their truths were always meant well. I'd rather be told I look like shit and given chance to change it than be told I look lovely and have everyone laugh at me behind my back.

Bianca likes me anyway. She was the one who pointed out which salsas were the mildest and which were most likely to prolapse my anus. Raf told me she never did that for Tina. I'm one of the pack now. Mi corazón, mi luz y mi joya preciosa, she calls her kids. I get a special name too. Mi cielo, she calls me. It means 'my sky'.

'I don't mind helping out vaccinating *some* of the people. It's ones like Marji Blumkin and that mad tramp who lifts his kilt at the lights I can't abide.'

The solitary woman had a coughing fit and left the auditorium. I caught a glimpse of her as she walked out – she was Black with short hair. Tight suit.

Like Géricault. My chest tightened.

'Rafael told me you want to move out, get your own place,' Bianca said, breaking me out of my state of panic.

'Yeah, well, eventually. Once we've saved up.'

'It's not the best start to married life, living with your mother-in-law, I know that. You want to be free to . . . love each other without me getting in the way, I know. And I will be OK when you have gone.'

I thought about what I should say and about what I wanted to say and for once, both were the same. 'Thank you.'

She smiled, cupping my cheek. 'You make Rafael very happy, mi cielo. He once told me he could see his children in your eyes.'

Probably after the night he spunked on my face, was what I *wanted* to say but didn't. Check me out for growth. Instead I replied: 'That's lovely' and glanced around for the woman with the short hair who may or may not have been Géricault. It bloody looked like her. And she was with a man now – where had *he* come from? Getting popcorn, seemingly. Or alerting back-up.

'He really loves you, more than he loves himself.'

'Who?'

'Rafael.'

'You say that about the dogs,' I scoffed.

'It's the same kind of thing. Uncomplicated devotion. When

you were in the hospital in Mexico after your arm operation, he stayed by your bedside every night. Wouldn't leave without you. That's true love.'

The film was boring af for the most part and a bit too curtseys-and- harpsichords for my liking, but near the end, a gunshot goes off which made us jump and alerted us back to the picture – Albert and Queen Vic are on a carriage ride and some dude in the crowd has pulled a gun. Albert leaps across her in the carriage and takes the bullet for her.

'That is exactly what I mean,' said Bianca, pointing up at the screen – 'the way Prince Albert dove in front of that bullet to protect her. True devotion.'

'I don't expect Raf to do that for me.'

'But he *would*.'

The couple over the other side were sharing their popcorn (how do people do that – eke out their snacks to the end of the movie? I've never managed it). The man wasn't looking at me – but the woman had glanced across. Because I had glanced at *her*. I almost went over and ask her what she was playing at when the theatre was only meant to be open for us when—

'—you remember when we went to the beach in lockdown to have a picnic?' Bianca asked. 'Last summer? There was a moment that day when I really didn't know if I liked you at all. I almost hated you.'

'You did?' I checked. 'Why?'

'It was the day I realised I had lost Rafael. I leaned across to move the hair out of his eyes but you got there first. And I knew then that he was not mi joya anymore – he was *yours*. When a mother loses her son to his partner, she loses a slice of her heart. But I am so happy for him. For you both. I have had that love and it must be protected.'

'You must miss Michael a lot.'

She nodded. 'Life is darker now. I miss our jokes, our dancing, our plans. I miss his hand holding mine when we were watching a movie or at dinner. There's an empty space now. But I carry on. I have to, for my family. I thank God for them.'

'Aren't you angry though?'

'It is nobody's fault. He got Covid, he got weak and he had a heart attack. But I made the most of him while he was here. We grew up together. Had wonderful parties, holidays. Grew our businesses, our babies. For thirty years, I knew beyond a doubt I was loved, without exception. Like you are.'

That hit me like an arrow to my throat. Raf would never love me like that. He only knew about 25 per cent of me, and he might love that 25 per cent but the other 75 per cent he'd never know anything about. And if he *did* know, that would be it for us.

Bianca smoothed my tear away with her thumb. 'Don't cry, mi cielo. You are beginning your journey of love. No more sad eyes. Why do you still wear your brown lenses by the way?'

'I prefer my eyes brown like yours and Raf's.'

'But it was the hitman who made you wear those lenses. I thought you would want to be yourself now with your *green* eyes?'

(I made up some *LA Confidential*–inspired hogwash that the cartel had cut me and changed my eye colour to look like Penelope Cruz. They bought it like they bought all the whore stuff.)

'I've got used to them now,' I said. 'I think my eyesight's

77

better with them. My mum always said my eyes were evil anyway. Green for evil.'

'She was wrong,' she chided. 'They are beautiful. Like the sea in Cancún.'

I linked my arm with hers, like she did to me, and she pinched my cheek like she did with Liv and the boys. 'He's safe with me, you know. I'd never hurt him, I swear.'

She patted my hand. 'I know.'

A bubble of emotion welled in my throat when I'd said it so I pretended to root around for popcorn in my empty box so she wouldn't see my shining eyes. I cry more easily these days, no idea why. I didn't realise how much I meant it until I'd heard the words out loud. 'I would do anything for him. Or you.'

She looked down at my wrist brace in the darkness and gave it a rub. 'I know you would, mi cielo, but you don't have to do anything for us. You already fit in. You are family and we love you.' And she didn't say anything else for a moment, until she mumbled, 'Unless you could be like a magician and make Edo disappear, of course.' She laughed.

I swallowed another gulp of emotion and turned my attention back to my popcorn. 'I could do that. I *would* do that.'

She laughed again, stroking my cheek for a moment, then turning back to the film as if she hadn't said anything. So I didn't say anything else. But I couldn't forget what she said.

'Can you make hot chocolate tonight? Like at Christmas?'

'Mi champurrado? With the cream?'

'Yes please.'

I kicked my feet in excitement. The woman behind us wasn't Géricault, it's just a woman with her man, on a date, feeding each other popcorn and enjoying the film. I am loved too and

I'm happy. Everything sparkled again; like on a Saturday night watching *Dancing with the Stars* with her and Liv as we stuff our faces with Gansitos, while sitting on our fat asses, scoring on our notepads. When she brings me hot drinks in bed and smooths Vicks on my collar when I'm sick. When we go shopping and she's waiting at a table in a café with my drink order. When she strokes my face and calls me 'mi cielo' – my sky.

I'd forgotten what having a mum is like. It's better, second time around. But I couldn't forget what she'd said about Edo. Ophelia laughed along with Bianca at her flippant comment. But Rhiannon was not laughing. Rhiannon was seething.

Saturday, 11 September 2021

1. *Twitter accounts who occasionally drop in the old 'In case nobody's told you today, you are loved.' How the fuck do you know? Not everyone is loved. Not everyone is that lucky. Patronising cunt.*
2. *Edo*
3. *Elliot from the pool*
4. *The entire judging panel of* America's Got Talent

It's been 830 days without a kill. Go me.

But after tonight, I know I'm on borrowed time. Whenever I read about some random rape or pederast in the local news, my Ophelia side has learned to ignore it or at least not let it 'in'. You come for me personally even, like old Bag of Dicks at work, Ophelia can usually laugh it off and move on. But you hurt one of my family, Ophelia disappears slowly offstage, fading into the background, and Rhiannon steps forward to eat you up and shit you out.

And tonight, Rhiannon is hungry.

This evening is one of our noche de la burbuja, or 'bubble nights'. We had them all through the pandemic as a way to stay together and forget what was happening in the world outside for a few hours. We'd play games, have pool parties, Michael would fire up the barbecue or we'd all sit around the fire pit drinking, playing cards, cuddling the kids or dogs, and talking about anything and everything into the night.

After Michael died, the bubble nights stopped for a while – it didn't feel right to Bianca – but lately she's been dropping hints about how much she misses them, so tonight we're having one. Me, Raf, Bianca, Nico, Ariela, the three kids, Liv and Tiny Mike, Liv's eight-month-old baby boy, whom Big Mike never got to meet. But even Tiny Mike can't make Liv glow like her usual self tonight. Nothing can. Not the card games, not guessing the scores on *America's Got Talent*, not even alcohol.

I see it in her face the moment she steps through the door. I can always see it. From the first time she said she wasn't coming to bubble night because Edo wanted 'quality time at home'. From the silences that followed things she would definitely laugh at. It was an Edo-approved silence. Had his name all over it. What I couldn't work out was why it had come over her again. She'd shown him the door months ago when he'd threatened to 'kick the baby out of her'. I wondered if he had slithered back in.

She's been avoiding my gaze all night but later I corner her coming out of the bathroom. She jumps when she sees me.

'God, quit creeping up on me like that!' She laughs but the laugh is hollow and she walks straight past me.

'He's back, isn't he?'

'What are you talking about?'

'Quit pretending, I'm not stupid.'

'OJ, I don't know what you're talking about.'

I nod. 'OK. Help me finish the tacos?'

We chop and dice and salt and dice again, sashaying past each other to the oven, criss-crossing each other from the hob to the fridge, talking about everything but Edo until we stand side by side at the sink.

'He's living with his mom,' she whispers, rinsing lettuce while I chop tomatoes. 'Tried to get a job with his friend in Anaheim but it didn't work out so he's back in town and he's got a job here in a garage near El Cajon. But we are *not* back together. I told him that in no uncertain terms. He came by to see Mikey last week. And we talked. He wants to be better. We have an arrangement – once a week.'

'Once a week to see Mikey? The baby he threatened to Lionel-Messi out of your womb, you mean?'

'He was jealous. He thought me and Chim had a thing going on.'

'Did you?'

'No.' She frowns but I can smell the lie through the sizzling meat aroma around us.

'So he's living with his mum but he wants to move back in with you two, I take it?'

She doesn't answer. I know this lack of answer. It means they've had the conversation at least.

'Jesus Christ.' I sigh.

'The fuck could I do?' she says, throwing her knife onto the board. 'I'm on my own, trying to run the salon, trying to raise a kid and he said—'

'—he said what? He's changed? And you're just waiting to see how red the flag can get, are you? He broke your fucking *jaw*.'

'I fell against the sink; that wasn't entirely his fault.'

'And the G-force it took to get you to hit the sink at that speed, where did that come from?'

She ignores that. 'I can handle him.'

'Yeah, to a point. But he'll still get the better of you eventually if you don't put a stop to this once and for all.'

'When it's good, it's great. It's like it was when we first met. As long as I don't . . . Edo's in a good place with his work; he's mostly . . .'

'Finish what you were going to say. "As long as I don't" what? Make him mad? Go out drinking with anyone with a penis? Put on too much weight?'

'Please don't tell Mom or the boys. They won't understand.'

'Oh they'll understand,' I tell her, keeping one eye on the living room where they're sat round on the sofas watching *Dancing with the Stars*. Nico and Ariela holding hands and laughing at some chick who's tripped over her dress. The boys painting Raf's toenails and Bianca feeding Mikey his bottle; him looking up at her with his Disney eyes and getting snoozier.

'I saw what worrying about you did to Bianca when it all kicked off the last time,' I say, lowering my voice. 'Don't do this to her.'

'Please, OJ, it's better if they don't know. Why do you think I've not been coming round here as much lately? Nico and Raf will kill him. I want to give Edo a chance to be better. Everyone deserves a second chance.'

'Normally I would agree [I wouldn't] but we were not in Second Chance Land with Edo, are we? I've lost count of where we are.'

Traumatised Bob runs in from the living room and yaps at me for a bit, then runs out again when I yap back.

'Raf gave you a chance, didn't he?' says Liv, after waiting to see if anyone has followed Bob in. 'You were living with a cartel hitman, doing God knows what, and you came good. Ariela's done jail time and Nico forgave *her*.'

'Ariela got a couple of DUIs. She's a recovering alcoholic. She did not persistently beat her wife into submission or threaten to kick the baby from her uterus. Don't get me wrong, I wouldn't piss on the bitch if she were aflame but at least she's trying – Edo is an irredeemable fuck-nut and he needs—'

'—needs what?'

'He needs to . . . not be around you. He needs to not be around our family. And if he hurts one hair on Mikey's head, Liv, I swear to God, I will kick him back up his own mother. Do you hear me?' Her face changed. 'What?'

'Your eyes are . . . black.'

'Good. Then you know I'm not kidding. Do not put that baby in danger.'

'I'd never do that! And he's *my* son, Phee, I know what's best for him.'

'No you fucking don't.'

We both snap our heads towards the doorway to see if anyone has heard our raised voices but they are all still in situ as before, except Raf who is having a junior mani now his pedi is finished.

'Stay here tonight,' I suggest. 'Don't go home if he's going to be there. Let him have the fucking house; just don't be alone with him.'

'I can look after myself.'

'Then leave Mikey here.'

'I'm not going to leave my baby here.' She's insulted by

84

the very suggestion, which I can understand, but what I *can't* understand is why anyone would put their son in the same airspace as the bastard who tried to murder him in utero. I saw the way Edo looked at that child. It was the same way Nico looked at Edo – like a burner at a spark.

Liv shakes her head and takes the bowl of pico de gallo out of my hands before I have the chance to put it on the tray. 'I know what I'm doing.' I follow her into the dining area with the cooked chicken, guac and warm tacos from the oven. She doesn't say another word to me all night.

The boys have switched over to a Padres vs Dodgers game so they take their loaded plates to the sofas while we ladies stay at the table, making small talk about embroidery and hairstyles.

No, really. It's all wedding chat.

I love it when Bianca plays with my hair to show Liv how she thinks she should do it on the day. Caressing my cheeks to show how it will look down, then scraping it back to show how it will look up. I feel like a daughter when she's doing that – it was the same way she always touches Liv and Ariela.

'Niña, you should take someone with you when you go for your dress fitting,' she says when I announce I'm going alone this time. She has that face again – the one she had when I told her my mum used to say my green eyes looked evil.

'I'll be fine. You've come with me every time before – I know what I want now. And I've seen one in Cordelia's window that might work if it fits. All lace and flowers and buttons up the back.'

'Oh, with the silk buttons!' she says. 'Yes, I've seen that one – it's beautiful. Perfecta. And it would cover your shoulders for church.'

I'd watched Liv's and Ariela's faces intermittently throughout this exchange – Liv concentrating on Mikey, but Ariela studying me intently. She doesn't like me at all. There's one in every circle I've found myself in who doesn't. There has been since school, even with teachers. First there was Mrs Fitch, the Maths Bitch, whom I heard talking about me one parents' evening to Miss Welford the art teacher. Welford said I was 'going places' to which Fitch replied, 'The only place Rhiannon's going is Broadmoor.'

Then later on it was Craig's older sister Kirsty. Then at the *Gazette* it was Claudia. Even in that ill-fated church group I joined with Craig's mum Elaine, I'd had everyone eating out of the palm of my hand except for Edna and Doreen. At the realtor's it was old Bag of Dicks. I even had it in my own family (my mum, both grandmothers and, for the most part, Seren).

In the Arroyo-Carranza household, it's Ariela, Nico's wife.

There are a couple of reasons Ariela doesn't like me. Firstly, I get on with Nico. It's nothing sexual, we just get along. He's like the older brother I never had and I love him. Secondly, I once told her daughter to smash a bottle over the head of a guy always hanging around outside her school the next time he touched her ass without permission (she'd given him two warnings; two warnings too many for my liking). This ended up with her getting suspended for a week while the school 'investigated'. And thirdly, because my backstory involves being a 'whore for a cartel'.

At least, that is the thread I've spun them.

Initially, she hadn't even wanted me around her kids once she found that out. Like I'd breathe syphilis on them or something. She still isn't ecstatic now, but I am a convenient babysitter when she has to work and one of them is ill or she needs her hair did for the weekend, or someone's dying.

But me being me, I decide not to care. I airdrop Raf a dirty pic I took in the shower that morning and watch the back of his head as it lands.

Ping! He turns to me – his face is a picture.

You are a bad bad girl Ophelia White.

Don't you know it 😉 I throw back.

'Ana, any more problems with that guy outside school?' asks Bianca, dealing another hand.

Anahid shakes her head. 'Nope. Hasn't been near me in weeks.'

'Adda girl,' I cheer as we high-five. Ariela gives me daggers as I sink my teeth into my third taco and feed Tigre a chunk of meat under the table.

'He's still bothering other girls though. He offers them drugs.'

Bianca rages. 'Ugh, these pendejos – it's everywhere in this town.'

Anahid chews her lip. 'I won't ever mess with drugs, Abuela, you can count on it.' Then she turns to me. 'Will you help me with my English homework after dinner please, Tía? We have to read *Frankenstein*.' She rolls her eyes. 'It's so boring.'

'Ophelia's not your tía,' says Ariela. She must have recognised how that sounds because everyone is looking at her. 'Not *yet*, anyway.'

'No, but she will be,' says Anahid. 'After she and Tío get married.'

'*Frankenstein*'s awesome,' I tell her. 'And did you know Mary Shelley wrote it when she was nineteen? Nineteen years

87

old and wrote the greatest horror story ever told. I tried to write a book once. Never got anywhere. Shelley writes one book, sells it into every language, then checks out. Utter boss bitch.'

'Why's it so amazing?' scoffs Ariela, tucking into her fourth (I counted) taco. She has a shred of lettuce dangling from her curls but I'm not going to tell her. 'The monster comes to life and kills its creator. Seen it a dozen times.'

'Yeah, you've seen it because of that book,' I say. 'It all started there. And he's not a monster. He's a creation that comes to life and bites its megalomaniac creator in the ass.'

Ana giggles and checks her mum's face for a reaction to my use of the swear word. There is none, so I continue.

'Victor thought he could control his creature but he can't so he abandons it. It's a metaphor for society – we don't know what we unleash until it's too late and then we turn our backs on it without thinking of the effect that will have. If the "creature" was shown any compassion at all from his creator, would he have murdered people? Murdered Victor's brother? Would any of us do bad stuff if we were treated better? Fuck no.'

Ana's eyes widen as she glances again at her mother's face. Ariela sinks her virgin marg and gets up to take her plate out to the kitchen, as a cheer for a home run erupts up in the lounge. 'How do you know so much about *Frankenstein*, Tía Phee?'

'Because, my dear . . .' I begin, rolling up the sleeve of my hoodie and flashing my bare wrist before her eyes, 'I too am something of a monster. "I am malicious because I am miserable. Am I not shunned and hated by all mankind?" Mwah ah ah!'

Bianca and Ana chuckle.

Ariela does not, obvs, cos of the whole hating me thing and all.

The baby grizzles so Liv takes him upstairs to his travel cot – I didn't hear her laughing so I guess the quote didn't land on her as it had on Bianca and Ana. Liv would normally join me in ganging up on Ariela and when the margs hit home, we'd do karaoke to Beyoncé and Lady Gaga, but not tonight. Her silence is deafening; her unease stinking like a corpse in the corner.

Raf comes over to the table to see what we're laughing at and stands behind me, playing with my earlobes which always makes me shiver. 'Like my nails?' he whispers.

'God yes,' I whisper back. 'All we need to do now is get you a tutu and tie your hair in a little topknot and you'll look just like Harry Styles.'

'Isn't it time you got over that?'

'Isn't it time you fucked me again?' I whisper in his ear and he does a barely audible sex moan, just for me.

God some days I want to dress him up like the sexy lil doll he is and play with him all day. But I won't, because he's not a piece of meat and I respect him as a person and yadda yadda yadda.

So a bit later on, round about the eighth inning I think, me and the boys are shooting the breeze on the sofas and cuddling with the dogs and Mateo and Elijah start falling asleep in my arms and I can tell Ariela doesn't like it one bit. She goes out and helps Bianca and Liv with the washing-up and Anahid follows suit. The game on TV is super boring but Raf and Nico have a lot to say about it, talking in riddles about triple plays and frozen ropes and moon shots and I don't have a clue how this becomes interesting to watch. I prefer playing it. I zone out and think of when me and the boys and Michael were out playing catch in spring of last year before he started coughing. And then I zone back in and do what I normally do when I want to be with Raf but he's watching sport: look for a baseball player to fancy to take my mind off the sad. There isn't one.

'Is Nick Bosa playing in this one?'

Nico frowns at me. 'He's a 49er. That's football.'

'Oh yeah. And that's *not* football. That's heavily armoured rugby.'

'Hey, don't start with me, OJ,' he says, doing the eyebrows. 'Don't you come in here with your Britishisms. You in *my* land now.'

'Bitch.'

'Jerk.'

And then he does what he usually does when we've exchanged *Supernatural*-inspired insults and resorts to tickling me. Now I am many things, but one thing I'm not is ticklish. No idea why – never have been – but Nico is the only person who's ever managed to make me giggle by tickling. He has very strong hands and he sort of pinches you at the sides when he tickles and it makes me feral. Then the boys join in with their dad and it's a pile-on.

'Raf, help me! You're supposed to step in and defend me from attack, Soldier Boy!'

Raf laughs at us from his armchair, wafting his hands. 'Can't, babe, my nails are still drying.'

Nico and I are more similar in personality than me and Raf. But he's not as good looking as Raf and he knows it so he makes up for it with muscles. We'd be terrible together – like

Mickey and Mallory. Fun at first but a bit like that Eminem lyric – a tornado meeting a volcano – and this volcano needs a coolant. And that coolant is Raf.

When I come out of my sex-haired revelry, Ariela has her coat and bag and is standing beside the sofa, ready to go home. That means the kids and Nico have to be ready to go too.

'You don't have to go as well, do you?' I say as Liv appears with Mikey in his car seat. She has her coat on too.

'They're giving me a ride,' she replies, not looking at me. I bend down to tickle Mikey's irresistible cheek and he beams up at me, as usual because he knows damn well I'd die for him. I open my mouth to ask Liv again to stay over when the others are out of earshot, but she turns away. She actually turns away from me. And so Mikey turns away too.

I stay in the kitchen washing up as they are doing the good-byes in the hallway. After a while, Bianca comes in with some dirty coffee cups and sets them down on the side. She stays beside me.

'He's back, isn't he? That . . . hijo de la chingada.'

'Who?'

'You know who. That animal, back in my daughter's bed.'

I wipe my hands on a dish towel. Bianca is looking at me. And I am looking at her. And I'm not the best judge of what someone else is thinking but on some level, it feels like she is telling me what to do. She looks out of the window into the garden and stares at my brugmansia plant, posing so elegantly in her pot. And then Bianca stares at me, for the longest time. She doesn't need to say one more word.

And as I sit in bed tonight with my husband-to-be snoring soundly beside me with all his fingers and toenails painted bright pink with silver stars over them, all I can think about is getting into work tomorrow and putting down a deposit of dirty money on that house on Roadrunner Ridge. The one right up in the hills where no one will hear Edo scream.

It's been 830 days. I'm definitely not going to make it to a thousand. I don't fancy my chances of making it to 831.

Sunday, 12 September 2021

1. *That British MP who didn't want that guy to get those cats and dogs out of Afghanistan*
2. *Man in park who snapped the elastic of his baby daughter's sunhat in her face and laughed at her when she cried.*
3. *Women in porn who lick a man's asshole – please, please stop doing that. No woman in real life wants to do that. No normal woman, anyway.*
4. *Edo*
5. *Elliot from the pool*

I went out walking the dogs this morning and every single one of them pooed within the first ten minutes so we hit the dog park for a run around in the secure bit and I bought them some puppaccinos for a treat.

And then Seren called me.

This was quite unexpected – Seren calling *me*. We have this understanding, my sister and I: I am allowed to call *her* once a month on her cell only to check up on Ivy as though she lives in Vermont; she is regularly in touch with Claudia in England and I am not. They do Christmas together, send holiday cards, have happy little Zoom calls with my daughter, that kind of thing. But when *I* call it has to last no longer than five minutes and I can't be around anyone when I do. As far as my sister's concerned, there's nothing more that needs saying – our communication is about Ivy and that's it. She doesn't like talking to me at the best of times so imagine my surprise when her number flashes up on my phone while I'm admonishing a corgi for trying to fuck one of my chihuahuas.

'What's happened? Did Hell fire an ice cube out of its vagina?' I laugh as the corgi finally gets the hint and buggers off back to his nonplussed sunbathing owners. There is silence on the end of the line. 'Seren?' Silence is never good with Seren. She went all silent just before she told me Dad had collapsed with neutropenic sepsis. She went all silent just before she told me she was leaving England for good. My stomach churns. Something's wrong. Maybe with Ivy. She promised me she'd tell me if there was even a hint that Mitch Silverton had done what I always knew he would. My teeth grit.

'Seren, answer me. What's he done?'

Seren's voice drops to a hush. 'Géricault called me. She called me here, at my *house*. Asking how I was, asking if I'd seen Ivy. Asked if I was going over there for Christmas. She told me two bodies were found at Honey Cottage.'

My heart comes out of arrhythmia. 'Christ, is that all?'

'What do you mean, "is that all"?'

'I thought something was wrong with Ivy. So Géricault's called you, big whoop.' I sit on a shaded bench out of earshot. 'I'm dead, and loving it, and she's grasping at straws again. How are the tortoises, by the way?'

'They're fine. Look, if she's got evidence that you're still alive, I'll go to jail for lying about you being dead! I cannot go to jail, Rhiannon. I cannot do that to my kids.'

'Or the tortoises.'

'This isn't funny!'

I know it isn't but it's my default setting whenever I'm anxious – to make light of things – and this whole conversation tugs on my anxiety. My breathing goes all shallow and it feels like I've eaten a sack of worms and they're writhing around in my guts. I front it out as best I can. 'Géricault's a laughing stock, saying I'm alive when everyone knows I'm brown bread in some Vermont cemetery as of two Januarys ago. You know nothing else. It's rinky dink.'

'What do you mean "I know nothing else"? Of *course* I know things. I know I didn't *kill* you. I know you're still alive and living on the other side of the country under another name. I know we speak to each other on the phone every month about Ivy. I know too much!'

It is worrying. I'm not worried about Seren, but she has appealed to my Achilles heel – her kids. And if Géricault *has* rumbled me, then any risk to Seren affects Mabli and Ashton. Their mum was the one who 'killed' me and 'identified' my bullet-riddled corpse after all. What shits on me, splats on her.

'Géricault thinks there's more bodies at Honey Cottage,' she says. 'Well, at least one more – that third lawyer. I don't remember him.'

'Obvs. You'd leave the room whenever Dad talked about that stuff.'

'But she knows I'm lying about *you*, I can tell. And she hates how famous you are in the UK.'

I snigger. 'I bet.'

'Some of your . . . sites have become places of pilgrimage. It's sickening. They treat your crime scenes like Disneyland. There's YouTube videos of them sweeping a blacklight over the ground, taking souvenirs.'

'Like where?' I ask, though I had already seen them all and saved them to my bookmarks bar.

'Jim and Elaine's, that canal . . . the park. They scan undergrowth for things the police may have missed. One guy went to the Well House with a GoPro strapped to his chest to look for more bodies.'

'Shame they had it demolished, eh?'

'He put a couple of bricks on eBay. They went for thousands.'

I'd seen the latest two-person amateur crime sleuth episode *The Darkest Crimes* hosted by media hack Guy Majors in which he turns up at various deposition sites in his wax Barbour and Hunter wellies and glances around sadly at 'where it all happened'. Close-up on the tear in his eye. One episode saw him shining a torch down the well where I'd sent Patrick Edward Fenton and Marnie's husband Tim to their slow, lingering deaths.

These men died painfully, slowly, knowing nobody was coming to save them. What kind of person puts another human through that kind of torture? What kind of person laughs in the face of another's pain?

I often wonder this whenever I watch James Corden. I chuckle.

'That car park where you killed the taxi driver has become the number one tourist spot in Birmingham, after the Bullring. People pose hanging out of car doors there. It's vile what you've unleashed onto the world.'

'Hey, I'm not the one hanging out of cars and stealing bricks and bidding on Mrs Whittaker's bathtub.'

'You started it. You've brought out all these ghouls.'

'They were already there, creaming themselves to Bundy and Dahmer and the like.'

'There've been copycat killings too.'

I'd heard about these – the guy who visited his paedophile sports coach in the nursing home and wrung his neck in front of *Flog It!* The girls who sent a pig's penis to a chef accused of manhandling his female staff. The man and woman who lured their molesting uncle into woodland and electrocuted him with a car battery. Each one made my heart soar. Secretly, of course.

'Géricault knows I'm lying. If she gets a whiff that you're still alive—'

'She knows nothing. Trust me.' I stop to round up the dogs and drop our litter in a trash can. Ugh, not a trash can, a bin. 'Why don't we change the subject?' I suggest before she can fold her tits over the bloodstained unicorn hoodies with my face on you can buy on Amazon. 'How's my baby?'

'She's fine.'

'Fine or *fine*?' I check.

'She's doing great. Claudia keeps in regular contact. Really great. She can write her own name now. She's intelligent. Talkative, funny. Sassy. Hell of a temper. Like you when you were a child.'

'You remember me back then?'

'You know I do.'

'What about Mitch?' I ask through gritted teeth.

'He's great with her. Claudia's in remission now and Ivy's happy and safe. They call her Dolly Bird. Mitch adores her.'

My chest aches with the remembrance of what he's done in the past and how far away I am from her now. 'He better do.'

'Claudia would tell me if anything was wrong, I promise you. Mitch has got flexible working hours now he's a personal trainer so he's not as short-tempered as he was. And he's a great dad.'

I had to admit, I was somewhat relieved by this, as much as I still despised the guy for his past misdemeanours. If Ivy was happy, that was all that mattered.

'How's Rafael?' Seren asks.

'He's fine.'

'So you still haven't told him you're wanted for serial murder, I take it?'

'I tell him everything *else*,' I say in defence. 'Well, I tell him what happens to *Ophelia* – he knows nothing about Rhiannon. None of them do. They still think I spent my former life as a cartel cum dump.'

'That's all?'

'Raf knows I've killed . . . someone. In the UK. A paedophile.'

'A paedophile?' Seren scoffs. 'Singular? What about the other twenty-several you maimed or tortured or chopped up?'

'That was another me. Rhiannon, not Ophelia.'

'How do you separate the two? Ophelia *is* Rhiannon. You *are* her!'

'I can't afford to be. If the twenty-several people I've killed don't put him off me, the necrophilia will. Anyway, I'm a good girl these days. I walk chihuahuas. Do chores. I donate old clothes to Goodwill – granted I'd donate better ones if I was nicer. I'm happy in this new skin.'

'But that's all it is, isn't it? "Ophelia" – a skin. You know

Géricault – once she's got the bit between her teeth, she will not let go.'

'But what does she know?' I say. 'Let her ask her questions. Just keep your shit together, Seren. That's all you've got to do.'

I know I sound like this isn't all getting up my ass like the throbbing haemorrhoid it is, but I am edgy af. If my sister has one failing it is that she is hopeless at keeping her shit together. She has hair-trigger anxiety, has given up smoking eleven times and like a cheap Post-It note, always comes unstuck. She's dreadful at pretending everything's OK. Seren's going to slip up, and when she does, the rug will be pulled from under me as well.

Somehow, sometime, she is going to rat me out. She's going to say the wrong thing to the wrong person at the wrong time and then *thwip!* out will come the rug, with her and me standing on top of it and we'll both come crashing to a hard, hard floor. It is going to happen.

It's just a question of when.

Monday, 13 September 2021

1. *Kev on the counter at Subway who lisps and spits straight on my lettuce. If I want it lubed up, I'll ask.*
2. *People who call their umpteenth child the 'miracle' baby – like, you know what causes it, you're constantly having unprotected sex, where's the miracle?*
3. *Woman I saw scrolling Tinder as she drove her son to school this morning. Almost threw my frappé through her window. I didn't because growth.*
4. *People who say 'let's circle back on this another time' – aka Wilmer*
5. *Edo*
6. *Elliot from the pool*

Miraculously, I have made it to 832 days without a kill. Probably because I am fighting every urge to go round to Liv's house with the biggest knife in Bianca's knife block and turn Edo into a one-man carvery with amputated veg on the side. Though 832 days is a good dry spell for any serial killer, every day is an uphill climb now. And something happened today which doesn't bode well. I became unstitched. I had the means, the motive and the opportunity.

And I bloody well took it.

I wasn't meant to be there – the mall. I'd taken an extra-long lunchbreak to go shopping, a pastime that became pleasurable during the first stay-at-home order. Fewer people = fewer chances of ramming someone's head through a pane of glass. I'd needed to get out of the office. Take my mind off things. Off Edo. Off Seren's call and Géricault's constant face on my homepage. But, most of all, Edo.

I've had this before but I've dowsed the fire burning inside me; dowsed it and distracted myself with literally anything else. Babysitting. Gardening. Injecting people with the vaccine and watching their faces as the pain hits.

That helped a lot.

And today I tried retail therapy. I enjoyed trying on wedding dresses the first time our wedding was booked, the frillier and more meringue-y, the better, but there were so many plunges, low backs, spaghetti straps, sleeveless, off-the-shoulder numbers or high slit, thigh slit, scalloped keyhole rags and I never thought I'd find The One. I did find a Morticia Addams-esque number that looked sleek and stunning with a long black veil but everyone talked me out of wearing black on my big day. Shame. Raf would have looked edible in a Gomez-inspired chalk stripe suit and tache.

Anyway, I saw a white dress I liked in Cordelia's window so I went in to check if they had it in my size. It had long lace sleeves, tulle-lined bodice, crystal-beaded waistband, silk buttons up the back. Around the meringue skirt were lace flowers and butterflies which caught the light. The lady said I'd look 'mesmerising' in it. Clearly, she'd seen me and my wad of cash coming.

So anyway, I'm on my lunchbreak, standing in the cubicle of this wedding dress boutique, trying on the seventy-eighth wedding dress I've tried on in the past two years, and it looks good, unlike all the others. It pinches me in at the 'taco trap'. The bodice is boned so I have a decent silhouette. Even with no make-up on and my hair all work-y and dull, I look angelic. The dress makes me feel like the proverbial princess. Beyoncé comes on over the speakers – *baby, I can see your halooooo* – as though the queen herself is giving me her approval. I feel like crying when I see myself in the mirror on the back of the cubicle door. It's a perfect moment.

Or it *should* have been.

Because in the cubicle next to me is a bloke having a wank.

Oh yeah, you better believe it. Of all the changing cubicles, in all the malls, in all the world, he has to wank in the one next to mine.

So the dress fits like a glove and I'm crying at the door mirror. Shit hair and greasy face as per but neck down, I'm a vision. I'm thinking about the day itself when I'd be sur-rounded by the people I love, standing on petals, 'Halo' playing on the church organ. For a moment, that cubicle is my altar, and the coat hook above the mirror is the minister. I think about Rafael's face when he sees me coming up the aisle.

Then comes the grunting.

On the whole, I've ignored the assholery of people and their habits with a rictus grin and a 'No problem' for the past twenty-one months. Tried with every fibre to not sweat the small stuff – our four wedding cancellations, the stock-pilers, price-gougers, the secret BBQ-ers during the lockdowns, the Capitol-stormers, the anti-vaxxers, even as I watched my family say goodbye to our beloved papi Michael over FaceTime as he wheezed his last breath in the ICU. I had also chosen to ignore the fact that twenty-one months ago I learned my child was living 5,478 miles away with a convicted sex offender. I have mastered the art of being OK with not being OK.

But the heart that beats inside this ribcage is Rhiannon's. And sex offenders still make my shit itch like nobody else. It was always going to be a sex offender that caused Rhiannon to break soil again.

A pair of sneakers appears in the gap beneath the cubicle wall. Sneakers with a phone wedged between them. Someone stands against the wall and the wall is juddering. The phone's camera is angled so it's looking up through the gap; looking up at me. Up my wedding dress.

I wipe away my tears.

Nobody should be in there anyway – all the stores have rules about this. Every other cubicle is marked with a big red X. I don't know how long he's been waiting in there for some poor unwitting bride-to-be but today's his unlucky day.

I swing my arms, trying to shake out the fury, trying to concentrate on my heavenly appearance in the mirror. I have to turn a blind eye. Turn the other cheek. Gloss it over. Shake it off. Let it go. Draw a veil. Do the right thing. I recall my daily affirmations:

It's a good day and I am happy.

Positivity is flowing into all my veins.

Out with anger, in with love.

It's not working.

I can do this – I am better than I want to be. In with anger, out with love.

It was too public. I should have left.

Breathe. Breathe. Hold for seven, out for four. Or was it the other way round? I can't fucking remember!

But the more I try to ignore it, the more I don't want to. The toxin has seeped in too far now and I'm feeling its effects.

At least I've tried to give up. It's more than Dahmer was willing to do.

My sword hand sings as the cubicle continues to judder and the grunts increase. Hurried breaths. Shuddering wall. Pumping fist.

I want to see what he looks like. I want to be close to him. Close enough to squeeze that pecker till it snaps off in my hand. I crouch down, the skirt of my dress bunching around me – the silk cold against my legs. I talk into the phone. 'You want me to help you cum?'

The juddering stops. The wall stills.

'I can do that for you. I can make you cum hard if you want me to.'

There's a beat of silence; then a chuckle like he can't believe his luck. 'You serious? You a freak?'

I climb out of my wedding dress and zip it back up in its plastic body bag behind me. I stand in my underwear. 'Oh yeah. I'm a *big* freak.'

'Can you . . . take your panties off?' he whispers. The wall starts juddering again.

'Come in here. With me.'

There's no CCTV overhead. No security at all at this end of the store. The assistants are way up the other end with the cash registers.

I look into the lens. 'You can cum on my bridal lingerie if you like.'

He's like a cat on cheese Dreamies – all I have to do is rustle my bag and he comes a-runnin'.

His door unlocks; my door opens and in he walks – a kid really, I'd take a fat guess he's twenty-one, max. He stands before me – scrawny af – I've seen more meat on a dirty fork; his chode clearly at the limit of what it can endure. Poor thing looks battered, like a battery hen. He has myriad acne along his Lord Farquaad jaw – some of it popped and scarring, some of it about to. An odds-on school-shooter. No stranger to a Comments section. I almost feel sorry for him, until the door closes. No way back now.

'That for me?' I ask, staring at his, I guess we have to call it, dick.

He can't do direct eye contact but he nods emphatically, his acne-ridden cheeks aflame. He drops his sweatpants, abused hen red strangled in his fist. Too small to get any real purchase on but he's doing his best. I get right up close to him and nuzzle him gently, the way Raf likes me to before we kiss. Raf always smells delicious, even when he's been working out – so good I wanted to take great big bites out of him.

But this guy smells of onions and smegma. No matter. I still want to ram a coat hanger through his eye socket.

'Can I cum on your tits?' he moans breathlessly as he pumps.

'Uh-huh.' I nod, my lips grazing over the rubbery tip of his nose. I tongue it lightly all over, ignoring the foul taste of his sweat.

'Oh God.'

'Do it,' I whisper, as my teeth graze his nose again, my mouth opening wider and with no more thought, I clamp down **hard**.

'JEEEEEESUUUUUUSSSS   AHHHHHH
FUUCCCCKKKKKKKK GETTT OFFFFF MEEEEEEEEEE!
FUUUUUUUUUUUCCCKKK!'

I spit out the chunk against the cubicle wall. He scrabbles around, pulling up his underpants, screaming, and darts out of there, holding up his sweatpants with one hand and the end of his spurting nose in the other.

My door closes so I don't know what happens at that moment but it sounds like all hell. Banging, crashing. Concerned voices.

> *Oh my gahd, what happened?*
>
> *Is that someone's blood?*
>
> *Another junkie?*
>
> *Ugh, call the cops,*
> *Brittany, call them! He's*
> *getting away!*
>
> *We gotta do something about*
> *these guys!*

All the reactions pointed to the fact that the guy has yanked up his wank-stained underpants and hobbled out as quickly as he'd cum in his fist.

I wet-wipe my face and neck, then apply copious amounts of hand sanitiser over both. I stuff the bloodied cloths in a dog poo bag, redress myself in my happy-go-lucky Ophelia outfit: dungaree dress, floral T-shirt and sneakers, and drape my long black-and-blonde plait teasingly over one shoulder. I strap on my brace – because who would accuse someone in a wrist brace of such a heinous offence – and fit my unicorn face mask on, arranging my dress over my arm. As I open the cubicle, I notice the guy has forgotten his phone. The camera's still on. All his social media accounts are open. I can even see his name and address on his Walmart app: Brad Pfister (yes, really).

When I surface, all dressed and hair fixed, I perform a masked-up impression of the Confused Travolta meme, then saunter along following the blood-spot breadcrumb trail through the store towards the cash registers. To all onlookers, I look like I'm entering the BAFTAs on the arm of Benedict Cumberbatch, happy to be there and slightly bemused. I join the throng of customers wondering what the hell's happened.

'Just some junkie' seems to be the consensus, helped along by me saying I'd 'seen a guy with a needle in the cubicle next to me'.

Prolly hit the wrong vein.

Some hobo.

A whackjob.

*We're so sorry for the
mess. Brittany's going to
clean it now.*

'How awful,' I add to the mix.

I take my bagged-up fairy-tale dress to the cash register and the assistant rings it up. 'Beautiful choice.' She smiles, handling it carefully by the hanger as I thumb through fifty-dollar notes. 'Did you find everything you were looking for today, ma'am?'

'Yes, thanks,' I tell her, as a thrill runs all the way up my back like those silken buttons. I pop in a discreet tab of gum under my mask to take away the taste of his blood and exit the freezing cold shop, allowing the sun to beat down on my face. Melting the snowball of anxiety that I'd got when I first saw the news about the bodies, which had grown bigger at the news of Keston's arrest, and bigger still with every Géricault interview or awkward silence with Liv. Now it has disappeared.

Gone completely.

I stand outside the shop, staring at the blood trail on the sidewalk and try to take stock of how I feel. I have my family, I have my wedding dress and I have bitten half the nose off the face of a sex offender who's left behind his unlocked phone.

And if the photos in his albums are anything to go by, he will do anything to get it back. Anything.

This is not a good thing. This is not a good thing at all.

— *Click. Phone call for Prisoner 45367. Select the hashtag to answer. Click.*
— Hey sis.
— Keston?
— Denise?
— It's not your sister. It's me.
— [long pause] Me who?
— Rhiannon.
— [voice lowers to a whisper] I don't believe it. I don't fucking believe it!
— Well, you better.
— [laughter] [a bit more laughter] [indecipherable swearing] You are one jammy little cow; I'll give you that.
— I walk in through the out door, what can I say?
— [laughing] I think they had the SAS out looking for you at one point.
— Are you cross with me for running out on you?

- I *was*. Water under the bridge now. How d'you know I was in here?
- Google. Your brief's appealed, hasn't he?
- Yeah. May as well stick it out for now. I know a couple of the lads in here so it ain't all bad. So where are you? They said you was dead.
- No, I'm still around. I kept your name out of it, my confession I mean.
- I know. I read it. Cheers.
- I need to know what you're telling people, Keston. I need to know what I need to worry about. I'm spinning a fair few plates these days.
- I can imagine. I ain't telling 'em nothing.
- Yeah but they're still looking for me. Géricault's finding bodies and stalking my sister for answers. I wondered if she'd come to you yet.
- Nah, I ain't a grass. And I sure as shit wouldn't grass on a mate's kid. I still think of you as that little girl with the lunchbox of snails who used to sweep the floor of her dad's gym and watch me and him sparring.
- I used to watch him do a lot of things.
- I remember *that* n'all. Anyway, Géricault's not on your case no more. They binned her off last year. They proper chewed her out – did her real dirty. She had a bit of a breakdown, I think. They put her back on cold cases but she found them two in Wales last year so they'll be throwing resources at her to find more now, mark my words.
- So if she came looking for me, she couldn't do anything, right?

- She'll still have arresting powers but nah, I wouldn't worry about her.
- Good. That's something at least.
- Nah, the bloke you wanna worry about is Amarkeeri. Little wet head, fresh out of Hendon, real brown-noser. If they've put him on your case he'll be pulling out every stop going. Out for blood, that one.
- I'll bear it in mind. Thank you, for trying to help me. And covering for me. The papers said you're looking at ten years.
- Nah. Five, max. They can't make any of the Sweetpea stuff stick, as hard as they're trying. Bit of fraud. It's a Cat D and I'm in a protected bit cos of being an ex-copper, so it ain't all bad. Shit, my time's up.
- Yeah, so's mine.

Wednesday, 15 September 2021

1. *Sting – all that sex and yoga and he's still a miserable bastard*
2. *Elliot from the pool*
3. *Edo*
4. *Patty Filbert*
5. *Brad Pfister (yes, really)*

Once upon a time I was a really nice child with a curl in the centre of my forehead. I trusted easily, loved even more easily and believed in all those things kids should believe in like Santa and heaven and that good luck will follow if you avoid the cracks in the pavement. But with every shitty person I met who treated me shittily or left me in the shit or showed me that actually, life is one crushing blow after another, I've become a little shittier myself. That curl became a scar and that scar made me want to be nasty. That's how a shitty person is created. And it takes a lot of love to unshit that.

And what's worse still is that I've had that – love. All through the lockdowns, the Arroyo-Carranzas have loved me to death. Rafael means more to me than Craig ever did and he loves me more too. And I've screwed it all up. By biting that idiot's nose off when I should have ignored it. I should have walked out of that cubicle with my dress folded over my arm and reported it to the nearest cop. That's what a normal person would have done.

But it's not what *Rhiannon* would have done. And after all, I am she. She is me. And now the whole thing is Fucked Up Beyond All Recognition.

No, no, wait, it's not quite FUBAR yet – I am still at 834 days without a kill. I can still do this. I can forget about Brad Pfister. I can take his phone to the cops, say I found it on the street; let *them* deal with it.

But then he could report me for de-nosing him.

And they could take my fingerprints.

And they'll recognise me from the news or the TikToks or the pix of me that flash up when they're doing those kill site pilgrimages on YouTube (800,000 hits for The Well House and counting) or one of the myriad documentaries – *Killer in My Family, Evil Up Close: The Rhiannon Lewis Story*; *Britain's Most Evil Killers*, episode 95; *World's Deadliest Females*; *Countdown to Murder*, season 15, episode 3; *Born to Kill*, season 7, episode 12; *Root Cause: The Blooming of the Sweetpea Killer* (a Panorama special); *Why Psycho Bitches Kill*, episode 2; *Murders That Shook Britain*; *Cruise Ship Murders: When Tanning Turns to Terror*; *Killer Fandoms: Sweetpea's Bad Seeds*; and *Little Girl Lost: Making of a Monster*.

I *can't* go to the police. But I can't do nothing either. The guy's photo album comprises multiple upskirtings, downblousings, sneaky shower shots in female changing rooms and multiple videos of him wanking over girls he was spying on while riding public transport. He is a sexual predator.

And I am a sexual predator's worst enemy.

But I have to stay under the radar. I have to curb my baser instincts or else I will lose everything. I'll lose Raf. No, it can't happen – I won't let it.

But what the fuck do I do now?!

I went to work, that's what I did. I went to work as usual. Grabbed a coffee and a muffin for a treat, on the way. Got in early. Fed the fish. Made the coffee. Opened the post. Opened Duolingo and parroted a bit of Spanish conversation to the Fat Jesus mural on the wall. Replied to emails. Answered the phone. Sent a few sexts to Rafael. Tried to masturbate in my office chair under the desk but it's hard when the chair has arms and your desk faces a window onto a busy street. And I tried not to think about that thing I was not meant to be thinking about.

Late morning, there was an urgent message from Wilmer:

Phoebe – can you call me when you get in. Want a quick word . . .

No please, no thanks, and Phoebe? Fucking Phoebe? People don't even get my name right when it's a *fake* name. Will this purgatory never end?

Then Pfister's phone started blowing up at my desk. It was Pfister himself (yes, really), whom I haven't quite decided what to do with yet but he's still on the fringes of my life like an unholy fart clinging to the wallpaper. He's using an old phone and he's giving me filth over text because I played a trick on him and sent him to a brothel downtown to pick up the one I stole.

You think it's funny send-
ing me to a fake address?
You won't think it's funny

when I'm fuckin' your ass,
bitch.

How's the nose?

GIMME MY FONE
BITCH.

How did you explain it to
your folks?

I WANT MY FONE.

I will contact you again
when I'm ready. Hassle me
anymore and I'll take it to
the cops gift-wrapped in
a fucking bow. Bitch.

Then after lunch, Patty called.

'Good morning, Wilmer Pinchot Real Estate Los Abrazos, here for all your real estate needs, this is Ophelia speaking, how may I help you today?'

'Ophelia, hi, it's Patty.' Oh Christ, I thought. I could really do without another instalment of 'Tales from Coma Hub's Bedside.'

'Hi, Patty, how are you?' Sure enough Patty regaled me on the life and times of old piss-the-bed hubs and his permanent chapped lips and her reading out the sports scores for him in the hope he might respond for the first time in four years, and I made all the right 'ahhh' and 'bless him' noises, while scrolling the Calico Critters catalogue on eBay.

'Ophelia, I need that portfolio for 30665 Roadrunner Ridge, hun, could you send me a scan?'

'Uh, the one in Julian?'

'Yeah, that's the one, do you remember me saying I have a couple who might be interested?'

The one I've already put a deposit down on, in case I decide to kill my brother-in-law and possibly Brad Pfister too, yes.

'It's gone,' I said. 'A guy called . . . um, Bradley Pfister. He paid the first two months' deposit a few days ago. He's moving in shortly.'

'Really? That's strange, it's been vacant for such a long time. Typical, isn't it? You wait years for interest and then three people all desperate for it come along at once!'

'Isn't it the worst!' I laughed along.

'Is it the one guy, Mr Pfister?' Patty asked. 'It seems such a waste for a four bed, one person in there. We should have shown him something smaller.'

'It's the only one available in Julian and that's where he wanted to go. He's an amateur photographer. Loves outstanding areas of natural beauty.'

'I'd better talk to him. The Roadrunner property's more of a family home,' she said. 'My couple, the Petersens, are willing to do it up. If we can find another place for Mr Pfister, I'm sure he'd move.'

'He got there first, Patty. He was so happy to have bagged it. And he's been through a lot lately – he's had facial surgery and he was recently mugged too. Be a real shame to kick him out now.'

If you don't pipe down and start following my line of thinking, Patty, I will visit Coma Hubs in the night and ride his face through the wall.

'Well, send me the portfolio anyway, would you? And I will pass it on to the Petersens.'

'OK,' I said, 'no problem. I'll look it up now and ping it across.'

'Thank you, dear, talk to you soon.'

I slammed the phone down as hard as I would if it were on Patty's own head. 'FUCK. FUCK. FUCK.'

No way could that gym couple view that house. *I* wanted that house. I didn't quite know why I wanted it yet – all I knew was if things were going to go the way they usually did, I'd need a place to hide and that property was perfect. With its basement and mahoosive garden with panoramic views of the Cuyamaca Mountains.

And somewhere to hide the fuckton of drain cleaner, lye and latex gloves I would need to store there too.

With the office quiet again, I sat back in my office chair and tried to look through the figurative crystal ball at the consequences of doing this. Of luring someone like Brad Pfister to Roadrunner Ridge and killing him. Killing people had brought me here – to San Diego. It had taken me away from my baby. It had trashed any hopes I'd ever had of a happy relationship with my ex. No good could come of this. Maybe this was a sign *not* to kill Brad Pfister. The universe was telling me to hit the brakes, get out and walk in the other direction.

I compiled the email to Patty with the shareable link to Roadrunner Ridge. It was the right thing to do. But it felt wrong. The anxiety flooded back into my chest cavity, as before. I saved it to Drafts and made another coffee. I gave myself until one o'clock to send the email.

I ate my lunch – corned beef, sauerkraut and Swiss cheese on grilled rye from Ike's deli. One o'clock came and went. I made more coffee. I fed the fish again. I googled a couple of old school friends I used to hate (both have deeply dull-looking husbands and one's house has been repossessed, so result). Did a few BuzzFeed quizzes to ascertain which Squishmallow, Christmas movie or *Stranger Things* character I was (some frog thing, *The Santa Clause* and Barb, bloody cheek). Arranged some viewings, relabelled files, made even more coffee. Three o'clock came and went. It was an afterthought so maybe Patty would forget she'd asked for the portfolio anyway.

And then *I* forgot about Roadrunner altogether. Because my mobile blew up. Liv's number. She hadn't called me in weeks.

I let it ring four times before I answered. She knew that I hated talking on the phone, especially if I wasn't being paid. I told her to only ever call me for two reasons – money or murder.

I answered on the fifth ring. 'You better need money or—'

There was a sniffling sound at the other end. Scraping and scruffling. Clothes, like the phone was in her pocket.

'Are you pocket-dialling me?' I laughed. 'Liv? You been on the margs? What you playing at?'

There came more scraping and scuffing and then heavy breaths.

'Ew, babe, I'm not into that, I told you.'

'Hey, is that Magic Chicken on Columbia?' she said eventually. 'Yeah I'd like to order a bucket of chicken please.' Her voice was weird.

'What?' I looked out the window at the chicken shop across the street. 'Wrong number, dumbass—'

'Yeah, I'll have the Chicken Tenders Mega Meal with biscuits . . . and a choice of dipping sauces.' Her voice was shaky and faint. And she was never this polite. And then I got it. A familiar cloud descended.

'Is he there?' I asked.

'Yeah. Chicken tenders.'

'Have you called the cops?'

'No. Dipping sauces too please.'

'Are you injured?'

'Yeah.'

'Has he raped you again?'

'Yeah. Please. And a couple slices of pound cake.'

'No sprinkles!' Edo called out in the background.

'No sprinkles please.'

My lips retracted over my teeth. 'Is the baby OK?'

'Yeah.' Her voice broke.

'Does he have a knife or a gun? Cough once for gun, cough twice for knife.'

She coughed once. 'Can you hurry? We're pretty hungry.'

'I'm on my way.'

I am crap at most things: maths, board games, using a Xerox, small talk, dieting, singing, sincerity, hand jobs, rolling my tongue and absolutely all sports, even though I do have a surprisingly strong pitching arm, according to my late papi, Michael. But one thing in which I truly excel is thinking on my feet. Especially when it comes to a situation like this. My sister-in-law is no shrinking violet – she's kicked her husband out before, many times; at least once for attacking her while pregnant which proved to be the last straw – unfortunately for Liv, this time he wouldn't go.

And unfortunately for Edo, he had me for a sister-in-law.

'Yeah, can I get one of those "no-contact delivery" receipts with it?'

The girl behind the counter looked at me funny behind her plastic visor. 'But we're not delivering.'

'I know, but could you staple one of those "no-contact delivery" notes to the bag when you've put it all in?'

'But—'

'Can you just do it?' I dropped her a fifty and she shut her questioning yap and just did it.

'Have a nice day,' she said with a meek smile.

I took the bag and drove immediately to Liv's house – two blocks away from the office. I parked around the corner, left my wrist brace in the car (because Velcro and crime scenes don't mix, remember?) and walked the rest of the way. I had Amy Winehouse's 'Valerie' ringing through my ears from playing it loud in the car. I was strangely nervous, like I was about to have my virginity taken. It's not a good nervous and it was because I hadn't had time to rehearse this. No time to think, I had to act. I was rusty. I hadn't killed anyone in a long time. I assured myself that when I got in there, it would all come flooding back. So far, I'd remembered my No Velcro rule but the others eluded me. Defend the Defenceless. That was the main one.

Except Liv *wasn't* defenceless. She'd kicked him out before. I had first-hand knowledge of her seeing off assholes in clubs and bars with one flick of her acrylics and she once held a broken glass against a bouncer's neck when he was feeling up her drunk friend's ass. This was no wallflower.

But bit by bit, Edo had found her fragmented parts and poured his poison into them. And it had weakened her. And when Mikey came along, although she was still fierce as a lion, he had declawed her, one at a time.

I left the bag on their doorstep, note facing inwards, rang the doorbell and fled to the side of the house. I peeked through the living room window to assess the situation. Liv sat on the sofa, looking out towards the hallway. Her face was, as always, flawless, but her hair was undone from its bun and one of her earlobes was earringless and bleeding. Her eyes filled with tears when she saw me. I shushed her and she went back to watching the TV as he returned with the chicken bag. They were watching football. He sat down, not offering her any, and set about the chicken like a dog on hot chips. I snuck around to the back door and tried the catch – it was unlocked.

Sports results were being read out on the TV – some guy was losing his mind over a 'bump and run'. I located the knife drawer, and bided my time. Minutes passed. I gripped the knife in both hands – it would have to be Righty; I still couldn't trust my left – too weak. I overheard him talking shit about her. Threatening to take the baby as soon as the game was over.

'Do you want a beer?' came Liv's voice around the corner.

'Yeah.' I opened the fridge and had a double IPA waiting for her. She frown-nodded and took it, then saw the large kitchen knife in my hand. She turned to leave but at the last second turned back, taking the kitchen knife from my hand before I could stop her.

'Whatever happens, save my baby,' she whispered.

'Liv, wait—'

She marched back into the lounge. When I got in there, Edo had started on the pound cake – one mouthful. Two mouthfuls. Four, five, six in a row.

Liv stood beside his chair, watching him eat; knife poised behind her.

'I'm going,' she said.

'Nah, uh, no you don't,' said Edo, reaching for her. She stepped away.

'You ain't going nowhere.'

'I'm leaving. I'm going to Mom's with Mikey.'

He swallowed another mouthful of pound cake. 'You deaf, bitch? Sit down.' He grabbed her wrist and pulled her again until she's on the sofa, knife still behind her. 'We're gonna sit here while I finish this, then you are gonna call that divorce lawyer of yours and stop that right and quick. You know what'll happen if you don't.'

'Please Edo—'

'Please Edo, I'll do what you say just don't hurt the baby!' he mimicked.

'You don't even want him!'

'He's my son, Olivia. You can't do nuthin' about that.'

'YOU KICKED MY STOMACH WHEN I WAS PREGNANT!'

'You get me all riled up, what do you expect?' He laughed. 'Babe, it's your own fault, I told you.' Cake crumbs littered his T-shirt. He flicked them to the floor as he delivered his parting blow. 'I've been decent so far but if you push me, I'll tell child services about your coke habit, the drinking.'

'You liar! It was <u>you</u> ripping line after line while I was in labour, not me!'

'I'll make up some more shit; I ain't proud.'

She stood, knife shivering by her side. 'Mikey's not yours! He's Chim's!'

This was news to me too. Chim is one of Rafa's best friends. He's also a complete twat who is thirty going on thirteen but let's put a pin in that one for now.

Edo's head turned slowly to face her, like an incredibly angry owl. He got to his feet, grabbed her throat but before he could land the punch, she thrusts the knife into his belly, once, then pulled away; hands to her face, screaming; the knife sticking out where a knife shouldn't be.

'You . . . you stabbed me, bitch?' he yelled, bent over, hands around the handle. He tried to pull it out. 'You stabbed me!'

That was my cue.

'Oh my God, Liv! What have you done?' I cried, hands to my cheeks, trying to do the shocked-face thing as I pretended I'd popped round to see the baby. 'Holy moly, Edo, are you OK?'

'She stabbed me! She fuckin' stabbed *me*! Call the cops . . . paramedics!'

'Oh no, what are we supposed to do in these situations, I forget. Huh Liv? Do we . . . do we take it out?'

'No, no!' cried Edo, struggling to his feet. 'Don't touch it . . . Aaah shit, it's in deep!' He tried to make for the stairs. I blocked his path.

'You need to sit down so I can administer some first aid, OK? Come on, let's sit you on the sofa, that's it. Now we should take the knife out . . .'

I stood in front of him, face-on, and grabbed the handle, twisting it hard to the left. He screamed. 'No, don't!'

'Oops, sorry, wrong way.'

I twisted it to the right and he yelled again, calling me every name in his vulgar lexicon. 'Is that any better?'

'What are you doing to him?' Liv sobbed, holding onto herself for comfort.

'Pain is weakness coming out, isn't it? That's what the poster says at Nico's gym.'

'I don't think it applies to knife wounds,' Liv sniffed, shaking like a leaf.

Edo stumbled to his knees onto the carpet as I reached once again for the knife and with a great heave, I pulled it clean out, which also released a scream loud enough to rattle the china they don't have because it gets smashed in every argument. I held the blade above his head – his own blood dripping onto his face. He groaned and writhed. Then stopped.

Liv gasped. 'Is he dead?'

'Nah, it's a belly wound. It'll take him hours to die from that. Is there any chicken left?' I handed the dripping knife to her and picked my way through the bucket. It's all scrag ends and half-chewed bones. 'Grim.' The baby was crying somewhere upstairs.

'Call someone . . .' Edo wheezed from the floor.

'I wouldn't bother,' I said, changing the channel to BBC America. 'Ooh, *Overboard*. Great. She's still on the yacht.'

Liv got her phone out to call 911. I sprinted over to her and knocked it clean out of her hand. 'What are you doing?'

'He's dying, OJ!'

'I don't care if he's singing acapella with BTS, he's not going anywhere. Did you really sleep with Chim, by the way?' She nodded, tears streaming down her cheeks. 'Oh well, there's no accounting for taste.'

'Aaarrgghhhh!' Edo yelled, rolling about on the floor like a louder Mexican Mr Orange, mouth foaming.

I walked over and, in my most patronising trill, said, 'Are you all riiiight?'

'You bitch . . . you put . . . her up to this!'

'I didn't actually. I think this is what's known as the last straw.'

Without another word, he puked all over himself.

'Cough it up, might be a gold watch.'

'What's happening to him?' said Liv, coming over and standing close beside me – too close for comfort.

'He's dying, obvs,' I said as we stood over him, watching him convulse. 'What's Chim's dick like?'

'Small,' she replied, distractedly.

'Figures. I wish you'd have let me handle this. I'd have stabbed him in the heart – you get a much shorter swansong. Also, I would have stabbed him in the kitchen on the tongue-and-groove. We'll be up all night scrubbing the rug now. Hey, remember when we did "Telephone" by Gaga and Beyoncé at Nico's birthday? This reminds me of that. You and me, teaming up, *Out in the club, and I'm sippin' that bub* . . . remember?'

'Focus, OJ, what the hell are we gonna *do*?'

'What does Beyoncé do in the video . . . she rocks up in the Pussy Wagon and she says, "You've been a very *very* bad bad girl, Gaga." And then they go to a restaurant and poison everyone and do a dance.' I started doing the dance but Liv didn't join in – she's too busy staring at old Convulsing Ken on the lounge carpet. 'OK, not the time.' Edo was screaming in pain.

'I can't watch.' Liv turned away, but turned quickly back as though it's so horrible she couldn't *not* look at it.

But at that moment, when I was worrying about the

neighbours hearing him, Edo stopped convulsing and lay still. Foam billowed out of his mouth but his body didn't move. His eyes flicker closed.

Liv clutched my hand – my bad hand – and it hurt. 'Oh my God. Is he . . . ?'

I bent down and poked him hard in his stab wound. No reaction. I wiped the blood on his T-shirt and checked his pulse. 'Ding dong, the lil bitch is dead.'

'Oh my God. What are we going to do?'

I brought Edo's car around to the side of the house and we dragged him through the kitchen and out to the boot – no, *trunk*. My left wrist killed from doing that so it's all on Righty from now on.

There were more squawking noises from yonder – Mikey was fully awake, summoning a boob.

'Go up and see to Mikey. I still can't believe you slept with Chim – he's like Raf's least good-looking friend. Why not Joe or Mase?'

Mikey's still crying over yonder. 'It was a rebound thing.'

The longer Liv was gone seeing to Mikey, the more my mind raced down blind alleys and dead ends which all lead to one place – the police putting me and her in jail. Or worse; they still have the death penalty in this state. And there won't be no funky outfits or dance routines in there. But the longer I sat there, the more a plan formed in my head like the pieces of a smashed window. I had the money, the means and bags of motivation.

All I had to do was wait until dark.

*

'Don't forget to sponge down that foam when it's dry. Damp cloth. Do it until it's gone. Then shove everything you used to clean it in the fire pit out back. Then shower and bleach your tub.' In her arms, Mikey smiled at me and I kissed his irresistible hair tuft. 'See you later, Michelangelo.'

'OJ?' said Liv, as I unlocked the driver's door. 'Is he really dead? Are you sure the cartel will be able to—'

'—I've got this. Stop talking about it now. All right? As far as you know, he was here, playing with Mikey, eating takeout and then he left.'

Yeah, so I told a porky that I had a cartel contact helping me with this when in fact, all I had was an idea, a set of keys and a teenth of scopolamine carefully harvested from my brugmansia in a Ziploc pouch in my bag.

Gloved and masked, I took Edo's car and pulled into the dark, dusty drive of 30665 Roadrunner Ridge around half an hour later. The headlights swept across the front of the house – it looked like it did in the portfolio. I got out and made sure the keys worked – lit my way through to the basement door and checked it out.

It was perfect. Seriously. 'Casa Sweetpea' – the dream serial-killer duplex. *A remote, charming desert homestead surrounded by manzanita, pine and oak trees in a breathtaking location. Cargo containers allow for storage for desert toys, plus a private water well, propane, power and septic tank provide for a mostly off-grid lifestyle. Soundproof basement, ideal for those noisy hobbies you want to keep away from the main living space. An ideal home for anyone that requires a quiet bolthole, away from it all!*

Sold. Well, rented.

Back out at the car and a voice hollered from the trunk. I snapped on my gloves and mask and stood back to open it and sure enough, he was wriggling like a fish on a line. He went, 'Nnnnhhh pfffttt uggghhh' behind his ball gag and I emptied the powder over his face. Thank God for it – me and my one good hand were no match for a twelve-stone Mexican with biceps like boulders.

'I knew this would come in handy. Thanks for being my first guinea pig.'

He took in a good lungful, coughing and spluttering on the powder, and in seconds, he was still again – eyes open and staring, but paralysed. Alive, not kicking. But not for long – there wasn't enough scopolamine for it to last.

'Nnnnnnngghhhh!' he muttered weakly behind the gag. 'Nnnnnggghhh—'

'NNNN-Nighty night,' I said, slamming the lid down on his head, once, *BANG*, twice, *BANG*, three times *BANGBANGBANG* until he was spark out. Dead.

Well, dead-*ish*.

Saturday, 18 September 2021

1. *That guy who got massively pissed and changed his name to Celine Dion*
2. *Anyone who partakes in the Milk Crate Challenge*
3. *Joe Exotic*
4. *Brendon Urie*
5. *Prince Andrew*
6. *Wilmer Esposito – my ex-boss*

One might wonder why after spending over two years kill-free I suddenly decided to jump back into the old routine. Because it's what I do, duh. Why do smokers start up again? Why do drug addicts relapse? Some psychologists say there's no such thing as a 'cooling-off period' for a serial killer anyway. Even Nnedi Géricault said it on that podcast – '*Serial killers are either killing, thinking about killing or planning to kill. They never, ever stop.*'

Even though I *did* stop. And I *can* stop, whenever I want. I've proved it. But she's right: I haven't stopped thinking about it, not while Edo's been around. In the back of my mind there has always been that thought circling – the right time, the right set of circumstances, I could take him out of the equation.

I don't feel the urge to do it all the time, like I used to when I was with Craig or working at the *Gazette*. Most mornings it was odds on someone was going to get a staple gun to the temporal lobe or at the very least a rage fantasy about shoving their head into a urinal.

But Edo is a special case. He's hurting my family. He could hurt Mikey. I can't let that happen. I *won't*.

I just hope my left wrist is up to the task. Time will tell, I guess.

I controlled every aspect of Edo's sudden disappearance. I drove his car to the Coronado Bridge where I scrawled a brief suicide note about not being good enough for his family, using a scratchy pen I found in the glove box. I accessed his social media and found some good suicide memes and liked a bunch of them, using his phone. I reposted one to his Instagram – a particularly pertinent one from *The Catcher in the Rye* where Caulfield talks about how he hopes he gets dumped in a river when he dies and that no one brings him flowers 'and all that crap'. That would do. Then I walked to the nearest payphone to call an Uber, having slung his phone into the drink.

The only aspect of Edo's disappearance I *couldn't* control was his family, namely his mother, Josefina, with whom he was meant to be staying in Escondido. He hadn't been in contact for three days and she was worried.

Liv called me this morning, before my eyes were fully open.

'OJ, I gotta talk to you, I'm going out of my mind . . .'

'Sure, what is it?' I said, making as sharp an exit from my marital bedroom as I could without waking Raf or tripping over one of the snoozing dogs on the carpet. I scrambled downstairs and out on the patio where I was promptly blinded by the morning sun. 'OK, hit me with it.'

'It's Edo's mom, Josefina. She came round to the house this morning, asking questions. Edo was supposed to go back to her place last night for dinner but he didn't show, and she was asking me all this stuff: when did I last see him, has he called here, what was his state of mind. What do I do? She said the cops told her he jumped off the bridge.'

'Great.'

'It's *not* great. She said he left a note – did *you* write a suicide note?'

'Yeah.'

'She said the writing on it wasn't his, she's sure of it.'

'Well, when you're in a depressed state of mind, you're not overly worried about your punctuation or grammar.'

'No, it wasn't his handwriting.'

'Well, obviously not, it was mine. There's no body to find anyway so we're in the clear.' I rubbed the sleep crusts from my eyes. 'Seriously, is that all because I'm still half asleep and I need coffee like five minutes ago.'

'Phee, this is serious – she's not taking their word for it. How can you even sleep – I can't close my eyes. Every time I do I see his face!'

'Edo's mum doesn't know *anything*. She's grieving and grasping for answers. Suicidal people don't tend to broadcast their intentions anyway, they just do it. It's perfectly believable.'

'He wasn't suicidal though, was he?'

'The police won't care. All the signs he left behind will point to him tossing himself off that bridge cos he couldn't handle being a husband and a father. All the dots connect. You're fine.

You've got to pull yourself together. The cops have nothing. *Edo's mother* has nothing. Scrape him off. You're gonna give yourself an aneurysm if you keep this up.'

'But she won't leave me alone! I can't take it anymore. And whatever Edo did to me, he was her kid. She needs answers. This doesn't come easily to me, covering up a *murder*.'

'Not murder, self-defence.' I took a quick sweep behind me to see Bianca yawning and putting the coffee on in the kitchen. 'I have to go.'

'Why don't I tell Josefina what he was really like – how he came to the house threatening me; threatening Mikey? She might understand why—'

'—you can't say a word about anything, do you understand? You stick to the story – you saw him that morning and he was threatening to kill himself if you didn't take him back. You told him to go away and he did. We've just got to hope none of your neighbours saw me driving his car away.'

'No one's said anything if they did.'

'Good. I've fixed his socials to make it look like he'd been thinking about doing this for a while. If you deviate from the plan, they'll investigate and you'll only see your baby through bulletproof glass. If you're lucky.'

'OK,' she mewed.

I walked over to the brugmansia and gave it a quick spray with the hose. 'Don't go getting loose-lipped on me, Olivia – it won't end well for any of us.'

Later that afternoon, I found out what that urgent meeting with Wilmer was about. I knew from his first sentence that I was not long for this job.

'Hi, Phee, are you pressed right now? Wanted a quick word . . .'

His voice went down at the end of his sentence and a familiar dread descended: I knew that voice drop. I'd been on the receiving end of that voice drop before. 'A quick word?' And that word would be *sack*, I guessed.

I'd guessed correctly.

Wilmer's going all through the gears of an endless, unrelated speech. I catch the odd phrase but I'm not quite listening.

'. . . difficult decisions . . . restructuring . . . financial sustainability . . .'

'Right . . .' I said, putting my coat on. I could smell the fumes of disrespect coming off him like rotten meat.

'And because of those reasons, it's meant we have to think about how we plough the road ahead . . .'

Oh just spit it out, Vadge Face.

'You've been wonderful, really an awesome member of the gang, holding the fort for us there – *really* wonderful – and I don't want you to think we've taken this decision lightly but we're going to have to let you go . . .'

They're kicking me out. Goodbye holiday pay. Goodbye healthcare top-up. Goodbye free dental.

I'm taking the coffee though, I decided. *And* the fucking fish.

'Do I get a redundancy payout?' I asked.

'Erm, well, because you haven't worked for the company that long, it wouldn't be legally onerous for us to provide you with any sort of—'

'Maybe I could call up Gigi and ask her about it. Didn't she used to work here too? I found some of her emails on the hard drive . . .'

Was he silent, or had he been sil*enced*? 'Gigi?'

'Yeah. You know – shapely brunette, about five-eleven? Lives in La Jolla. Cums on your face when your wife's at Pilates?'

'How the hell—'

'—keep thinking about that payout, Wilmer. It might cost you more in the long run if you don't. Bye, Felicia.'

Suck my wonderful tits, you philandering canker sore. See, it pays to be the receptionist who keeps her eye on the ball and her nose on the sexual whiffs coming off her boss's face.

I'm about ready to kill a bitch today. I don't think Edo will have to wait in that basement for much longer. Bless 'im.

Sunday, 19 September 2021

1. *Edo*
2. *Mark Cordero – a dog killer in Texas*
3. *Roxanne Peach– a baby killer who just got a whole life tariff in the UK*
4. *Men who shop with their wives but don't help or look interested and spend the time sauntering along, hands in pockets letting The Wife fill the trolley and wrangle the kids. STAY HOME, PRICKS.*
5. *Andi Smith-Lansing*

I noticed an empty fish tank in the basement at Roadrunner the night I'd taken Edo and unceremoniously tied him to a pole down there, so when I went to feed him this morning, I nabbed it and gave it a good clean.

The office fish are still alive, by the way. And so's Edo. That stab wound didn't come to much, but I don't feel like finishing him off yet. There's a part of me that wants to drag this out – the Rhiannon part, I guess. But the Ophelia side of me wants to wait. Keep him alive, look after him like a pet. Rhiannon just wants to hurt him. Torture him. Hear him scream. It's a constant tussle. I am still a psychiatrist's wet dream.

And anyway, Edo doesn't deserve the sweet release of death just yet. So instead, I feed him, give him a few sips of water, provide a bucket for his ablutions and supply constant musical entertainment. I've taken the time and trouble to hook up Brad Pfister's iPhone to a speaker on the stairs to play 'C'est La Vie' by B*Witched for him. Every day. On a loop.

'They did this at Guantanamo Bay, apparently, to break detainees. It's called "noise torture". Me and my sister Seren made up a dance routine to it once in happier times. Still a banger. Count yourself lucky – it was a toss-up between this and "Cotton Eye Joe".'

'You can't just leave me,' he panted, as the song played for a third time.

I turned it up. 'Let the fun begin . . .'

Late afternoon, I stopped off at the office to clear my desk, get Richard E. Grunt from the top of my computer, nick the rest of the coffee, transfer the fish to their new tank, and grab a few reams of A4 paper and anything else in the stationery cupboard that wasn't nailed down.

Raf finished early today so after leaving a few farts in Wilmer's office chair, I swung by the Food Gnome to pick him up. He was out front in the parking lot, carrying a large box of groceries, accompanied by a short, limping Mama Fratelli–lookin' woman heading to a red Volvo.

I've encountered this woman before and I do not like her. I park a few spaces away and walk towards them. He sees me first and waves. Even with his uniform on and his mask pulled up over half his face I would still suck him through a hosepipe and back again.

'Hey, baby,' he says, placing the grocery box in her trunk as directed, then pulls me towards him for a sneak-kiss under our masks before re-fixing them. 'What you doing here? I can get the bus.'

'Thought I'd surprise you. And I needed fish food. I got the sack. And I nicked the office fish.'

'Ah shit baby, I'm sorry . . .' he begins before he's rudely interrupted.

'Did you cram the wine in against the toilet rolls?' Mama Frat hollers from her driving seat. She has badly-drawn-on eyebrows. I try not to laugh.

'Yes, ma'am,' he calls back. 'And I put the peas between them to keep them cool and stop them rattling too.'

She grunts in place of a 'thank you' and fumbles in her handbag for what I think is a tip but turns out to be cherry-red lipstick. God knows why. She's already a rolling turd in glitter wearing acrylics. She applies her lippy in the rear-view as Raf steps back from cuddling me and bends down to pick up a couple of stray pieces of litter. . He works so hard and she's born rude. I'm on a steady simmer.

'Boy, did you put the eggs on top?'

'Yes, ma'am,' says Raf.

'Who is she calling *boy*?' I scowl.

'Leave it, Phee. She's going now.'

'What about the strawberries? Did you put crap on top of 'em?' she squawks. 'I don't want them all squashed like last time.'

'No, ma'am, they're right on top there with your eggs and I've buffered them with your two loaves of bread, see?' He points inside the back seat. 'You're all good to go, OK? Have a nice day now.'

'Are you giving me cheek, boy?' she barks.

'No, ma'am,' he says, stepping back again. 'I wished you a good day.'

She mutters under her breath and I distinctly hear the slur.

It's my turn to step forward to the open driver's window. Unicorn face mask down. Horns out. 'Oi! Eyebrows. What did you call him?'

She looks at me like I'm the lump you find in your tit. 'Excuse me?'

'I said what did you call him?'

'Butt out, girly, this don't concern you.' She starts the engine.

'If it concerns him, it concerns me.'

'Phee, come on, don't start anything.'

'No, Raf, it's OK, I don't remember this bitch saying thanks as you helped pack out her bulky-ass Volvo with saturated fats. Why don't you say it now, Mama Fratelli?'

'I ain't saying nuthin', that's his *job*.' She looks back at Raf. 'Are you gonna call off your attack dog or am I gonna have to take this further?'

I want to do her here in the car park. Shank her in the spare tyre. The top one. Slice her down the middle. Open her up. Guts to the floor.

'Take *what* further?' I snap. '*You* being an ungrateful old cunt whose breath smells like ARSE or me defending my husband?'

'Y'all married? Ugh.' She looks at us in turn. I recognise it as disgust. 'Got enough of 'em over here already without you two breedin' another MUTT. Leviticus 19:19 – Do not mate different kinds of animals. Do not plant your field with two kinds of seed.'

I wished I remembered my Bible study days and then I'd have launched the perfect counterattack; something like, *Doth it not also sayeth in Leviticus 19:33 that 'when a foreigner resides among you, treat as your native-born. Love them as yourself, for you were foreigners in Egypt'?* But instead I yelled:

'Oh get down off your cross and give us all a fucking break.'

And I swing at her, fist flying wild but I can only get one jab in, which doesn't land cos she buzzes up the window and I'm buffered by a handsome Mexican wearing a grey uniform that I ironed.

'A mutt with a muzzle on.' She laughs behind the glass, looking at Raf and then back to me. 'I'll be speaking to your manager about this, Poncho.'

Mama Frat cackles like a witch. I can't stand it – she drives off without a second look. Nothing I can do but stamp my feet and eat her dust.

'I'll kick your tits off your chest, you BITCH! ¡NO TE METAS CONMIGO, PERRA! ¡NO ME CONOCES!'

Raf's hold on me is total. The moment it's over, I'm still spewing, but she's gone, out of the lot and up the road. And cos of me, Raf's probably lost his job as well.

'It's all right,' he coos softly as I struggle against him, fists clenched, eyes on stalks. We breathe together as I watch the road where the Volvo went in case she comes back. 'Easy, easy. Remember what I said last time: lose your temper, lose the fight. Breathe it out.' He loosens his embrace, snapping off his gloves and mask and shoving them in his pocket. His forehead is against mine, hands smoothing the sides of my face. 'Cálmate, it's all over. It's all over.'

'Fuckin' . . . eyebrow . . . bitch!'

'I know, I know, ssshhh.' I hated that Raf had to deal with this but this is what we'd become. Me on fire and him putting me out. Me flying off the handle, him pulling me back down. Like he's the Mandalorian and I'm Grogu and he has to keep stopping me from doing stupid shit that could get us both killed. We're rocking back and forth. He keeps hold of me till my arms go limp.

Sometimes if he'd had a sesh with his brother at the gym, he'd come back and take an ice bath in the garden. One time I got in with him – never again. But as anxiety suppressants go, it removed every atom of anger from my body. Being with him in that ice bath – deep belly breathing, holding onto one another, it was the only other thing that worked.

Apart from killing, of course.

'Why doesn't she make *you* angry? I've seen her here before, talking to you like that, calling you and Luiz names.'

He shrugs. 'She's a rat-licker. Just gotta keep your distance from 'em. Smile and nod, keep your triple-layered mask up and let them do what they gonna do. Quien se enoja, pierde – that's what my dad used to tell me. The one who gets angry loses, always.'

'But you got angry and they kicked you out of the army, didn't they? So you didn't take the advice.'

He is momentarily flummoxed. 'Well, no, but I should have. It ruined my life, not taking that advice. But I learned from it. What's the point of getting angry? You ain't gonna change an attitude like hers. I try to kill her with kindness, and the occasional Spanish platitude, which she *hates*. "Speak English; you're in my country now, boy!"' he screeches, impersonating her.

I smile. 'What's her name?'

He side-eyes me. 'Yeah, like I'm really gonna tell *you*.'

'Come on, I'm not going to do anything, am I? She's gone.'

'She's been on our Wall of Shame since we introduced a vegan aisle. Kept puttin' steaks and burgers between the tofu and beefless bulgogi.'

'Wasn't she one of the ones who showed up for the No Masks protest?'

'Yeah. She's never worn one.'

'Or a bra by the looks.'

'Imma go clock out. You wanna wait here?'

'No, it's all right, I'll come in. I need to pick some things up anyway.'

When I'm done, I linger outside the break room while he's at his locker, rubbing in hand sanitiser and talking to a colleague. There are a few others in there, sipping coffee and reading magazines, chatting behind their masks.

I glance at their noticeboard, at their list of dos and don'ts, their cleaning rotas, their Wall of Shame. I clock Volvo Bitch instantly – Mama Fratelli, glaring up at the CCTV. Her name is Andi Smith-Lansing.

Hmm. She had a few stone on me but I reckoned I could take her.

But, *steeples fingers*, one does not simply walk into the Food Gnome and murder Andi Smith-Lansing, oh no. This one could afford to simmer for a while. A low heat, a steady rolling boil, and when the time is right, I will turn up the heat and watch that dirty birdy squawk.

On the way home, we hit traffic. Raf's driving and chowing Red Vines. It normally takes us twenty minutes to get home

– today, it's an hour and twenty. Plenty of time for me to boil and bubble over Mama Fratelli and her massive audacity and crusty mouth creases. I search for her on social media but she's not there.

'He was going to flush them down the toilet. What else could I do?'

He gazes back at them in their shallow tank. 'They can't jump out of there, can they?'

'Not if they have any sense.'

'I'm sorry you lost your job, baby.' He holds my hand across the gearstick. He chows his Red Vines and flicks through radio channels. I stare at him. He has the most beautiful side-of-face I've ever seen. He has a good back-of-head too. And he's so happy. We're stuck in traffic-a-geddon and he's singing along with Don McLean.

'God, that woman really got on my tits.' I scowl as the memory drifts back in with the car horns outside.

Raf has already forgotten about it. 'Who?'

'Mama Fratelli.'

'Scrape her off. She's not worth going full-tilt John Wick over. Seriously.'

'She's on our list though, right?'

'Oh yeah, she's queen of the list. Once The Purge happens, it'll be her door we're knocking on first.'

'I ain't knocking,' I scoff. 'I wish I was more like you – I wish nothing bothered me. But there's some things in life you're not meant to have – for me it's true peace. And being able to run upstairs without my thighs giving me a round of applause. How do you do it? How do you just let things go?'

'I'm sitting in my own car, I got my best girl by my side, I'm eating my favourite candy, I don't need the bathroom, don't gotta be anywhere . . . and "American Pie" is on the radio. It's a matter of perception.'

A wise old Instagram account once said, *Before you marry someone, sit in traffic with them for hours.* And my soon-to-be husband Rafael is one of those strange people who doesn't get riled up by it. He says, 'Lot of waiting around in the army. You get used to occupying the mind, else it occupies you.'

'How many people did you kill when you were a soldier?'

'No idea. Why?'

'Just wondered.'

'My job was mainly to walk around in blazing heat with a bunch of heavy shit on my back trying not to die.'

'And learning Backstreet Boys routines . . .' I say.

He throws me a look. 'Sometimes.' He smiled. Oh that fucking coy smile got me every time. 'Anyway, air support got all the kills.'

'I can't believe someone as emo as you in high school was a soldier.'

He chuckles. 'You're not going to get over that yearbook picture in a hurry, are ya?'

'Nope. I look at it every time I need a laugh. Ooh there's that bastard again. Honk him, Rafa.'

'No way. If you start an altercation, I'm the one who'll lose, guaranteed.'

'You can take him. You're a trained soldier.'

'I'm also Mexican.'

'You were *born* here. Your brother and sister were born here.'

He picks up my hand, kissing each of my knuckles in turn,

saving the longest kiss for the scar around my wrist, before setting it back on my lap. He sings along to Don McLean's 'American Pie', as I continue to wish unspeakable acts of torture on the occupant of every car we pass. He's so beautiful as the sun beams in onto his face that I forget what I'm pissy about. I want him to pull over and hold me, cos when I'm touching him, all the stress vanishes.

'You OK?' He notices me perving at him.

'I'm sorry I'm such a bum hole.'

'You got nuthin' to be sorry for. Turns me on, you defending your guy like that. Anyway, I know why you're on demon time.'

'Why?'

'Well, it's been a nightmare, hasn't it? Covid. Losing Dad. All the wedding cancellations. The whole Edo shitshow. And now losing your job.'

'Oh, I couldn't care less about the job. We've still got *your* job, hopefully. And we've got the Tenoch cash, of course . . .'

'We're not relying on that.'

'It's clean money, Raf. The paperwork clearly states the money was left to me in a New York City deposit box by a distant deceased Mexican uncle once removed. There's even a death certificate and a form that states all taxes have been paid. It's clean as a whistle.'

'If it came from *him*, it's dirty af.'

There's an awkward silence for a few wheel rotations. We have this fight all the time about Tenoch and what he 'put me through'. About the dudes I 'had to turn tricks for'. The violations that never happened but that keep him awake and in therapy. That filthy $100k. He hates that especially.

He'd hate it even more if he knew about the other $900,000

in the safety deposit box in New York that I had to leave behind.

'Who *is* worthy of my rage then?' I ask.

'Hitler?'

'He's dead.'

'The Turpin parents?'

'Oh yeah, big time.'

'And Edo. Wherever he is.'

'Get in line, babe.' I laugh.

'Liv doesn't talk about him anymore, to me or Nico. Has she said anything to you?'

'Nope. I think he's long gone.'

'She looks so sad lately. Like she was when he was there. She hasn't done something stupid like taken him back, has she?'

'Not that I know of.' I start playing with his ear. He nuzzles against my hand and as if by magic, the cars around us start moving again, like we've unlocked the world. 'She'll be OK, Raf. There's nothing to worry about.'

The ache in my hand has gone and the acid in my chest has dispersed.

We pull into the drive and Raf's barely turned off the engine when there's commotion. Bianca, his mum, runs screaming out of the house in slippers, scurrying up to Rafa, babbling in Spanish, faster than I can translate. She grips his arms. He tries to soothe her, like he does with me, but she's too wired. Spit and tears and clawing fingers. I pick up some words—

Olivia. Edo. Bastard.

And one complete phrase that I don't understand at all but that makes Raf do a face I didn't like on him at all.

144

'¡Mi niña ha intentado suicidarse! Mi niña ha intentado suicidarse!'

'What's she saying? Raf, what's she saying?'

'It's Liv. She's tried to kill herself.'

I don't know why Liv felt so guilty about offing Edo (or *thinking* she'd offed him). He was a scumbag and got what had been coming to him for a long time.

But then, I don't process emotions the same way normal people do. Sometimes, I don't think I process them at all.

Anyway, Liv didn't try very hard to kill herself – it was the old pills and scotch routine – but she didn't take enough pills nor drink nearly enough scotch. A neighbour called round and caught her in the act, forcing her to puke it all back up. She was taken to the same hospital where Michael died so it was a bit of a fraught evening. Raf, Nico and Bianca went – I waited at the house to look after Mikey with Ariela and her three kids, Mateo, Elijah and the eldest, Anahid. They were taking it in turns to laugh at that fart noise on TikTok, dress up the chihuahuas and channel-hop through all my favourite Eighties movies on cable – they landed on *Crocodile Dundee*.

'Awww, leave it!' I said. 'I used to love this as a kid! My dad used to quote from it all the time.'

'I thought you grew up in care?' said Ana, sprawled across the couch, who'd momentarily stopped scrolling through *Frankenstein* cheat essays to pick me up on one of my rare boo-boos.

'Yeah, before I went into care this was,' I corrected. 'When I was, like, three. I barely remember him actually.'

'But you remember how the film made you feel,' said Ana.

She's one of those kids who understands the world. She also tore apart the film for me in a few comments. I was barely watching anyway; too busy earwigging Ariela's phone call out on the pool terrace.

'He's casually sexually assaulted a trans woman and all the guys in the bar have slapped him on the back and laughed about it.'

'But the crocodile bit was good, wasn't it? When he leapt out the water?'

'*She* was the one in the wrong. It's the croc's river.'

I nodded. 'I can't argue with that either.'

'And why does he have to save *her* all the time? It's sending such a bad message to girls. She's all weak and feeble and he's all macho and douchey.'

'Yeah, he is a bit.'

'There's a lot of casual racism against Australians too.'

I nodded. 'Yep, no doubt about it. With modern eyes, this film is toast.' Jesus, you ever want to hate the world, talk to someone twenty years younger than you. They'll suck all the pleasure out of everything you do, watch, say, eat or believe. And they'll be right about it too. Having said that, I ain't showing her *Rocky* anytime soon. Or *True Romance*. Or *Die Hard*.

'Could you apply some of that wisdom to your *Frankenstein* essay?'

'I have but it's harrrrd,' she whined. 'It's all about revenge I guess.'

'Yeah and you're talking to an Olympic champion in revenge so hit me with your questions . . .'

Mateo interrupted, batting his lashes. 'I'm hungry, Ophelia.'

'You've polished off a family-size bag of popcorn, Greedy Guts!' I said, pulling him in for a tickle session as he squealed in delight.

'I like the bit with the knife!' said Elijah, leaping from the armrest of the sofa. '"That's not a knife – now THAT's a knife!" Cool dude!'

'Mine's bigger,' I muttered into Mateo's ear, getting up to check on Mikey in his bassinette. I checked his breaths on the back of my hand. 'Ana, keep an eye on Mike the Tyke for me?'

'OK,' she said, setting down her phone.

Outside, the sun was setting. I left the kids watching Crock-o-shit Dundee and stepped onto the patio, drawn towards a persistent buzzing on the fence. A bumblebee was trapped in a spider's web. I carefully pulled the bee out by her leg, laying her down on the grass where she writhed to free herself from her bonds. After a rest from her exertions, she sat catching her breath in my palm. So shines a good deed in a weary world.

'She's OK,' said Ariela on a sigh, clicking her phone off. 'Had to have her stomach pumped. Nico's staying with Bianca; Raf's on his way back.'

'Mikey's still asleep. Shall I make dinner? The kids are hungry.'

Ariela took a long, slow drag of her cigarette, sucking it almost all the way to ash. It was ageing her – she has smoker's lines around her mouth already and she's only in her mid-thirties. 'They're always hungry.'

'We could order in?' I suggested. 'I know Bianca doesn't approve but she won't mind. We could get some of that birria stuff again, that was amazing.'

She turned to me and her mood gear-shifted into an even

pissier one. 'Is that all you can say? Don't you care about Liv at all?'

'Yes, she's my best friend. What do you want me to say?'

'I don't know. Something to show you're a human being with *feelings*.' She burst into tears and shoved another cigarette in. 'I saw you when Michael died. You didn't cry once. Not once. Everyone was in pieces but you – nothing.'

Christ, she must've been watching me like a hawk. I did *try* to cry. But it doesn't get me like it gets normal people. I do care about the family – *all* of them, except her of course. But grief just doesn't hit me like it hits normal people. Never has. I was mildly hurt she'd seen through my fake tears though.

This outburst had clearly been building for a while and now she was Vesuvius and I was that Pompeii dude they found under a boulder.

I sat down next to her at the pool with the fatigued bee in my hand.

'Don't touch me.'

'I was going to show you my bee. I saved its life.'

She looked at the creature, struggling to get her second wing out of the sticky web, and went to flick it out of my hand into the pool. Lucky for the bee, I had quicker reflexes.

'Why do you hate me so much?'

She reached behind for her Gucci slides, as though ready to walk away. 'I don't get how you can be so torn up about a bee but this doesn't affect you at all. We were saying goodbye to Michael on FaceTime and you were on TikTok, showing us some fucking tortoise.'

'It was ninety-eight years old. And it had a little cowboy hat on. I thought it might cheer people up.'

She snorted and sucked on her cig. 'I've known Liv since she was Ana's age. I guess you feel things more deeply when you're a mom.' Two tears fell in quick succession.

'Oh right, you're playing the mum card.'

I could have said I knew the second Ivy was a poppy seed stuck to my womb lining that I wanted her. How much I loved her. How I would wrench Mitch Silverton's heart right out of his chest and eat it if I found out he'd touched her. But I didn't want to. She'd pissed me off trying to drown my bee.

'You know what happened to me in Rocas Calientes,' I said, more to the flowers than to her. 'At the Hacienda?' I waved my arm in front of her face.

Her slides were on, but she stayed where she was. 'You know I do.'

'No, not the prostitution stuff. What put me in hospital. My hand?' I reached across to place the bee safely on a lavender patch, out of harm's way.

'He said they tied you to a fireplace and tortured you for money.'

'*They* didn't do anything – it was one guy called Paco. He handcuffed me to a fender and kicked my head in. And he said that if I didn't tell him where the money was hidden, he would kill three children in front of me.'

Ariela reeled back.

'I didn't know where the money was, but I sent him to the wrong place to look for it to buy me some time. And I knew that when he came back, he was going to do exactly what he said and kill those kids in front of me. Kids are my one weakness. Kids and dogs.'

'Nico didn't tell me that. This Paco . . . cut off your hand?'

'No. I did that myself, to get to the kids he'd locked in a cupboard.'

'*You* cut . . .' She didn't finish – just looked at my left hand.

'As it turned out, their mother had already broken in through an upstairs window. *She* was the one who killed Paco before he got to them. Took his head clean off. I was already passing out with blood loss by that point. But she saved all of us. So that was a waste of an arm, wasn't it?'

Ariela lit up a cigarette and sucked it away before I said another word. Yeah, suck on that, you endless *endless* bitch.

'So I may not be a mother, Ariela, but I have seen the lengths a mother will go to in order to save her children. And I know what I would do to save a child from certain danger. Because I'm a good person, despite what you *think* you know about me.' I got to my feet, flicking Vs behind her back whenever she turned away.

'You've stopped wearing your wrist brace.'

'On and off, yeah. It's mostly fine now and I've been doing my physio exercises.' I showed her how I could oppose my thumbs, despite Old Lefty aching. I wasn't going to let *her* see the weakness though. 'Dr Zweig says I'll probably never have the same grip strength but otherwise, it's all right.'

'I like what you've done with the garden,' she said, throwing the muted compliment out there like a handful of mouldy crumbs. 'I hate gardening. There's so much bending over. How do you get rid of all the weeds?'

'I weed it. Little and often.'

Beyond the pool, I had been tasked with creating a cottage garden, like Bianca had seen on *Downton Abbey*; a patch of England with Southern Californian nods but mostly roses.

Nico and Raf had built me two large raised beds with irrigation lines, filling them with topsoil, grit and well-rotted manure. I stuffed them full of herbs and canes for chillies and tomatoes, and around the borders we'd spent the long lockdown evenings digging out, I planted Bianca's favourite colours: red, peach, yellow, as well as lavender, sunflowers, marigolds, alstroemeria and bougainvillea around the patio doors, as well as individual pots of mint and coriander for her cooking. The smell when the sun hits it all at midday is out of this world.

'That's the one we have to keep the kids away from?' asked Ariela.

I nodded. 'Beautiful but deadly.'

In the large Ali Baba pot I'd been given for my birthday, I planted something for myself – brugmansia. It was quite a beast now – taller than Mateo and Elijah – with branches outstretched like Dracula's cape, and dripping in peach angel's trumpets, loaded with sinister intent.

'The seeds have scopolamine in them. The powder can kill people.'

Ariela scoffed. 'We should get Edo here. Sprinkle it on his pancakes.'

Finally, she was talking my language. She smiled and it sort of broke the ice. Way ahead of you, babe, way ahead.

By this time the bee was free of her sticky bonds and had both wings flittering, ready for take-off. I settled her on top of the verbena and she lifted herself up and away. While out of view of Ariela, I checked my messages. All from Pfister, all begging. He had cut his leg and sent me an Ick Pic.

I did the cutting thing you
psycho.

                              I want my phone. You said
                              I could have it now. Your
                                              a thief.

It's YOU ARE a thief. Y
O U apostrophe R E. If
you're going to threaten
me, at least get it right.

                              Fuck you. Where's my
                                              phone?

I'm texting you on it,
Numbfucks.

                              You can't do this! That's my
                              property. You're a thief.

And you're a pervert,
what's your point?

He didn't reply for a long time, but he'd definitely seen the
message.

Then the *Typing* . . . message came up.

I'm horny, that's all.
I meant no harm.

                              Horny people use porn. They
                              don't remove air vents from
                              women's toilets to create
                              holes for cameras and bore
                              spy holes in girls' locker

152

> rooms. I deleted the vid of me
> biting your nose, btw.

There was another long silence before . . .

> You've disfigured me for
> life. I could sue you.
>> How did you explain it to the
>> folks?
> Dog bite. They wanna sue.
>> Haha.
> You bitch.
>> You can get nasal surgery,
>> Brad. What you can't get is
>> anal virginity surgery and
>> that will be long gone the
>> second a prime piece of ass
>> like yours gets behind bars.
> If I find out you've shared
> any of those photos, I will
> kill you.
>> Stay tuned, Liam Neeson.

Ariela finished her cigarette then came up to join me. 'Is that Raf?'

'No. Someone from work asking where the fish went.'

'I'm worried about Nico, Ophelia. I'm worried he's lying to me.'

'He's not.'

'You saw how he got after Michael died. I'm worried the

Coronado Bridge story is a lie. What if Liv's protecting Nico? What if he killed Edo and he's struggling to handle it? I know my husband – I know when his head is heavy. And you know what? I hope he *has* killed him. But if the police find out . . . He's on his third strike . . .' Her words petered out as Ana appeared in the doorway.

'Mom? Is there any news on Tía?'

'Liv's going to be fine. She'll be home soon. Daddy's staying at the hospital with her and Abuela for now.'

'The boys are hungry.'

'Mija, put some cartoons on.' Ariela moved her sunglasses down from her hair to cover her eyes and handed her daughter her cell. 'Place an order at Margaritas. Same as last time. I'm not hungry.'

Anahid looked at me.

I smiled, swallowing the saliva that had run into my mouth at the mention of takeout. Ana sloped back inside. I waited until the doors closed. 'What do you mean Nico's on his "third strike"?'

'There's a three-strikes rule in California. If you've committed one or more serious crimes, you get jail time. Nico's got two strike priors, one for running with this gang when he was a kid making fake IDs. The second was the fight in the café after Michael's funeral. Assault and battery.'

'He barely touched the guy.'

'He broke his jaw. He only got off with a warning because we re-mortgaged to pay his bail. One more slip-up; he's looking at twenty-five to life.'

I stared at her neck mole. I think it had got bigger. She noticed me staring and self-consciously covered it with her hand.

'You don't know him like I do. He talked about killing Edo last year when Liv "fell down the stairs". He took up MMA to calm his rage but the moment his family are hurting, it's there.'

I knew the feeling well, like a pet rabbit I stroked regularly. Nico was a middleweight champion in MMA. He's won trophies, state championships, you name it. Nowadays he trained up wannabes but he told me once he'd 'never lost the fire that drove him'. Very much like myself.

'Rafael is more balanced,' she continued. 'Cos of his army training.'

'He still suffers,' I told her. 'He's in therapy.'

'I didn't know that.'

'Yeah, residual PTSD. He kept having nightmares about his dad dying, and Syria and what happened to me at the Hacienda. He's doing OK. Got some coping strategies. Breathing, ice baths, and this "grounding" thing where he squeezes a stress ball. He still gets anxiety but he can cope better now.'

'But you're not in therapy yourself?'

'Nah, it wouldn't touch the sides with me. Being here's my therapy. Sunshine. Gardening. Walking the dogs. Bianca's hugs. Hanging with the kids and Liv and Tiny Mike. And Rafa. All the therapy I need.'

'What the hell are we gonna do?! I can't lose Nico, I can't . . .'

'You're not going to lose him,' I said, stroking her arm like I would if she was a friend and I actually liked her. But it was Nico I was thinking about – my big brother. Figuratively, it was his arm. 'He's going to be OK – I'll make sure of that.'

Monday, 20 September 2021

1. *Noel, Adam and 'Thom', the baristas at the Hot Bean Café who talk through the milks so quickly I need a fucking DeLorean to hear them*
2. *Kelly with the nose hair at Avenue Dental*
3. *Kate Beckinsale – are you planning on ageing ever or . . . ?*
4. *Doctor Scott who did my smear test and lost my cervix, mid-exam. He eventually located it 'to the left'. I made the obvious Beyoncé joke – 'Everything you own in a box to the left' – but he didn't laugh.*

Nico didn't come back with Raf and Bianca that night, or the next morning. Nobody could find him. Raf went out early with Chim and Mase and a few of the other guys from the gym and servers they used to know at the restaurant to look for him. Bianca cancelled her hairdressing appointments to sit by the phone. As I was coming out of the en suite, Ariela was sitting on my bed.

'The fuc— Is there any news?'

'What if he's done something stupid, Ophelia?'

'Like what?'

She bit her lip as it wobbled. 'Torrey Pines.'

'Who's she?'

'No, it's a hiking trail, on the coast road. Michael and him used to hike along there when he was a kid. He goes running there sometimes. I found him up there once on the edge of the cliff.' Her face changed. 'I'm so scared.'

Why was she telling *me* this – she hated me. People did this sometimes, opened up to yours truly. Presumably because I don't overemote like other people do. I take on what I'm told and sort of file it away, like any good admin assistant would. My understanding is efficient. And my advice, even though I do say so myself, is often pure fucking gold.

I hitched my towel under my arms and sat next to her on the bed. I wasn't keen on my naked, wet foof being so close to her but I gauged the need for closeness. 'Does anyone else know about Torrey Pines? Does Raf?'

'No. I just thought of it. If he's . . . I can't see him like that, I can't . . .'

She broke down, leaning towards me in what I realise now was a hint for a hug. But I didn't want to hug her. She was still way too close to my naked foof for comfort and besides which, her hair stank of cigarettes. And she'd wished death on my bee. I gauged that this was a situation which warranted some form of physical contact, though, so I patted her bony arm.

'I'll go,' I said, placing an arm around her shoulder and holding my breath from the stink of cigs. 'I'll go and look.'

She nodded and gripped my hand. 'Are you sure? Would you really do that?' I nodded. 'Where will I tell Bianca you've gone?'

'Say I've got a rehab appointment. Stay here and keep her calm.'

And wash your fucking hair.

*

Torrey Pines lies north of Los Abrazos and twenty minutes away along Highway 101. A wild stretch of coastline with sheer-drop bluffs and hiking trails, it was named after the strange trees that grew all over its sandstone canyons – like children's drawings of Christmas trees on the surface of Mars, misshapen and bent over by the wind. I knew Nico wouldn't have headed to the golf course so I hit the high road to the nature reserve.

The parking was twenty dollars, which luckily was the only bill I had on me.

'Bloody cheek,' I grumbled as I placed the ticket on the dashboard and pressed the lock. I had put that money aside for a resin pirate shipwreck I'd seen for the fish tank. Nico's black jeep was parked at the far end under some overhanging trees. I walked over and stared inside. A couple of coats in the back. Litter in the footwells. Scraps of paper. I tried the handle. Locked.

I caught two brightly coloured hikers on their way back from Yucca Point. 'Hey, if someone wanted to kill themselves, where would they go?'

They gave me the look people normally give me when I open my mouth.

'No, not me, *I* don't want to kill myself. My . . . brother-in-law. We think he might have come up here. Had a tough year. All the lockdowns and what-not. Where's the steepest drop?'

'Razor Point,' said the dude, pointing behind him in a vague northeast direction. 'Follow the signs. Do you want us to call somebody?'

'No, it's all right. Thanks.'

The woman nodded. 'Do you want us to wait for you?'

'Nah, he's probably topped himself by now.' I eye-rolled theatrically.

The woman gasped and they both had this synchronous furrowed brow thing going on – I keep forgetting that Americans don't get my sense of humour. 'Sorry, no, it's OK, I doubt he's even up here. But thanks anyway!'

They eventually took the hint, leaving me to traverse the wooden bridges and staircases along the trail, following yellow signs for warnings of rock falls and steep inclines and brown info signs for Razor Point. I eventually found it. And I found Nico. The absolute unit that he was, curly brown hair blowing in the wind, and very much alive, standing on a precipice – the French Lieutenant's Hench Mexican Sidepiece With Calf Muscles For Days.

Cue the Denzel Washington relief GIF.

He'd stepped over the barrier at Razor Point, looking out over the undulating sea far below. Black Padres T-shirt, waterproof coat, shorts and he was shivering. Imagine a thick-set Oscar Isaac in white LeBron Witness 5s. One of his laces flapped in the breeze.

'You owe me twenty dollars,' I called out. 'It's outrageous, just to see a few cliffs.'

He turned to me, as though he had heard my voice but didn't know where to look for it. He was always so clean-shaven and smart but today he had a beard and his curly hair was greasy.

'How the hell did you know I was here?'

'Lucky guess?' I stepped over the barrier to join him.

'What are you doing? Get back, you'll fall.'

'S'nice here, innit? Should have brought a picnic.' I overtook him to look over the edge. 'Blimey, this is higher than I thought.'

'Get back here, Ophelia, it's dangerous.'

'No. If I want to stand on a rocky precipice watching the waves crashing hundreds of metres below me, I'll stand on a rocky precipice watching waves crashing hundreds of metres below me, thanks.'

'Please, come back. I don't want you up here.'

'You'll keep me safe though, won't you? You're my big brother.'

He stared out to sea, eyes watering. I checked my Notes app but none of the questions I had down for him – *How's life at the gym treating ya? What do you bench these days? Tell me more about HIT training again?* – seemed appropriate in that moment.

'Are you gonna top yourself?' I asked. He didn't answer. I reached out and took his hand and he squeezed it tightly, his throat wobbling but he still wouldn't look at me. 'If you go fish-side, you'll have to take me with you. And then you better *hope* you die because Rafael will fucking kill you.'

'I'm not gonna jump.'

'You're doing a great impression of a man who might.'

'I needed to clear my head.'

'You won't look so good when you bloat up, you know. Mind you, with those muscles, you'd make a terrific lilo.'

'I told you, I'm not gonna jump. I needed to think.'

'About what?'

'Looking over the edge at a place like this, it brings everything into focus, you know?' He walked forwards so we were level.

And I *did* know. I'd been there myself, on the cliff edge at Monks Bay when pregnant with Ivy. It had been a fleeting thought on the cruise as well when all other options seemed absent.

'My sister almost died. And I could have stopped it. But I didn't. I let her down. I let them all down.' His foot slipped suddenly and the edge of the cliff gave slightly beneath his feet as he backed away.

The shock of it made me lose my temper and pull out my knife. 'Right.' I thrust the point right up to his neck and nicked the skin. 'I've done about as much happy-clappy Oprah bullshit as I can do, so are you gonna come back from this ledge voluntarily or am I gonna have to stab you?'

That did it. Within moments, we sat side by side on a nearby bench watching a roadrunner pecking at dirt.

'Meep meep,' I said as it ran off. I put the knife away.

'Why the hell are you packin' knives?'

'A knife,' I said. 'For protection. I need to keep myself safe from predators lurking on remote hiking trails. Or daylight robbery parking charges. You owe me twenty dollars by the way.'

His face changed. I didn't understand it at first but then his mouth broke out into a smile. And then it split wide open and he laughed, loud and clear like a radiator bleeding off steam. It was one of those 'life is beautiful' moments – pure happiness, like when I find an episode of *Ramsay's Kitchen Nightmares* I've never seen. Like when we're all laughing at the same joke on *Ted Lasso* and I look around and everyone's smiling, even me. Like when Beyoncé came on stage at Glastonbury and I was in the front row. Or when Adele dedicated her Grammy win to her, though technically she should have given every one of those trophies to Bey.

'What's funny?'

'Just thinkin' back to Salomé's birthday,' he said, referring to their arty auntie who lived in Rocas Calientes, 'and you whining about the parking for that restaurant.'

'I'm British. It's in my DNA to moan about parking. And litter. And missed penalties. We're miserable bastards really.'

He laughed again. Then his face changed back to how it was before. 'What do I do, OJ?'

'Why is it on *you* to do anything?'

'Because I'm Papi now. It's my job to take care of everyone. I didn't know how much Liv was hurting.'

'Ariela said you have this three-strikes thing over your head.'

'Yeah, I do. Edo didn't report me for beating the shit out of him then but he could have. I got the impression he *would* have. But he's gotten away with it, hasn't he? He's done this to her and rode off into the sunset and he doesn't even give half a shit.'

'I wouldn't say "rode off into the sunset", but he's gone. And he's not coming back. Liv killed him.'

His jaw fell open as he turned back to me. 'What?'

'Edo = brown bread-o. Belly up? Bit the dust?'

'When?'

'Last week. There was a fight; Liv called me. He'd gone round, hurt her, tried to take the baby away. When I got to the house, she stabbed him.'

I left out the whole later section where he wasn't quite dead and I had been torturing him for days by tying him to a pole in the basement at Roadrunner, cutting off his fingers and playing B*Witched for him on repeat.

'And then he was dead. We covered it up. I drove his car to

the Coronado Bridge and left a suicide note on the dash then flung his phone into the water.'

'*You* did that?'

'Yeah. I got an Uber back. Then we all got on with our lives. Well, I did. Liv's been a bit ropey on the whole thing. Bereaved, guilty and stuff.'

'Why didn't you tell us? Why didn't *Liv*?'

'Do we really have to go through all this? The guy's dead, period.'

He looked behind us, to make sure all the millions of people who had been near us were definitely gone. 'Does Raf know about this?'

I shook my head. 'No. And I'm trusting you won't tell anyone.'

He didn't agree but he didn't disagree either. 'Why tell *me* before him?'

I wasn't sure why I told Nico in that moment – a strange mix of wanting him not to feel guilty anymore and liking the look on his face whenever I said something shocking. I wanted to impress him too – the way little sisters want to impress big brothers. I wanted him to be proud of me, like Seren never was.

But instead I said, 'Because you need to know the most. And because you're my family. And because he's hurt this family. And he deserves to die. *Deserved.*'

He nodded. We were most certainly on the same page. 'Did the cartel help you get rid of the body?'

Ah yes, the cartel: my faithful imaginary wingman that handily takes the rap. 'Yeah, I know plenty of dudes from my whoring days in Cartelville. I called one of them up. They have these barrels they dissolve people in. Leave no trace. Sweet as a nut.'

He rubbed his mouth. 'Shit.'

'It's dealt with, Nico. So you can't tell anyone. And I won't tell anyone about . . . this.' I gestured to the endless expanse of blue ocean beyond us.

'But his mom's reported him missing.'

'There's no *body*. The last time his phone was used was on the Coronado Bridge where his car was found, fingerprint-free days ago. As far as the cops are concerned, he went shark-side, beset by mental health issues. The End.'

'What about the Chuck n Buns?'

'What's that?'

'We had a whole-assed brawl two months ago. I banged him out in the parking lot. I just know there's a tape. If he turns up dead, that's evidence against *me*, OJ. What do I do? I could blackmail the manager, get the tape. Maybe threaten him a bit?'

'While cops aren't looking into his disappearance, it's not a problem. I wouldn't sweat it,' I told him, giving it the big *It's all gravy, baby* shrug and nonchalant sweep of the hand when all the time I'm thinking what a complete and total ball ache I have in store for me now, clearing up his fetid mess.

'But what if the cops *do* look into it? What if his phone shows up or his mom gets them to re-investigate his disappearance? What if the cartel—'

'—it's not going to happen, all trails are cold, I assure you. Don't worry. Be happy.' Drop it, you fucking idiot.

'It's a loose end though, OJ. I am on CCTV threatening to kill him. Then two months later, he goes missing. People have gone to jail for less.'

The cogs continued to turn in my mind. 'When was this again?'

'July ninth. Midday. I drove by and saw his car in there and . . . I lost it.'

'OK, leave it with me, I'll sort it.'

We saw the roadrunner again, pecking at empty peanut shells, on the way back to our cars but apart from a brief stop to laugh at its funny waddle, we didn't say a word. Our cars were the last two in the shaded lot. As I broke away from him to get to mine, he clutched my hand and wouldn't let go.

'First you make Rafael happier than he's ever been, then you keep Liv's secret; now you . . . save my life. We all owe you one, OJ.' And he hugged me – the kind of all-encompassing big-brother hug I've never had before. I couldn't remember ever being hugged like that, even by Dad. I was surprised by the sincerity of his touch and swallowed hard against the inevitable emotion about to betray me.

'I'm not doing this for payback. I'm doing this because you're my family. And I love you, *all* of you.' My heart did a leap thing and my throat went all sore when he let me go.

He laughed and shook his head. 'You're entering your villain era, aren't you, Ophelia?' he said as he got into his own car and slammed the door. I watched him drive out of the car park.

I thought hard at the steering wheel as I watched his dust in the rear-view. There was no stopping it now. I was in too deep and the feeling of wanting to be good and remain out of trouble had been roundly suplexed into the crash mat by the need to protect my family. And Nico was my big brother. I switched on the engine and revved it hard.

Entering my villain era? Well, I never really left it, did I?

Tuesday, 21 September 2021

1. *Bitches who talk too much about their boyfriends/ husbands – aka me. I am the bitches* 😎
2. *Any celebrity who Instagrammed holiday photos while the rest of the world locked down*
3. *Ellen DeGeneres*
4. *Tom Cruise – there is nothing behind that guy's eyes. I should know.*
5. *Boris Johnson – you can take the gal out of England but you can't take the need to smack this guy in the face out of the gal*

Honestly, is it me or are human beings easier to deal with when they're dead?

It's one thing after another with the living. No sooner had I got back from saving Nico's arse from the jaws of clifftop death than I had a response to my *How you doing?* text to Liv.

Not good. Please don't call me for a while. I need to think x

So now I have a broken arrow there as well – Liv is 'thinking'. Thinking about what? Thinking about whether to go to the cops and tell them she stabbed Edo or thinking about whether to implicate yours truly into the bargain? In the meantime, she's taken Mikey and they're staying with her friend Sam. Sam works from home so she's around to keep an eye on her.

We would have kept an eye on her. But I think there's more to this than I'm being told. Maybe it's me. Maybe I'm the problem.

Everyone thinks her suicide attempt is the culmination of divorce malaise, the baby blues and the late processing of her dad's death. Only she and I know the real reason. Guilt. She thinks she killed Edo. She sort of did – he wouldn't have survived for much longer. Not with me around.

But now she wouldn't even let me reassure her that in fact she *didn't* kill her hubs – she merely made him compliant enough to transport to my kill house so I could do it for her. But with her now resolutely refusing to read my messages, she'd jettisoned any hope of mental composure on the subject.

Nothing I can do about that now.

The thing is, a sister-in-law with an itchy trigger finger was one thing but if she got an itchy 911 finger, I was doomed. I tried a bit of meditation to breathe out the new onslaught of anxiety in my thorax. It didn't work. I tried cleaning, playing with the dogs, baking Bianca a red velvet. Nothing worked. So I did what I always did in these situations: watched an old ep of Gordon Ramsay shouting at someone and stayed angry.

I got the whisk going in the bowl but between that and some loud-assed old-school grunge on the radio, I could barely hear the voice on the line. I switched the mixer off, pulling the whisk out too quickly and spraying wet batter over the kitchen cabinets. 'Ahhh-cock-bollocks–shitbags-and-scrotums-ya-fuckin-Yankee-Doodle-piece-ofoh hi there, may I speak with a Mr Brad Pfister [yes, really] please?'

'May I ask who's calling?' said the sus-sounding matriarch.

'My name is Alison Chan-ey, Alison Chaney. I'm returning his call. He contacted us about the enquiry he made recently at the La Jolla Institute of Plastic Surgery. He filled out our online form?'

'Oh, OK, one moment please.'

I finished mixing in the eggs and started scooping in the flour. By the time I was at the 'spoonable mixture' stage, a man's suspicious voice has answered.

'This is Brad.'

'Hi, Braaaaaad,' I said, still in my faux American drawl as I licked the spoon. 'I have a job for you. And not a *nose* job.'

'Who is this?'

'I think you *knows* who it is,' I sang.

His voice lowered to a whisper. 'I want my phone back.'

'OK, well, I'm about to tell you how you can make that happen. So is Mommie Dearest still within earshot?'

'No. I'm upstairs.'

'OK, listen up, Buttercup – I *knows* where you live, in case you were thinking of ignoring me. And if I *knows* where you live, I *knows* where Carole, the pharma rep, and Andy, mortgage loan coordinator at the Bank of America, live as well, don't I? And Mackayla? Your little sister who does gymnastics and has curly red hair and who you whore out on social meed for hearts and follows?'

'Yes,' he mumbled, clearly through gritted teeth.

I dropped the accent – I sounded much more sinister in my British voice anyway, as all good Disney villains will attest. 'OK well, I'll come to the point. For your first task, I need you to put on a performance for me.'

'What performance?'

'Are you aware of the charmingly named Chuck n Buns on the corner of Fletcher and Edwards? The one with the neon sign and the parking lot always covered in garbage where the guy was caught fucking a pie?'

'Yeeahhh.' Again, the suspicious note to his reply.

'I need you to be there this lunchtime. 12.05 p.m. On the dot.'

'Why?'

'To cause a disturbance for me.'

'What do you mean?'

'Like, a ruckus. A melee. A hullaballoo, if you will.'

'A hulla-ba-what?'

'Go in, smash things up a bit, upend some tables, rant and rave – maybe you had bad service there once and you've gone full-on Michael Douglas.'

'Who's Michael Douglas?'

'Ugh, foetus,' I muttered. 'Just lose your shit, OK? But make it good and take your time. I need at least . . . seven minutes.'

Five is too short, ten is too long, seven is perfect.

But I was greeted with an audible sigh. 'Why do I have to do this?'

'To keep your Peeping Tom ass out of jail, oh precious one, that's why. Unless you want to eat slop and get forcibly buggered for the rest of your days.' I spooned in the sugar and two drops of vanilla essence. 'I read all your Facebook rants about why women deserve to be raped, by the way. You'd be quite the speechwriter if you knew how to use a fucking apostrophe.'

'I'm not doing this. They'll call the cops.'

'They won't call the police if you're unarmed. Shout and

bawl, complain about the lack of coleslaw or stand on a table and deliver a speech about why all cherry pies deserve to get fucked in the tin tray, I don't care.'

'But if I get arrested—'

'—you'll get off with a caution. You're not going to cause any real damage. You're only going to raise your voice a bit, throw some chairs, squeeze ketchup on the tables. For seven minutes. Police don't respond to anything in seven minutes, especially a scrawny white dude.'

I pulled down the oven door and slid in the two mixture-filled tins, before setting the timer.

'And that's all I gotta do to get my phone back?'

'For now.' I went to lick the spoon then thought again. Hips and all that.

He sighed again. '*When* am I gonna get my phone back?'

'When I am good and ready to give your phone back. I hold the cards here, remember. Now do we have a deal or do I pay a visit to Andy at the Bank of America on National Ave and cut off an appendage from *his* anatomy?'

His voice was all a-quiver. 'Don't you fuckin' touch my dad.'

'Then be at the fuckin' Chuck n fuckin' Buns on fuckin' Fletcher and Edwards at 12.05 p.m. and I won't fuckin' have to, will I?'

I pull up at the Chuck n Buns ten minutes before noon. No sign of Pfister (yes, really) but I know he'll be here. Being inside the place made my stomach turn over. The air stinks of fryers that haven't changed their oil in months and the music pumping out is scratchy and in need of a bullet to the speaker.

'Hey, I have an appointment with your manager at midday?'

I say in my perkiest Reese Witherspoon squeak, selecting the simplest-looking dirtball shovelling fries to announce my arrival.

'Oh sure yeah,' he says, like he's suddenly awash with responsibility and doesn't know what to do first – put the mop down, put the scoop down, or take the order from the woman behind me. I delight in the wind beneath his flapping baby wings. 'I'll go grab my manager.'

A portly fellow around twenty-one years of age appears in a doorway labelled 'STAFF ONLY' and his badge proudly says 'ROY' – next to it is a cartoon of a worried-looking bull splayed flat inside two sesame seed baps. Roy doesn't look happy to see me. His shirt is wet under the arms and all down his back in a wide V. 'You've come about the job, right?' He sweeps me into the office with all the gusto of a guy who's gonna hang himself right after I leave.

He's not prepared. Computer's off. Can't find a pen or something to write on. I'm waiting patiently, glancing around the room. The CCTV monitor sits on a bracket jutting out from the wall behind him, showing footage from six separate cameras – two above the drive-thru windows, one at the entrance, one at the exit, one above the counter and another outside the bathrooms. There's a VCR too, pretty old school, which means there must be a new tape every day. Nico's brawl will be on one of those tapes – ninth July. One sits on top of the VCR where it has been switched that morning. The others must be in the cabinet behind Roy's desk.

This was only supposed to be a recce but it's going to be much easier than expected.

And there are the keys, a whole bunch of them, on the desk

before him. Colour-coded so even the most idiotic of store managers can identify them. The red one must be it because the cabinet lock has a red sticker on it. This is going to be fucking child's play. There isn't even a lock on it.

'OK so I'll run through the job description for you, though you prolly already seen it but we're looking for people who are friendly, who'll greet the customers, send their orders through, make sure the orders get out quickly, and make sure cash register tallies at the start and end of each shift . . .'

'Yeah that sounds straightforward. I've done this before, if you look at my resume you'll see I worked at the Food Gnome for six years as a cashier.'

'Yeah, it's on the email you sent, right?' He scrolls through the computer to find it. 'There are also some cleaning duties . . .'

'Fine with me. I love to clean. I'm quite a neat freak at home.' He stares at my wrist brace. 'Oh, don't mind this. I get a little RSI sometimes. I volunteer down at the mission, dishing out soup for homeless veterans. I'm my own worst enemy sometimes! It doesn't affect my paid work, of course.'

He nodded, searching for my email. 'Very commendable.' An imaginary glint sparkles from my toothy smile. 'What was your name again?'

'Giselle,' I said. 'Giselle Carter.'

'Hmmm, I can't find it here, Giselle, when did you send it in?'

'Last week. Thursday, I think. I also attached my high school diploma which I think was your minimum requirement?'

'Yeah, I think I remember.' He gave up looking. 'OK, no bother, um, why don't we run through a couple of the usual questions, see how you would cope with the following: so you're at work and a guy comes in and he's salty cos we've run out of chicken. What do you do?'

'I would smile sweetly and say we have a delivery coming imminently and that he is welcome to peruse our menu to see if there's anything else he would prefer in the meantime.'

'He's still angry. Starts throwing his weight around. What do you do?'

'Offer him complimentary fries and tell him he's seen and appreciated?'

He smells my special fried lies. I need a distraction. Luckily, I have a puppet on call and right on cue, I hear my pre-ordered extra-spicy hullaballoo.

'Excuse me, I won't be a minute.' Roy frowns, marching to the door like he's finally awake for the first time today.

Oh yes you will. Soon as the door closes, I can see all manner of hurly-burly going down on the CCTV screen – chairs yeeted across the room, Pfister shouting off, ketchup a-squirtin. My minion, doing the Lord's work.

I open the piss-easy cabinet with no lock and scan each tape until I find the one marked ninth July. There aren't any others with that date – so I shove it into my bag, slamming the cabinet back up and retaking my seat on the other side of the desk. I check my pulse – barely troubled. I was expecting much more of a thrill, maybe even an attempted seduction of Roy while I fiddled with the lock but there was no need. It was like sex with Craig – all the right moves, all the anticipation but absolutely no climax.

By the time Roy returns to the office, I'm sitting in the chair looking exactly as I did when he left – meek, pretty; the sweetest of all possible peas. First rule of hoodwinking a man – make yourself as small and innocent as possible. And smile. Smiles cover a multitude of sins.

'Sorry about that, some guy day drinking.' His sweat patches had doubled. 'Weird dude. He came in, threw some chairs around and just left.'

'Well, it takes all sorts,' I say. 'Listen, I've this moment had a call from my husband saying he needs me to pick the twins up from day care so Imma have to bounce. But thanks so much for your time, Roy.'

'Job's yours if you want it,' he calls after me.

Gordon Ramsay clap DONE.

I called straight round to Nico's gym – an intimidating place at the best of times due to its black-and-red walls, abundance of chains and grunting, and music videos where the men are all in puffa jackets and the women are reduced to breathy choruses, baby-oiled arses and pneumatic tits. I stood in the doorway and hollered at him over the racket, beckoning him out of the way of the CCTV. Nico was in the ring, giving a Ronda Rousey to the back of some scrawny guy's head.

'Hey, how you doing?' he called out, a lot happier than when I last saw him. 'I've been meaning to text you.'

'I'm glad you didn't. Paper trail and all that.' I removed the tape from my bag and handed it to him. 'Your brawl, sir. You want fries with that?'

'What?'

'The tape of you and Edo, at the Chuck n Buns. I stole it.'

He wiped his sweaty brow on his wrist and frowned. 'How?'

I shrugged. 'It was piss easy actually. I thought it was better

174

to have than not have, so do what you want with it and then you're in the clear if the cops *do* come knocking about Edo, aren't you?'

His jaw just wouldn't close. 'H-how the hell did you get this?'

'I went over there and pretended I wanted a job, got access to the office and . . . Roberto es tu tío.'

'I can't believe— OJ, you are amazing.' He laughed, tucking the tape inside his hoodie pocket and pulling me into a steel-strong hug – a full, warm big-brother embrace which even though it was a stiflingly hot day and we were standing on pavement that was melting the soles of my trainers, I still enjoyed. 'I don't know what to say. That's it? That's the whole thing?'

'Yeah. Do with it what you will.'

'I got a hammer out back I'd like to introduce to it. OJ – you're a warrior.'

'Better a warrior in a garden than a . . . whatever it is . . .'

'. . . a gardener in a war,' he finished, hugging me tightly again and kissing my hair. 'Thank you, mi hermana. Thank you.'

Thank you, my sister. Just those four words made up for that horrible Craig interview in *Hello Magazine* where he'd asked how anyone could truly love a woman like *that*. It made up for all the times Seren had called me toxic. All the times someone had called me a freak or a weirdo at school or work. And when Nan had called me a cancer in our family. *This* was my family now. Nico and the kids and Bianca and Liv and Mikey and mi hermoso Rafael.

And nobody was going to take them away from me.

Daily Mail

10 January 2021

Sweetpea Killer: identity being 'protected' by sick fans, say detectives

The Sun

5 April 2021

Police – Killer's fandom is actively damaging our investigation

The Times

27 June 2021

Detective Sergeant Jai Amarkeeri from the Met's Homicide and Major Crime Command warned the killer's die-hard fans – who call themselves Bad Seeds – 'your loyalty will cost innocent lives'.

Daily Telegraph

17 August 2021

Crimestoppers have raised the reward for information leading to justice for Sweetpea's victims to £300,000 – the biggest single reward offered in the charity's history.

Sunday Sport

2 September 2021

I CUT OFF PERVO BOYFRIEND'S SCROTUM AND BAKED IT IN A PASTY: SWEETPEA MADE ME DO IT

Wednesday, 22 September 2021

1. *R. Kelly*
2. *Anyone on* Teen Mom
3. *Ted Cruz*
4. *The guy who's bid £8,000 on eBay for a Christmas card I sent Imelda seven years ago, the one covered in glitter. Imelda hates glitter.*
5. *Imelda. Nice interview on* The One Show *by the way. Those horsey hair extensions take the emphasis away from your shit fillers.*

I took the dogs to the park for a good run around this morning and saw Liv out with Mikey in the buggy, and her friend Sam walking alongside. They'd got coffees and paper bags of pastry. Liv saw me but she didn't wave. She and Sam talked and laughed – the kind of laugh that says, *I saw you but I have another friend now so whatevs*. Seventeen texts she'd ignored. Seventeen.

Fuck her, I thought. You keep on carrying that guilt, babes. I ain't letting you off no hook.

When I sat on a bench to let the dogs run about, my phone went and I momentarily thought it was Liv but instead it was Seren. Again. Twice in one month. This was unheard of.

'This is getting awfully regular . . .'

'Rhi?' came the quietest voice. 'Géricault's been here. At my house.'

That shut me up. 'Whut?'

'She turned up, on my doorstep again. She's only just left.'

'Maybe you shoulda shot her, like you did your last uninvited guest.'

'Not funny. She was here for two hours. Said she was on vacation but I know she came here to see me. She sat in *my* living room, Rhiannon. Drinking out of *my* glass.'

'She's not the devil incarnate, Seren.' I threw the tennis ball for Diablo who then rode roughshod over the others to get to it first, causing an insane amount of anguished squeaks and a mini pile-on. 'STOP. FUCKING. FIGHTING!' I yelled out in my best Tommy Shelby voice. Amazingly, they did.

'No, she's not the devil incarnate, she's worse – she's the woman who could put me in prison if she gets a whiff that you're still alive . . . I shouldn't have called. I'm at a public payphone down the street in case she's bugged the place.'

'She's going up a blind alley. I'm officially dead and she's the only person in the whole world who thinks I'm not.'

'Aren't you freaking out right now?' asked Seren. 'She got on a plane, flew all the way across the Atlantic and came to my *house* in the middle of a pandemic – she wouldn't do that, go to those lengths, unless—'

'—unless what?'

'Something's different.'

'Tell me exactly what you said to her and try to remember every single place in your house that she went.'

Seren went over it – where Géricault sat, what she drank,

how long she was in the bathroom for, everything. I got a bit bored with all the minutiae and put her on speakerphone so I could round up the dogs. Then we walked back home.

'Check every place she went in the house, every bit of furniture she ran her hands over. If she *has* bugged it, it'll be a small silver or black sphere, no bigger than your nail. Check lampshades, switches. Do you have an iPhone?'

'Yeah.'

'She may be tracking you. It'll tell you if there's an AirTag nearby. You'll get a notification and then you can disable it. Was she ever out of your sight?'

'Well, she went to the bathroom. I couldn't exactly follow her in.'

'Do a sweep in there – see if anything looks odd. Kids' rooms too.'

'Sweep? With a brush you mean?'

'No, Seren, with your *eyes*. Check and see if anything looks out of place, like an ornament or a book. Listen out for a low buzzing; a hum. There might be an app you can download to detect them too.'

As we came into our street, I waved pleasantly to Marji Blumkin and kids, leaving their house across the street for soccer practice. She didn't wave back. I flipped the bird behind her back and her daughter saw it from the back seat.

'How do I google it if she's checking my phone?' asked Seren.

'Mmm, good point – in which case maybe invest in another phone?'

'Do you know how much new phones cost?'

'Oh, shut your hole up, you're loaded. Stop whining and just sort it out, will you? For both our sakes.'

Seren's phone call didn't concern me that much – it would have, a few weeks ago before I'd begun down my primrose path of dalliance again, but when I'm in a killing cycle, generally I don't worry about things like nosey detectives on the other side of the country. I'm in control. I'm happy. I'm loved.

And still, technically, dead.

Which means, amongst other things, that I still have access to Target. Aka, my favourite place in the world. I like to go quite late at night, when the moon is full, the car park almost empty, and there's not so many human traffickers around looking for lone women.

But even that risk is worth it for the reward.

Don't get me wrong – I still hate that they call crisps *chips* and all the *'erb / cilantro / arugula* bullshit but one of the things I love about American life is that you can go to a big shopping place like a Walmart or a Target and buy anything you want. You could go in there looking for Band-Aids or a birthday card and come out with cheesecake, a hoverboard, an inflatable baguette, an engagement ring, a sequinned pillow of Danny DeVito, a top hat and tails for a chihuahua, and even a rust-resistant fourteen-piece knife set complete with slip-proof grips. All of these I have bought in the last few months.

Take a fat guess which one was my favourite.

Obviously, I couldn't go to the Food Gnome to get supplies for Edo today so I hit Target, then swung by old Basement Jack to feed him and change his bucket and music. The fucker still hasn't had the decency to die so he's getting another dose of B*witched to send him on his way. Three straight days of 'C'est la Vie' should be enough to kill anyone.

When I get home, there is a new thing to worry about. A taxi has pulled up outside the house and paying the driver is a stocky guy in combats with a rucksack, looking like a Wish version of Colin Farrell. He smiles at me; a smile that would moisten the most menopausal of gussets.

'Oh fuck,' I mutter.

So this would be my undoing: aka Billy, aka William O'Shea. The heavily tattooed ex-squaddie from the west of Ireland who could ruin my life. He has dark brown hair shaved at the base and the top is scraped back into a tiny topknot. He has on a short-sleeved Hawaiian shirt and cargo shorts covered in army patches. He holds out his hand in greeting.

'Hey, it's Ophelia, right?' he says.

I smile pleasantly, noting my mask is flung on the passenger seat, out of my reach. Still, he doesn't seem to recognise me so I leave it and instead offer my hand. 'Billy O'Shea, I assume?' I frown, as though I don't know who he is or what he might know.

He shakes my hand, staring at the scar on my wrist. 'Yeah. They used to call me Colin Feral in the army.'

'Why's that, cos you're overrated?'

He laughs. A lot. 'No, cos I'm Irish. And cos I get through more pussy than the Cats Protection.'

'Lovely.'

'Ahh sure, is it my fault whenever I open me gob their knickers come flying off?'

I hate him already but I have to admit, he does have that infuriating way about him – the way that said, *I could laugh you into bed and you fucking know I could.*

'Ahh but seriously though, it's great to meet you at last, Ophelia. Raf never stops going on about you on the old group chat. Your pictures don't do you justice though. He's a lucky guy.'

'Pictures?'

'Yeah. Raf sent some pictures. You and him on some beach after your engagement party?'

'Oh yeah. *Those* pictures.' For a second, I'd assumed he meant the ones doing the rounds on certain sites, threads and true-crime documentaries. The ones *pre*-surgery. As long as he hasn't seen me pre-surgery, there is a good chance I'm in the clear.

'Yeah, you're a stunner all right.'

Oh, he's charming all right – he more than passes the vibe check. I can see why Raf said he's a big hit with the ladies. He has the twinkle, the humour, the smiling Irish eyes but something about him riles me.

Oh yeah. That's it. The fact he might know I'm a serial killer. Annoyingly though, his charm does work on me and to my everlasting shame I blush. It's amazing how quickly feminism flies up the chimney when a man calls you pretty.

'Are you staying with the Arroyo-Carranzas?'

'No, no, I've got an Airbnb in town; didn't want to intrude with all the wedding preparations going on,' he says.

'Ah right, well, it all starts in earnest next week. Everything's been booked for a while – it kept getting pushed back so fourth time's a charm.'

'Yeah, Raf told me. What a fuckin' nightmare.'

'Oh no, it's fine, I *love* dealing with people and I'm a dab hand at organising things so it's been a real joy.'

'So it's still all set for the twenty-ninth then?'

'Yep. Come what may.'

'No more "single ladies" dance for you then?' He chuckles, with added Beyoncé hand movement.

Why would he do that? Why *that* song in particular? Had he read the biography? Does he know about my love of Beyoncé?

'Uh, nobody's home at the moment,' I say to change the subject. 'Raf's working until four and Bianca's vaccinating so it's just me.'

Billy pays his driver and sends the cab on its way. He stands on the pavement as though waiting for me to say more.

I know what I *should* say next – I should invite him in for a drink or some lunch but I don't want to be stuck there all day making pleasantries with a stranger. Not least a stranger who lived in London, had probably seen my pre-surgery mugshot on every news report pre-Covid and could rumble me at any moment.

'Well anyway, we can get to know each other at least, can't we?'

'Can we?' I say, unlocking the front door and immediately unleashing the onslaught of six yapping chihuahuas whose noises reverberate from every wall in the place, turning up the dial on my existing anxiety.

I'm nervous, that's what it is. Billy makes me nervous. On top of Liv and Nico and Géricault and everything else, I do not need this today.

'OK, well, I've got a lot to do but you're welcome to come in and I can make you a sandwich if you like?'

'Sure, that'd be great,' he says, as I hold the door open wider for him and he swings his bag onto his back and saunters past me, a stupid grin on his face like he's just so happy to be here.

He turns to me in the hallway. 'I could do with a slash as well, if that's all right?'

I point towards the downstairs bathroom and head on into the kitchen. I set about topping up the dogs' water before breaking into the crate of Guinness cans that Bianca had got in for him.

I place his Guinness on a coaster on the coffee table in front of the TV – I even switch the TV on especially so he doesn't feel the need to come into the kitchen and make small talk.

'Ah that's grand, thank you,' he says, striding in and reaching for the can but not sitting down. 'Is there any baseball on?'

'Padres White Sox, I believe. Raf wanted to be back for it,' I say, handing him the remote. His finger grazes my hand as he takes it. He's still looking at me as I watch the screen, waiting for Nick Bosa to appear with his thick thighs in his tiny leggings before remembering that this is still not his sport.

'Right, well if you're OK I'll go make your sandwich. Won't be a tick.'

God I hate being faux-nice to people. It reminds me of the me I used to be during the days of The Act. All Bo Peep and pleasant but I had to keep this interloper sweet for fear of rumbling the sweetest of all possible peas.

The pea that is Me.

Next thing I know, the interloper's standing at the kitchen island, watching me make his sandwich. The baseball game is blaring in the next room. He tries engaging me in small talk about Raf and the family but I give short answers – one word if I can get away with it.

Yes. Fine. Yes, we were all heartbroken when Michael died. No it wasn't an open casket. Yes, Rafael wants kids after we're married. No, he can't spike the wedding cake with the toad venom he bought from his cab driver.

I've never made a sandwich so fast in my life. I hand it to him, urging him with my eyes to go back into the lounge and fuck the fuck off. But he remains at the island while I am all at sea.

'Ahh thanks, Ophelia. I could eat a racehorse and go back for the jockey.' He sinks his glass of Guinness and sighs contentedly. 'Ah, well it's not on the backdrop of an Irish airneál or a cloudy sky but you can't beat the old liquid Viagra, can you?'

'How long are you staying for?'

'Why, you bored of me already?' he says with a wink. 'I got an extended Visa so I can stay up to ninety days. I'll keep out of your hair, don't worry. Me and yer man have got some serious drinking to get done while I'm here.'

'Don't you have a job to get back to? Or . . . family in the UK?'

'Nah, not really. I've got an aunt and uncle back in Ireland who I visit sometimes but no other fam left. Jobwise, I'm a bit of a drifter. Ran a few bars, did some hotel work in Dublin and London, had a couple of wives but I've got like ADHD so I struggle holding stuff down like relationships and jobs. I did a bit of travelling around Europe for a bit as well, worked at Euro Disney – one of the most popular chipmunks they ever had . . .'

My GOD he talks fast.

'Yeah, I like to travel, don't much like staying in one place – I get bored easily. Don't like to be, you know, rooted.'

Was that a dig? Was he dropping floral hints that he'd sussed my true identity? No, I reasoned. Tenuous at best.

'So you don't spend much time in the UK then?' I hedge.

'Ah on and off, you know. When there's a bit of work around.' I was about to probe him further on this when he strode over to the patio doors. The garden looks amazing. Was that you?'

I stare at him, heart freezing. 'Yeah. How did you know?'

'Raf told me you were a bit green-fingered. It looks gorgeous.' He gazes out the patio doors but there were no lingering looks at me at least.

Still not proof he knows me, I reason again. Annoyingly, he seems a genuine sort of character. 'Raf told me about your hand. How is it?'

'Fine,' I say, self-consciously pulling my hoodie sleeve over my left wrist. 'Is there anything Raf hasn't told you about me?'

'Oh I'm sure there's plenty,' he grins. 'The science is getting better all the time. I try and stay on top of it all, see what's available. I mean, prosthetics are all well and good but, in a few years, they'll be able to start re-growing severed limbs in a lab I shouldn't wonder.'

'Right,' I say, distracted by making myself a glass of orange juice.

'Yeah, they can do all sorts now. They've got titanium implants that they can actually clamp onto the bone, how about that? Technology's getting better all the time. It's exciting.'

'Yeah, it must be,' I say, with added side-eye. I don't know why he's so obsessed with amputation but he sure seems to know a lot about it.

He mooches around the place as we chat – I say 'chat' but it feels more like an interrogation. His eyes are on me the whole

187

time as he paces the kitchen, staring intently at Bianca's clay ornaments along the windowsill, and the fridge pictures of Mikey in his late grandfather's arms.

'So sad that,' he remarks. 'How are they doing, coping without him?' He points to the picture of Michael in his baseball cap at a game, sitting between Nico and Raf.

'They just get on with it, you know. They're a strong family. Resilient.'

'Good job,' he says.

I learn a few things about Billy in that excruciating hour – I learn that dairy products make him fart like the *Titanic* saying goodbye to Southampton docks, but he refuses to stop eating them. I learn that he lives on his army pension, money from dead parents and divides his time between London and Ireland, doing odd jobs and sleeping on mates' sofas. He spent some time in prison for 'general assholery' when he came out of the army but he sometimes goes into prisons now to lecture on how to go straight. He can still feel his feet sometimes and he loves the Irish band B*Witched.

Well how about that? I know a cosy little basement party for two he might like to attend later.

'Is Nico still off the booze?' he asks.

'Yeah. He's pretty clean-living these days.'

'Shame. Got no one to go out on the pull with anymore, now they're both settled down. It used to be a case of Lock up yer daughters with us three.'

'I'd sooner castrate the sons,' I add, watching with disgust as he takes an unashamedly huge bite of his sandwich. He continues talking while a smidge of mayonnaise sits at the corner of his mouth. I don't tell him.

'Rafael's told me all about you. Well, not *everything*, obviously.' I break stare before he does. The Padres hit a homer.

What did *that* mean – *obviously*?

'Raf said you had convictions in Ireland.'

'Yeah, I do. A few years ago now—'

'—convictions for what?'

'Being a bad lad. Bit of drunk and disorderly. Criminal damage to private property. Some burglary when I was down on my luck.'

'Oh is that all? I'm surprised they let you in the US.'

'Ah well, I had to do a bit of form filling and a bit of sucking up to the Gardai back home but they know I'm fierce sound at the end of the day. I'm not in to cause trouble. Just a . . . bit of a Bad Seed, you might say.'

I freeze – he knows. He fucking knows. Even though bad seed is just an expression, with it following all the other stuff he's said about being rooted and the garden it is too much. He *knows*.

'And they still let you out of the country?' I say, trying to keep my voice calm. 'Must be mad.'

'Yeah, I've behaved myself since and with the GBH I demonstrated no intent, cos I was drunk. I did some rehab, paid my dues, picked up a lot of litter. Bought myself a clean slate.'

'Good for you,' I say, one hand absent-mindedly stroking the handle of the knife drawer. I'm not thinking straight now. I'm just panicking internally and trying to take the deepest breaths I can without him noticing.

His stare lingers again. 'Ah it's really good to meet you finally, Ophelia. I'm a big fan of your work.'

I'm as itchy as a bitch in a ditch and just as I'm about

to walk out and go and tidy something that doesn't need tidying, the front door flies open and the dogs all get up out of their beds to scamper around and bark the place down again. Raf is home, calling out for me, but the second he comes into the kitchen he sees Billy at the island and the two of them bound towards each other and embrace like the old friends they were.

'Bill! How you doing!? Long time no see, brother! Ah it's been too long!'

'Ahh it's good to see you too Rafa, seriously, you're looking well, man!'

'I thought you were clocking off at four?'

'I asked Luiz if I could go early to see Billy. Hey man, how long are you staying? Can I get you another beer?'

'I'll get it,' I say, taking the empty Billy proffers me and heading back to the fridge, feeling slightly relieved Raf is acting as the bridge over our troubled water.

The baseball game warbles on in the background as I with the beer and see them both gabbing on the sofa about army people I've never met but they both know so intimately they can identify them from their farts.

'So you two met in the army then I take it?' I ask, handing Billy a fresh Guinness when they finish tossing each other off.

'Yeah, our platoons worked closely together in ISAF,' explains Raf. 'Our paths crossed a couple of times – first in Kosovo on a peacekeeping deployment, and then later during the Operation Herrick missions to train Afghan soldiers.' Whenever Raf talked about his army career it impressed me. I forgot he had a whole-assed important job once upon a time.

'Yeah, when you're in the army and you're on the same side, you fight like brothers,' says Billy.'

'We lost too many brothers out there, didn't we man?'

Raf nod and slaps his friend on the back. 'A friendship forged in hell.'

'Ain't that the truth,' says Billy, swigging from his can. 'I miss it though, don't you? I miss it every day.'

'Why did you leave if you loved it so much?' I ask.

'Got legless, didn't I?' He grins.

'They can't chuck you out for drinking, surely. If they did, we wouldn't have an army left in the world.'

'No, literally,' he says, moving around the side of the kitchen island and pulling up the hems of both his combat trousers to show me the metal rods where his legs used to be. Rods and shoes are all he has left.

'Ahh right,' I say. Hence all the knowledge on amputation. He didn't walk like someone who had nothing going on beneath the knees and you couldn't tell either, until he sat down and his trousers shaped around them differently. He was so positive and the only thing that seemed to bother him about it was that now and again he had to take one of his legs off cos the stump was rubbing. It put all my moaning about my slightly numb-fuck left hand into proportion.

I leave the boys to their fond reminiscences about fun times in Helmand Province and go upstairs to get my dog-walking combats on. As I'm getting the leads on, I hear Billy and Raf talking about me on the patio, passing around a spliff. The bifolds are open.

'Ah man, I'm happy for you, you're one lucky bastard, you are. You weren't this happy at your first wedding.'

'Yeah. I feel like I won the lottery, ya know? Like, when I'm with her, I forget everything else. She's poured herself into my soul and filled me up.'

'She's filled you up, has she? Didn't know you were into all that.' Billy laughs. Cue an endless pun fest about pegging.

Raf doesn't engage. 'There's no point trying to get into deep stuff with you is there, ya prick?'

'Hey, I can be deep. How about this then: a life without love is like a sunless garden when the flowers are dead. The consciousness of loving and being loved brings a warmth and a richness to life that nothing else can bring.'

'That's beautiful.'

'Oscar Wilde, my friend. One of the finest Irishmen who ever lived, other than meself of course.'

'I'll drink to that,' laughs Raf.

'*Sláinte!*' says Billy, which Raf repeated over the tap of their beer cans.

It was such a contrast to when I heard those two bitches talking about me in the toilets at the *Gazette*. I can't even remember who they were now, but I remembered every word of what they said.

She's so quiet and starey.

I've never taken to her.

Very weird.

I've never been comfortable around her.

Absolute freak.

Raf's never thought of me like that. Never made me feel less. I love many things about him but that thing I love the best. I snuck in on him in the shower tonight, fully clothed, and washed his hair. I hadn't planned to – I saw him in there and I wanted to make him happy.

'Hey, what you doing in here?' Raf smiles as I lather the shampoo in my hands and rub it over his scalp, around his ears and forehead and down his neck. He closes his eyes and makes bed noises.

'Wow, I don't know what this is but I know I like it.' He laughs.

I rinse his head gently under the water and do the same with his body wash, massaging it into his chest and back, creating large blooms of foam all over him until he's sudsy. Then I wash it all off with freezing cold water as we are kissing. I'm naked, soaked inside and out and exceedingly satisfied by the time I step out of there.

'Whoa. What was *that*?' he gasp-laughs.

I towel my hair. 'Dunno. I wanted to jump into a moment.'

'Well you did that!' He holds me around my waist and cuddles me in. 'I don't think I've ever felt like that before.'

'Like what?'

'Like I've died and gone to heaven.'

I'm fully aware of the irony of what he'd said but it's like only when I'm killing can I be the person I need to be the rest of the time.

'I saw a TikTok, all about cold water and the vagus nerve. Makes you feel brand-new. Like when we took an ice bath together.'

'Well, vague me up, baby.' He smiles. 'Maybe we should do another ice bath some time.'

'*You* can. I'm not risking a stroke.'

He rolls his eyes. 'God, you see one TikTok and it puts you off anything, doesn't it? Oh, that reminds me.' He grabs his phone from the jeans he'd thrown down. 'I was scrolling the vacation tag for honeymoon ideas. I know we'd sort of decided on Cancún but what do you think of Hawaii? We did jungle warfare training there once and I know a few people still out there. Or Belize? We did some training in the jungle and helped build this school. Or Billy suggested Phuket. We've got a buddy who lives there. He owns a bar—'

'—if you've been to all these places, why do you want to go again?'

'Because they're beautiful. We did some work with the National Gendarmerie in Madagascar and there was this place where we could hire boats and stay in this beautiful cabin right on the beach. We had a tour once and we saw all these lemurs and tiny green frogs—'

'You miss travelling, don't you?'

'Yeah, I do,' he says. 'That was the best part about being in the army, seeing all these cool new places. I wanna show you them, see it all again through your eyes.'

Aww bless, I thought. I fucking hate travelling but travelling with Raf it might not be so bad. Shame I already had a plan in mind.

'How about San Francisco?' I suggest.

'We can go to San Francisco anytime, it's only up the coast. Why there?'

'I just fancy it. I saw a film on National Geographic about this giant park they have with bison in it.'

'Bison?'

'We've lost so much money on lost deposits, babe, I just thought we should keep this one simple and fairly local.'

'Yeah but it has to be special. It's our honeymoon. And it *is* going to happen this time. I want to spoil you. I want us to go to a prime honeymoon destination.'

'What is a prime honeymoon destination then?'

'Somewhere quiet with beaches, cocktails, a desert island. Ooh, what about The Maldives? You'd love it. We were stationed there for a month after I first got drafted, doing some work with the MNDF exchanging medical training and tactical combat casualty care but in the time off, we got to explore and the beaches are the nearest thing to heaven you'll ever see. They got these crystal-clear lagoons and the sand on the beaches is like—'

'Great sand, yeah, I got it, but San Francisco's got Alcatraz. You love that level on *Call of Duty* . . .'

'Okaaay,' he said. 'But do you really wanna spend our honeymoon in the place where Al Capone once shit in a bucket?'

'The Unabomber was from San Francisco as well.'

I caught him looking at me. 'Are you serious right now?'

'Yeah. It looks like a fun place. Nob Hill and all that. Did you know eighty per cent of San Francisco was destroyed in the earthquake of 1906?'

I'd done a bit of research.

'And there's Haight-Ashbury and all the Summer of Love stuff started there. *Pride* started there too. The Zodiac Killer was from there. And the Golden State Killer. Nightstalker. There's a walking tour of the murder sites.'

He was still looking at me. *That* look. I knew I needed to flip the switch and say normal things now.

'*Zodiac*'s a great film by the way,' I added. 'We should watch it. It's the only time I've been able to stomach more than two solid hours of Jake Gyllenhaal.'

'Focus,' says Raf.

'Sorry. Oh and best of all, *Sister Act 2: Back in the Habit* was set there. St Francis Academy. They won the All-State Choir Championship, Raf.'

'It's a fictional school, you do know that, right?'

I didn't know that actually; I genuinely thought it was a real school. Sometimes you invest so much in a movie, you forget it's just a movie.

'Well anyway, there's some amazing hotels in San Fran with spas and stuff. We could have a sensual couples massage. One hotel's got beautiful views of the ocean . . .' He nodded. I had to say more things like that. I opened my Explore San Fran app. 'We could stroll through the Golden Gate Park, hand in hand, and visit the Conservatory of Flowers. Take a bus tour of the city. Chinatown. Eat Chinese food. There's a romantic rooftop bar where we can have cocktails. Like our first date . . .'

I got an eyebrow raise for that effort. He was softening.

'More to do there than some beach.' I hugged him and played with his ear which he loved. *Come on, ear, do your thing.* 'And if you *did* want sand between your toes, we could take a bus ride to Carmel. There's beaches and museums and these fairy-tale cottages like big doll's houses. Aren't they cute?'

I showed him the screen and he took my phone from me and scrolled down to the honeymoon couple walking on the beach at sunset, arm in arm with their shoes dangling from their hands.

'You've already started planning this, haven't you?' he side-eyed me.

'No, I haven't, honest. Ooh I know, how about a road trip? Share the driving, stop off at places along the way – Malibu, Santa Cruz – go see where *The Lost Boys* was filmed. How about that?'

'Baby, I don't have time to plan a road trip and I only got one week's leave, that's it. Everyone's isolating, we're hella short-staffed.'

'No, I'll do all the planning. I'll make sure it's no more than a week and I'll map our journey every step of the way.'

'We could rent a car,' he suggested, studying the app, scrolling up and down the screen a few times, landing on the honeymooners staring longingly into each other's eyes again. *C'mon, honeymooners, do your stuff!*

'San Fran's pretty touristy, Phee. You hate that. We need more time to ourselves, baby. Peace and quiet, not murder walks and bus tours.'

'We can do the mushy stuff on the way.' I deploy a neck nuzzle to sweeten the deal, breathing in his Hugo Boss and kissing away beads of water.

'It's a lot of driving,' he whined, scrolling.

'We can take it in turns. Rent a car, maybe a Mustang, eh? Pick it up from San D, drop it off in San F and fly home. Flight's only an hour or so. It'll be an adventure, RIGHT? Pleeeeeeeeease . . .' I quit the neck nuzzle and venture my hands south to his crotch, cooing softly in his ear like a siren. He can never resist that. And with a twitch, I had him.

'All right, all right, you win. We'll do a road trip to San Francisco and wear flowers in our goddamn hair.'

Yay yay, I get my way. Rule Number 1 when asking for something from a man: make sure they're cum drunk when you ask. They're more likely to meet your request with approval.

'You won't regret it, baby,' I said, snuggling against him and scrolling the street map on my app, zooming right in to the street I had pinned as one of our must-sees. 'You really won't.'

Thursday, 23 September 2021

1. *That woman who sells her farts online*
2. *People who are unnecessarily in a hurry. Unless you're in labour or delivering blood, ease off the gas, Lando Norris.*
3. *Lily James*
4. *Lily James's agent*
5. *That fish with human teeth*

Hi hi, hi ho, it's off to kill a bitch I go.

My remote hillside hideaway 'Casa Sweetpea' – aka 30665 Roadrunner Ridge – allowed me, for the first time in a long time, to plan properly. There was no 'act' at all. It was 100 per cent Rhiannon. That was why I loved going there. It was like letting out a corset or undoing a belt buckle. Roadrunner let me release the pressure, for a short while, so I could go back to being The New Me: Ophelia. Loving wife-to-be, wonderful daughter-in-law-to-be, much-cherished family member. I love them and I want to be good for them but sometimes, I need to be me. And they can't know who me is. Dr Jekyll leaves the basement – just as Hyde enters.

I focused my attention on my target, wrapped to the

basement pillar, a bloodied, shit-stinking version of the man he once was – Eduardo Ochoa. His head hung over as a string of red drool oozing to the carpet.

'Please . . .'

'Please what?'

'Kill me . . .'

'You still have seven fingers left. Well, seven and a bit.'

My dad had taught me how to snap off fingers, with a bolt-cutter he'd picked up on a building job. He said when you're torturing someone, they can either make it easy on themselves and tell you what you need to know, or you have to get nasty. He used to break their fingers, one at a time. He'd learned it from *Reservoir Dogs*. But sometimes breaking wasn't enough. Sometimes, you want to hear them scream louder.

That's how it began with Julia. I wanted her to scream, like she'd made me scream at school. That's the one good thing about getting older. Big Me can burn down all the houses that Little Me didn't have the matches for.

I hadn't laid into Edo properly until the second day and even then, it was a case of going to work and leaving Pfister's phone playing the 'Macarena' on a loop. For a guy who had a knife wound to his belly, which turned out to be not as deep as we'd hoped, he was surprisingly strong. But the brugmansia kept him prone and the bucket kept the floor semi-clean.

The place had first gone on the market in 2010 when it was listed at $225,000, but it hadn't sold so the owners, the Nguyens, moved back to Vietnam as intended but kept it as a rental property on our books. Interest had largely come from film companies needing remote homesteads for horror movies or families needing a stopgap between house moves. Nobody had stayed there for long and the place had become rundown and soulless. There's no carpet throughout, just tiled floors – except for a large brown checkerboard rug in the hallway which the Seventies rejected for being ugly.

In short: it's a shithole, but it's a remote shithole so I love it.

The enormous soundproof basement is fitted with repurposed kitchen cabinets all along the back wall, a toilet and even a pull-down queen-size bed (broken). Apparently, the guy who owned it in the Seventies was a drummer and he pulled a lot of all-nighters. There are no drums down there now – just piles of leftover car parts that Mr Nguyen kept there.

Best of all, there are no neighbours. Nobody's even close. Which means nobody can hear the screaming of the teeny tiny wife beater whom I currently have tied to a pole down there.

'Kill me,' he wheezed. He'd developed something of a tic since I'd last seen him. It was mildly amusing.

I stopped sharpening my knives, marching right up to him. His face was turned away. I went to the other side and he turned again. I held up my knife to his neck and prodded his Adam's apple with the point.

'I'll make you feel every inch of this, Edo. Isn't that what you used to say to Liv? She told me about your technique in bed. "If you're not in pain, you're not doing it right." She told me all about the choking too. She hated it.'

His Adam's apple bobbed. I learned early on that Edo, as with all the greats, was a coward when it came to real confrontation. The snap of a glove. The creak of a door. It can wither them on the vine like a time-lapse grape.

I smelled his fusty spunk and blood aroma; his piss-soaked jeans. With my good, gloved hand I grip his throat.

'"Is this good for you? Does that take you to the edge, bitch?"'

'NO!' he screamed.

'Oh you want me to stop? You want me to go away? Does that hurt? THAT'S WHAT LIV SAID BUT YOU DIDN'T FUCKING LISTEN, DID YOU? If you don't listen, why do you have ears? Tell you what, I can get rid of them for you. How about that?' I selected the boning knife from the block.

He spluttered in my face and I left him to go sanitise with multiple wet wipes. Fuck the planet – I wasn't dying of plague for this cum wad.

I went to the back and grabbed one of the three five-litre drums by the handles, bringing it over to him. I sat down on it and tapped the label. 'Know what this is? Did you see *Fight Club*? You know that stuff that burns through his hand? Caustic soda. I got it in Target, a tub at a time. This is what I'm going to dissolve you with.'

He sobbed. I scroll the playlists again. 'I can get you money.'

'The only thing I want is you dead,' I said.

'So why stitch up my belly? Why give me painkillers?'

'To keep you alive so we could have some fun first. Duh. Gotta make sure the meat's nice and tender, don't we? Although, I have kept you fed and watered which is more than most serial killers would do. You've had it easy really. But then I'm a woman, aren't I? Easy peasy.'

'It's infected,' he whined, nodding towards his belly. I lifted up his shirt. It did not look like a healed cut. Looked more like something green that slithers out of the ground when it's been raining.

'Well, I did my best.' I scrolled through Pfister's playlists.

Load of hip-hop horseshit but he did have some old-school Madge. 'Anyway, I'm bored of this now. What's your fave Madonna song?'

He screamed HELP – the pure, plaintive caterwaul of a man who's desperate. Not Bob-De-Niro-in-a-Warburtons-commercial desperate – more staring-death-in-the-face desperate. He crouched down to the floor, yanked at his restraints, cuffs clanking on the pillar. His voice cracked to a whisper.

'Please! Help!'

'Madge didn't sing "Help". How about "True Blue"? Favourite Madonna song, quickly, or I'll slit your throat unaccompanied and you'll hear your own voice box screaming. I HAVEN'T GOT ALL DAY.'

'"Borderline",' he said, all husk; lips so swollen I could barely hear.

'You can pick any Madonna song in existence and you pick "Borderline"?'

'I don't care,' he whined, sinking down the post to the carpet – narrowly avoiding the seeping patch of his own piss. 'I swear I'll never come back—'

I crouched down to face him. 'Fucking right you'll never come back.'

'I WANNA SEE MY WIFE. I WANT TO SEE OLIVIA! I want to see my son. I won't touch them again, I swear.'

'You will.' I snapped on my gloves. 'You're a shit. That's what shits do.'

'Someone will find me . . . my mom will be looking for me. Mis amigos, mi mami, mi mami, mami, please, look for me . . .'

'Nobody's looking for you. They all think you're dead.'

'What?'

'I left your car on the bridge with a goodbye note to your mother on the dash after posting some truly awful suicide-inspired poetry all over your social meed. Then I yeeted your phone off the bridge. Police think you jumped.'

'NO! NO, they don't!'

'They do. We've started building the fiction that you had mental health issues. You threatened it a few times. "Let me see my son or I'll kill myself." "If you divorce me, Liv, I'll kill myself." We'll all swear to it. Mami's filed you a missing person but the cops aren't concerned. They're taking your last text as a suicide note. I didn't send her any of your videos, by the way. Last thing the woman needs right now is footage of you spooging on the edge of your bathtub.'

'You fucking bitch!'

'Yeah, yeah.' I tied my mask around my face.

'I swear on a stack of Bibles, I'll leave town. You can trust me—'

'Anything else? You'll say your prayers every night, no more swearing, you'll join UNICEF and parachute into Uganda with pencils for school kids?'

'. . . you're a . . . psychopath.'

Now that's where he was wrong. I've actually had it clinically diagnosed from an Argentinian psychologist on YouTube that I'm *not* a psychopath – I am, in fact, possibly, a sociopathic narcissist. I have all the symptoms:

- Grandiose sense of self-importance ✓
- Disregard for the law ✓
- Lack of empathy ✓
- Moody or hostile and/or aggressive ✓

- Callous treatment of others ✓
- Selfish ✓
- Pathological lying – who me? *cue Rita Hayworth hair flick GIF* ✓
- Constant need for attention and/or admiration ✓
- Manipulative ✓

Although I do buck the trend as most of those diagnosed as sociopathic narcissists are cruel to animals and work in top jobs whereas I like dressing chihuahuas in top hats and am destined to work in admin forever.

I settled the phone on the speaker. The music started. I brought the knife block over to him and placed it on the floor. The song began its haunting intro.

'Please! Ophelia! Please, God, no!!!'

Edo made one last attempt to wrench free of his bonds, but though his arms were weak, his voice was louder than I'd ever heard it – one last attempt to bring me to my knees. 'YOU FUCKING WHORE, YOU FAT UGLY CUNT, I'M GONNA KILL YOU' and then he flung a load of fast Spanish insults at me that he didn't think I knew.

'How are you gonna rape me, you're tied to a pole?'

'I wouldn't fuck you, perra gorda, asquerosa!'

'I'm an ugly fat *dog* now? That's not what you said at your anniversary party. "You look so good in green, baby. Wanna go upstairs?" Remember wheezing that into my ear at the finger buffet?'

'I wouldn't fuck an ugly puta like you!' he spat.

'Aww, my vagina is crying right now, I hope you know.'

Then it was back to appealing to the soft side I didn't have.

'PLEASE OPHELIA! NO, OPHELIA. PLEASE! I WANT TO LIVE!'

I set the knife block down on top of one of the lye barrels. I stroked the handles, left to right. 'Shipped all the way from France. Almost a grand's worth of the finest stainless steel, forged and polished crosswise by skilled artisans from the Thiers region and hand-finished with slip-proof riveted handles. Perfection. Well, they *would* be but the company couldn't guarantee delivery in time so I got this shitty-assed set from Target for $49.99 instead. They'll do the job though.'

He made a last-ditch attempt to free himself of his bonds but nothing worked; they were too strong. And he was too weak. So he cried again. 'Pleeeeeease, I don't waaaaannnna diiiieeeeee!'

'Paring knife, chef's knife, bread knife . . . cleaver.'

'NO! PLEASE! I'M BEGGING YOU!'

'Yeah they usually do.' I sang along to Madge; the sweetest harmony, completely ruined by his screaming.

'Did you hear about that Tudor chick who . . . did treason or something? Her executioner was ham-fisted and drunk I think, and the axe was blunt . . .'

'Pleeeease . . .' he sobbed again.

'. . . and it took several blows for her head to come off. Hack. Hack. Hack. She would have felt every one. Now if I do this with my shitty left hand . . .'

Christ, I felt so powerful in that moment. A master of two worlds – a giantess. One foot firmly in the Ophelia camp; the other in Rhiannon's again, with full control over both. Mistress of two worlds. The me I *am*, and the me I enjoy pretending to be; united at last. Sometimes, being Ophelia alone is not enough – I need Rhiannon to feel truly complete.

'Pleeease, Ophelia, please *please*, Ophelia, don't do this . . .'

'Begging doesn't work on me.' I slid the cleaver from the block. 'Actually, you could try saying, "Please no, I'm begging you, RHIANNON."'

'What?'

'Say, "No, please don't. I'm begging you, Rhiannon." Go on.'

'No, PLEASE! RHIANNA, NO, NO, DON'T!!!!!!!!'

'NO, NOT RHIANNA, *RHIANNON*. MY NAME IS RHIANNON!'

'Please, Rhiannon, please don't . . .'

He called my name – my *real* name – and it felt like home.

And with a wide arc over my head, I switched the cleaver to my right hand and slammed it down hard against his bent neck. *Crack*.

'Nnnnnnnn,' he said, like a robot on low batteries. I did it again.

And again. *CRACK*.

'You look so pretty in red, baby.'

And again, until he was quiet and his body made involuntary noises; the pump of an artery, the wet splat of flesh as it drops to the stone floor; the crack of his spine as his head fell away.

I hadn't heard my post-kill laugh for so long but it came from my throat so suddenly I jumped with the sound of it. God, it was like getting into your own bed again after a trip away or putting your own shoes on after you've been bowling. Everything felt right again. I was whole. I was level.

And his blood spurted against my face, splashing me all over like a warm summer rain after a long-ass drought.

Friday, 24 September 2021

1. *The Rock – how does he keep getting away with playing himself no matter what film he's in?*
2. *David Cameron – I might not live in the UK anymore but I'll never forget.*
3. *Covid – people keep cancelling my wedding cos they've gone down with the latest variant. Just fuck off already, Corona. And take the lot of them with you for messing up my place settings.*
4. *People who bang on about the advantages of ice baths.*
5. *People who bang on about the 'need to be seen'. Why does everyone have to be 'seen' nowadays? I never saw myself in the media I consumed as a kid. Never did me no harm.*

It was mostly just boring wedding stuff to do today. Liv wasn't up to doing any of my beauty treatments – still 'thinking' about stuff. Still ignoring my texts. Still staying with her friend Sam because she doesn't want to go inside her own house – so I went into town with Bianca and she introduced me to a friend of hers called Sylvie who gave us a good rate. I got the Top to Toe package:

- Mani/pedi ✓
- Facial ✓
- Full-body salt and oil scrub ✓
- De-stressing aromatherapy massage ✓
- Eyebrow shaping ✓
- Complimentary glass of champagne ✓

And after that I set about ticking off the rest of my to-do list:

- Dress fitting – it's tighter than I remember. Damn you, birria tacos ✓
- Chasing up RSVPs ✓
- Practise vows ✓
- Pick wedding playlist of artists before the allegations drop and we can't listen to them anymore ✓
- Drive to kill site to check Edo's headless body there and police not ✓

Normally I'd have enjoyed all of this and the ongoing build-up before the big day but with Liv still out of action and Billy constantly keeping Rafael in bars and away from me, the more the splendour of Edo's demise played on my mind. The freedom of it. The sounds his flesh made as I hacked it. The sound of his skull hitting the floor. The little après-mort gasp he did as I rolled his corpse into the corner of the basement so I could sluice the floor. The fact he called me Rhiannon. I wish I could be Rhiannon all the time. Every time I see one of the invites come back with Ophelia on it, my heart sinks.

Nnedi Géricault was right – it *is* what I always wanted: to be wanted. To be loved. For someone to say it and mean it for once. To be seen instead of ignored. That's why everyone has a Mental Elf problem or cries noisily on their YouTube over a mean comment or their guinea pig dying, isn't it? To be seen.

I sent those diaries to Freddie so I could be seen. So people would love me. The hybristophiliacs, the loners, the abused and my bouquet of stans: the Bad Seeds, those still spreading their love for me on social media like an engineered infection. The professional chef who baked me in cake and sliced through my head on his Insta, sending his follower count soaring.

The true-crime docu makers who ensure I'm included on all the most pertinent specials. The T-shirt makers. The macabre museum collectors. The ones who go to my deposition sites to take pictures and maybe the odd bit of gravel, which then sells on eBay for ridiculous amounts. Even, on some level, I was enjoying the fact that Nnedi Géricault was still looking for me. Still talking about me on any podcast who'd have her on. Any breakfast TV show that would patronise the crap out of her. I liked it.

I liked being Rhiannon. I missed her.

That's what we all want, isn't it? A bit of Look At Me, Aren't I Special?

But I want one person to see me as I am and love me for that. To be proud of me. And if I can't get that from Rafa, I can get it from my public.

Then there are the 'witnesses' who claim to have seen me killing Canal Man that New Year's Eve; the bitch who claims we were bezzie mates at school who spent the entire coach trip to Morwellham Quay pouring Ribena down my collar (count your days, Ribena Bitch) and there's another doppelgänger claiming to *be* me – same hair, same voice, but way too thin to lug bodies.

Everyone I've known has shoved their oar in about me

during guest spots on *Up at the Crack* or features in *OK!* mag. People I barely said two words to, like Johnny at the *Gazette*. According to him, I'm a 'monster'.

Oh rly, Johnny? *I'm* the monster? At least I didn't fuck my wife's sister and spend my youth tying fireworks to cats. Well, one cat. And one maimed cat is one maimed cat too many in my eyes.

Guy Majors, a Partridge-esque TV news cuck who is so wet for me he could open a Center Parcs in his underpants, finally pinned Claudia down for a sit-down chat in April. His show – *Guy Majors: The Real Deal* – visits someone key in a big crime story and 'digs deeper into the human story behind the headlines' (translation: pays through the nose to wade about in someone else's sewage for clicks and likes). I only watched it to see Ivy but Claudia keeps her out of the limelight as much as possible. I guess that's a good thing.

There are interviews with anyone who's ever had anything to do with me. Anni and Pidge, my former friends. Three of the WOMBATs, Jim and a space-cadet Elaine, stroking my furry Judas of an ex-Chihuahua Tink on her lap. Anni and Pidge are appearing at Murderpalooza next year, signing autographs. People I went to college with are signing *autographs*. Probably selling stickers saying, *We Knew Sweetpea Before She Was Evil* and charging £60 for a selfie on their own phones.

An old school 'friend' I'd completely forgotten about gets her fifteen minutes too – Stephanie Rouass. I think I spoke to her maybe twice in the time I was at St Judith's – the private school my parents sent me to when I started earning them decent money. And as Stephanie speaks, I'm put in mind of the science lesson where I refused to gas a frog and cut it up. 'She never hurt animals,' said Stephanie. 'There was that spaniel at

Priory Gardens who lay next to her as she lay dying. Maybe that was why she was kind to them.'

Cut to pictures of the sandy-coloured, sad-eyed Molly, being carried out with red-dipped ears. I always wondered what happened to that dog. I hope they didn't kill it like they did with Dennis Nilsen's.

I tell you who's really sucked the bereavement teat dry and that's the wife of the taxi driver I sliced up in Birmingham. My God, there isn't a news network she hasn't spoken to nor a chat show she hasn't trotted out on nor a fun run in his honour she hasn't walked. Every time I see her speak, it's the same low-hanging clichés – my 'world fell apart', 'our hearts broke that night' and 'you don't expect it to happen to people like us'. Not one original comment. So too with the mum of the guy, Troy Shearer, who tried to rape Marnie in Cardiff. 'It hit me like a tonne of bricks. Everything happened in slow motion.' Cue the close-up of the hideous white marble headstone and the family standing around with cheap-assed teddies and cans of lager 'so he can have a pint in Heaven' *voms*.

'Troy was a top lad,' says one of his mates, breaking down into sobs on another mate's shoulder. *Top Lad* – translation: Troy knew how drunk a woman needed to be before he could force one up her. Cheers, Troy.

The Christians are the worst – like the WOMBATS [aka the Women of Monks Bay and Temperley, a Christian ladies guild of which I was briefly a member during my gestation period living with Craig's mum and dad]. They go on and on about me being 'such an unassuming girl' with a butter-wouldn't-melt face and that 'none of them had any idea what an evil person we had let into our midst'.

I'll be forgiven. They're Christians. It's in their interest.

But all these interviews are months old now, some of them two years. Once upon a time I was on all the magazines, all the front pages. Then Trump took over, and later, coronavirus. 'How I Beat the Rona'. 'How My 99-Year-Old Mum Beat the Rona.' 'How the Rona Turned My Wife into a Sex Maniac.' Every now and again, a qween will get her own back and the #IStandWithRhiannon hashtag is all over Twitter again, but that's about it. Freddie's biography was serialised in one of the tabloids, then the hoo-ha died down and the book dropped out of the bestsellers as fast as it had gone in. Let a reality star take a shit on a keyboard and it's odds on *they've* got a bestseller. And but for a few YouTube true-crime nut jobs and their latest theories, I cease to exist except in the odd Netflix docu or Tumblr appreciation post or copycat killing by some noob who makes rookie errors like wearing Velcro or forgets to check for CCTV before knocking on some paedo's door.

Turned out to be a podiatrist. What a waste.

A psychologist on YouTube said I craved fame because it gave me back what I'd lost as a child: support. Happiness. Love.

But he's wrong about that. I don't think that's all I want at all, because I have the best family in the world right now and all the love I could wish for. And I'm happy every day. But it's not enough. I can give up killing for 830 days. I could probably give up for a thousand days but there will always come a day when the clock has to reset because someone has to die. Someone who's hurt me or my family. I know I'm my own worst enemy. But the enemy of my enemy is my friend.

And right now, she's the only friend I've got.

Saturday, 25 September 2021 – my unofficial birthday

1. *People with overly white teeth*
2. *Larry Nassar*
3. *That perv gynaecologist who used his sperm to impregnate his patients*
4. *That Hitler fanboy who shot up a school in California but didn't have the decency to shoot himself*
5. *The people who tweeted about microchips in vaccines from phones with whole-ass GPS trackers in them*

Brad Pfister has been texting me relentlessly all week and I've been watching the texts getting longer and angrier and more beggy and it's been mildly entertaining as he's gone from threat to accusation to threat to beg to full-on *I'm going to commit suicide if I don't get that phone back right fucking now.*

Like that kinda threat ever cut any ice with me.

But I had a job for a certain someone to do and for some reason I thought it would suit him, what with him being so eager to get his grubby little wank bank back. So I called him – I was outside watering the plants.

'I did what you said last week. I want my phone now.'

'Do you want ten thousand dollars?'

'What?'

'Answer the question first: do you want ten thousand dollars?'

'Yes.'

'OK, so I have one more task for you—'

'—no, nuh-uh, no way, I want my phone back, right now.'

'Well, I thought you might say that so that's why I mentioned the ten thousand. You could have it in your bank account this afternoon, how bow dah?'

'What's the catch?'

'I have one more task. You did the last one beautifully, by the way. The ketchup squirting was on point, bravo, seriously.' I stroked the soft orange bell-shaped flowers on the brugmansia, all fat with new seeds.

'What about my phone?' he said. 'When do I get my *phone*?'

'I'll give you ten thousand dollars today, and, let's say, another forty thousand plus your phone, intact, *after* you complete the task. Then we're done.'

'What the fuck?'

'Ten grand now, and another forty *and* your phone when you're through.' I text him the photo of the open shoebox. 'Think what you could do with all this. Think of all the women's locker rooms it'd give you access to.'

'Why the hell would you give me fifty thousand dollars? And how can I be sure that's not some stock image off the internet?'

'Oh you need proof? OK, here's a live image of the same box.' I snapped another photo with my middle index finger in shot and pinged it his way. The message connected. Two blue ticks.

'Are you serious right now?'

'As cancer. So will you do this or not?' A bee buzzed in the lavender patch. I think it was my bee. I like to think that buzz was saying, *Hi, matey! Thanks for saving me!*

'What do I have to do?'

'Is that a yes or a no?'

'Depends. I don't trust you.'

'I don't *blame* you. OK, so I need you to go to San Francisco for a week. Take Carole and Andy if you like. Tell them you won a competition. Most Prolific Upskirter in the Bay Area . . .'

'What am I supposed to do in San Francisco for a week?'

'See the sights. Treat your folks. And spy on a guy for me while you're there. You're good at spying. You know all the tricks, clearly.'

'Who do I spy on?'

'Well, sadly for you, it's not a chick. It's a guy called Elliot Mansur. Although he has several other aliases he goes by: John Adams, Mike Tucker, Joe Purvis. According to a fairly deep dive on social media, he's currently going by the name Jimmy Joe Maxwell. I want you to stalk him and make a note of everything he does; everywhere he goes.'

'Why him?'

Ugh, questions questions. 'He's my ex. And he's claiming disability benefit while not providing for our child. I need evidence for the courts. Evidence he is pulling a fast one.'

I also need to tie him to a post and cut off parts of his body, one after the other with no anaesthetic, if you really want to know.

'I can't afford to stay in San Francisco for a week,' Pfister whined.

'You'll have your ten thousand for travel money in your PayPal this very afternoon, dumbass. And a further forty to look forward to when you get back. I'll text you an address and leave it in the mailbox out front at a specific time.'

'Am I gonna lose my hand when I grab it? Is that the game?'

'This is not a game. I need that information. I am trying to build a good life for my child and he is the one thing standing in my way. Please. *Please* help me, Brad.'

I was fully channelling the mum in *Home Alone* at this point when she's giving the woman her diamond earrings and begging to swap plane seats so she can get back to Chicago, little voice wobble and all, but nevertheless it seems to land.

He didn't answer for a while. Then he said, 'There's a gaming convention on in SF; happens once a year. I could say I need to go for that. Mom and Dad won't check the dates. So I track this guy?'

'Track him, make notes on his habits. I'll send you a photo of him – he may have changed since it was taken but for reference, he's about ten stone wet through – like a human weasel – and he has a scorpion tattoo on his neck. He lives on Turk Street in the Tenderloin district.'

There was a long sigh on the other end.

'Make sure he doesn't see you at any point. You've got to be clever about this, Pfister – don't go bumbling about in your size twelves.'

'And this is all I gotta do? And you'll give me my phone and fifty thousand dollars?'

'Yes. I give you my word that when you've done this, I will give you your phone *and* your money and that will be the very last you hear from me.'

'OK.' He sounded surer now. Confident even. 'I'll do it.'

Maybe all Brad Pfister needed was a job and he'd become a contributing member of society, rather than a lazy, sponging, Daddy's boy of an upskirting predatory shit nut. Or maybe, this was a stopgap.

Either way, it was too late. Pfister's future was set in stone. And lye.

Two days later, Brad Pfister (yes, really) was boarding a flight to San Francisco. I asked him to send me regular updates and photos of him at the airport, on the plane and with a specific SF landmark in the background – the Golden Gate Bridge, the *Cupid's Span* sculpture in Rincon Park, St Patrick's Church, so I could be sure he was doing as I was 'paying' him to do.

You have pleased me, minion, I sent back after receiving the selfie of him at Arrivals. God he's such low-hanging fruit it's almost too easy.

It's my fake birthday today – aka, the birthday on all my medical forms and passport. Even though I privately celebrated on the actual day I, Rhiannon Lewis, was born in April, I celebrated with the family who think I'm Ophelia White, soon to be Ophelia Arroyo-White. They pulled out all the stops – balloons, cake, pile of presents, all the dogs had outfits on (*details below) and at night we drank cucumber palomas and toasted marshmallows around the fire pit, snuggling up listening to Bianca's stories about when she and Michael dated as teenagers. The drink flowed, the lights twinkled and our laughter rang out around the garden. I liked this birthday better than all the other ones I've had.

But it still made me think of Seren and the treasure hunt of presents she made for me once. And her bloody awful singing voice as she sang me 'Happy Birthday'. I thought about Ivy too – it didn't matter how many times I looked around that firepit at those smiling faces, none of them were my Ivy. And that made me sad.

See what I mean about humans. They're so damn complicated. And I include myself in that.

Billy was there too tonight. He's 'part of the family', said Bianca. I caught those steely greens of his staring at me again a few times across the flames. Bianca had made us all 'spice bags' in Billy's honour – some Irish delicacy I'd never heard of – and handed them out. The gesture almost made him cry. I didn't like that he was so in with the family – didn't like her hugging him like that. Was I jealous? Jealous of her treating him like one of the family?

Yes. I think I was. Because any attention on him was attention Bianca wasn't lavishing on me. Jesus. I'm not going to dwell on that.

Oh and Raf came clean about where he'd been earlier that day when he had to 'dip out'. I thought he'd bought me a puppy – I listened in the garage for muffled squeaks all afternoon. But there was no puppy.

Just an abomination.

What he came back with was a tattoo. On the left side of his torso, on his ribcage. One word, in cursive, threaded with pink flowers: *Ophelia*.

'It's still sore.' He smiled, displaying it proudly to the gathered assembly who 'Oohed' and 'Aahed' at how romantic his gesture was. All I could see was some other woman's name tattooed on his skin. And it made me unspeakably, wordlessly, hot-coals-kind of angry.

'Why'd you get it there?' asked Nico, swigging his beer.

'I asked the dude for ideas of romantic tattoos and he said one couple had gone in asking for matching ones of ribs because of Adam and Eve.'

Bianca nodded. 'Because God used Adam's rib to form Eve.'

'Yeah, like she was made of the same stuff as him. But a tattoo of a rib wouldn't be special enough. And I thought, Well, what *is* special enough: Ophelia. That's it.' The firelight made his eyes shimmer. 'Do you like it?'

I smiled, despite the expression my face naturally wanted to do. 'I love it.' My teeth clamped down after the three words escaped so nothing else could, like a scream. Fortuitously, tears streamed down my cheeks at that precise moment, so it looked like I was deliriously happy. Isn't it funny how deliriously happy and unspeakably angry can look the same in different people's eyes?

'Aw baby.' He laughed, setting down his empty beer bottle on the patio and cuddling me. 'I wanted to show you how much I love you.' He took my face in his hands. 'Cos I really do, you know. And I always will, Ophelia.'

'I think you've had enough of these.' I fake-laughed, picking up his bottle. 'I'm gonna fetch some more smores. Anyone want anything?'

'Yeah, I'll take another beer,' said Billy, handing me his empty bottle. 'A cold one. You like 'em cold too, don't you, Phee?' He winked when he said it.

What with the tattoo and that comment, my power base had now completely slipped beneath this rogue Irish legless wonder. I was done for. He knew – he knew what I knew and it was only a matter of time. He was going to ruin everything for me if I wasn't careful. And as much as I knew it would hurt Raf, it was either kill Billy, or have Billy open the can of worms that would choke us all.

He was signing his own death warrant.

I strolled inside, smiling until I was sure I was out of view. I waited until I was in our bedroom before burying my head into my sequinned Danny DeVito pillow and screamed my lungs raw.

*The Dogs' Outfits

Chonk – *Chunk from The Goonies, obvs. Hawaiian shirt and Babe Ruth candy bar in his pocket.*

Giblet – *Ballerina with a drinking problem*

Diablo – *Satan, with red horn hoodie*

Pandora – *Butterfly, with tiny wings, one of which got eaten by Satan*

Tigre – *One-eyed Spider-Man*

Traumatised Bob – *wouldn't wear a costume but he did keep his tiny sombrero on long enough for a photo op so bless him for trying*

Sunday, 26 September 2021

1. *Overly nice retail staff*
2. *Overly rude retail staff*
3. *The entire cast of* Grey's Anatomy
4. *Infomercial creators – they're on every single five min-utes. Forget investment in any decent drama or breaking news story; not when there's Magic Mesh screen doors and NeverStick cookware to flog.*
5. *Medical firms – especially the meds they sell you to counteract the effects of the stuff the infomercials tell you to eat*

I could have called it quits at Edo, valeted my mind like I valeted that basement. Like the moment on a diet when you come to terms with eating the doughnut and resolve to start again Monday. Clean slate. But that's the thing about doughnuts. Even though they're loaded with stuff scientists say will kill you, they taste like good sex feels. They taste like Otis Redding sounds. They taste like a peachy autumn sunset looks. You don't wanna stop feeling or hearing or seeing it cos it's just so damn good.

Digging a hole out back proved impossible with one good

hand. At home I had to rely on Raf or Nico to do all the hard stuff in the garden, while I settled for a trowel and one-handed secateurs, but that was only for plants. A whole-assed body was a different story so I left Edo where he was for the time being, wrapped in a tarp in a corner of the basement. I'd idealised a six-foot square hole in the ground at the back of the house; I'd have shoved him down there – one part lye, one part liar, one part water – and that would have been that. Kinda like an extra-large outdoor pozole, except you don't take the meat out of its jeans. Five hours, beginning to end, and he'd have been dust.

But I couldn't do it.

Old Lefty wouldn't play ball or help me drag his ass up those twelve basement steps, and I can't even wear my brace to support it because Velcro. I've never been so frustrated in my life. I haven't sweat that much since my gravedigging days in Mexico.

OK, I wasn't *that* hot. But it was still damn hard work and with one not-playing-ball hand, it was even harder. The hardest thing of all was the realisation that things were different now. It's like when you realise you're too old and scared to do cartwheels anymore or run any distance without wheezing. Those days were over, just as the days of having a good left hand that could help lug bodies or dig graves were over. I'd have to chop him up instead, I surmised, but I couldn't face that yet, not on top of a dress fitting at midday.

I called Seren on the way there to see if she saw the Nnedi Géricault interview and to ask if there was any update on the bug or not a bug sitch – nothing. This time she wasn't even picking up. She'd done this before, freezing me out. Ghosted without a word. But *she* called *me* last week, so what's changed since then? I wished it was like the old days when it was just me and my own boo-boos to worry about – now I had to worry about hers too and one boo-boo afficionado was enough for any family. But she was the weakest of all links. It's why Dad purposely didn't tell her things. Only me.

When she didn't pick up, I wondered if she'd had another breakdown. I wouldn't put it past her. She did come from the Queen of Breakdowns herself: our mother.

I don't remember our mother Joedi being anything other than odd, and she thought the same of me. There must have been a time when things were different because I've seen photos of us laughing; me burying her feet in the sand on holiday. Me hugging her neck. Me smiling up at her from my cot. But I can't remember any of that. That's from The Time Before the Hammer Blow.

Mum had it easy with Seren. The worst she got from her was the odd dodgy boyfriend or a hissy fit over a bad exam result. With me, she got backchat, maiming and arson. Did I get worse because of my mum or did my mum get worse cos of me? Maybe we brought out the worst in each other, but she wasn't the easiest to get along with, even before I got hammered.

She seemed to hate life. She couldn't stand her job, she didn't like chocolate or parties or loud noises (I feel you there, Ma). She struggled with eye contact, even with us. She'd moan about other people's kids and dogs and parked cars in the street, and she'd have these manic cleaning sessions where she hated us being in the house until it was done. Then she'd show it off like we were seeing our house for the first time and we had to laud her like a peer of the realm. But the one thing she despised more than anything was sickness. If we were ill, she wouldn't come near us. I'm talking booking into a hotel till we were better and the house had been deep-cleaned. *That* bad.

Nowadays, she might have been diagnosed with some disorder and we could have got help for her. At the time, I think we enabled it. Anything for a quiet life. But sometimes we'd fuck up. I fucked up more than most.

I was let out of school early once – sent home with a bug – and I'd waited so long in the school office for Dad to pick me up that I got bored and walked to the bus stop. When I got back, the house was alive with music. I walked in on her dancing in our living room. She'd pushed back the furniture, turned the volume up and let herself go. Madonna – 'Like a Prayer'. She was smiling and swishing scarves back and forth; bare feet, hair down, in her own world.

And then she saw me in the doorway and screamed, scrabbling for the remote and switching off the music, shouting her head off at me for scaring her. I told her I'd been sick at school and she bunched her scarves up against her face and poked me in the back with a broom all the way up the stairs and told me to stay in my room until Dad got home. Dad left my meals on a tray outside my room for a week. He wasn't allowed to come near me either. I had to piss and shit in a bucket, which he'd empty before and after work. I'd love to see how she'd have dealt with Covid.

Now whenever I hear 'Like a Prayer', I dance. When I killed Edo, I danced in his blood as it flew out of him; as it coated the walls, floor and ceilings. I felt as good as she must have, dancing with those scarves before I ruined it.

These days I am almost the woman I always wanted to be:

contented. Happy, even. I dance almost every day, me and Raf around the kitchen, with the dogs. Salsa. Merengue. I have people who love me and for whom I want to do things. Whom I want to protect. Nnedi's right about that – decent human relationships. Do I need to kill as well? Not habitually, no, or else I'd be at Roadrunner right now, catfishing perverts left, right and centre and kicking their comatose bodies down those basement stairs. I need it like I need doughnuts – so maybe I don't need it at all. I just enjoy it.

What I *do* know is I need Rafael. I need him constantly.

'Wash your face,' I told him after tonight's sweaty session. His mum was doing the late vax shift so we'd been in bed since he'd got home from therapy.

He loomed towards my face again. 'Nah, there's no need.'

I held his neck. 'Raf, I've told you before, I love you to pieces but I'm not kissing my own biff on your face. Wash yourself, tortuga.'

'No.'

'I'll swap you for a dildo.'

With some degree of huff, he rolled out of bed and walked to our en suite to do as he was told.

'How was therapy?' I called out. It was a daily question I had to remind myself in my Notes app to ask him. As much as I love him, I don't give a monkey's about anyone's day. 'Get a gold star for your worksheet?'

'Hardy har,' he said, flopping back down on the bed. 'He said a profound thing today which I remembered: he said that sometimes love is violence – you can kill a plant with too much water, or too much light. What the plant needs is understanding of what does it harm.'

My chest constricted – what had Billy been saying to him? What seeds of doubt had been planted in my absence? 'Why did he say that? What were you talking about?'

He threw me a look. 'What goes on in therapy stays in therapy, baby. Come on, you know that.'

'Oh yeah. Sorry.'

'That's all right. Play with my ear.'

'Too tired.' I did it anyway, half-assed.

'You know why I'm in therapy, don't you?' he said.

'The Hacienda, the army, all that jazz,' I said.

'Partly. When I found you at the Hacienda and you were covered in blood and your hand . . . Honestly, I thought you were dead. And that fucked me up seeing you like that. It fucked me up as much as what I saw in the army did. And it was threatening to take me down. But it didn't take you down – you just get on with it. And I knew I needed to be stronger for you. I had to strengthen myself, so I can be your wonder wall.'

I turned to look at him. 'Are you serious?'

'Yes.' I couldn't believe how much I loved him at that moment. I wanted to bite him; take chunks out of his skin to get as much of him inside me as possible. Not to hurt him – just because that's the way I show love, I guess. It's how I show any form of emotion. But I didn't. I snuggled instead.

And then, as often happens when I'm happy, an intrusive thought slithered in and I, like a twat, let it. This time it's Billy. My chest pulsed painfully. *If he ruins this wedding . . .*

'Ear please,' Raf reminded me, cos I'd stopped. I resumed the twiddle.

Caro, my old-timer friend I had made on the cruise, told me I deserved to feel love. I didn't believe her at the time. But when

I put my anger to one side and allow myself to bathe in it, right up to my neck like in these moments with Raf, I realise how special it is. And not just with him – his whole family. They're always telling me so, showing me so. Well, most of them.

'Your mum always looks after us whenever we're sick, doesn't she?'

'Yeah,' he said, a note of suspicion in his voice. 'Why do you say that?'

'I haven't had a mum for ages. It's nice. She smells nice. Like a mum.'

'Aww baby,' he said, leaning over to kiss me.

'Last time I had a hangover, Bianca tucked me up warmly on the sofa and put on *Sister Act 2: Back in the Habit* and made menudo with fresh bread. She stroked my hair until I fell asleep.' I stroked Raf's hair. 'Can we have a gospel choir at our wedding? Maybe we could get Frankay to do a rap?'

'I doubt we'll be allowed,' he murmured, falling back to sleep. It was one of the few things about him that annoyed me – he could fall back to sleep in minutes, a skill he'd picked up in the army.

His eyelashes fluttered in the air-con as his breathing deepened. I traced the vein down his neck from his ear, found his pulse, pressed my fingertips against it. Time was, lying on a dead man was the highlight of my life. Now the man had to be living. I had to feel that heart beating against mine. And it had to be his. My, my, hadn't Sweetpea grown?

But I couldn't relax: I was scared. Scared that any day, I'd fuck all of this up. Maybe I already had. Maybe the consequences of my actions and my past are both marching up the driveway right now with their sleeves rolled up. Maybe Billy will drop a bollock at the next family barbecue or I'll blow my top and that will be that. Or one day Raf will do a Google images search and he'll find the motherlode: Rhiannon Lewis. Two words lay between me and certain abandonment.

Rhiannon Lewis was a freak, 'an abomination', according to Guy Majors; 'a cancer', according to my own sister; someone to distrust, to avoid. Someone to give That Look – that look Mum gave me that day I caught her dancing with the scarves and was quarantined in my bedroom. Raf would be no different. The second he knows; he'll look at me the same way. That golden smile will disappear and the cloud of dread will descend and he'll take a step away. And I'll never get him back. I have to drink up every inch of him while I can and do my best to be the exact kind of wife he needs: Ophelia.

At least, to his face anyway. And, in my own way, I can show exactly what he means to me.

I'd been lowkey following the 'Elliot Manning' thread ever since Raf had told me about the incident at the pool. And all the things I'd learned about him were from news articles. For a start, Raf had misremembered his name; it was Elliot Man*sur*, and he'd remembered the aftermath incorrectly too. It was a few months after molesting him that Mansur had left the job as a lifeguard and started as a janitor at an RV campground at South Carlsbad Beach, around forty-five minutes away. It was *there* that he kidnapped another boy, also ten, and carried out a sexual assault in his trailer while the boy's parents were at a barbecue. He was arrested soon after.

Everything else about Mansur was deep underground. There were no social media accounts obviously associated with him and any comments about him on Facebook were derogatory ones from years ago, mainly middle-aged mothers from Ohio and Minnesota, commenting on what they'd do to him if they could get hold of him.

Sure you would, Sue.

Other than that, there were no digital footprints to follow, until I got to the Megan's Law website. Where there is a search function. And there I hit the jackpot: Elliot Paul Mansur.

Date of Birth: February 2, 1969 (Age: 52)
Sex: Male
Height: 5'9"

And a picture, of a lizard-looking fuck, like Raf had said.

He was sent to Coalinga State Hospital for sexually violent predators in 1994 where he admitted to twenty felony counts of lewd acts against boys at various settings, from playgrounds to zoos, but 'through a process of therapy and regular counselling' persuaded authorities he'd change his ways upon release. He was ordered to sign the Sex Offender Registry for life.

But he had aliases, hence why I haven't been able to find him online.

Known Aliases: Paul Elliott, Joe Elliott, John Cooper, Jon Geoffrey Cooper, Geoffrey Johnson, Paul Manning, Jimmy Joe Maxwell
Weight: 140lb
Eye Colour: Dark brown
Build: Slight
Ethnicity: White

Description of Offenses: kidnapping, rape of a minor, attempted rape of a minor, solicitation of sex with a child under the age of 14

Year of Last Conviction: 2017

Offense: Attempted child abduction, Topeka, Wichita

Risk Assessment: This registrant is deemed to be moderate risk.

Marks/Scars/Tattoos: pockmarked face, webbed finger on left hand, tattoo on neck behind right ear of scorpion

Last reported address: San Francisco CA 94102

Monday, 27 September 2021

1. *Kelly Clarkson – shut up and let your guests speak*
2. *Anyone who vapes – sick of walking through your strawberry-flavoured mouth-farts*
3. *Elliot Paul Mansur*
4. *The judge who decided Elliot Mansur was* only a moderate risk *to society.*
5. *Andi Smith-Lansing*
6. *The composer of Baby Shark. Count your days, do-do-do-do-do-do . . .*

There's a herb garden in Briercrest Park that I used to sit in on my lunchbreak sometimes, in the days when I had paid employment. I liked to sit and smell the air, listen to the breeze rustling the treetops and the gentle tinkle of a wind chime in the children's play area. Run my bare feet across one of the mosaic jungle animals in the art installation. Except today, a homeless guy was pinching one off in the bushes. And it killed the moment stone dead.

So instead, I sat there tugging on the Velcro straps of my brace, smelling the fug of a fresh turd and trying to find the happiness in the day. Nearby, three kids cackled over a dancing racoon on TikTok, some Karen screamed about a needle in the sandpit and two nurses from the medical centre sipped coffee and chitchatted about a guy whose two-pound arse boil had burst, drenching an intern. Beauty's where you find it.

Liv had texted that morning, out of the blue, wanting to talk. At least one of my estranged sisters had remembered I existed. I tried Seren again while I waited for Liv – still no luck. I tell the churn in my stomach to pipe down – it doesn't mean anything, her not getting back to me yet. My sister had pretty much ghosted me through my twenties so I should be used to it – but I can't stop the knot beginning to tie. She called *me* about Géricault possibly bugging her, so what's the latest? Was she bugged? Had she been arrested? Did Géricault find some cold hard evidence? Was Ivy OK? Ugh, the silence was maddening. If she's in trouble, *I'm* in trouble. If I'm in trouble, *she's* in trouble. We are inextricably linked now. She could bring this whole thing down with one interrogation meltdown.

'Fucking hell, will you ANSWER YOUR FUH. KING. PHONE!' I shrieked into the echo of the park. A couple of people glanced my way but not many. Mostly kids. Apparently, so I've found, you can lapse into any length of public break-down and people will leave you the fuck alone. They just think you're tweaking or having some paranoid delusion and give you a wide berth.

Liv turned up late and in no rush, as usual. She'd had time to do her *Clockwork Orange* eyelashes and have new acrylics but not to meet me at the time *she* suggested. I stared at her mutherfuckerly, so the hint landed, but I didn't hold it against her, especially when I saw the mint green Bugaboo she's pushing and heard Tiny Mike squawking inside. I couldn't wait to hold him – it's all I could think about. It'd make all the stuff I was pissy about float away.

'You came,' I said.

She flicked her hair back. 'He filled his diaper as we were leaving. I thought we were getting coffee?'

'I thought you'd like to sit first and chat. Sit down and relax awhile. Breathe in the glorious fragrance of tramp turd.'

She looked around. 'Gross.'

I checked my Notes app for something to say to her – about the salon or Mikey or her suicide attempt. None of them seemed right at that moment. I had to confront the elephant in the park. And not the mosaic one.

'So you wanted to speak to me finally? I'm flattered.'

'I wanted to clear the air, yeah, before the wedding. I feel so guilty about . . . what I did. And I don't know where to put it, Phee. And it all got on top of me and one day I couldn't face going on anymore. I don't wanna die – but I don't wanna live knowing I did that . . .' She looked down at Mikey.

'Edo's mum still hassling you?'

'No, I got a restraining order. She can't contact me and she can't come within a hundred yards of me or him. I took your advice and finally grew a pair of tits.'

'You already *had* a pair of tits – he was just standing on them, that's all. Good for you.'

'Is it? Then why do I feel so bad? Mikey's her grandson. And she's right, I *did* have something to do with Edo's death. I caused it.'

'Do you wanna say it a bit louder, I don't think the shitting tramp quite heard you.'

'Sorry. But she didn't do nothing wrong. She just misses her son.' Liv reached into the buggy and stroked Mikey's sleepy cheek.

'The police have nothing to go on,' I said quietly.

'It doesn't make any difference. I've got this pain in my chest all the time. I'm on antidepressants.'

'Oh who isn't,' I grumbled.

'I *hate* what I've done. I've started seeing the psychologist Rafael recommended but I talk and talk and it doesn't change how I feel. I thought I'd feel better but—'

'—you *will* feel better. It'll take some time but you will.'

'I know he was an asshole. And he would have hurt me again, Mikey too. I wish it could've been different. I wish he'd listened to me when I kicked him out at Christmas. I wish he hadn't been such a—'

'—cunt?'

She sat down on the bench, wheeling the buggy nearer. 'I told Chim. About him being the baby's real dad.'

'And?'

She went to speak, but the words got stuck. 'He cried.'

'*Chim* cried?'

'Yeah. He's low-key, quite a sensitive soul. He was so happy. He's asked if he can see him. Mikey adores him already.'

'Can I hold him?'

She pulled the buggy towards her and lifted Mikey out, placing him in my arms. 'Dinky lil nug, isn't he? He reminds me of Papi. There's a pic of my dad as a baby with Abuela. He's his mirror image, down to the chin dimple.'

'The pic hanging on the stairs?'

'Yeah. Same dimple, same smirk.'

Tiny Mike snuggles in cos kids love me and know innately

they're as safe as houses while I'm around. A deep sigh comes out before I can stop it.

'What did you see in Edo?' I asked her.

She looked at me. 'Why do you ask?'

'Well . . . you make Ariana Grande look like a seventy-year-old unshaven prison lifer called Big Frank. And Edo was a scrawny, zitty twat who hit you, had side hoes you knew nothing about, monitored everything you ate and drank, and as if that wasn't enough, blackmailed you with pictures of your own biff so you wouldn't leave him.'

'He only did that once. Maybe twice.'

'*And* he farted all the time, even in front of your mum.'

'We *all* fart in front of Mom . . .'

'*I* don't fart in front of her.'

'You must do! Not even in front of Rafael?'

'No way. He might have seen more of me than a gynaecologist but I can't go there yet. The only time I fart when he's around is when we're walking past traffic or the TV's on loud. Have to time it just right – like Andy Dufresne beating his rock against that pipe in *Shawshank*. Got to wait for the thunderclap before I let rip.'

She almost collapses into hysterics but I don't know what I've said that's so funny because it's the truth. And then I think: why *don't* I fart in front of him? Am I afraid that if I break wind, I'll accidentally let something else out of the box, like the fact I'm a mass murderer? It's so silly. I resolve to fart in front of him as soon as I get home, even if he dumps me on sight (or smell).

Or maybe I won't.

It crossed my mind to ask her advice about Billy but it's

not like I could – one stitch would unpick and then the rest of them would yank apart too and suddenly my whole blanket of lies would come undone. I wished I could tell someone – it was needling me like, well, a big needle.

Liv was still laughing at the fart comment. I haven't *ever* seen her laugh like that. 'I don't know,' she sighs, pulling herself together. 'I was with Edo for a long time. He was eighteen. Bought me all this stuff – make-up, jewellery. Took me for spins in amazing cars. Mom and Dad didn't know for months. I was too young to know he was a valet.'

'How old were you?'

'I don't know, like, fourteen?'

'Wow, he really groomed the shit out of you.'

'Yeah, but it was exciting. Dangerous. I didn't tell the fam about him for a long-assed time. I knew what the boys would say. But as I got older, it was just scary. I didn't realise how unsafe I felt with him. He conditioned me to feel like that. And when you have a good day, you think as long as I can keep him like this, give him what he wants, I can be happy. Our wedding day was happy. But it wasn't right. I'd look at Mami and Papi and now you and Raf and you guys just . . . work. It looks easy. You belong together.'

'You were always different when he was around – quieter,' I told her. 'And you didn't laugh as much. It was like you had to check with him if you *should* laugh sometimes. I hated that.'

'I hated that too.'

'My nan was like that with my grandad. Edo reminded me of him. Like every time you talked to him, you were diffusing a bomb and might hit the wrong wire. You are a warrior for killing him like you did. You did that for yourself and for Mikey. Don't you dare feel guilty for another second, Liv.'

Liv kissed Mikey's fist, smearing away the delicate ring of pink lipstick left behind. 'Well, at least you don't have to worry about Saint Rafael. He's practically perfect in every way. And he'll be an amazing husband.'

'Oh Raf's not perfect,' I told her.

'You said he's got all five.'

'He *does*. Communication skills, faithfulness, over five-nine, displays emotion, doesn't watch sport all day *plus* his dick is . . .' *chef's kiss*.

'Ew please!'

'But I came home one day and he was laughing his ass off to *White Chicks*. I realised then he wasn't perfect. And he burns everything he cooks. And he doesn't have a single Beyoncé track on his phone – not one – and . . .' I tried to think of something else. 'And . . . he gives me beard rash?'

She frowned. 'You don't have beard rash.'

'Not on my face, no.'

Liv laughed. 'But apart from all that?'

'Apart from that, yeah, he's perfect. You know what I like the most though? It's the little things – the way he touches me. The way he plays with my hair when we're watching *Squid Game*. And the way he smoothes my back when I get cross. I've never been touched that way before. My dad used to encourage my . . . bad behaviour. You know, acting out and stuff. Ex-boyfriends . . . found it funny or just plain ignored it. But not Raf. He holds me accountable. And I need that. I need *him*.'

'Aww babe.'

'He picks me flowers. And he holds me. And he listens.'

'That's so sweet.'

'And when he puts my legs up on his shoulders when I'm edging, I just fuckin' wilt.'

'Like seriously, enough with the information about my brother in bed, dude.'

'I'm serious. I never thought I had it in me to be a pillow princess – I usually have to do all the work – but with him? Game-changer. I can squirt like a jet hose now.'

'Oh. My. God!' Liv chuckled, pretending to vom.

We laughed together, like we used to before everything happened with Edo. It felt good to have my friend back.

'You know that Klimt painting *The Kiss*? The guy standing behind the girl in a flower field? I was reading an article about it the other day . . .'

'TikTok?'

'Yeah, TikTok.' I smiled. 'But that's how I feel when I'm with Rafael. Like all around me is golden. That's how I feel. I feel golden.'

Liv's finger traced down the baby's ski-slope nose. 'Are you guys trying for one of these yet?'

'Raf wants to wait until after the wedding. Suits me. I'm much happier when I'm bleeding anyway.'

Be it myself or someone else.

'I got Magic Mikey a tuxedo onesie,' I told her. 'Ordered it online. You are going to piss yourself – it's *so* cute.'

She cackled. 'They make them in his size?'

'They make them for fucking hamsters so finding one for him was no sweat. He looks chonky today.'

'Yeah, he's really putting it on. Of course, I'm doing everything wrong for him. I should be encouraging him to walk more. I shouldn't be talking to him in English so much.

I shouldn't be giving him so much cheese, even though he screams the fucking place down for it.'

'Who's saying all that?'

'Mom, Tía Julieta, Tía Xóchitl. And I got no desire to eat healthy – I want shit. Shit and sugar, the whole damn day. Someone needs to follow me around and knock it all outta my hand, I swear.'

'Well, I'm unemployed at the moment.'

She smiled. 'I know I gotta be realistic about what that's gonna do to my body but come on, I'm not about to give up chilaquiles or margs anytime soon. But my belly, OJ. Look at it. Look. At. It!'

She lifted her sweater and pinched about half an inch of fat on her torso. I'd seen more meat on a butcher's pencil.

'I am never going to find another guy if I'm fat.'

'As long as you've got holes, most men are happy.'

'That's very misogynistic.'

'No, it's true.'

'A woman is more than her holes, Phee.'

'Yeah I know. We've got the vote, joint custody, pockets, what more could we ask for?'

She chuckled. 'Te extrañé, Louise.'

'Missed you too, Thelma.'

I liked this. I didn't want to tell her that she was, in fact, *not* the one who finished Edo off. I had intended to today, to clear the air, but I got the feeling it was too late. She'd hate me now, cos I'd waited too long. Also, I wanted her to get to a place where she felt good about doing it herself. The way *I* felt about killing. In control. Powerful. Untouchable. I wanted her to feel the same way. I did at one point go on a flight of fancy in my mind and imagine us hitting the road, two murderesses together, and that maybe she'd feel as invincible as I do when I snuff out a life. But unfortunately, Liv's a normal person, and normal people don't feel like that when they kill. They, generally, regret it.

'So how's it all going with the wedding?' she asked.

'I've noped out of a lot of it. Bianca and your aunties have taken over.'

'Yeah, they tend to do that.'

'I don't mind. And thanks to my Spanish lessons, I can answer them back now when they're taking the piss out of my British accent or calling me gordita cos they keep having to take the dress out an inch.'

'Who's doing your service?'

'Father Salvador. And Salomé's on aesthetics – strings of fairy lights, ornate candle centrepieces for all the tables, swag for the entrance, petals along the aisle. Bianca and Julieta are doing the food and they've roped Matthias and Leandro into bar duties. There's going to be a beanbag area for the kids and all the suits and dresses are on order. Me and Raf just need to show up now.'

'Where you guys going on honeymoon?'

'San Francisco. Road trip.'

She frowned. 'Don't you want a beach and some bottle service, dude?'

'Nah, I don't need frills. As long as I'm with Raf, that's enough for me.'

'I always needed the frills. The big holidays, the flexin' on Instagram, the diamond ring.'

'What happened to the ring?' Liv kicked the wheel of the Bugaboo. 'Nice.'

Around us sit picnicking families, medical centre staff

eating lunches and children clambering over grassy knolls and a dry creek bed. It reminded me of the day my friend Marnie and me had gone to the boating lake and scoffed pick 'n' mix in the shade of a weeping willow. We both had baby bumps then. It was a good day, but I still wasn't happy. I wasn't entirely happy now either – still too many lies buzzing around. I wished that Raf knew the truth but still loved me anyway. Was that possible? Sometimes I thought it might be but then I came to my senses.

No sooner had I put that thought out into the universe did Brad Pfister's phone buzz in my bag.

It was a selfie of him on Haight Street, shortly followed by another of him outside a café called Wild Bean. The message underneath came through – *This is where he works, btw.*

Keep it up, I sent back with one hand – my shit hand – so what I actually managed to type was: *Kreep id upl*. I turned the phone off.

Liv caressed Mikey's soft scalp with her acrylic. She was thinking about it all again, I could tell.

'None of the heat will fall on any of you,' I told her, in no uncertain terms. 'And if there *is* any heat, I will take the rap.'

'Are you serious?'

'Yes. You're my family. That's what family does, isn't it?'

'I'm still a killer, Ophelia. I killed someone. I can't shake that off.'

'You can and you will. He won't ever be found.'

She hugged me, sniffling against my shoulder, before drying her eyes on the sleeve of her hoodie and taking Mikey to feed him. 'I don't know what we'd do without you, OJ. I really don't.'

We sat in companionable silence while Mikey chugged on her knocker.

'So do you want coffee and doughnuts then?' I asked.

'Yeah, but not here. It's too expensive.' She placed Mikey back inside the Bugaboo. 'Let's walk to the Food 'n' Home. We can use Raf's discount.'

When we got to the Food Gnome, we masked up and headed for the freezers to raid them for Ben and Jerry's. En Vogue came on the overhead system and we both started vibing down the aisles, tossing nachos and Lay's and any dip in which you could feasibly dunk a crisp into our cart.

And they *are* crisps, not chips.

It was when I was choosing six differently flavoured Krispy Kremes for our selection box that I heard a familiar voice echoing down one of the other aisles, shrieking like a banshee's louder sister.

'I don't give a fuck about your rights! You're in my country now, buddy, and *I'm* the one being disrespected! I've told you my husband died of cancer because he had to wait so long for a goddamn doctor's appointment!'

'What the hell?' Liv murmured behind her face mask, as Mikey wailed inside the buggy.

'Fuck,' I gasped behind mine. 'It's Mama Fratelli. Raf says she comes in regularly having a go at them cos they stop her licking apples and shitting in the freezers and stuff.'

'Ugh!'

'She's a *nightmare*.'

Andi Smith-Lansing marched up the candy aisle with her dumptruck ass bouncing along behind her, like the

Shrek-looking bag of bitch that she was, followed by two members of staff – Rafael and Luiz, the deputy manager.

It looked as though they'd come from the office, fresh from a bollocking. Raf saw me and Liv in the line and snuck over, kissed me full on the lips and swiped his discount card against the scanner.

'Thank you, boo.' He scuttled back to Luiz and continued to escort Smith-Lansing towards the exit. More staff ran to cover them. She was surrounded.

But Mama Frat wasn't done. '*Cancer*, did you hear me? People dying of *cancer* and all y'all care about is wearing a mask to protect yourself from a disease that don't exist! My husband had it in his balls—'

'Face masks are mandated in this store in line with govern-ment—'

'—I don't give a rat's ASS about the government! The government ain't done me no good since they put that old fart in charge! People ain't dying of this – it's all a CON. Nobody's dyin' . . .'

Cálmate, I think. *Focus on the breaths . . . focus on what matters. Deep in . . . deep out. I am here. I am loved . . . Deep in . . . deep out . . .*

We were still in the line, eyeing up the scene, subtly grooving to Grande, and I was poised to light the be-eyebrowed bitch up if she touches Raf in any way, shape or form. I was a coiled spring, ready to pounce. Ready for the kill.

I bent down to the buggy. 'Like dead things, Mikey, dead things.'

When I looked up, Mama Frat had got violent. She was coughing right in people's faces. Anyone who passed by

– a woman on her phone. An old dude on a cane, a young girl holding her dad's hand.

And Rafael.

That's when I lit up, heart thumping, teeth grinding; arsehole as tight as a fist. There was no going back now. I was going to do it – I just didn't know what 'it' was. I scanned the aisles for something pointy.

'Aww, look at y'all, so scared of a cough!' she was shouting. 'Grow up, it's all a lie! You're so scared! It's pathetic! You're PATHETIC!'

I kept walking.

She pushed Luiz who stumbled against a tower of garbanzo beans. All stacked up neatly, and they tumbled all over the floor.

I kept walking.

'Grab her!' yelled a security guard as he and Raf got her hands behind her back and frog-marched her towards the doors but she was a big woman – stocky – and she wasn't being manhandled by 'two ponchos' so she hit out. She headbutted the guard before turning to Rafael, the ex-soldier. She pulled a flick knife out of her pocket and held it out in front. He backed all the way off. She kept jabbing the air with it until he increased his distance.

I kept walking.

The cans of garbanzo beans she'd knocked over rolled all over the floor between us – on special, thirty cents for two. I grabbed the one nearest my feet.

'HEY!' I yelled. I'd left Liv and Mikey in the line and was about ready to fuck shit all the way up.

'YOU!' she shrieked. 'You watch yourself, Gutter Slut. You and your Beaner. You scared too, baby? You scared of a cough?'

'No. Cough away. Sooner your genes are out of the pool, the better.'

'You want a piece of me, bitch?' she yelled.

She was coming for me, jabbing, sliding through the cans. I eyed her, top to toe. Drew up to my full height. Side shoe to the rubber, just like Papi had taught me. Left leg up. Back hip guiding my stride. And I flung that can straight at her melon head.

And it smashed her right in the face, first attempt.

Stick that up your bunghole, Crocodile Dundee.

Winning an Oscar wouldn't have topped that moment. I'd left the house that morning an ordinary run-of-the-mill chick – I would return as a goddess.

The cheers around me were deafening as an unconscious Mama Frat was scraped up off the floor and dragged outside to the parking lot where the cops promptly drew up and handcuffed her. I kissed my right arm, right on the bicep, like Raf always did when he was flexing his muscles.

Raf couldn't close his jaw, and grabbed hold of me, lifting me clean off the floor and burying his face in my neck. 'I can't believe you did that!'

'I have hidden depths, baby.'

Strangers slapped me on the back, shook my (good) hand, gave me high-fives with the bad one. Liv hugged me, Mikey screamed the place down but in his own way he was cheering. They all were. For me.

There was one problem: I didn't realise it at the time – too swept up in the adoration – but I had made one of my world-famous boo-boos.

Because this was 2021. And nothing happens in 2021 unless

people record it. Close-ups of Smith-Lansing's diatribe, her jabbing knife, my (thankfully) masked-up face. The whole event was on YouTube within the hour. The only thing between me and internet superstardom was my unicorn face mask.

Thank heaven for Covid.

Wednesday, 29 September 2021 – our wedding day

1. *People who call football 'soccer'. That other thing is rugby in leotards.*
2. *Marjorie Blumkin*
3. *Elliot Mansur*
4. *The account called 'Jamie Dornan's Fleshlight' on TikTok, which is convinced Craig was to blame for my crimes, not me. Bloody cheek.*
5. *Raf's friend Chim, who lit his own fart at my wedding feast*

I called Seren again today, just on the off-chance that she would want to talk to me. I call her most days and it's always the same – no answer. I've even tried calling her landline – sod the rules – but it keeps ringing out. I learned from Facebook she'd gone back working part-time at a medical supplies facility so I tried that number instead – it rang out too. I surmised that my sister had gone underground, disappeared off the planet altogether or worse, she was ignoring me.

What I couldn't work out was why. I made myself a cheese toastie first thing, cut into toast points like she used to make me when we were little. Blob of salad cream on the side. I only ate one toast point – couldn't stomach the rest. I'd made it to remind myself of her but as soon as I put it in my mouth, my stomach rolled over. She'd salted me up, ignoring my calls, and now I was in panic mode on the happiest day of my life. I launched the plate against the wall where it smashed satisfyingly into lots of fragmented pieces. A bit like my skull. Nobody heard the smash – everyone in the house was too busy bustling to and fro with plates of canapés, crates of glasses and strings of fairy lights.

'Where *are* you, you bitch?'

Even so, I wasn't going to let Seren's casual ignorance ruin my big day. I made do with her voicemail message and imagined her saying *Congratulations* to me as Liv pinned up my hair. I could even imagine she meant it.

Liv went out to get more pins from the salon and handed a grizzling Mikey to me from his bassinet. I wandered over to the window to show him all the comings and goings downstairs but I don't think he was impressed. By the look on his face he was either having a shit or an existential crisis.

'There are all the aunties with the food. The suits and dresses have arrived, there they go. Oh and here's the band. We're going to dance a lot today, Mikey. Are you gonna show me your moves?'

At one point, Marjorie Blumkin sashayed out of her house across the street, her buttocks far too rounded in her Fabletics leggings, and pulled her trash cans in off the kerb.

'That's Marji – the Thanos of Karens. She has those leggings in every colour. Soon as you're old enough, me and you are gonna kick razorblade footballs into her yard.'

Blumkin is everything I hate in a human who isn't a sex offender. A shrill, racist harpy who not only bought a puppy during lockdown but gave it up to a kill shelter six months later when her kids got bored of it. Marji had complained about us four times since I'd lived there and she's had ICE out twice on the Arroyo-Carranzas, convinced nobody's documented. She'll go off about anything; nothing we do is right. Our trash cans are always in the wrong place, we have too many cars, and any dog shits on the kerb must belong to one of ours even if the turd in question is too big to have possibly come out of a chihuahua. The latest one is she wants us to cut down the maple in front of our house cos the birds sing too loudly in the mornings.

Oh yeah, she's fracking for a hiding.

And yet the Arroyo-Carranzas just tend to laugh her off. They laugh most things off – so does Billy. I can see why the Irish and the Mexicans get on so well – they take very little seriously. If it's not their fault or their problem, they don't worry about it. I wish I could be like that. I smelled Mikey's head as he fell asleep against me – every ovary I have goes up in smoke. I know Raf wants kids, someday, but that whole subject is part of the avalanche. I gave up Ivy so I could carry on killing, knowing it wouldn't be good for her to be around me. I've never killed so bloodily as when I was expecting her. Panic rose in my throat.

And suddenly, I dropped him. My weak-as-shit left wrist gave out and I dropped him. Only onto the bed, thank God, but it's a good long ruler's worth of a fall so for him it must be like dropping from a building. He immediately started crying and I picked him up again and held him against me.

He must've felt my heart shredding with guilt but he still screamed.

'Oh Mike, I'm sorry! I'm so sorry!' And I actually meant it, for once. It hurt me as much as it did when I'd accidentally step on one of Tink's paws when she'd follow me around the kitchen.

But he wasn't having it, he was proper pissed with me. He trusted me and I let him down. I stared at him screaming, kicking out, fists balled in fury.

Liv came back with the spare pins, seeing off a spiral of impending motherhood panic. 'Aww, did he shit himself again?'

'Uh, no I don't think so. Liv – I dropped him.'

'What?' she said, giving me that look people always give me.

'Only onto the bed. My wrist gave out. It was only about a foot but. Oh God, he hates me—'

'—he doesn't hate you,' she said, scooping him up with her two strong af wrists and rubbing his back. 'You're shaking, don't worry he's fine!' Mikey nuzzled in and stopped screaming the second he felt his mother's skin against his, all the while still giving me baby evils. 'It'll be you next, you know. You wait till you get that fertility lazo around you. You won't be able to stop pumping 'em out. Tons of 'em.'

Perish the thought, I thought, but all Liv got was a hopeful smile in the midst of my panic. 'Aren't you pissed that I dropped him?'

He'd stopped crying. She shook her head. 'You said he didn't drop far, and you couldn't help it so no, it's OK.'

I was glad she didn't mind but it took me a good ten minutes for my heart to pick up its normal rhythm. I resolved never to pick him up again.

The one good thing about this incident was that for the first time in forever, I hadn't equated the baby's screaming with Priory Gardens. I hadn't gone back there in my mind on that shrill glass-breaking din. I stayed in the room, in the moment, and tried to soothe him.

By the time she'd finished plaiting and studding my hair with diamond clips, draping my velo over me, and Liv had done my nails, I was serving some serious lewks. I know life was supposed to be all about beauty-is-on-the-inside crap but come on – I was a stunner. There in the mirror was a girl who knew the assignment and was eating it up, every crumb.

'Ay, Papantla, tus hijos vuelan!' said Bianca as she and Liv cried together, admiring the vision before them that was me. I'd never understood why people cry at weddings. I still felt bad about Mikey, who was by this time sound asleep in his bassinet completely un-brain damaged.

'Todo listo, hermana,' Liv announced, adding a last cheek highlight.

'Mi hermosa hija,' said Bianca, cupping my cheek.

My sister and my mum then hugged me. What did I need Seren for when I had *them*?

I could see Raf in his blue suit as soon as I walked through the church doors. Jesus Christ, I didn't think he could look any more gorgeous and then he pulls the navy tuxedo look out of the bag. He stood at the altar beneath a floral arch, alongside Nico and his two army buddies, Mase and Billy, and Chim, Liv's baby daddy, and before them, the pews decorated with blue-and-orange flower bunches.

Billy was in my good books again – as far as I knew, he had said nothing to no one about who I really was and I started to think I had imagined it all; the signs, the staring, the cheeky winks of those emerald eyes. Maybe he *didn't* know my true identity. Maybe the cosmetic surgery and contact lenses had worked their magic. In any case, I pushed the possibility of otherwise to the side of my mind where I had also pushed my sister and determined to enjoy my day.

Our wedding was the first big event the whole Arroyo-Carranza family had been to since Covid first flew out of that bat's arse. I'd missed the all-night danceathons, beer pong contests, the card games under the veranda. I'd missed getting drunk with Raf's friends and cousins. I didn't normally like my boyfriend's friends – I'd positively despised all of Craig's – but I liked Rafael's. Or maybe it was because I liked Rafael that I could tolerate them. And I could understand most of their conversations now – when they spoke slowly enough, which wasn't often. But I slowly got the gist. It was nice. I felt part of things, rather than the wallflower I'd been when I first met them all.

The vows were like I've always seen in movies but could never imagine saying myself but I meant every one of them – I *do* declare my consent before God. I *do* take this absolute king to be my husband, and I *will* be true to him in good times and bad, in sickness and in health, all the days of my life.

He meant them too, to a point. He didn't even laugh when he said them – he looked straight into my eyes as he pushed that ring onto my finger. And he said, 'Ophelia, receive this ring as a sign of my love and fidelity.'

He promised *me* – well, he promised Ophelia. I tried to hear my own name in my head when he said it and imagine he was saying it to her.

After we'd said our vows, Bianca wrapped the wedding lasso around us – a chain of orange blooms – first around me and then around Rafael, binding us together in an infinity loop, the traditional symbol of our unity and fertility.

'What God joins together let no one put asunder,' cried Father Sal to the gathered throng. And then we were officially husband and wife.

Me! A Wife! Who thought *that* would ever happen?

And then we all went back to the house and partied. We had tables and chairs set up in the garden, and Salomé had decorated the place all over with orange and blue flowers, same as the church, along with silk chair coverings and strings of fairy lights which lit us up as the sky grew darker above our heads. Somehow, the roses I'd planted smelled stronger too.

We feasted on all our favourite foods – an Anglo-Mexican combo of delights. There can't be many weddings that feed their guests tamales, polvorones and chilpachole alongside jam scones, miniature cod bites and chips and Yorkshire puddings. We had an open bar with tequila, agua frescas for the kids, fruit platters with chamoy and Tajín, Gansito ice cream and on the top of our traditional three-storey iced Victoria sponge stood a Calico Critters bride and groom.

There were three best men – Chim, Nico and Billy. Nico's speech was the best – I can't recall all of it exactly as I was too busy trying to look like an angelic bride not choking on a Yorkshire pudding too big for her mouth, but he mentioned my Bean Qween glory at the Food Gnome. Oh and there was this bit:

'Ophelia, before Rafael met you, he didn't know where life was taking him and he didn't care. You've given him purpose.

He was drifting. Now he's tethered. Before you found him, he was lost. Thank you for making my brother happy again. You're not just his maniac, you're *our* maniac now too.'

The applause rang out around the whole garden, bouncing off the garden fences. The six chihuahuas skittered out from underneath chairs, dressed in tiny tuxedos and frilly skirts, darting all over the place. The kids ran after them, one by one, rounding them up.

I hugged Nico after the toast while they were still clapping and he whispered in my ear – 'I hope you know how much you mean to us.' Then he kissed my forehead. Mi hermano.

Then Chim got up and gave *his* best-man speech – he was the comedy relief and basically entered into a ten-minute spiel about drinking binges that he, Raf and Mase used to go on in their twenties. Binges like the time they got deep fat fried on some hokey weed and hadn't been able to blink for seven hours. Chim's like the shorter, tubbier version of Raf – where Raf's voice is deep and luxurious, Chim sounds like Minnie Mouse.

And then Billy stood up. I sank another tequila to kill the nerves I had about this one. Was this going to be the moment where he unravelled me – where he dislodged the snowball that would bring down the landslide?

'If anyone deserves to be happy, it's this guy,' he announced in his warm Irish brogue. 'If it weren't for Rafael, I wouldn't be here. I owe him everything. He was an amazing soldier and his army career was shot down way too soon. He had a lot more to give. Rafael saved my life a few times. He's saved lives, too many to count. Cutting down snipers nobody else spotted. Calling out IEDs nobody else knew were there. Raf does a lot of things on instinct – he knows when something's right, and when it's wrong.

'This one patrol, we'd gone out to clear a route of IEDs around a patrol base and we were crossing this ditch and Raf saw this thing glinting in the sun – the Taliban used wires to trigger IEDs. He held me back. I was like, "No way, man, I'm gonna check it for traps." But Raf held me back. He picked up a rock and tossed it towards this wire, and the entire road blew like feckin' Nagasaki. If I'd gone two metres forwards, I'd be a name on a wall right now. I never see the danger, but Raf does. Thank God.' Billy turned to Raf, tears in his eyes. 'So it's a bit of a shame that he got himself kicked out the week before I went out and got me two feet blown off really, isn't it?'

The crowd roared with laughter, cutting right through the grim reality of the speech and as though to underline it, Billy propped one of his fake legs up on the table and lifted his trouser leg to show everyone. Then he picked up his half-full beer glass. 'In Ireland we say that love is blind but marriage is an eye opener – you get to find out what you've signed up for . . .'

He looked directly at me.

'. . . and I think what these two have signed up for is worth celebrating. They're both astonishing people who I am proud to call my friends.'

What's he after? I thought.

'Ophelia – there's only one difference between in-laws and outlaws. Nobody wants the in-laws.'

That nearly brought the house down.

'But in your case, you've married into a terrific family who'll look after you and help you grow into the best version of the person you are. Bianca calls Rafael her jewel and she's absolutely right – the man's a diamond. He'll look after you like you're the most precious thing on earth. You've done what my granny always said I should do – marry the one who'll help you flourish . . .'

His stare at me was pointed – flourish? Flowers? Sweetpea? Or was I just reaching now?

'So everyone, please raise your glasses to the best friend I ever had and his fragrant new wife – Rafael y Ophelia!'

'*Rafael y Ophelia*!' everyone cried back, to a deafening applause glittered with whoops and hollers. All I could think about was the word *fragrant*. Like a flower. Like a sweetpea. I downed another tequila. Don't tell Raf but I can't stand tequila – I've always just found it incredibly handy if I needed to get pissed in a hurry.

Our mariachi band serenaded us into the night. Raf's uncles Sam and Felipe are cops and somehow managed to keep the neighbours off our backs so we could enjoy ourselves. Our dance floor emerged in the centre of all the tables, and we were up first for our wedding song – 'Bonnie and Clyde'. After that, it was a free for all and I danced till my feet bled and I had to take off my shoes.

'Mind if I cut in, mate?' asked Billy, tapping Raf on the shoulder and Raf didn't hesitate to hand me over to his friend. When Raf had disappeared through the throng towards the bar, Billy held me too closely against him as the lager fumes hit my face.

'You wanna lose your dick as well as your feet, I suggest you back off a smidge, O'Shea.'

He laughed, stepping back slightly. 'Sorry. I'm a bit heavy in me cups. You look beautiful.'

'Duh, well, I am the bride. Thanks for the speech.'

'Meant every word. It's good to see him happy – he deserves to be happy.'

'What does that mean?'

'Nothing.' He shrugged as he spun me around, inadvertently yanking on my weak-as-shit wrist. I tried to mask my pain. He moved too close to me again, swinging me from side to side, holding me close so he could whisper against my ear. 'Are those flowers on your dress?'

'Yes.' I looked down. 'Embroidered.'

'Nice.'

'Some people have commented that I look like an angel today,' I said, leaving the statement hanging and posing coquettishly as he scoped me up and down.

'Yeah, I can see that. It suits you.'

'Thanks.' I relaxed in his arms as he twirled me around and we did a little waltzy-twirl thing as the music slowed. He held me closer and we swayed and he looked down at my dress again. 'What flowers are they? Pansies?'

'Daisies, I think. Or possibly peonies. There are roses on the back. They're Raf's favourite.'

'I thought sweetpeas were Raf's favourite.'

We stopped dancing, while everyone around us carried on. I felt like he had dropped a lit bomb down the front of my dress.

Billy smiled. 'Oh yeah. I know exactly who you are.'

I cleared my throat – my voice had momentarily left the building. 'I think you should ease up on the tequila, mate.'

He pulled back. 'I know who you are, *Rhiannon*.'

I'd often heard that expression 'my blood froze' but I'd never felt it until that moment. I couldn't deny it now – he knew. He had hold of me and I was stuck between several jostling family members on the dance floor so I couldn't even run away. I had to stand there, smiling, dancing, like the bride I was on the outside, while the serial killer I was on the inside imagined that cake knife slicing his head clean from his shoulders.

'How?' I mewed. 'How did you know?'

'Don't worry,' he laughed, holding me as we twirled, 'it's not obvious. But Raf sent me a picture when he first met you – before your surgery.'

'When . . . when did he take a picture of me? I only met him once before. 'There's no way . . .'

'At the airport. He took a photo of you. Said he thought he'd just met his future wife. Asked me what I thought of you. I didn't recognise you at first but then eventually it became clear who you were cos of all the stuff on the news. I didn't tell him, obviously.'

'Oh my God.'

He laughed. But then his tone changed, as did his face. He was happy? 'You're a fucking legend!'

Even with the copious tequila and swirl of love all around me, I felt sick with nerves. I wanted to run – through the garden, through the house, grab my car keys, get in the car and flee for literally anywhere else. But Billy had me in his grip and he wasn't letting go. I couldn't go anywhere – I had to face him and I had to say it.

'Yes. I am Rhiannon.'

He loosened his grip and spun me around again but my feet couldn't keep time with the music – or my mind couldn't keep time with my feet.

'You've no need to look so worried; I'm not going to tell

anyone. I'm a huge fan. I know a lot of people who are. I know you wouldn't hurt the family.'

I was so cross – not *killer* cross but brewing. 'Am I that obvious? You knew from one photo?'

'Not at all. I have an aunt who's mad on true crime. She's a big fan of yours too; always watching documentaries and listening to podcasts about you. She was the one who got me interested in your story. Signed me up for the fecking newsletter and everything. You don't look much like your old self nowadays.'

'What newsletter?'

'The Bad Seeds. You must have heard of them. It's a massive fan forum where people meet online to enthuse about you – they organise conventions, print T-shirts. They're obsessed. There's even talk of a mini-series being made about you, did you know that?'

'I won't hold my breath,' I scoffed.

'We think the world is better off with you in it, Rhiannon.' He checked around the immediate area for prying eyes, then pulled open his suit jacket to reveal a couple of badges – an Irish flag, some army medal, a Pride badge and a black teardrop-shaped one with a gold crack running through it. The Bad Seeds – the dark mark of a Rhiannon stan.

And then words came out of my mouth which my brain hadn't parked there. 'Do you think Rafael should . . . you think I should tell him?' I asked.

But then Mase cut in and stole me away to dance with him so I never heard Billy's answer. The next time I saw him, it was hours later and he was passed out in a rosebush wearing Liv's floral crown, which is just as well – I'd been nervous all night at the amount of tequila he was necking and I feared any moment he'd grab the mic and let all my squawky, blood-soaked gatitas right out of the bag.

The day was a weird-ass Mexican fairy-tale of drinking and dancing and laughing and spinning and people getting yeeted into the pool in a whir of flowers and twinkling lights. And apart from that moment with Billy and another when I overheard some of Raf's aunties talking about Rafael's first wife and her 'tetas más grandes' it was the best day of my life.

Raf was dancing with baby Mikey in his tiny tuxedo when I came back from a make-up touch-up and it was hands down the cutest thing I'd ever seen. Mikey fell asleep in Raf's arms, despite all the noise, and I put my head on Raf's shoulder and we were all dancing then, like we were a family, dancing with our baby boy, just for a minute.

'Wow,' I said.

'What's up?' smiled Raf.

'I think one of my ovaries exploded. Not like me at all.'

'You wanna . . . sneak inside, make one of our own?'

'I thought you wanted to wait until after . . .'

'. . . we're married? Well, you are now, mi esposa.'

'They'll notice we've gone. We're the stars of the show here, mi esposo.'

'You think they'll care?' I looked around the garden – every table, someone was up dancing or singing or laughing in a drunken haze.

'Go on then,' I said, and Raf handed Mikey to a nearby auntie who'd been dying for a smush all night, and led me indoors.

At that moment, I was too pissed to be concerned about all

the impending motherhood stuff I'd hated when I'd been having Ivy. All that vaginal pokery and sore tits and constipation and postpartum periods that look like the black goo that comes out their mouths in the *Thriller* video. At that moment, there was nothing I wanted more than to have a piece of Raf inside me. I wriggled out of my knickers and sat up on the washer in the laundry room waiting for him to wedge the door shut. A part of me knew that this time, whatever went wrong, there would always be someone around to care for my baby. Endless Mexican relatives, all over the state, a few more in Tijuana and several hundred in Baja and Sonora. It would be OK this time. It would be better.

'Hey, Mrs Arroyo-White. Do you realise this is the first time we're fucking as man and wife?' he said, right into my ear, then he bit my lobe.

'Mmm, that feels nice,' I sighed. 'My husband.'

Neither of us had cum by the time the clock chimed midnight and our magic ran out. No fairy-tale is ever complete without the bad fairy, is it? And for once, it wasn't me.

We heard a commotion outside. The band had stopped and someone was shouting; screaming even.

'The fuck?' said Raf, pulling up his suit trousers as I scrambled my pants back on and straightened my hair. As we came out of the laundry room, the dogs scampered past as though running from an incoming tsunami.

Cue the *Kill Bill* sirens.

It was Edo's mother, Josefina, at the end of the garden, appearing as suddenly and as unwelcome as the bedraggled old bag who boos Buttercup in *The Princess Bride*. She was lashing out at anyone who came near and as we got outside,

I saw she was carrying a handgun. Nobody had been hurt yet. Bianca was closest to her, trying to talk her down.

'Fina, cálmate, por favor entra a la casa y hablamos.'

Liv was shouting at her, clearly at the business end of a margarita marathon. 'Why can't you let him go, you fucking bitch, coming here, insulting my family, I didn't do nuthin' to him! Tell him, Ophelia.'

Even the flowerheads turned to look at me. 'What?'

'I didn't kill him, did I? He was alive . . .'

'It's OK, Liv, it's OK, you need to calm down now,' I said, knowing how loose-lipped she got when she'd been drinking. 'Can someone take her inside please?' To which, Nico stepped up.

'What is she talking about?' cried Josefina, looking straight at me and pointing the gun. Rafael immediately stepped in front of me. 'What did she mean she didn't kill him? What do you know?'

'I saw him. Well, I saw his car. On the bridge that day. Coronado Bridge. I was driving past and I recognised it. I saw a figure standing beside it, only for a couple of seconds, but I'm pretty sure it was Edo.'

'You saw him on the bridge? You saw my Eduardo? Mi niño?'

'He was throwing an object off.'

Everyone looked at everyone else. Rafael looked back at me. Bianca looked at Nico who looked at Ariela whose boys were asking each other what it all meant. Billy and Mase did the Tom Hanks face into their beers. Aunts put hands to their mouths. Uncles, cousins, kids and chihuahuas all seemed to look at Liv and their faces said the same thing: you poor woman.

'He wrote a note,' she replied, her lower lip wobbling. 'He said he wasn't good enough as a husband or a father . . . and said goodbye.'

I nodded. 'This isn't Liv's fault. You can see she's hurting too.'

'It can't have been him; it wasn't my Edo!' Josefina screamed.

'It was his car,' I said again. 'That's where the police found it, wasn't it?'

Josefina nodded, struggling to find one of the many rumpled tissues inside her green cardigan pocket. And she stood there, hole in her slipper, crying in the middle of the garden. Bianca placed her arms around her, taking her inside the house on a promise of a warm drink.

I smiled fakely at her when she passed me but when I looked up, Raf was staring at me with an expression I couldn't read.

'You saw him? Why didn't you say?'

'Can we talk about this later? We have a garden full of guá who all need to get way more drunk than they already are.'

'What else aren't you telling me? Why did Liv say that about not killing him and why did you cut her off?'

'Because she didn't kill him. *I* did.'

Thursday, 30 September 2021 – early morning

1. *Americans who don't understand any other accent and think Wales is in England. Buy a sodding atlas.*
2. *Gwen Stefani and husband*
3. *Quiz show hosts who spend an age finding out about the contestants – just ask the fucking questions, Steve!*
4. *TikTokkers who film themselves giving out food to the homeless or helping old funts cross the road. Put the camera down and assess whether it really matters to you.*
5. *Woody Allen*

It was 2 a.m. when I found him, punching the guts out of one of the bags at Nico's gym. Raf's teetotal uncle Felipe got the short straw in driving me around as I refused to stay at home so everyone else could go out looking. I knew he'd gone there. When he was angry, he'd normally paint something or hit something. Tonight, he was hitting.

He carried on punching the bag, left right, left right, left-right-left-rightleftrightleftright, ignoring me in the doorway.

'It's all calmed down now at home. Your mum and Josefina were doing shots with your army friends. Your uncle Alfonso was twerking on your uncle Dante. And our priest was flexing with some backflips. For a man of the cloth, he's surprisingly extra.'

Raf still didn't answer.

Still no answer from the man on the bag.

'Are we going to talk? Raf?' He had on his tuxedo trousers but was bare-chested and sweaty with boxing gloves strapped tightly to his hands. All his poise and cleanliness from the day had vanished. He moved away from me, walked towards the boxing ring, and hung his arms inside over the ropes. I climbed inside and sat down on the edge to look at him.

'Your dress'll get dirty.'

'It's already torn,' I told him. 'I sat down a bit quick after the dancing and I've ripped the back. Bloody thing only just fits anyway.'

'Talk, Ophelia.'

'Liv called me up, two weeks ago. Edo had gone round there and refused to leave. He was trying to get her to call off the divorce, trying to get access to Mikey, worming his way back in. He'd raped her.'

Raf's eyes banged shut. 'Where was Mikey?'

'Upstairs asleep.'

He looked at me properly for the first time. 'Why didn't you tell me?'

'What would you have done?'

'I don't know. Me and Nico could've gone round there—'

'—when she specifically told you not to, yeah that would have been a good idea, wouldn't it? She didn't want you two in trouble. Anyway, before I could do anything, Liv stabbed him with a kitchen knife.'

'She *did* kill him? Josefina was right.'

'Well, *kind* of. He was out cold – lost a lot of blood – so we waited until it was dark and loaded him into the back of his car and I . . . disposed of him. *And* the car.'

'How? The cartel?'

'No, not the cartel, *me*. I did it. *I* got rid of his body.'

'Where?'

'It's not important. But he wasn't dead when I put him in the boot – the *trunk*. Liv started it but I finished it – I had to. He'd have gone to the cops about her stabbing him and then he'd have got custody of Mikey, wouldn't he? I did it for the family.'

'*You* killed Edo?'

'Yes. She'd have gone to jail. *Nico* would have gone to jail too—'

He ducked down and stepped through the ropes to sit beside me in the ring. 'What's Nico got to do with it?'

'Um, a small thing called threatening to kill Edo in the parking lot of the Chuck n Buns two months ago? I've sorted that too. I stole the CCTV.'

'What? Why?'

I shrugged. That didn't go down well so I had to elaborate. 'He's my brother too now. I care about him. I care about Liv. And your mum. And Mikey and the other kids. I love you all. Your therapist said that sometimes love is violence, right? This is how I show love.'

'Talk to me. How did you do it?'

I told him what had happened – I added in the detail about finding Nico at Torrey Pines but I didn't tell him about the brugmansia powder and the musical basement torture. The truths came thick and fast – to a point.

'It seemed easier to make it look like Edo had committed suicide. Fewer loose ends than pretending he'd just gone away.'

Raf ranted and raved, banged his fists on the canvas and stood up, yelling that I should have been careful, that I shouldn't have spent the Tenoch money on the Roadrunner rental. That I'd put everyone at risk. It was the lies more than anything – he didn't seem to mind the fact that I'd killed; only that I'd lied to him about it. 'I can't take any more lies, Phee. I can't. You keep all this from me? How many other guys you killed? TELL ME.'

'No one. Just him.'

'I don't get this – I don't get why you couldn't tell me earlier.'

'I don't think like a normal person, Raf. I thought you understood that.'

'You can't bring cartel stuff here; it's too risky for us.'

'IT WAS NOTHING TO DO WITH THE CARTEL!' I yelled. 'IT WAS ME!' I nearly said it; nearly spilled the whole tea about Rhiannon Lewis, serial killer extraordinaire, and how he'd underestimated me for the last time. But I had to hold back the avalanche a bit longer. He wasn't ready. *I* wasn't ready.

'How did you . . . kill him?' he asked, sitting back down, closer.

I wanted to tell him the whole truth and nothing but the truth at that moment but I couldn't say the words. Not because I thought he'd punch me out but because of how much *my* verbal punches would knock him flying. My God how he'd changed me – time was, I couldn't wait to tell Craig that I'd broken his favourite football trophy while dusting or that yes, his penis *was* too small for me. But with Raf – I couldn't bear it. So I stuck to what I thought he could cope with.

'I took him to the house . . . tied him to a pole in the basement. That's all you need to know.'

'No, I wanna know it all. Tell me.' He stared me down, not one blink.

'I tied him to a pole in the basement. Drugged him first, obvs. And I left him there, for a few days, to die alone of his injury. I wanted him to suffer.'

Raf's face changed. I couldn't read it.

'And then, eventually, I went back and he was still slightly alive so I killed him. With a cleaver. One short, sharp strike, to the back of the neck. It was done.'

He looked away from me. I didn't know what that meant either. I guess I was testing him on the whole 'forever' part of our vows now. All that sickness and health crap didn't amount to a hill of beans if he couldn't handle the fact I'd offed the odd rapist or two.

Or twenty-eight.

'I told you the truth. That was a good thing, right? I knew you couldn't handle it.'

'Oh I can handle it. I just forget sometimes that you're capable of that kind of thing. This ain't your first rodeo, huh?'

'Old Cartel Kate and her wily ways, that's me.' I winked. Despite my grin, I felt all rancid again. That beautiful face did not deserve this. But I needed to know: I needed to know if he *could* love me like he loves 'Ophelia'.

He didn't say anything for a long time. Then he pulled off his boxing gloves with his teeth, throwing them to one side. The look he gave me was like the one my dad used to give me.

All *Oh Rhiannon you didn't*. But he didn't call me a psycho or threaten me with the police like I feared he might. He said the perfect thing. 'How do I protect you from this?'

Something in my chest broke in two; the pieces fluttered away. 'What?'

'The cartel nearly killed you once. I couldn't bear it if someone took you again. You wouldn't make it back.'

'There's no trail back to me, to *us* from that house. I paid the deposit under another name.'

'And the body? What did you do with Edo's body?'

'It's still there. In the basement.'

'We need to bury it. Or burn it.'

He sat down next to me, sweat dripping down the side of his face. I wiped it away with my finger and was relieved that he didn't flinch.

'Do you still hate me for not telling you?'

'How can I hate you? You've saved my brother *and* sister from jail and death. And you did it all by yourself.'

'I'd rather I went to jail than they did or you did. And I'd sooner die myself than let someone like Edo bring up Mikey. They're my family too now, you know? That's how I feel anyway. I feel closer to them than I do any of mine.'

He kissed me on my temple. 'I'm sorry.'

'What are you sorry for?'

'Well, lookit – my army career's in the toilet. I got a shitty-assed job helping shitty-assed people pack groceries. You nearly get killed by a drug cartel and I almost get there too late to save you. My brother-in-law could have killed you *and* my sister—'

'—I don't need you to save me, Raf.'

'—and now you've single-handedly dug her *and* my brother

out of the shit they both created. You deserve so much better than me, Phee.'

'Don't torture yourself, Gomez. That's my job,' I tell him nibbling his ear.

'I mean it. I'm a waste of space.'

'Al right then, why don't we go home, sign you up for organ donation now, chuck the toaster in the bath and be done with it, hmm?'

'Don't joke.'

'Don't talk crap then. Raf, when I met you, not a single person in the world cared about me, least of all myself. Now, I have a husband who's an action hero. I have a mum and a big brother, and a sister who's like my best friend. I have nephews, nieces, cousins, aunts, uncles. I have game nights and movie marathons and someone who brings me chocolate and gives me cuddles when I'm menstruating and hot drinks when I'm sick. I have karaoke and dancing, so much *dancing* . . .'

He smiled. 'Yeah, we do dance a lot.'

'And last Christmas, I came downstairs to a sea of presents with my name on and a row of people all dressed in the same pyjamas as me. There isn't a day goes by where I'm not hugged or kissed or told how loved I am. And don't give me that useless former soldier crap again – you're a trained soldier with about a million transferrable skills. You can mend or build anything. You can survive *anywhere*. You can kill someone with your bare hands!'

He did the De Niro nod of agreement – I knew that one.

'You're incredible. So don't say you can't give me anything – because you've given me *everything*.' I held up my left hand

and stared at my wedding ring. 'Including this. And I'm never taking it off.'

We lay down in the boxing ring, Raf cuddling me against him.

'You'll get all sweaty,' he said.

'Good.' I looked down at our intertwined fingers, two solid gold rings. I'd told him I'd killed another person and he was still there. Not giving me The Look or walking away and calling me a freak. I wish I could be myself with him – my Rhiannon self. But this was as close as I'd ever get. It's not enough – it never would be until he knew me as I truly was – but it would have to do because I couldn't lose him. I *wouldn't* lose him.

And then he kissed me. 'You asked me once what I saw in you.'

'I know exactly what you see in me. Your dick,' I scoffed.

'Be serious for a minute. For a long time I didn't know what it was, it was so many things, but I've narrowed it down from a hundred.'

'A *hundred* things you love about me?'

'Yeah, I've got it down to ten. You wanna hear them?'

'Go on then.'

'Well, in no particular order, you make me laugh. You always got my back – there's no one I'd want next to me in a war situation more than you.'

'Seriously?'

'Oh yeah. It's the way you give me butterflies. It's the way you love kids and dogs, go out of your way to protect them, even if it means causing yourself pain . . .' He kissed my left wrist where my scar was.

My skin tingled all over like he was leaving a sprinkle of

magic wherever he went on my body. I couldn't believe that ring on his finger symbolised me now. That he was mine and that, by law, I was his. It's all I'd ever wanted – someone who stayed. 'Keep going.'

'I love how we watch TikToks in bed and end up in hysterics. I love how much you want to impress my family, even if you go to ridiculous lengths to do it sometimes . . .'

'. . . it was your mum's birthday and no Target in the state had that cake in stock. I *had* to go to Phoenix.'

'I know, I know.' He laughed. 'You're learning Spanish for us, you're looking after us. I love how I've never met anyone like you.'

'Three more.'

'I love your eyes, your *real* eyes. The green ones. I love that sweet ass. And I love how I want to be the best version of myself for you.'

'Wow,' was all I could say. 'You didn't say any of that in your speech.'

'Because it's just for you – you're the one who needs to hear it; it doesn't need an audience.' He kissed me again. 'No more need for secrets, OK? You can talk to me, about anything. *Anything*. I will never judge you.'

'You promise?'

'I promise.'

'Thank you.' I cuddled against him and closed my eyes.

'I'm going to make you as proud of me as I am of you. Even if it takes me the rest of my life.'

Monday, 4 October 2021

1. *Elliot Mansur*
2. *Brad Pfister (yes, really)*
3. *Patty Filbert*
4. *The prick who invented pop-ups*
5. *James Charles*

So someone *did* upload a YouTube video of 'Bean Qween Taking Out Racist Karen' which I all kinds of loved but again, thank God for masks. Nobody in the comments section had mentioned Bean Qween having a passing resemblance to that wiley old minx Rhiannon Lewis, so the coast was clear of any nosey old boats. For now, at least.

I kind of like being in the spotlight again though. Watching the 'like' count on the video going up by the hour. People saying nice things. Wondering who 'that amazing babe' was. Seeking me out. But that was just the problem. I *couldn't* be found. I could not afford to step back into the spotlight. It would be the boo-boo to end all boo-boos.

And someone *did* find out – it was leaked online that my name was Ophelia White from Los Abrazos and they had used my picture from the realtor's website – sunglasses and smile in my business suit as I helped Wilmer cut the ribbon on the new office last year. Zoomed in on my face. Quite grainy and I had a face mask on but it was the same build, the same hair. And to the wrong eyes, it was the same person – Ophelia Jane White, aka Rhiannon Lewis.

I just had to hope and pray that my extensive facial reconstruction and general happier demeanour didn't give my sordid little game away.

I managed to put Rafael off from coming to Roadrunner with me to bury Edo's body by saying I'd already done it days ago. That was the lie part. I said I didn't want him anywhere near the place because of fingerprint identification – that was the truth part. He didn't like it but he got it. Off to see off Brad Pfister (yes, really) now. There may well be Pfisty Cuffs . . .

There's been a boo-boo. Quite a gigantic one. The meeting with Pfister did *not* go according to plan, all thanks, once again, to my crappy left wrist. I'm starting to wish the bloody thing had never been sewn back on.

I had already been at Roadrunner for an hour when Pfister's red Prius came beetling up the dusty drive. I stepped out onto the doorstep with the Adidas shoebox in my hands and a small Sabatier tucked into the back of my waistband. He did that palm-on-the-steering-wheel pish as he doughnutted to a stop on the gravel driveway, then got out, slamming the driver's door, and circling his keys around his finger before pocketing them. His nose had healed somewhat in the past week – still a bit scabby – but the bruises had come right out. He loped towards me, notepad in hand.

'So what did you find out?' I asked, stopping him from coming too close.

'Money?' he said. I lifted up the box to show him the stacks. He nodded. 'I got everything you asked for,' he said. 'He lives on Filmore Street in Cow Hollow, and he works in the Tenderloin at some liquor store on Turk Street. I wrote it all down.' He showed me the notebook, but didn't let go of it nor make any attempt to hand it to me. 'Phone first.'

I plucked his iPhone from my pocket and threw it over. 'New passcode – treble six, treble six.'

Once he's caught it and punched it in, he checks through his photos; all his snatched gusset and side boob shots intact. 'Nobody else seen this?'

'Nope.'

'And you haven't told the cops?'

'What do *you* think?'

He sighed and shoved the phone in his pocket. 'OK, so the money?'

'Notebook first,' I said, clicking my fingers. He threw it at me and it landed with a dusty splat at my feet.

'The only day he doesn't leave the apartment is Sunday. Well, he didn't when I watched him. He's one ugly dude. Real skinny lil bitch.'

'I know. Anything else?'

'He drinks in a bar down the street from his apartment called Grizzly's. Goes there most nights and he gets the bus, the 38R, and he doesn't drive. At least, I never saw him drive while I was there.'

'Got pretty close to him then?'

'You told me to. I had my parents with me so it didn't look

sketchy. I said I had to go off for lots of photo shoots cos I won a gaming award. They didn't mind. They did the touristy stuff. Kinda saved their marriage in a way.'

'You're welcome,' I said. 'And he definitely doesn't live with anybody?'

'Nope. Doesn't seem to have any friends either.'

'CCTV outside the apartment?'

'Nope, not that I could see.'

'And you're sure he didn't see you at all?'

Pfister (yes, really) vehemently shook his head, like he was getting rid of a fly. 'Nope, I made sure of it. And if I thought he might have, I changed my routine up, followed him another day. He gets a lot of Door Dash.'

'What sort of food?'

'Pizza and fried chicken. From what I could tell.'

I flicked through the notepad at all of Pfister's scrawly assed notes then shoved the book in the back of my jeans. I picked up the shoebox. He came forward to take it, stopping short of arm's length.

'Can I ask you somethin'?' he said. 'And will you answer me honestly?'

'Maybe.'

'Why not get a private detective? Why did you ask me to do this?'

'You were cheaper.'

Brad's mouth laughed but his eyes didn't. 'They were charging more than 50k to spy on this guy for a week? Boy were *you* ripped off.' He stepped forward again to take the box. It was as close as we'd been since the day of the nose biting. He took it, but the second he did, I pulled the tissue from my hoodie and tossed it against his face so the powder could fly out and stun him—

—and herein lies the inevitable boo-boo.

Roadrunner Ridge is up fairly high. It's half-surrounded by trees and half by a wide expanse of dry grass. This has always been its allure to me. But a wind tunnel blows up the driveway and this breeze has been known to take my breath away when I step out of my car. In this instance, and having thrown the powder using my gloved left hand (aka, the shit one), every speck of the brugmansia powder missed Pfister and disappeared into the desert air.

'FUUUUUUCCCKKKKK!' I yelled.

There was a scuffle. The box skittered away on gravel and dust but none of the money came out. It wasn't about that anymore though – this was now a fight to the death.

He hit me, I hit him. There was a whole load of struggling and punching and the fight wasn't pretty or well-choreographed and I couldn't grab my knife to save my own life. It's much less easy than it used to be now, wrestling with predatory men, but back in the good old days I was younger, had more stamina, had pile-driven far fewer tortillas and guac and had two working hands.

In one hot moment, he had mounted me, his hot hands either side of my neck, pressing; and I was flapping about hitting him as much as I could but for a nerd, he was hella strong. Particularly strong wrists.

Well, a man who spent as much time wanking as he did would have, wouldn't he?

Anyway, I was there scrabbling about the dirt for a rock to hit him with and eventually finding a palm-sized one. Almost losing consciousness, I managed to pull in a breath as he released his grip on my neck to gain better purchase and before he could react, I bashed the side of his head with it – partial frontal lobotomy to the left temple – and *BOOM*. He collapsed on top of me like a heavy sack.

Thank God for old Righty. I couldn't feel my left hand at all – it had gone all pins-and-needlesy and seized up.

'Jesus!' I gasped, clamouring for air, tasting blood as I scrabbled out from under him and got to my feet. The tissue tumbled away into the brush, meaning he was going to wake up any second, perfectly sentient, and go at me again, full throttle. I made to run inside the house but the second I was on my feet, he was on me again before I knew what was happening, yanking me back to the gravel and getting on top of me again on the Seventies hall rug. We wrestled and writhed and groaned, like poorly edited porn, until I wriggled away from him and made a grab for my knife. As I did, the Lord was with me as he stumbled over a kink in the rug and fell, face to the floor.

I've always liked that rug. And at that moment, that rug was my shaggy, filthy old wingman.

And then I had him, and I was on him and he didn't stand a chance – there's something about killing someone who needs to be killed. It fills me with the adrenalin I need to momentarily forget my age, my weight and my shitty-arsed left wrist and I went at that fucker like a championship balloon-popper when the first prize is a Lamborghini. I stabbed and stabbed and stabbed that scrawny arsehole like I'd never stabbed anything before. It was frenzied and fast and full of fear that this bastard almost got away from me. Almost left the building, got in his Prius and ruined my life. Every plunge of that knife was loaded with terror. I didn't stop until his pulse had and I shook as

I straddle him. I didn't cum as he shuddered to a halt beneath me. I waited for it but it never arrived. That hits different now too.

I don't know how long I was sat there but all of a sudden, the atmosphere changed. New sounds. Outside. Gravel crunch. A voice.

'Coo-eee!'

'Oh my fucking holy fuck.'

It was Patty Filbert from the office. The front door was ajar, swinging slightly on the breeze. And I just sat there, slightly hidden, straddling Pfister, covered head to toe in his aortic spurt and cringing into my next life.

'Cooo-eeee! Is anyone home?'

I was literally red-handed, red-faced, my formerly white T-shirt all soaked red now too, and sitting astride a twenty-one-year-old man full of holes I've made and holding aloft a carving knife dripping with his blood. What do I say? We're rehearsing a play? Enjoying a sex game with red food colouring? Truth was – I can't. At all. This was it. She was gonna catch me.

She was walking up to the door. Voice and gravel crunch louder. 'Is anyone home? It's Patty Filbert from the Wilmer Pinchot agency. I was just driving by—'

If she made it across the threshold, the nosey old bint who wouldn't take no for an answer was going to get what was coming to her. I had no choice: I would have to break one of my golden rules – Defend the Defenceless. But in this case, I had to protect myself, protect Rafael, my whole family. It was her or them. So no contest.

I remained sitting on Pfister (yes, really) and waited for the inevitable screams. The crying. The hastily dialled 911. The gravel crunch run. The sirens.

'I came by last week but nobody was around. Is anyone home?' Patty's voice grew distant as she walked around the other side of the house. She must have seen the blood trickle on the doorstep by now.

'Is somebody hurt?'

Yes, you, if you don't sod off. Go home and change Coma Hub's pissbag.

I rolled silently off Pfister and crept towards the door, standing behind it, waiting with my knife poised, dripping.

The knife, not me.

I watched through the crack. She was standing there, looking around. I didn't want to kill her – she was the only one at that office who showed me how the photocopier worked. She was a good person. But I was screwed. Needs must.

'*Leeeeeave,*' I whispered through the crack. It was ages before I heard the gravel crunch again. And then heavy breathing.

'Oh my God. Oh Lord, oh Lord, no, no, no, oh my God . . .'

The gravel crunching sound got more urgent – I peeked through the crack to see her running back to her car. What happened? What did she see? She glanced back towards the house as she ran. The engine gunned and the car sped off from the scene of my crimes. I didn't see her for her own dust.

The drive was dusty but empty and I was all alone again at Roadrunner Ridge. I walked outside and looked around. There was no one around but trees and birdsong echoing in the valley.

And then I realised – the fucking shoebox had gone. A shoebox full of money. Forty grand's worth. That God-fearing bitch clearly had a price and forty grand was it.

But then there was a more pressing matter to deal with – a noise from behind me. An echoing groan from the hallway floor. Pfister (yes, really) was still alive.

'Oh for fuck's sake!' I yelled, stamping back inside to finish the job. It was like the end of *Rocky* 6 when the Russian kept getting up. 'Die already!'

I slit his throat from left to right. That did the trick.

Once the gargling starts, it doesn't take long for everything else to shut down completely. For the struggling to cease; for his eyes to close.

He was long gone, and so was Patty with my money. Where would she go from here, I thought – she'd seen Pfister's blood on the doorstep; his car parked right outside. I'd parked *our* car around the back so she wouldn't have seen that – I ain't no rookie – but I knew she was gonna tell somebody about this. Her conscience won't let her keep this silent. And if she told the police, they'd go up there. They'd find Edo's body under the basement stairs. They'd find Pfister's too.

They'd find my fingerprints everywhere.

There's no way I have time to dig a pit and dissolve them both and sanitise everything after. And there's no getting the blood stains out of my Seventies wingman in the hall – they're ingrained in it forever like the smell of pot and old rocker jizz. I would have to burn it all – the whole place, to the ground. That would take care of that.

But what would take care of *me*? I didn't realise it until I looked at myself in the hallway mirror but I was a complete mess. Not only was I covered in blood, Pfister had gone to town on my face and neck. There was gonna be bruising. Marks. Cuts. And as I showered, I felt every single one of them.

Using a rubber tube from the cornucopia of car-part crap in the basement, I siphoned the petrol from Brad's tank like Daddy Dearest and his 101 Ways to Cover a Crime Scene taught me. And I burnt it all – I drove Pfister's car straight through the front door and set it alight, the whole fucking place.

I rinsed out my jeans and T-shirt as best I could but they were soaked through with blood so I threw them into the fire too. But I couldn't hang around to watch it burn. I sped home wearing nothing but my (thankfully) black bra and pants and an old faded beach towel I found in the basement.

I prayed all the way home that no one would be in. That I could sneak upstairs, wash, apply a ton of make-up and hopefully, no one would notice me wincing in pain all night. But they were all there, and Billy, eating steak ranchero around the kitchen island and laughing together like the family I'd always wanted.

And I stood there, barefoot in the beach towel, wet hair, cuts and bruises all over my face and neck, looking like I'd been mauled by a pack of coyotes. A thought flew in that I could pretend I'd been at the beach and been mugged but it flew in too late cos as soon as Raf looked at me, I started to cry, quite naturally. Like he had inadvertently reached in and turned on a tap I myself couldn't reach.

He hugged me first, peppering me with questions and kissing me all over, asking if I'd been mugged, been assaulted – they all did, in turn. Even Nico's kids. Even *Ariela*. They all thought I'd been raped.

The pain in my face and in my left wrist was too great to care about coming up with a genius explanation. So I let some truth out. They wanted answers so I gave them answers.

Freud claims there are no accidents – he'd say my unconscious mind *meant* to create this clusterfuck of a situation whereby my family found out about my dark side. My conscious mind didn't *want* to tell anyone – I didn't *want* Rafael to know I'd told him another lie either – but subconsciously, I was screaming to let it all out.

'Go into the garden,' said Ariela, when Anahid came in, holding her phone, asking what had happened to Tía Phee's face.

'But Mami, she's got blood on her—'

'—I said get in the garden, now. And keep your brothers out there. Go!'

The kids refused to budge from my side, God love 'em, so Billy did the decent thing and suggested a game of poolside Giant Jenga and he was so damn charming about it they followed him like the Pied Piper, even Ana, although clearly she was concerned about my mashed-up face.

Rafael sat me down on a stool at the breakfast bar and looked me over, stroking my face so gently it almost tickled after all the punishment it had received that afternoon. 'What happened? Who did this to you?'

'I'm OK. I'm fine,' I insisted, even though my head was banging and a quick glance in the mirror told me I'd gone six rounds with Meatball Molly.

Rafael was clearly more concerned than I wanted him to be and he'd stopped touching me when Nico quietly reminded him the cops might need to swab me. I tried telling him that wasn't necessary and that what I needed most was his arms around me but he kept his distance and bit his nails instead.

'You're bleeding. You got a gash on your head, a split lip. Baby, who did this to you?'

'Was it the cartel?' said Nico. 'Is this payback for Edo?'

'She's been attacked,' said Ariela. 'I knew this would happen. She has brought trouble here. She's brought *the cartel* here!'

'*I* DID THIS TO ME!' I yelled as everyone but Rafael moved away and stood around like a herd of cows, staring. 'I brought this on *myself*.'

'Are we in danger with the cartel?' said Ariela. 'Are my kids in danger? Because I swear if you have got this family involved in anything—'

'—I haven't got any of you involved in anything. And it's nothing to do with the cartel either. This was all me.'

With the kids safely ensconced outside, Nico, Ariela, Bianca, Liv and Raf all gathered around, waiting to hear my tale of death-defying courage and utter stupidity. Ariela stood furthest away from me at the fridge – it looked like the ice that had started to melt between us had frozen over again. It hadn't taken much, had it? One sniff of trouble and I was back out in the cold again. Anyway I didn't care about her – it was everyone else's opinion I was concerned about, namely Raf's. Lies sandwiched between truths has been my method of choice in previous situations such as this and I figured this strategy could work for me again so there I went, telling them (nearly) everything:

How a guy called Brad Pfister had upskirted me in a bridal changing cubicle [true] and I had stolen his phone [true] and when he'd tracked the phone to the house on Roadrunner Ridge where I had taken Edo, he'd seen what I was up to and blackmailed *me* [false].

How Edo wasn't dead when I took him from Liv's house but that I 'did not know that at the time' [true].

How I'd tied Edo to a post and beat him for what he did to Liv, thinking he would die pretty quickly but he did not – he lasted another week [true].

How I'd taken $40,000 of the Tenoch money to Pfister in one of the shoeboxes [true] but we'd fought [true] because he'd wanted more [false] and I'd had to kill him [true].

I could see Billy, through the living room, standing on the patio, one fake leg through the sliding door, clearly trying to earwig the discussion as he monitors the kids' Jenga game. He may as well have been snacking on popcorn – he was bloody loving it. He still hadn't said anything to the others though, even sober, and he hadn't dropped anymore floral hints around them so for some reason, he was onside. Still didn't trust him though.

It was at this point, upon learning that *I* was the one who'd finished Edo off and not *her*, that Liv stormed out of the kitchen and went to fetch Mikey from his travel cot under the stairs. When she returned, Nico begged her to stay but she refused. She opened fire on me.

'You made me believe *I* killed my husband!' she sobbed. 'I haven't slept, I haven't been able to stop myself feeling guilty and . . . I almost took my own life, you fucking BITCH!'

'I thought you'd eventually feel good about it.'

'Good about it? I am *not* a killer,' she spat. 'I've been racked with guilt for weeks and all the time you made me believe it was *all* me! You evil CUNT!'

I didn't argue. I *was* an evil cunt, she was right. As far as I was concerned, she was just stating the obvs. I hated that she wasn't my friend again. No more Thelma and Louise. No more bubble nights with *Ted Lasso* and us doing Roy Kent impressions (I'm the best) and seeing how dizzy we could get on mezcal. No more karaoke to Beyoncé and Gaga.

'WHY DID YOU DO IT?'

'Because he deserved it. He beat you up enough times. I thought he deserved some payback.'

'He could have gone to the hospital – you could have saved his life. He was Mikey's dad . . .' The words petered out on her tongue.

'Oh, like you really care about Mikey,' I scoff.

That one took all the air out of the room. 'What did you say?'

'If you cared about that baby, you wouldn't give Edo a second thought. If I'd taken him to hospital, you know what would have happened? He'd have been back within the week, getting Mikey taken away from you, your house, your business, everything would go. He'd have ruined you. Because that's what men like him do. Look at what you did, almost taking your own life over defending yourself. He made *you* feel like it was all your fault.'

'It *was* my fault! I fucking stabbed him, didn't I?'

'Yeah, you did. You stabbed him. And in that moment, I thought you were magnificent.'

Liv thought I was taking the piss but I was deadly serious but she carried on yelling and pointing her accusatory acrylics at me, as Nico held her back from punching me square in the face. Blaming me for her being on antidepressants. Saying it was all my fault she nearly committed suicide. And when she ran out of things to blame me for, she loaded the baby into his car seat and they left.

'You cannot drive like this!' yelled Bianca, followed by

a quick-fire back and forth in Spanish between the two of them and a slam of the front door.

I've never had a best friend for long. I had Marnie from the baby group for a while, and a couple at school for about the span of a free period or a conversation about our mutual love of miniature houses, but they never stick around, friends. I'm too difficult. And it always ends this way – they find out what I'm really like and they leave me alone.

A silence fell as Bianca returned to the kitchen and Billy returned from the patio to join us.

'What happened then, with Pfister?' asked Nico.

'We got into a fight, over the money, and I stabbed him to death. He'd seen Edo's body in the basement. I had no choice.'

'How?' asked Rafael, still holding my hand at this point. 'You told me you buried Edo. How could Pfister have seen him?'

'You *knew* about this?' said Ariela.

'I knew she killed Edo – I didn't know about this other dude.'

'He was too heavy to drag upstairs. My wrist let me down. So I had to leave him in the basement.'

Ariela shook her head in disgust and folded her arms across her chest, cursing and cussing in super-fast Spanish under her breath. 'You all see what she is now?' she screeched at Nico and Raf. 'I warned you about her – I *warned* you not to marry her. She is a *monster.*'

'She saved Liv's life,' Billy barked back at her. 'She saved your husband's arse too, by the sound of it.'

Ariela stared at him. I stared at him. Raf stared at him – why had Billy backed me up but my own husband hadn't? Still,

I wasn't entirely surprised. I knew the avalanche would start coming down one day – I just never thought it would be on a Monday afternoon.

Nico sighed as he told his wife the truth about the CCTV at the Chuck n Buns. 'She stole the tape for me. I didn't ask her to, but she did it before the police could put two and two together and make eight.'

'How?' she gasped.

I couldn't be bothered to waste my breath explaining myself any more so I sat on my stool and said nothing, like an uncooperative gnome.

Nico continued the story. It sounded better coming from him. He made it sound like I was the family hero.

'Seriously, if it wasn't for OJ, I'd be in the slammer, Ari. Liv could be dead; Mikey with Child Services. And now she's almost gotten herself killed to keep our secrets. We can't be mad at her. OK, she lied . . .'

'. . . but she's looking after all you guys,' added Billy. 'You've got to give her props for that at least. And you said she was a rock when Michael died last year, wasn't she?' He looked to Raf who nodded silently.

'Butt out, Billy. This has nothing to do with you!' Ariela manoeuvred closer, pushing Nico to one side but he held her back from reaching me.

What's he after, I thought, side-eying Billy. I can never be too sure when people are being nice to me, or about me. There's always a catch, like when you're getting a new mobile phone deal – seems great at first but somewhere in the small print you learn you have to sell your first born for extra texts.

Rafael was doing his usual thing of not looking at me and

thinking it all through. He'd dropped my hand as well. But then, out of the blue, he said: 'She came through for us. All of us. Sometimes lying is about protection as much as it is about deception.'

Nico nodded. 'That's deep, bro.'

But Ariela wasn't biting. Some people will always see the bad in you, no matter what you do.

'All it says to me is that she is a nasty piece of work – the lying, the blackmailing, renting out kill houses. Cartel money handovers. Me hierve la sangre, Nicolas! She is a devil woman! Why did she do all this, don't you wonder? Think, Nico. This is how women like her operate. They latch onto a family like ours – good people – and they destroy us from the inside out.'

'What do you mean, "women like her"?' said Raf, locating one of my spare wrist braces from the kitchen drawer and strapping it on for me. The relief was immediate.

'She's a narcissist. I read about this on the internet – she weaves her way into a family, trying to make friends with everyone, then one by one, she will KILL US ALL. There is a group of women, in Brazil, they go around drugging men in bars and stealing their wallets, their phones . . .'

'Must have been what they were wearing.' I yawned.

Ariela set her phasers on me to kill. 'I knew it the second you said she lived with a cartel, Nico,' she continued. 'She will bring shame on all of us.'

I sighed. '*Retired* cartel hitman, that's all Tenoch was. He was harmless [ish]. And if I wanted to kill you all, wouldn't I have done it by now?'

'Look what you've done to Olivia! She could have killed

herself. You need a . . . headshrinker or putting away. Locking up. Serious help.'

'Maybe she could see a doc at the place you go to, Raf?' suggested Nico. Raf didn't respond.

I did. 'Therapy? That's a bit like bolting the stable door after the horse is in the Pritt stick, isn't it? And if I didn't need therapy *after* cutting my own arm off, I sure as shit don't need it now.'

Ariela scoffed. 'She takes nothing seriously. You can joke about this? You can joke when Liv almost died? She thought she killed her husband and all the time it was *you*, plotting to torture him like some . . . maniac.'

'That's a bit harsh,' said Billy, tattooed arms folded in the doorway.

'You will ruin this family then leave nothing but the carcasses. You are a monster! I told you all this when we learned of her living with the cartel, I told you all!'

'Yes, well done you, very clever.' I slow-hand clapped.

'How many people have you killed, Ophelia? How many? You killed Edo, now this Pfister guy. How many did you kill when you were with the cartel?'

'One,' I said [true]. Billy gave me the eyebrows.

Ariela bitter-lemon laughed. 'Bullshit. Esta chica solo dice estupideces. She is a serial killer. She killed three people AT LEAST. Did she try to kill that woman across the street too? The one they think was poisoned?'

'Marji?' said Bianca. 'Did you put Marji Blumkin in hospital?'

I didn't answer. Ariela answered for me.

'And she is living under *your* roof, Bianca! Estás loca o qué.'

Bianca had had one hand on the countertop as though

balancing to stay upright; the other holding the locket around her neck – the one containing the picture of her and Michael when they were young. 'Whatever Ophelia does, it is always with the family's best intentions in mind.'

'Bullshit!' Ariela spat.

'No, it is true. When Michael died, she was there for us. Cooking, cleaning, looking after *your* children when we were at the hospital all the time. She helped out at the restaurant . . .'

'. . . the restaurant we lost during lockdown, you mean?'

'That was not Ophelia's fault.' Bianca turned to me, holding out her hand. 'You poisoned Marji because of her complaints against us, didn't you?'

I felt Ariela's laser eyes burning through one layer of epidermis.

Bianca sighed. 'Come on, let's go upstairs and get you cleaned up.'

I felt like kicking my feet in excitement, like I did whenever she made her hot chocolate or played with my hair. And I was about to have her lead me upstairs when Ariela delivered her parting blow.

'No, she's a freak. She doesn't belong in this family. She's a killer. She goes around killing people and bringing the devil on all of us. What, do you think you are above the law? Who do you think you are, Ophelia?'

The bubble had been pricked. I shook away Bianca's hand and jumped down off my stool, walking slowly towards her, my brain bulging out of my skull with the pain but my rage as tall as the house.

'Who do I think *I* am? I'm the woman who tells the guy rubbing himself on the bus to put it away before I cut it off. I'm the woman who follows the man who follows *your* daughter home from school to keep her safe. I'm the woman who watches the men who hang around playgrounds, outside stores, slow down in cars, take photos up the skirts of women in supermarkets. Do you know what I found on Brad Pfister's phone? Hundreds of pictures of underage girls. Girls in changing rooms. Girls in supermarkets. Girls in school uniforms, not much older than Anahid. Close-up photos on buses, in shops, on the street. Secret shots in changing rooms, in toilets, in bars. Between their legs. Down their shirts. If I'd had longer with him, his bollocks would be hanging from a streetlight now. Men like Brad Pfister and Edo – *they're* the monsters. And if there was any justice in the world, you would let me put men like that down *legally* with no comebacks. But there isn't that justice. There's only me. *I* am the only karma that's coming for them.'

Billy silently punched the air behind them all and beamed. I couldn't help but reciprocate. Raf let out a rattling sigh and got up to locate alcohol.

'*I'm* insane for wanting men like Edo and Brad Pfister and any other man who abuses women or children dead? How about this: maybe *I'm* the only sane one of all of you.'

Ariela snarled and slung her handbag across her body. 'I'm not staying here a second longer with a murderer. Go and round up the kids.'

She was barking at Nico but he didn't move. And then some sort of Jedi mind trick happened and he walked out to the garden, and rounded up his kids. Nobody said anything. Ariela waited in the hall.

'I wish *she* was dead,' I muttered.

When Nico came back, he looked about to speak, but clearly

the weight of expectation placed by his wife was too great and he remained silent. He looked at Rafa, then left. I watched them through the window loading the kids in their Jeep, with them still asking questions about me and what had happened. Nico got in the driver's seat; she put on her sunglasses, going the full diva, and they reversed out of the drive without a second look back.

That left Bianca, Billy and Raf.

'I'll draw you a bath, Ophelia,' said Bianca on a sigh. 'You must be in a lot of pain.'

'Thank you,' I mewed.

'You're OK with this, Mom?' said Rafael.

'We have already lost Papi before his time. I am not losing any more of my family. We close the circle and we look after ourselves and each other and we carry on, stronger than before. I will run you that bath.'

Bianca headed upstairs. Soon after, I heard the taps running strong in the bathroom and an aroma of Dettol antiseptic came wafting down the stairs.

'Thanks for standing up for me,' I said, to Billy. Rafael thought I was talking to him.

'Meant every word of it,' Billy replied, arms folded, looking at Rafa. 'Look, you two must have a lot to talk about, I'm gonna head off. Got a date tonight with that sort from Nico's gym. The one with the thighs that can crack walnuts.' He picked up his green hoodie from the back of one of the stools and shrugged it on. 'I'll see yous both tomorrow, all right, buddy?'

Raf nodded, giving him a weak fist bump in return.

When Billy had gone, I leant against the counter, waiting for a verdict or the presentation of divorce papers. 'Go on, say what you're going to say.'

'I'm just wondering what else is gonna come out of the woodwork when I least expect it.'

He removed the first-aid box from the cupboard above the hob, bringing it to the island, moving aside the stacks of bandages and painkillers until he found sterile gloves, alcohol-free cleansing wipes and antiseptic cream. He stood in front of me, tending the wounds on my face and hands and checking my wrist movement, my eye movement and looking for signs of concussion. When he was done, he put everything back in the box, threw the used stuff in the trash and snapped off his gloves. He came back to my stool and he enveloped me in the longest, warmest hug I'd ever had.

'This is how it's gonna be with you, isn't it? Unpredictable. Lies which don't turn out to be black lies exactly but pretty big grey ones at least.'

'It's just the way I am. Spin the wheel of fortune and see what version of me you're getting today – comedian, gardener, porn star, mass murderer . . .'

'I just want you,' he says and my chest pulses painfully. 'The *real* you.'

I nearly said it. I nearly tore the Band-Aid off right there. But he interrupted:

'Where is the house? The one where the bodies are?'

'Up on Roadrunner Ridge. I drove Pfister's car through the front doors before I left. Everything's on fire.'

'Fuck me!' he spat.

'I had to. I can't dig a hole with my crappy hand and I couldn't move the bodies outside and bury them like . . . the cartel used to do. And before you argue, I didn't want you to come up there helping me. I didn't want you near the place.'

'Stop deciding what I can and can't handle!'

'*You* have always said to me you don't want any involvement in anything dodgy. That's why you wouldn't spend the Tenoch money on anything significant like a place of our own. Blood money, you call it.'

'Yeah, well I'm right about that—'

'—but not about *this*. This was a one-off, or so I thought. I get rid of Edo, I destroy all the evidence and wipe the slate clean. Pfister was a complication but he's gone now too. It's over.'

'How can it be over? Your kill house is sending smoke fumes high into the sky above the city right now. It'll be crawling with cops.'

'They won't find anything.'

'How do you know?'

'Because I cleaned it before I torched it. I doused both bodies with petrol and lit them first.' I tried not to blink as he stared me out with his shining eyes. 'I covered my tracks.'

'They should be buried. The cops will find their remains, and if they find them, they'll find *you*.'

'No, they won't.'

'They *might*. What about dental records? What about *prints* . . .'

'—I always wore gloves. I smashed Edo's teeth in before I set him alight. And both bodies will be burnt to a crisp by now. If they do identify either of them, they'll think Pfister killed Edo, or vice versa. It'll be fine. I'm not worried about it. And nor should you be.'

He stared at me for the longest time. And then, thankfully and without further prompting, he enveloped me again in his arms and just held me, like I needed him to.

Friday, 8 October 2021 – honeymoon

1. *The I Love Your Accent crowd*
2. *The American pronunciation of the name 'Craig'*
3. *The American obsession with the Royal Family. You do know the old king once kicked a corgi across the room? And that, basically, Queen Victoria's bad parenting led to World War One, right? FACTS.*
4. *American true-crime podcast hosts*

Rafael had been quieter than usual over the past few days leading up to our getaway, as might have been expected when he'd just learned his wife was a bit more of a murderess than he'd originally taken her for. We weren't like two newlyweds, eagerly expecting our honeymoon, and all the endless sex we would have – we were more like housemates. He'd taken on a few more shifts at the Food Gnome using the excuse that we needed the extra money and every night had gone out with Billy or Nico to some bar, chugging beers and watching baseball; I'd spent more time with Bianca, volunteering at the vax hub and walking the dogs.

Neither Liv nor Nico nor Ariela and the kids had been near the house, nor had they phoned. It was like they'd all gone in one direction and Rafael, Billy, Bianca and I had gone in another, with Nico sitting on the fence in between, dangling his legs over the side. I know it makes Bianca sad that her family are at odds now, but she doesn't show it in front of me. I hate that I've done this to them. I hate that she doesn't smile or chatter so much around me now.

We hadn't said another word about my confessional earlier in the week, but at breakfast this morning, my new mother-in-law sat across the kitchen island drinking her coffee and pretending to read the paper. I knew she was pretending because her eyes didn't move across the page. Eventually she looked up and said, 'Is that drug dealer still bothering Anahid at her school?'

'Yeah, I think so. He bothers a lot of the kids. Mostly the girls.'

She nodded and looked at me.

'I could look into it,' I said, reaching for the newspaper and pulling it across to read the front page:

TWO DEAD IN JULIAN HOUSE FIRE

'No, you must recover first. You are still not back to your old self.'

'I'm fine.' I beamed. 'My bruises are healing; cuts are all scabbing over nicely. Even my wrist feels better this morning.'

She got up from the table and came over to me, stroking my cheeks as she inspected my facial wounds. 'Yes, they are looking good today. You concentrate on enjoying your honeymoon. That is an order.' And she yanked on my plait as though to put a full stop on things.

*

Me and Raf left before lunchtime from the Hertz dealership in Los Abrazos with our rented black Ford Mustang GT convertible, blasting out the radio and driving at top speed along Highway 1 parallel to the coast. He drove the first leg. We had our Calico Critters bride and groom taped to the dash and we held hands across the gearstick. My wrist didn't ache so much today, even out of the brace.

'*Some breaking news now in Julian where the bodies of two people were found inside a burning house up on Roadrunner Ridge on Wednesday. Thick smoke billowed up into the sky in the Julian area where the San Diego police discovered a scene of carnage up there on the old mail route . . .*'

'Do you want a Red Vines?' I asked, getting the packet from the glove box and switching stations to a lil Harry Styles number. I fed Raf his candy as he switched it back and listened to the end of the bulletin.

'*. . . derelict building was found fully on fire. The fire department was called and several trucks took over two hours to douse the building and put out the flames, after which an investigation found two bodies inside the residence. Early indications were that the bodies – both male – were already dead when the fire began and that one of the bodies is thought to belong to twenty-one-year-old missing man Bradley Pfister, whose car was found at the scene . . .*'

I switched the channel again to Harry Styles's 'Watermelon Sugar', hoping somehow the upbeat melody would make Rafael somehow forget he'd accidentally married Hannibal Lecter.

'You OK?' I asked.

'Yeah,' he said. Ray-Bans on. Staring ahead at the road as the traffic thundered past. No eye contact whatsoever. I had to second-guess the tone of every word that came out of his mouth, trying to read his mood, trying to guess the possibility of him just flinging off that gold ring of his and putting the car, and this relationship, in the past.

'Looking forward to all the sights we're gonna see over the next week? Golden Gate Bridge? Alcatraz? My pussy – a lot?' He didn't laugh. 'Oh come on, are we really going to start our honeymoon like this? You giving it the silent treatment.'

'I'm not giving you the silent treatment, I'm just thinking, that's all. Trying to clear my head. Trying to get some logic on all this. It's gonna be on my mind; you can't expect me to be casual about it all.'

'Do you want to ask me anything?' I said.

'Like what?'

'I've killed at least four people. One in England, one in Mexico, two here. I'm a serial killer. Officially. That's not OK with you so let's talk about it. Unless we're driving to the cop shop and you're going to hand me in?'

He looked across, reaching for my hand and holding it in his own.

'You know, I haven't done my wrist exercises this morning,' I said, all suggestive eyebrow. 'Maybe I could practise now?'

He kissed the scar on my wrist. 'Let's not add a public indecency charge to your already bulging rap sheet, OK?'

He smiled; I smiled. He was happy, I was happy. But above us, I could sense a shift. It wouldn't be long before the landslide came down on top of us, suffocating everything. I wanted to enjoy as much of him as I could before then.

I sighed, head back, breathing in the warm coastal air through the vents. It was one of those days where you feel like the world is doing its thing just for you. Nothing could touch me. I felt just like I did when we'd first met – not the time at the airport, but the time at the beach when I'd jokingly referred to him as Future Husband. Now he was Actual Husband and I loved him as much as a serial killer can love anything.

I turned around in my seat to stare at him as he drove. I watched him for the longest time, chewing his Red Vines, commenting on the scenery. Throwing out the odd dad joke. I felt all the tension leave my body. Being there with him made it all better. Like we were driving to San Francisco just to have a honeymoon; just to be in love. Like two normal people. A song came on the radio – 'Meet Me at Our Spot'. I started singing it. Raf joined in when the dude did. We surprised ourselves with how well we knew it.

'They play it a lot on the system at work.' Raf laughed.

'I like it. Where *is* our spot?' I asked.

He picked up my hand and kissed it. 'I don't know. Maybe the airport where we met?'

'Nah.'

'That bar where you got drunk?'

'Nah. I puked that night.'

'The beach? When I saw you again after all those weeks? And I couldn't believe how beautiful you were. And how lucky I was to find you again.'

I thought about it. 'It's a bit *Grey's Anatomy* though.'

'It's nice. The sun was going down. Everything looked beautiful. And I found you there. And life got good again.'

I smiled, despite myself. 'All right, that beach at sundown.' I shifted in my seat so my cheek could lie against it and I could watch him drive. 'That's our spot.'

We stopped for lunch at Huntington Beach (old-fashioned lemonades and fried chicken sandwiches – fuck you, arugula) and bought some Nerf guns and played on the sand with this other honeymoon couple who had them too and it was this strange hour of spontaneous fun; the kind you only have when you're a kid. I felt like a new Me. Not Rhiannon, not quite Ophelia, but this other girl. This wifey type who was relaxed and carefree and generous and—

'OI! GET A MOVE ON, YOU PRICK. YOU'VE GOT AN ACCELERATOR UNDER YOUR FOOT, FUCKING USE IT!'

All right, so I wasn't entirely relaxed and traffic did still tear my ass out but I was trying. And it was only that one outburst – the rest of the time I would temper my emotions for him. I didn't want him looking at me thinking, *I've married an axe murderer and she's gonna kill me one of these days.* I would be better for him. See? Progress.

By the time we arrived at our beachfront hotel in Malibu, it was late so we couldn't do any of the stuff I'd planned – the Hollywood homes tour, surfing lessons or a posh dinner. We couldn't get a dinner reservation anyway so we settled for an impromptu vending machine picnic on the beach and a walk in the waves. Perfection.

'I could get used to this,' said Raf, resting his chin on my shoulder and wrapping his arms around my waist.

'Get used to what?' I said, cheek on cheek.

'Being on a permanent holiday. Feels like running away from everything, doesn't it?'

'Why would you want to?'

'Don't you ever get those thoughts? Where you don't turn up to work or a party or whatever. No responsibilities. No worries.'

'No money . . . where would we go?'

'Anywhere. I can build us a shelter, I can feed us, do the hunting and gathering shit. Build fires. I got them transferrable skills, remember, baby.'

'Well, I could do the admin at least.'

I looked down at our hands – our wedding rings – and I couldn't believe he was mine. 'Let's keep running then,' I said.

He smiled and turned me to face him so we could kiss until the sky went dark above our heads.

The second day, I drove and we set off after breakfast on Highway 101, bound for Lompoc where I had booked us a private tour of the vineyards.

Even multiple murderers like day trips, you know.

Afterwards we headed up on Highway 166, ostensibly on our way to our next port of call – Carmel-by-the-Sea, but instead I veered off and headed to the Carrizo Plain National Monument. I remembered Craig's dad, Jim, talking about it when I was pregnant with Ivy and it had stuck in my mind as a place I had to go if I ever found myself near it. It was where the 'superbloom' was: a desert landscape packed with wildflowers – pinks, purples and yellows – rampaging wildly all across the landscape as far as the eye could see. It was a two-and-a-half-hour drive from Lompoc – a bit out of the way – but as Raf was sleeping soundly, he couldn't argue. And the closer to it we got, the more excited I became.

I was so excited and I'd memorised all the rules about going there – don't pick the flowers, respect the trails, don't litter or create desire lines or lie down in the fields however good it looks for the 'Gram. I couldn't wait.

But when we got there, we drove through endless dry roads between mountainous valleys of dry grass, no sign of any flowers at all. I kept on driving, expecting them always to be around just the next bend – a glorious panorama of purples and yellows – but they weren't there. It was definitely the right place – we'd passed signs for it – but not one fucking flower. The whole area was sun-scorched grass as far as the eye could see.

I got out of the car and stood by the side of the road, right by the sign, gazing out at the expanse of dry, natural brush. My throat constricted.

But I was good today.

> *You don't deserve pretty things, Rhiannon.*

But Mum—

> *—go away please.*

I want to stay here with you.

> *Get off me.*

Why?

> *Because I don't want you to cuddle me.*

I'm sorry.

> *DID YOU PICK THAT CAMELLIA?*

No.

> *YES YOU DID. I TOLD YOU NOT TO GO NEAR THOSE BUSHES.*

I smelled it and the petals
fell off.

                              Get out of my sight.

No. I want to help you in
the garden.

                    GO AWAY, RHIANNON.
                    I DON'T WANT YOU
                              NEAR ME.

I HATE YOU. YOU'RE
A BITCH, MUM!

                    Tom, I can't have her near me
                    today. You'll have to deal with
                    her. She makes me feel sick!

It's all right, Joedi, it's all
right.

                    No, it's not! I try and ignore
                    her but she's a horror!

It's all right, she's all right.

                    You ALWAYS say that, but
                    it's not all right! You let her
                    get away with bloody murder
                    and that's why I can't control
                    her. I can't do anything!

A park ranger pulled up in his jeep alongside the car.

'Everything OK here, darlun'?' he said, poking his head through his jeep window and breaking my trance. 'Y'all know where you're going?'

'Where's the superbloom?' I asked him.

'Ain't no superbloom this year, darlun'.'

NO SUPERBLOOM FOR BAD GIRLS WHO MAKE ME FEEL SICK!

'What?'

'Superbloom usually arrives in spring, around March or April, so even if it *was* happening this year, you'd still be around a season out of whack.'

'But . . . it said on the internet it's here; it should be here!'

'We've had a real dry summer and the wildfires ain't helped. We need a lot of rainfall in the winter to promote the spring growth and we ain't had it. We had a real riot of orange poppies back in March across the Antelope Valley but they didn't last long. Where y'all headed today?'

'San Francisco. We're on our honeymoon.'

'Ahh felicidades!' said the man, as Raf began to stir in the passenger seat. 'Hope y'all have a great time. You'll love Frisco Bay. And you gotta do Alcatraz Island! Took my wife last year for the first time. Great audio tour.'

'Thank you, I'll remember that. See if I can drag the old ball and chain along,' I said, trying to make light of the situation but there was acid rain in my chest. Expectation – it doth be the root of all heartache.

'Have a nice day, darlun'!'

The ranger sped off down the track with a friendly wave and a toot of his horn, leaving us alone with the Mustang. I turned off the engine and walked into the nearest field.

'Ophelia?' Raf called, getting out his side. 'Where are we?'

I walked into the field where a shaft of light had beamed down from the clouds like a sword. Her voice rang in my ears – *Keep her away from me. Tom, I can't deal with her. I don't want her near me.*

She needs our help, Joedi.
It's going to take time.

>She's uncontrollable. She lies,
>she steals, she hurts people.

She's all right with me.

>You have her then; take her to
>the site with you on Monday.
>I'm not having her here. I can't
>trust her here. I don't want to be
>alone with her.

That's a terrible thing to
say, Jode.

>I KNOW IT IS. Mum said
>she's got the devil in her since
>she came out of that hospital
>but I denied it; put it down to
>adjusting or growing pains but
>she's changed, Tommy. She's
>not our little girl anymore.
>And those bloody Sylvanians
>– they're everywhere. She's
>a teenager for God's sake, it's
>not normal.

Leave her be, they're not
doing any harm.

>I'm going to take them to the
>charity shop – she shouldn't be
>playing with them at her age,
>it's weird. They're all over the
>house—

'Phee?' Raf called again but I kept walking towards the shaft of light. The voices seemed to get louder the nearer to it I got. Stupidly, I thought I might see them in the light, like they might call me up to be with them again or some shit like that, but when I got there it was a plain old break in the clouds illuminating the dry grass. Dry grass where flowers should be. Dry grass because dry grass was all I deserved.

'There should be flowers here,' I said.

Raf looked back to the sign by the road. 'Carrizo Plain? We're at Carrizo Plain? There isn't a superbloom this year.'

'I KNOW THAT NOW, DON'T I?' I shouted. 'That's all I wanted to see, just some nice flowers but no, I've even messed that up getting the stupid wrong day, wrong month, wrong season. I can't even have that, can I? I can't even have *that*.'

I barged past him. There was nothing else to take my fury out on so I screamed – lifted my chin to the sky and let it all out into the air. I sat on the grass when I was done. I waited for him to come to me, and he did.

'I know,' I exhaled. 'Overreaction. I wanted it to be a nice day. I wanted to see the superbloom. I wanted to see beautiful flowers today. And they're not even here. And now we're going to arrive in Carmel late and we're not going to have time to see the fairy-tale cottages or walk on the beach all romantic. All cos I wanted to see the STUPID FUCKING FLOWERS.'

I pulled up handful after handful of dry grass and threw it around pathetically, then got up and stomped fully back to the car, far too wound-up to be near anyone, least of all him.

But as I got back to the car, he was there. He got to the door before I could and closed it.

'Why was seeing flowers today so important to you?'

'It doesn't matter.'

'In my last session with the psych guy, he told me that fury is pain in a hooded cloak. Talk to me.'

'What does *that* mean?'

'It means your pain is coming out as anger. And I get it. Stuff you've told me – about your mom. Why were flowers so important for you today?'

'It's her birthday today. And she hated me. Every memory I have of her is her hating me. Wanting to spend time with her, but her giving some excuse or just plain telling me to leave her in peace. I loved being in the garden and planting things and going barefoot in the soil but she stopped doing that with me. Said I wasn't allowed to help anymore. *Don't touch this, don't touch that. Why have the petals gone everywhere? You got thorns in your fingers, didn't you? That's what you get for ignoring me. You don't deserve flowers, Rhi—*'

I so nearly said my name. The name that would summon forth every demon I was afraid of. But Raf, if he noticed, did not pay it any mind. He leant against the driver's door, arms folded.

'You haven't seen any flowers today because the superbloom happens in spring and we made a mistake with the dates. If I'd known you wanted to see the superbloom, we could've come up here in March. We'll come next year. We'll come the year after. And we'll keep coming back until we see those flowers, how 'bout that?' His voice was treacly and my knees were weakening.

He opened his arms and I fell into them. 'My dad used to say, "Somos raíz, pero yo soy mi propio árbol." You know what that means?'

I wasn't in the mood to translate. My head was full of cotton wool. 'No.'

'It means, we are root but I am my own tree. *You* are not your mom, and your mom can't make you feel like that anymore.' He kissed my forehead.

'Everyone leaves me, Raf. That's how Mum always dealt with me – she'd walk away. *Oh she's having another of her tantrums, leave her.* She'd ignore me, which made it so much worse. Her and Seren, they're the same – Seren couldn't wait to leave me too.'

He stroked my hair. '*I'm* not gonna leave you.'

'Yes, you will, you *all* will eventually – they always do. I make some mistake, I take things too far, and you'll go. I'm meant to be on my own.'

'I won't leave you,' he repeated.

'You will. You *should*.'

'Well, I'm not going to. OK? Mírame.' He held my face between his hands and studied me. '*OK*?'

We smiled at exactly the same time.

'Come on,' he said. 'We got a date with those fairy-tale cottages. And it's my turn to drive.' He plucked the keys out of my hoodie pocket and opened the door. 'Your turn to navigate and think up a new game. No more I Spy or Punch Buggy though. Have we done the licence plate game yet?'

I strapped into the passenger seat and watched him as he did his mirror-signal-manoeuvre thing behind the steering wheel and adjusted his seat so he sat further back. I touched his arm as he started the engine.

'What's up?'

'I don't want to be like this. I want to be better.' And I forced myself to say the words that I almost never said and meant them. Because this time, I wanted to say them and I wanted to mean them. 'I'm sorry.' And with them comes a fresh wave of new tears. 'I'm *really* sorry.'

He lifted my chin and leant across to kiss me. 'You got nothing to be sorry for. And if you wanna stay fiery, baby, you stay fiery. Cos luckily, darlun', you got a cool-as-hell husband to put out your flames.'

We played our usual round of car games – Would You Rather . . . , Hypotheticals, The Suitcase Game – and then it all got a bit philosophical as we asked questions about the meaning of life and what's outside the universe. Our brains started to hurt after that so we stopped at a diner for doughnuts.

After about two hours, Raf said he didn't feel too good so we pulled in at a rest stop and he was in the bathroom for ages, which I initially put down to too many doughnuts. I felt OK – groggy from so much car sleep and itchy grasslands – but I started to worry. Nothing good ever comes from pains in the stomach. That's how my dad's trouble started.

And it got me thinking about his mortality again: what if he got hurt? Or sick like his dad? How would I cope? Bianca said that she was still angry at Michael's untimely death but that she was just 'so grateful to have been loved like that. Love without exception.' But they'd had thirty years together – Raf and I had barely three. You read about it all the time – people dropping dead of undisclosed conditions. Appendicitis. Tumours. Bianca said heart conditions run in their family. I would deserve it if Rafael died, but it would finish me. Now that I had him. The thought of losing him pricked me like needles. The intrusive thoughts grew bigger in my mind – I'd read about this stuff all the time on the internet. *Fit and Healthy Ex-Soldier Drops Dead of Natural Causes. Fit and Healthy Young Man Drops Dead of Undisclosed Heart Condition. Fit and Healthy Aztec God Drops Dead Cos His Stupid-Ass Wife Caused Him More Stress in Two Years Than One Man Can Handle in a Lifetime.*

When he got back in the Mustang, he was holding his stomach and blaming it on the wine at Lompoc, but he didn't even swallow any. I kept looking at him, and all I could think was, *Please don't leave me*. It cast a cloud over my mood all the way to Carmel.

Until we arrived singing 'Bitch I'm Loca', with him as Maluma and me as Madge, and his pain had mysteriously disappeared.

It was hella late – 11 p.m. – but despite the hour, a smiley woman called Catriona welcomed us to our boutique hotel with a plate of cookies and fresh coffee. We were shown up to our room, which had its own fireplace, hot tub, snack basket, Wi-Fi and complimentary robes, and the second she opened the door, I discovered that my husband was a big, fat, *not-dying* liar.

Rafael had spent every gas station and restroom stop liaising with the hotel and a local florist, and among them, he'd arranged to have our entire room filled with flowers.

And I mean FILLED.

Vases full of orange and peach roses, Matsumoto asters, carnations, yellow daisy chrysanthemums, sunflowers, spiral eucalyptus, hydrangea, yellow orchids, hot-pink oriental lilies, snapdragons, Amaranthus, lavender, alstroemeria, purple statice and a bed covered in scattered rose petals.

'Oh my God!' I said, unable to take it all in. There was too much of everything and the smell was astonishing. So fresh, so beautiful. And I just fucking melted. I couldn't believe what my eyes were telling me. No way had one person done all this for me. *Me*. Rhiannon Lewis. The freak. The monster. The cancer in the Lewis family. No way was I this loved.

Raf grinned from ear to ear.

'How the hell did you arrange all this?'

Catriona left us to it. Raf stepped forward. 'A phone and Wi-Fi, duh,' he said, gathering me up in his arms.

'This is for tonight? Just for me?'

'Yeah. Now is *that* a superbloom or what?'

'It's better,' I said, kissing him back and squeezing him against me as tightly as I could. 'It's so much better. I can't believe you did all this for me.'

'I'd die for you, Morticia.' He held me and kissed my mouth.

'I'd kill for you, Gomez,' I whispered back.

'Either way, what bliss.' And we fell onto the bed and lost ourselves amongst a blanket of Addams Family quotes and fresh petals. He was inside me all night – inside me, around me, against me and with me. All mine.

'You happy, querida?' he asked me as I lay in his arms.

'I've never been this happy,' I said.

But being happy makes me said. Raf nodded off so he didn't notice but I cried myself to sleep.

I was trying to lock that moment in my mind forever but the frustrating thing was it would soon be over. We'd both wake up, have our showers, get dressed, have breakfast and leave. Go out into the world again where all the madness was – where all the things were that made me mad. Nothing ever lasted. Nothing this perfect ever could. Especially not for me.

Sunday, 10 October 2021

1. *Thoughts and Prayers Twitter*
2. *That pioneer woman who cooks*
3. *The douchebag who's created deep-fakes of me swanning around Australian tourist attractions, even though I'm dead (and loving it)*
4. *Will Ferrell on* The Office *USA*
5. *Catherine Tate on* The Office *USA*

We didn't drink the champagne in the hot tub as Raf had wanted – there was a rather off-putting sign on the edge warning us of legionella, UTIs and 'hot tub lung'. Kind of a passion killer. But thanks to my ultra-thoughtful husband, our honeymoon was firmly back on track and after a night filled with flowers and far too much jizz-covered ecstasy to commit to paper, we spent our piteously short morning in Carmel walking off a caffeine buzz and eating cinnamon buns from a little bakery.

Thanks to our carnal abandon my wrist KILLS this morning, so Raf has insisted I wear my brace until further notice, which I don't mind cos even though it's an ugly-assed thing, it does relieve the pressure. I've overdone it of late, offed one too many sexual deviants, so old Lefty has taken quite a bit of punishment.

We strolled the area and found those fairy-tale houses, known locally as the Comstock houses – a collection of picturesque cottages that looked like real-life doll's houses. It was like Sylvanian come to life and I didn't want to leave.

The cottages all had their own names – Hansel, Gretel, Snow White's Summer Place, Fables, Curtain Call, and The Tuck Box (which was actually a restaurant). There was even one called Honeymoon Cottage where we took the obligatory selfie to further underline that yes, we were on our honeymoon and quite the normal, everyday couple.

'Can we live here?' I said, peering through the window of the one known as Fables to see if I could locate the lucky bastard within and make a cash offer on the place. Nobody about.

'Not much to do around here,' said Rafa.

'You and I could both get jobs, finally see what it means to be living,' I sang at him, cuddling his arm as a woman passed walking a dachshund on a lead. The little chap scampered over and padded up my shin for a squish.

Raf laughed. 'I could live with that.' He kissed me, and his arm around my shoulder felt like the pure safety I feel when I'm carrying a knife. 'This is your kinda place, isn't it? All cutesy and fairy-tale, warm buns every morning.'

'Totally, yeah. This is me in a glass. Nothing to get ragey about here.'

'You'd find something eventually.'

'Probably.'

'How the hell did someone who likes doll's houses and puppy dogs end up living with a cartel hitman?' He laughed.

314

I looked up from stroking the tiny dog and let the woman pass by us on the sidewalk. 'Life's what happens when you're busy making other plans.'

'That's good. I've never heard that.'

'John Lennon said it. My dad was a fan.'

'You know my therapist said to me that when people have deep connections to animals it's often a trauma response. Because animals love unconditionally – and humans don't.'

'Hmmm,' I sighed. I was still a little embarrassed about my meadow meltdown at Carrizo Plain. He didn't give up though – he seemed to be trying to winkle something out of me.

'Tell me more about your dad.'

'I've told you he was a boxer for the county. And he was a builder as well; had his own firm. Amongst other things.'

'What other things?'

Vigilante, I wanted to say, but there was only so much tea I could spill. And I'd already spilled *a lot* – about Ivy, about killing 'someone' in the UK, about Edo and Pfister. And, at this point in time, he still loved me so I was wary of shovelling any more snow down the mountain.

I sat on a wall, waiting for the valet to bring round our car from the hotel car park with our punnet of fresh local strawberries on my lap and eight vases of flowers rescued from the room. Raf stayed standing.

'Hey, you didn't answer that last Would You Rather . . .' he said, as one of the rosebuds fell to his feet. 'Would you rather get stuck in an elevator drinking gin with Ryan Reynolds or Chris Pratt?'

'Chris Pratt. And I wouldn't drink the gin; I'd smash him over the head with the bottle.'

Raf chuckled, holding the rosebud against his nose. 'Rosebud . . . *Rosebuuuudddd*.'

'What's rosebud?'

'*Citizen Kane*. Didn't you ever see it? Orson Welles, black and white.'

'Well, that answers *that* question.'

'What's *your* rosebud?' he asked as I tore another strawberry from its stem and fed it to him.

'I don't know what you're talking about.'

'In the movie, "Rosebud" was the last thing this tycoon said before he took his last breath. This journalist spends the movie wondering what it means and at the end you find out it was this sled he had when he was a kid. It's this metaphor for what he realised mattered to him most. He grew up and became this arrogant multimillionaire with all this stuff – antiques, treasures, big mansion, ex-wives – but ultimately, all he remembered was Rosebud. This perfect moment of innocence when he was sledding and his family were still around. It's like the end of childhood and the beginning of adult life. The loss of innocence.'

'You really wanna pull on this thread?' I said.

'Not if you don't want to.'

'We're having such a nice time, Raf, I don't think we should be talking about this now.'

The car appeared and we settled the vases in between various bags and shoes in the two footwells in the back and prayed they'd last the journey. Raf drove. He didn't say one more word and the drive was long. One of us had to speak soon. And it was my turn. I owed him that at least. I owed him some idea of why I was the way I was.

'When I was six, I got a bad brain injury. The Christmas before that – that was probably my "rosebud". That's when I last remember being truly happy. And loved. Though I barely remember it. Just flashes. Tinsel. And a Tickle Me Elmo. And snow on the trees.'

'Is this what you started telling me about yesterday? When you got sick and needed a lot of hospital treatment?'

'Yeah. One second, I was watching TV and dunking my biscuit in my milk. The next, lying in a pool of my own blood.'

There was a pull-in – he stopped. Switched off the engine. I was sure in the back of my broken mind I had told him about it before but the more I thought about it, the more I realised I hadn't. Tenoch knew. And I'd told Caro, that old woman I met on the cruise. But I'd kept Raf away from all things Priory Gardens. I only had to mention 'hammer attack on a nursery' and I was a Google search away from him finding out everything. I had to hold back the white mountain deluge for a bit longer. But I wanted to throw a few more snowballs.

'I used to go to this crèche at a woman's house, in the summer holidays. Dad had a lot of work on and Mum had started working from home again as a tutor. The woman who ran the crèche, Alison, was going through a bad divorce. Her ex wasn't taking it well. And we were there one morning when he broke in with a hammer. We took the brunt of it.'

'Jesus Christ.' He looked appalled but not actually shocked. It was the same face he had when a referee gave a bad decision.

'It was ages ago. I got sick of talking about it. No one ever asked me about the dog though. There was a dog there – a brown spaniel – he hid when the man broke in. But after, he came into the lounge and licked my face and it woke me up.

And he stayed with me – his ear all soft on my hair. He stayed with me as I lay there waiting for help. No one ever asks me about him.'

Raf squeezed my hand as traffic thundered past on the road.

'My dad always blamed himself cos he was the one who dropped me off that day. Two hours later, he was visiting me in hospital being told I'd never walk or talk again. All the other kids died.'

'Oh baby.'

'I had damage to my frontal lobe. My scar's further back now, since they brought my hairline forward. See?' I leant forward to show him and he cupped my face. 'It took a while to get back to some kind of normal but I changed. I went from being this happy, innocent six-year-old to this angry little goblin who my mum didn't know how to touch. She went from hugging me and tucking me in at night to not coming near me if she could help it. Left everything to Dad. I don't really blame her – sometimes I lashed out. Didn't have control of my emotions. I still struggle, as you know . . .'

Raf stroked the back of my head.

'You calm me down. You make me remember how I could have been. How I am *supposed* to be. So yeah, I guess that was my "rosebud moment". All innocence lost and I saw the world for what it was. Frightening. Uncontrollable. Killing . . . the paedophile in the UK. It was satisfying. It's never left me – that need to save the babies at the crèche. I was happy before that. I'd been kept away from the horrors of this world before that moment – because it is, Raf; it is a horrible world. I think I've been trying to claw back that innocence ever since.'

Rafael looked me, straight down the lens. 'No, it's not. That was a horrible thing that happened to you but there is still a lot of beauty in this world. And *good* people. For every asshole, there's a whole bunch of people who are shocked by what that asshole did. And I bet outside that crèche a day later, there were hundreds if not thousands of flowers and teddies, right?'

'How did you know that?'

'Because there always are. It's what good people do after bad stuff happens. Look for the helpers, remember what Mr Rogers said?'

'We never had Mr Rogers in England. We had an old perv in a shiny tracksuit molesting any kid he could get his hands on.'

'I can't bear to think of you being hurt,' he said, still stroking my hair with his warm hand. 'But maybe this is where life starts again for you. You got me now. And I'll never leave you.' I tried not to cry, but it was no use.

'Don't say things you don't really mean.'

'I mean every word. You got me forever, if you want me. Remember those vows we said a couple days ago? That's what that was about. Billy told me I've found a woman who'd kill for me and to hold onto you no matter what.'

A weight had gone from my chest. 'Billy's a twat.'

'Yeah but he's a truthful twat.'

I changed the subject. 'What's *your* rosebud moment?'

'Mine?' He gunned the engine again. 'Going to my cousin's birthday party in January 2019 and our plane getting delayed.'

'That's when we met at the airport.'

'Yep. Totally lost my innocence then.'

This caught my breath for a moment or two. If he hadn't met me, he wouldn't have to put up with any of my shit. A nice, smiley Bindi Irwin type could have sat down next to him and offered him normality and love and safety. Instead he got this. Poor fucker. I smiled, despite myself. 'For better or worse?'

'Oh so much better.' He tucked a rosebud behind my ear. 'Te amo más hoy que ayer, pero menos que mañana [I love you more today than yesterday but less than tomorrow]. Come on, Rosebud, let's keep going.'

There were lots of pull-ins all along the coast, so we could stop driving and take in the views of coastal fog and lashing waves against the craggy Big Sur cliffs. We had the top down the whole way to Santa Cruz, where we stopped for a lightning-quick caffeine break and a piss cos we wanted to get to San Fran before dark. That was easier said than done because the Target fairy had sprinkled her magic en route to ensure we couldn't resist passing all of them.

I bought a veil, Raf bought a top hat, I made a bouquet from my Carmel flowers and we gunned it into the city, belting out Scott McKenzie through the early evening traffic. My posy blew out of my hand, leaving a stream of petals in our wake. I kept one pink rosebud in my diary.

The rest of the flowers made it to the hotel and once we'd parked up at the entrance to our stately pile that would be our home for three nights, the concierge arranged to have our stuff taken up to our suite.

'Wow, what in the higher tax bracket is going on here?' Rafael laughed, staring up at the immense ceiling of the lobby.

The building was way bigger than it looked on Google Maps, and there were the flags of all nations at the entrance and even a red carpet.

'Welcome to San Francisco,' said a short, squat woman

in a too-tight maroon blazer called Shelley. She had a squint and a rack that would make a porn star jealous but seemed perfectly pleasant as I guess she had to be considering what we were paying to stay here. 'Is it your first time in the city?'

'Yes,' I said. 'It's beautiful from what we've seen.' I was in a good mood.

'Oh it really is.' She led us through the pillared lobby – which was so opulent and shiny it looked like Liberace had puked over it – furnished with plush lilac velvet sofas and armchairs, gold mirrors and enormous vases spewing out enormous sprays of roses and lilies.

Two floors up, the lift opened onto our floor and our room. Shelley let us in ahead of her, swiftly followed by a bellhop with our luggage trolley.

'This is our Golden Gate Suite,' said Shelley, leading us into a suite of rooms bigger than our house. We had our own hallway with an enormous vase of yellow flowers in the middle, two sofas in the living room area with an enormous glass table and a stack of those art books nobody ever reads. There was a marble-effect roll-top desk in the corner and a chandelier in the middle of the ceiling. I'd need an Uber to get to the other side of the bed.

'The balcony offers panoramic views of the city and bay, including the Golden Gate Bridge itself right over there. And your dinner is awaiting as you instructed, sir,' said Shelley, who tripped over a wrinkle in the rug and Raf's instinct was to catch her before she fell. I couldn't stifle my laugh.

'Thanks so much!' she cried, straightening her uniform out, trying not to look flustered.

'This is all . . . incredible.' Raf tipped Shelley, and the bellhop, as she showed us both out to the balcony where a private dinner for two was set out: In-N-Out Double-Doubles with fries and strawberry milkshakes.

'Are you sure this is all ours?' Raf laughed.

'Yep.' I kissed him. 'Happy honeymoon, darling.'

'We can't afford this,' he whispered, out of Shelley's earshot.

'Don't be silly. Look, there's Alcatraz, isn't it?'

Shelley joined us at on the balcony, like this was her honeymoon too. 'Yup, and you got the Coit Tower over there and the Transamerica Pyramid. In the morning, you can get a better view of it all through your telescope.' Shelley led us back inside the room and gestured towards the three-legged brass contraption in the corner: an actual-assed telescope.

'Whoa,' cried Raf. 'This is unbelievable.'

I wondered if I'd inadvertently booked Shelley as our live-in tour guide while I was scrolling Expedia as she didn't seem to want to leave.

Shelley laughed politely. 'It's pretty awesome, right? With all the lights in the city on, it's spectacular. And we have three restaurants downstairs – the Eastwood and Williams restaurants, and the Fossey Café, plus you got the DiMaggio Sports Bar, or the wine and oyster bars if you're looking for somewhere more sedate.'

She rattled through the other amenities the hotel had to offer, then it was on to the extras in our suite – Bang & Olufsen stereo, wireless internet, twenty-four-hour concierge, hot tub, complimentary dry-cleaning. The art on the walls wasn't the usual B&M range of shitty-assed horses running through waves or ears of wheat you usually find in British hotel rooms either – this was serious big tits and harpsichords in ornate gold frames. Proper art by people who could draw, or, at the very least, trace.

Once Shelly was happy that we knew how the TV worked and all the shower and spa settings, she finally left us to our own devices.

Raf turned to me. 'Baby, how much does three nights cost? Seriously.'

'Let me worry about it, OK?' I found the remote and pressed a button and this massive screen appeared from a cabinet in the wall. 'WOW, check this out!' The theme tune to *The Office*, US version, trilled out. I flopped onto the bed.

'Tell me you didn't use any of the shoebox money for this,' said Raf.

'I didn't use any of the shoebox money for this.'

'You did, didn't you?'

'Yes.' He wouldn't get out of the way of the screen so I got up and started on my burger, sauntering across to the stereo to find a radio station amid the white noise. 'Raise Your Glass' pumped out. I turned it up.

'What?'

I danced across to the balcony, pouring out champagne. I handed him a glass but he just stared. 'Come on, loosen up. Look through the telescope!'

I focused on the streets below. Down there in that throbbing city walked Elliot Mansur. I was probably looking in the wrong direction but since I'd hit the champagne, I didn't care.

Raf stormed out to the balcony, still in something of a mood about the money. 'How much of that money did you use on this place?'

'Not all of it.'

'Ophelia Jane . . .'

I always knew he meant business when he full-fake-named me.

'I put some of it into two separate bank accounts, Chase and Bank of America, just under the threshold where they'd ask questions, OK? Look at the art, isn't the art beautiful? Is that a Gentileschi?'

It didn't distract him. He kept staring at me. 'How much?'

The radio still pumped out Pink. *So raise your glass if you are wrong, in all the right ways* . . . 'I forget now,' I said, continuing to groove.

'OPHELIA . . .'

'All in, with our couples massage, valet parking and use of our solid gold telescope . . . about five grand.'

'Jeezus—'

'Per night.'

'WHAT?'

I shoved a burger into his open mouth before he could say any more.

Monday, 11 October 2021

1. *The health and safety warnings on every product: sleeping pills (May Cause Drowsiness); chainsaw (Do Not Hold Wrong End); Mikey's buggy (Remove Child Before Folding); and drain cleaner (Do Not Drink). Today in San Francisco, I saw 'Contains Hot Liquids' on a coffee cup.*
2. *Dwight's right – we need a new plague. A better one this time.*
3. *Hipsters and their 'art'*
4. *That YouTuber who banged their dementia-addled mother . . . oh any of them actually, they're all dicks*
5. *That guy who threw the alligator onto the roof of a bar*
6. *Grown-assed adults who use the word 'smol'*

On our first full day in San Francisco, we hit the tourism trail, walking to Pier 39 and grabbing funnel cake and cappuccinos and listening to the sea lions writhing around on their floating docks in the water in between scratchy bursts of Otis Redding from the boardwalk speakers. Raf was still pissed at how much I'd spent on the hotel but I managed to win him over with a combination of feminine wiles, gentle reassurance that we still had over $43,000 cash left in the shoeboxes and a gentle swaying along to Otis.

'Dance with me,' I said.

'People are watching.'

'It's not illegal. We're married now, remember?'

After a few turns around the boardwalk and a round of applause from the throng of people watching us, we went into Build-A-Bear and bought a Grogu for Mateo and a basketball Bugs Bunny for Elijah – before wandering along to the crystal shop to get a necklace and a box of taffy for Ana. Boats bobbed on the water and we'd stop every now and again to watch them.

After Ripley's Believe It or Not (highlights: a miniature Golden Gate Bridge made out of toothpicks, a donkey made from corks, and Princess Diana's funeral re-enacted by petrified ants), we rode a cable car to Rincon Park, ending up at the Museum of Modern Art, which thrilled Raf no end because there was a Diego Rivera exhibit on and an installation that was trash – literally, trash. 'Art' made from actual rubbish.

'I'm so glad I paid twenty-five dollars to see a rungless ladder, a suitcase with a broken strap, and a skirt made of Evian bottles,' I muttered under my breath as Raf took in the full majesty of it all.

'It's symbolic.'

'Symboll-*ocks*,' I muttered.

'Don't you think it's amazing? That they've used all this stuff again?'

'Yeah, and charged me twenty-five bucks to see it. Genius.'

Raf was practically crying at it – I was looking round for a can of petrol and a match to set it alight. Twenty-five dollars *each* to get in – EACH – and I tried, I really tried to get interested in rubbish I'd specifically thrown out which lots of floppy-haired hipsters were standing around in Birkenstocks drinking wheatgrass and wanking over.

'This is awesome, isn't it?' said Raf, oohing and aahing at every paint splash and overpriced bit of rag stuck to acrylic paint.

'Yeah,' I enthused, squeezing his hand. My God I was bored. But this is what you have to do when you love someone and know you've fucked up – you accompany them to boring-assed modern art galleries and pass the time feeling him up in the dark audio-visual installations. The only other thing I was staying alive for was the gift shop. But even that was crap.

We grabbed a burger in this restaurant which had robotic waiting staff – literally, robots, and they *still* fucked up our order – and then we were walking down this nondescript strip of shops when I spied a tattoo parlour. A light bulb turned on above my head.

'Hey, why don't we get matching tatts?' I cried, thinking, *And maybe you could get that floral abomination removed from your ribcage while you're at it?*

Raf was all for it. 'Yes, definitely, we are definitely doing this.' He smiled as he held the door open for me. Inside we were shown books of sundry ideas for matching couples tattoos, each one cheesier than the last. Infinity hearts, keys and padlocks, avocado halves, a girl with a crossbow and a guy with an arrow through his heart, but we settled on half-broken heart tattoos on our hands so that when they were together, the heart was whole.

Simple, cheesy af and cheap. Very much like ourselves. We even started walking in step for a while. Me and Seren used to do that when we were tiny.

Ugh. Just remembered how much I hate her ignorant ass at the moment. Bitch.

After that, we wandered for a while, hearts mended, hand in hand, in and out of parks and shops, buying stuff we didn't need – keyrings, candy, miniature snow globes, and, as most tourists do at some point in their lives, we inadvertently wandered into the rough part of town: the Tenderloin. We'd probably been walking for ten minutes before we noticed.

'Ah shit, I've heard about this place,' said Rafa. 'Stay close to me.'

He was straight back in army mode – eyes everywhere, tail-end Charlie, head on a swivel, all that. We passed a tent city and though it was grim, nobody bothered us. I mean yeah, there were a few people dotted about bent over double in some zombie-esque state of confusion. And there was a guy tightening a rope around his bicep and another giving a very old man a hand job in the front seat of a Ford. And some woman with her face smushed against a wall she'd been sick down. And the odd shoeless Joe roaming around asking for money.

Yeah, it was a pretty bad place. And it was no wonder Raf had transferred his usual golden retriever energy into pure German shepherd. The killer instinct from being a soldier was always there, under the surface.

It was nice not being the angry, alert one for a change.

'I say we get an Uber back to Chinatown,' he added. 'There isn't much more to see around here.'

'Let's have a look round this area first,' I said. 'We ought to drink in all the culture the city has to offer, Raf, not only the tourist places.'

Right on cue, a one-eyed woman who looked about sixty

but was probably my age, toppled headfirst into a trash can while scavenging for food. Raf briefly let go of my hand and upended her the right way.

'Hey! It's my chicken, let me get my chicken!'

She was after a box of half-eaten 'Flock' meal from Respectable Bird and once Raf had helped her retrieve it, he handed her a $50 bill and she was on her merry way, cussing him to the high heavens.

'I'll knock the rest of her fucking teeth out if she ain't careful,' I seethed as he came back to me.

'Baby, come on.' He smiled.

'She was hella rude. And you *paid* her for the trouble.'

'She's got nothing.'

'*Manners* cost nothing,' I said as we passed an empty shop front where a woman and a small scruffy dog sat outside on an old sleeping bag. I took a leaf out of Raf's book and handed her a $50 bill.

'Thanks, man, that's awesome!' she said.

'It's for the dog,' I said. She looked up at me.

We crossed the street, towards the liquor store.

'"For the dog"?' said Raf. 'Why did you say that?'

'Because it's not the dog's fault she's on the streets.'

'How do you know it's *her* fault she's on the streets?'

The peppermint deodoriser they were cleaning the streets with wafted our way from a flatbed truck outside the liquor store. 'Ooh someone had their Wokeabix this morning, didn't they?'

'Don't you care about anything except dogs and kids?'

'I can't care about *everything*, Raf. Adults will always screw up. Kids – usually not their fault. Dogs – never their fault.

I think we should go back and buy it off that woman. She doesn't deserve it.'

'It's the only thing in the world that she has.' We looked back and sure enough, she was nuzzling the dog's neck and he was licking her face.

'Come on,' I said, pulling my mask up and him into a store. 'Let's get some snacks for the room.'

He still couldn't get to grips with my thinking but like a good soldier he fell in line and pulled his mask up, following me into the grubby-looking store. Inside, the place smelled like cheese, though it wasn't obvious they sold any.

'OK so what do we want, wine? Beers? Cheetos? Dips?'

'Yeah,' he said, perusing the shelves as I walked the aisles. He picked up the chips and candy and we headed for the counter because all the alcohol was stored behind on shelves, dotted with neon 'Special Price' starbursts.

A shop assistant in a green apron and shabby grey trainers with frayed laces appeared from one of the back rooms, as if by magic, and I followed him to the counter. His face was no different from the mug shot though he'd dyed his hair black since. Jet black – but the same dark eyes, same jawline, scrawny neck, scorpion tattoo. Lizard-looking fuck. His badge said 'Jimmy'.

Aka Paul Elliott. Aka Joe Elliott. Aka John Cooper. Aka Paul Manning. Aka Jimmy Joe Maxwell.

Or to the people who knew him best, Elliot Mansur.

Pockmarks. Webbed finger. Tongue darting in and out his mouth to wet his dry lips. Stinking of pot. And on his neck, a tattoo – faded but unmistakable – of a scorpion.

Raf was looking at the chewing gum racks and hadn't

clocked him yet. 'Oi oi, what drink do you want, babe?' I called out, looking at Mansur and smiling my sickly sweet smile.

'Anything. You choose,' he said, still not looking.

'How about those?' I said, pointing to some in the fridge behind Mansur.

'Yeah, whatever,' he said, choosing his gum and bringing that and the chips over to the counter, as Mansur reached under the counter for some bags and rang up our total. When he stood back up, he and Raf made eye contact. No reaction. Raf looked down at the stains on Mansur's green apron. No reaction. His eyes flickered up to the scorpion tattoo.

Then we had a reaction. A slight one – all in the eyes.

'You OK?' I said behind my mask.

He nodded but continued to stare at Mansur's neck.

'$48.90,' said Mansur and as he said it, he looked directly at Raf. And without another thought, Raf turned and walked right out of the store, leaving me to pay.

'Thanks,' I said, slamming down a fifty and taking the bag and hurrying out to find him. He stood outside an empty store marked 'For Lease', mask off, breathing deeply.

'Hey, you OK?' I asked.

'Yeah,' he said. 'Couldn't breathe in there.' He paced the sidewalk.

'Yeah, it stank, didn't it? It gets so hot with these on.' I pulled my mask down. 'Stand still, catch your breath for a moment.'

He was quiet, in fact he was silent, as we made our way back towards our hotel via Nob Hill and Chinatown where a few bao buns accidentally fell into my open mouth at one of the bakeries.

'What's up?' I said, wiping my mouth with a serviette.

'I'm not hungry,' he snipped.

'Why?'

'I guess seeing a woman older than my mom covet a box of half-eaten chicken from the trash kinda made me lose my appetite.'

'That was ages ago. Hey, listen, we should do romantic stuff tonight. Fill our hot tub with rose petals or do a moonlit stroll.'

'Yeah whatever.'

'Don't whatever me. What's wrong?'

He stared at me, no blinks or anything.

'WHAT?'

'You really don't get it, do you?'

'Get what?'

'Nothing.'

So he was still being a little bitch as we boarded the tram, adorning our face masks. He spent the journey looking out the window. I kept my eye on a guy in his jimjams at the back of the bus in case he started wanking and flicked his spooge over me. He looked the type.

'Maybe we could do a carriage ride?' I suggested as one passed us in the other direction. 'That would be romantic, wouldn't it?'

'You're still trying to do romance?' He laughed. A bitter-lemon laugh.

'No, actually *not* a carriage ride. I don't want animals doing stuff for me.'

'Animals do stuff for humans all the time. Police dogs, service dogs.'

'Don't get me started on service dogs. How about a moonlit boat trip?'

'I'm not in the mood.'

'Why not? What's wrong?'

'That guy in the liquor store. You know who that was, don't you?'

'No,' I lied.

'Yeah, you do.'

'I don't, Raf. Who was it?' I checked out my pretending-to-be-shocked face in the window as the tram went under a bridge. I never got the mouth right. 'What was he, an old army bro?'

'No. He was the one who molested me as a kid. Even smelled the same. The Elliot guy.' His voice had gone all strangled and he blew out a long breath and rubbed his whole lower face so I knew he felt some type of way.

'Wow. Blimey,' I said. 'That's a turn up for the books, isn't it?' When I turned around, Rafael was staring at me – one of his hard stares. 'What?'

Rafael was really quiet all the way back to the hotel. He diligently placed our beers in the fridge, went in the bathroom, came out and sat on the end of the bed for the longest time, staring out of the window. I tried the coffee maker but my coffee tasted funny. Sort of like when you've licked the chain of a swing. I remember wrapping a Wham bar around a swing chain once and licking it off. It's no wonder I'm fucked in the head.

I made that exact comment to Raf but he didn't laugh; not even a fake one to show he still loved me even if I was no longer funny.

Eventually it annoyed me and I called him on it.

'Raf, if I've upset you could you be a doll and, like, spill some tea here so I can get a clue?'

He turned to me. 'You don't get it? You really don't get it?'

'Get what?' I took off my brace and gave my wrist a bloody good itch.

'I saw the man who molested me today. In public. Out of the blue. Have you any idea what effect seeing him would have on me?'

'No . . .' It wasn't a firm 'no' and when he could see I wasn't going to elaborate, he stomped around to my side of the bed and slid his hand under my pillow, pulling out my hideous washbag – the spare one I kept at the bottom of my suitcase that his auntie Camila gave me for Christmas. He chucked it across the bed.

Oh, I thought. *Boo-boo time.*

'Why were you rooting through my case?'

'I wasn't rooting, I was looking for Band-Aids. And I found *that.*'

I reached for the wash bag but he snatched it back. He yanked open the cords at the top and tipped out the contents. I tried to imbue my face with shock as I scanned each item. I was going down the route of *What on earth . . . I didn't put all that in there!* but Raf had already made up his mind.

'What the hell is this, Ophelia?'

'It's gaffer tape and a baggy of white powder, gloves, rope and a knife. It's leftover stuff from . . . when I killed Edo and Brad Pfister [yes, really]. I stuffed it in my case and threw a black jumper on it and I forgot it was in there.'

'Why is it here? What is this, blow? Heroin?' He picked up the baggy.

'Scopolamine. From the brugmansia plant in my Ali Baba pot at home. I dry out the seeds and petals and grind them up to make a powder. That pestle and mortar I got for Christmas from your cousins – I do it in the garage. You blow the powder into someone's face, it renders them . . . limp.'

His mouth wouldn't close.

'I cleaned it all up. You weren't ever at risk, I made sure I cleaned up the garage every time I made it.'

He stared hard at me.

'What? I'll shove it in the trash downstairs, now you've reminded me it's there.' I went to take it, checking that he wasn't going to snatch it away first. 'Stop it, I don't like you doing that face.'

'It shouldn't be here, with us, on our *honeymoon*.'

'OK, I'm sorry. The housekeepers' carts have trash bags on the ends of them – I'll drop it in one of them when we go down to the spa. All right?'

He let me collect it all up in the bag again and draw the string.

'Better go and wash your hands in case any of that stuff came out of the bag. It shouldn't have but just in case.' He did as he was told, standing next to me at our Jack and Jill sinks as I was washing mine.

'What now?' I asked.

'That knife – that's the one you used on him? Edo?'

'Yeah.'

'But why was it in your suitcase?'

'I told you; I forgot it was there. There's not many places to hide things at your mum's house. I shoved it in there and forgot about it.'

'Don't bullshit me. Tell me why you brought it on our honeymoon.'

'I. Forgot. It. Was. There. Calm. Thine. Tittàge.'

He sat on the edge of the tub. I put down the lid of the toilet and sat across from him.

'You were going to kill him, weren't you? Elliot Manning. You were going to do it for me. That's why you wanted to come here.'

That stopped me in my tracks. I'd never experienced this before – someone who could read me so well, he knew what I was going to do before I'd even done it. He was like a boo-boo sniffer-outer. But he wasn't shouting at me – his voice was level. Flat. Almost quiet. 'Mansur,' I corrected.

'What?'

'Nothing.'

'No more lies, please.'

I knelt on the floor before him, between his knees. 'Yes. I tracked him down. And that's why we came here. I just needed a positive ID before I—'

'Jesus Chr—'

'—I thought you might see him and feel the same way I do when I see people like that. I looked him up on Megan website. His name's Elliot Paul Mansur but he's living under the name Jimmy Maxwell. He lives alone.'

'How do you know all this?'

'I've done my homework. How did you feel when you saw him?'

'How do you *think* I felt? I was shocked. I was . . . scared for a short while. I wanted to throw up.'

'And then?'

'I . . .' He didn't say anything else for a long time. And then he looked at me, straight on. No blinking. 'I wanted to kill him.'

I stroked his face and smiled, hoping that he would mirror

me and smile too but he didn't. 'I love you. I want to *avenge* you. And I know that sounds like a Sarah J. Maas novel but I do. It's *all* I want to do. You'd do the same for me, wouldn't you? I knew you'd feel the same way.'

'No, no no,' he said, getting up off the tub and backing away from me. 'This is our *honeymoon*, OJ! A honeymoon is supposed to be romantic. Special. It's supposed to be about love.'

'And what do you think I killed Edo for, the fun of it?'

'YES.'

'I killed him to protect your sister. My best friend, at least she *used* to be. She hates me now. I killed Brad Pfister to stop him blabbing about Edo. I killed that guy in Mexico because he shot Tenoch. I killed that guy in England to protect my baby. Some people don't deserve to stay alive and free, Rafael. And one of those people is Elliot Paul Mansur. And yes, I wanted to come here so I could kill him. For *you*. Because I love you more than anyone else on this planet. I want him to die so you can live. We could kill him together . . .'

He laughed but it was not a happy laugh. 'So you're gonna go ahead and do it alone, are you? And I'm gonna let you do that? On our honeymoon?'

'Stop getting so hung up about honeymoons. It means nothing.'

'It does to me.'

'I'm sorry, I didn't mean it like that.'

'I don't want you to do this for me. I don't want *us* to do this at all. I told you what happens when someone like me gets involved in anything shady. Me and Nico – we get followed in stores by security guards all the time. We get pulled over in our cars for all kinds of crap. This is *my* America, Ophelia. An accessory to murder? That is real-assed jail time.'

337

'Only if we get caught. You really think Elliot Mansur deserves to live his life, free as a bird, unchecked, forever?'

'He's probably being monitored.'

'By who?'

'I don't know; people.' He sat back on the edge of the bath.

'Why is your face like that? You're sad.'

'Because this isn't right. *I* should be the one protecting *you* – this is crazy, you hellbent on doing all this for me.'

'It's not crazy. You hurt my Raf; I kill you. That's *my* love language.'

I crouched down to the floor between his legs. I held his face and stroked his ears with my thumbs, as he liked me to do. 'I've never loved anyone as much as you. And the thought of someone hurting you makes me want to hurt *them*.'

'But I don't want you to.' He closed his eyes as I traced my fingertips around his ears. He held his cheek close to mine; his breaths short and hot.

'I can,' I whispered, stroking all the way down his neck and chest. 'What if this was about me? What if he had hurt me? What would you do to him?'

'Kill him,' he whispered against my open mouth. 'I'd fucking kill him.'

'Would you?' I said, opening and closing my mouth over his.

'You know I would,' he growled.

'That's my boy.' I smiled, biting his lip, pulling his T-shirt over his head.

Angry Make-Up Sex on a bathroom floor is bloody uncomfortable by the way, even on priceless top-of-the-range heated tiles. There is such a thing as too hard, so once we'd had a back-bruising orgasm each, we retreated to the king size and went for a more sensual Round 2. It took two climaxes, two cum runs to the toilet and a bit of oesophageal bruising but I finally got Raf back into a level mood. Once he was relaxed, we headed downstairs for our massages, and I did as I had promised – dropped the washbag into a housekeeping cart trash bag en route.

'Happy now?' I said, as it fell into the cavernous black sack.

He squeezed my hand as we walked to the lifts. 'Don't get me wrong – I agree with you. Men like Mansur should be put down . . .'

'But?'

'But I don't want us to go down with him.'

'It's your call. We do or we don't.'

He looked at me. 'Let's . . . *not* do this. Let's forget about him.' He kissed me. 'Let's just be honeymooners.'

'Mm,' I moaned against his neck. 'Whatever you say, my darling.'

And he took my hand and we walked to the lifts and pressed the button for the lobby. But I was already thinking thoughts I couldn't tell him about. Thoughts I couldn't stop.

Tuesday, 12 October 2021

1. *Machine Gun Kelly*
2. *Elliot Mansur*
3. *Couple in the lift on the way down to breakfast oversharing their raw food diet. And their farts.*
4. *Woman in the boat queue for Alcatraz who picked her nose and wiped it on the handrails*
5. *All the Kardashian baby-daddies*

'Raf?' I whispered siren-like into his ear as we lay in bed the next morning. He was on his phone. 'Rafael?' I teased his ear.

'Hang on,' he said, distracted. He looked like he was thinking. Oh Christ, I thought. It's always dodgy whenever a guy is thinking. Whenever Craig went off to 'think' he'd come back stinking of fried onions and proposing we move closer to his parents. Then I see he's actually staring at some blocks of words on his phone. Bleeding Wordle.

'Sorry, I gotta beat my record.'

'Unbelievable,' I muttered, getting up to shower.

Citizen Kane was on the TV when I re-emerged – a classic-movie channel that seemingly played the same five black-and-whites over and over again until the end of time: *Kane*, the nuns in the mountains, the boring version of *Miracle on 34th Street*, *Rebecca* and some Cary Grant one where he's all suave and sophisticated, for a change.

I watched about twenty minutes of *Kane* before switching it off. Rosebud or no rosebud, that is one boring-ass film. If I'd watched it to the end to find out Rosebud was a fucking sledge, I'd have been pissed.

We had to get the first clipper across to Alcatraz Island from Pier 33 so Raf wasn't in the best mood anyway. He was always monosyllabic until he'd had at his second coffee or first blow job so I didn't think too much of it. But by the time we got to the prison, his silence was getting on my tittàge.

'Do you want a squirt of my hand sanitiser?'

Silence.

'Is that a body floating out there or a chunk of polystyrene?'

Nothing.

'Do you want to go down on me in Al Capone's cell?'

Barely an eyebrow raise.

Ugh. Might as well have come by my bloody self. Why is it no matter what I do, I am in the wrong? Even when I think I'm doing the right thing, someone's pissed at me. That hammer must have smashed my common-sense nerve ending to smithereens.

I tried Seren's phone when I lost him in the queue as he flounced off to get a soda. Predictably, there was still no answer. I don't know why I bother anymore. She might be the last link to my daughter but I was getting fed up of being ghosted by her. And a seed of doubt started to sprout in my brain. What if something had happened to Ivy and she wasn't telling me?

My sword hand sings for you, Sister Dearest.

The irony of that day's excursion wasn't lost on me – paying thirty dollars for a three-hour tour of jail when I could hand myself in and go around one for free, staying as long as I liked.

Alcatraz was on a pretty island – plenty of trees, nice views, birds warbling away on the rocky outcrops, shame about the bird shit everywhere – and it was a bright, clear day to visit. The water was calm, unlike me when the whiney bitch from Wisconsin threw up in front of us as we stepped off the boat, splashing my Nike high-tops with what looked like semi-digested orange emulsion.

'Shall we do the audio guide?' I asked him as we entered the main jailhouse, the whole place echoing with chatter and clanging metal doors. Didn't look like it'd seen a lick of paint since it shut in the Sixties. Wisconsin Wendy had given the place a bit of colour at least.

'Yeah hwarbbbubullover,' he mumbled, translated as *Yeah whatever you want I don't mind.*

'Bloody hell, you're like a kid who's had his dick confiscated today, what's wrong with you?'

'Nothing, I'm tired,' he snipped, taking an audio guide as our queue snaked through into the laundry area.

At least the audio guide dude was talking to me. In fact the narration came from various old timey guys who'd resided in Alcatraz at one time, correctional officers and ex-cons. It was peppered with the odd sound effect – clanging doors, echoing whistles, cries of 'New fish' and 'Fresh meat' and 'See you in the showers – heh heh heh!' That kind of thing to build up the atmos.

We walked along the blocks and in and out of the cells as we liked. I went in one to see if the sink moved in case there was an escape hole dug behind it, but it was fixed securely to the wall. When I turned around, Rafael was standing outside with the cell door closed.

I sat at the desk – which was nothing more than a shelf jutting out from the wall – and pretended to write a letter.

'Dearest Rafael,' I began in my best Nicolas Cage Southern fried drawl, 'I think of you always, your smile, your sweet ass . . .'

Raf stared at me from the other side of the bars, the head-phones of his audio guide resting on his shoulders. He wasn't playing anymore. His face told me the fun was over.

'You like it in there?' he said.

I looked around. 'It's not bad. Bit pokey. Could do with a few posters.'

'It's five feet by nine. They'd be in here for twenty-three hours a day.'

'Not all of them,' I said. 'If they had privileges, they could work in the laundry or the library, like that old dude at Shawshank with the crow.'

I went to pull the barred door back across but he held it in place and continued staring at me through the bars. 'What are you doing?'

'Stay in there a second. Look around. What do you see?'

'I see a rusty bed with no mattress, a tiny sink and a bog. That shelf must be for the chess pieces they used to make out of mouldy potatoes.'

'Imagine being in there for years and years on end. Only being let out for an hour a day. Only eating oatmeal that some guy's spat in. Or worse.'

'Prison ain't like this anymore, Raf. That's why this is

on the *tourist* trail. You get Wi-Fi and Open University and PlayStations.'

He stared me down. 'You don't get your freedom. That's one thing you don't get, ever again.'

I stood in front of him at the bars. 'I could handle it.'

'You couldn't. I know you.'

'Perhaps you don't know me as well as you think you do.'

'I know you lived with a cartel for a year. I know you've killed people. Got a taste for it. I know you engineered our honeymoon around locating a guy who molested me over twenty-five years ago . . .' He left that sentence hanging. 'I also know you're caring and considerate, mainly to me and your family and kids and dogs. I know you love miniature toys. Gardening. Getting outside. Fresh air. You would never see any of that again if they jailed you.'

'Yeah but no taxes,' I said. 'Food, lodging, full medical. Could be worse.'

'And you wouldn't have me.'

'You'd visit.'

'No Ivy ever again.'

He'd touched a nerve. 'I'm not seeing her now, am I? Let me out.'

'I don't want you to do anything else to jeopardise our marriage. Because that is what you're doing if you go after this guy.'

'For *you* . . .'

'Forget that it's for me. Don't do this.'

'I won't. I said last night, it's your call. If you don't want me to do this, I won't. *We* won't.'

He stared at me – he didn't believe me. I was beginning to read that glint in his left eye a little better now. That was the glint of doubt. And it was there because he could read my thoughts. He knew damn well I didn't mean a word of it. But I didn't know how to lie better with him – it had always worked on everyone else. But not Raf.

'I mean it,' I said. 'We'll carry on enjoying our honeymoon, maybe have some funnel cake when we get back to port. And we'll let Elliot Mansur live his life in peace and harmony, even though he has a lifelong addiction to raping young boys. How about that?'

Rafael stood silent behind the bars.

'He's not going to change. That's the way he is. Just like I am the way I am. But for you, because I love you, I'll stay away. If that's what you want.'

He licked his lower lip and looked away. Two tourists were behind us, waiting to look into the cell. He looked at me. 'It's what I want.' He pulled back the barred door and waited for me to step out.

'Your turn,' I said, standing aside so he could go in but he didn't.

'No thanks,' he said. 'I'll stay this side of it.'

I bought an orange T-shirt in the gift shop that said 'Psych Ward Resident 20267'. This offended him too.

'You think that's appropriate?' he said, as we boarded the boat to shore.

'Women's cut you mean? I shoulda got men's, shouldn't I? Much better to hide the bingo wings.'

That was all he said the entire journey back. It was like the San Francisco coastline had suddenly become the most fascinating thing and he had to give it his full concentration. Had finding the washbag and learning about my eighteen-month stalking campaign of Elliot Mansur rolled the snowball that would bring the rest of the avalanche down? Was it already rumbling along the mountainside and I couldn't hear it yet?

It was after five when we got back to the hotel room and I flopped onto the bed. 'What's on TV?'

'I don't know,' he said. 'I might go down to the bar for a while. There's a Giants v Pirates game on at six.'

'Oh right.'

'You can come with me.'

'No thanks.'

'You sure you'll be all right up here alone?'

'Ahh, all alone in our five-thousand-dollar suite, how ever will I cope?' I faux-moaned. 'I was thinking of booking a hydro-facial. Maybe a mani-pedi. They come to the room.'

'Cool.'

'You don't mind the cost?'

'No.'

'Are we OK?'

'Yeah. We're OK.'

'OK.'

'OK.'

We were so not OK.

He came to the bed and sat down. I levered myself up and we hugged.

'We bought beers yesterday you know. We could stay in the room and we could chug 'em together.'

'You'll be watching the baseball though,' I griped. 'And they have draft beers downstairs. You prefer draft beers.'

'Yeah,' he said. 'I'll be in the sports bar.'

'OK.'

Rafael had a shower and went down to the sports bar at 7 p.m. but I knew he would only be gone an hour, two tops, which wouldn't be long enough for what I needed to do. But I couldn't put this in reverse now. I'd already made my mind up that I was doing this. That I was going, with or without him.

At least getting a new knife wasn't a problem – I tottered through the dining room lost while they were laying up for dinner, doing my apologetic British tourist act. Shame about the Psych Ward T-shirt but I zipped up my pink hoodie to cover it. There was a waiter mincing through with a trolley full of wrapped cutlery and ornately folded napkins.

'Oops I'm so sorry, can you tell me is this the way to the beauty salon? The chap on reception said I had to head for the dining room?'

'No, ma'am, you've got to go back through those doors there . . . Tell you what, I'll show you myself.' He put down his basket of knives and forks.

'Oh it's no trouble, I'm sure I can manage, after all I got lost by myself, I'm sure I can get un-lost too!' I Hugh-Grant-babbled. Nobody questions you when you're English and posh – we get away with murder. Literally. Have done for centuries. Can't believe it still works.

'No problem at all, allow me to escort you, madam.'

I giggled charmingly, like an English rose would. Luckily, he was so in love with his own spiel about how the hotel was destroyed by fire in the twenties and how one of the Vanderbilts married here, that he didn't witness my sleight of hand as we passed the bread basket, set to one side on a service trolley, surrounded by half-sawed baguettes. I only took it out when I was behind closed doors in our suite.

Pretty decent blade. Five inches of scalloped Santoku steel with a triple riveted handle and a nice straight edge with a sheep's foot curve. And the mark of quality too: Sabatier. My favourite. Not the sort of weapon you want lying around on some dining table in a public place. Anyone could take it.

With almost everything I needed, apart from the brugmansia which would have made things *much* easier, I changed into all black, packing a bag of spare clothes in case of spillages, and removed my wrist brace. No Velcro, remember? Once through the revolving doors of the lobby, I stepped out into the warm San Francisco night with only two things on my mind: Elliot Mansur and a large, hot coffee.

Plan B, innit?

I started up the Mustang and consulted Pfister's notebook.

His generous note-taking made Mansur's address easy to find – at least the little pervert could do that right. If I hadn't killed him, he'd have made an excellent secretary. Much more suited to admin than me.

OK, I've had a few drinks and my hand is steady enough to write. So where was I? I waited under the veranda of a closed beauty store opposite and watched Mansur leave the liquor store after his shift – still the shabby grey trainers with frayed laces, black shaggy hair, severe jawline. I was mindful to stay several metres behind him wearing my face mask as he loped up the street towards the bus stop in his dirty blue jeans and faded yellow Ramones T-shirt, smoking a cigarette down in record time and flicking the stub in the gutter as he boarded the bus. I had to make sure he was definitely going in the direction of his apartment on Turk Street – and tonight, he was.

I jumped back in the Mustang and got a head start, parking in the shadows behind a Starbucks opposite the apartment and grabbing a grande black coffee as the bus drew up, around twenty minutes later. Yellow T-shirt got out, fumbling with his keys.

'Could you put it in another cup please? To keep it hot?' I asked the green-haired barista behind the counter as she prepared my Plan B. Mansur was at his door, fumbling with his keys. Time was running out – I needed to get over there before he shut me out. Green-Haired Bitch was taking an age.

'COULD I HAVE IT WHILE WE'RE YOUNG?' I shouted, which didn't go down well but did achieve the necessary speed and I dashed out of there the second she shoved the cup in my hand.

'Hey,' I said, placing my coffee on the sidewalk as he opened the front door. I started fumbling in my rucksack. 'You live here too, right? Never find the damn things when you need 'em!'

He sort of looked at me, sort of didn't. 'Don't worry about it,' he said, one foot inside, one out as he held the door open for me.

'Oh thanks, you're a lifesaver.' I chuckled charmingly, picking up my cup and readjusting the bag on my back. 'I don't suppose you got a door key for my place on there too, have you?'

'Sorry,' he said, his neck pulse going ballistic.

'They'll turn up soon enough, I'm sure,' I said, following behind him, careful not to make too much small talk in case he rumbled me. Paedophiles have an innate sense that someone's luring them into a false sense of security. I pride myself on getting the balance just about right.

349

As we walked up the stairs, lights above us flicked on, as if by magic, or rather a tight landlord who'd installed sensor lamps to cut costs. I lifted the lid to pretend-sip my coffee but it was so strong and my stomach rolled over. I kept climbing until Elliot stopped on the third-floor landing, and by this time I was fizzing like a can of shaken-up Coke. Yearning to get on him, get him alone, to straddle him and start plunging. The images flashed through my mind – what he did to my Rafael. What he did to that other kid and God knows how many more. Oh yeah, he's mine tonight, I thought. All mine. This was the right thing to do. Even if it does end my marriage.

Apartment 346 was where Mansur stopped walking and his keys jingled as he located the right one on the bunch. My fictional domicile would have to be somewhere on this landing too. He started unlocking his door, but waited until I'd passed him before opening it. I did, before turning around.

'Oh hey,' I said, catching my breath. 'I don't suppose you've had the letter about the structural investigation, have you?' He was close – close enough that I could smell his odours – pot and that liquor store cheese whiff.

'The what?' he said, one skanky trainer in the door. The TV's on inside the apartment – some game show – maybe he *didn't* live alone and Pfister had stiffed me? I couldn't think about it. I lifted the lid off my coffee and blew the surface cool, but not too cool. His voice was nondescript. Higher than I expected: the way I'd imagine a weasel to speak.

'Yeah, I've had a letter about a structural issue with the building. Something about land subsidence? The Facebook group mentioned we might all have to move out so they can carry out remedial works.'

'I rent so it's not my place, not my problem.' He gave me a patronising smile before continuing inside his place.

I drifted back towards his door. 'Oh right, well, I only mention it because I heard that subsidence can affect the structural integrity of a building and its paedophiles . . . I mean residents.'

I had seconds to play with. A guy standing shocked in his doorway and if I didn't act fast, I'd lose him. I flicked the coffee in his face but the second I did, another guy came out of nowhere, wearing a black hood and kicked him fully inside the dingy room, slamming the door behind them.

I stood in the corridor, reeling. 'The actual FUCK?' There was no one else in the corridor, nor anybody peeking out to check what the commotion was. I couldn't hear anything inside. I tried the handle and it opened.

And the hooded man was straddling him on the carpet, a sofa pushed to the side, the TV flickering on low in the corner – *Dancing with the Stars* – some soap actress struggling through a Charleston.

I got inside and stood by the door, watching this lone ranger go to work. And I knew it was him as soon as I smelled his aftershave.

'Oh my God.' I could barely breathe as I watched Rafael, hunched over Mansur, his bare hands pressing on his windpipe. Mansur's eyes bulged. His death rattle was exquisite – the choking, spluttering, gasping last noises of a man who should never have been born. Born to cause pain. I've never wanted to kiss Raf so much in my life. And when Mansur finally lay still – the quivering, shaking and spasming finally at an end – eyes open and bloodshot, no more noises, Raf got up, standing aloft, catching his breath, and I did. I kissed him. He grabbed me for a hug. He was the one shaking now.

'Jesus fuck!' he kept saying. 'Jesus fuck! We gotta go.'

'I can't believe you did that,' I said, tears in my eyes as I placed both my hands on his chest to feel his heart. A little further down his shirt, it was wet.

It was blood. He'd been stabbed.

'Shit! You're hurt!'

He looked down too, and lifted up his shirt to inspect what seemed to be a stab wound on his ribcage, right on the Ophelia tattoo.

'It's all right, it's not deep,' he says, gazing around the floor and finding the flick knife that Mansur pulled on him during their scuffle. 'Is there any blood on the carpet?'

I switched on the main light and studied the floor. 'Doesn't look like it.'

'Are you sure?'

It was then that I noticed the wall at the back of the room had changed. A door was open – the door to the one bedroom. About halfway up the crack in the door, there was a face. A boy's face.

'SHIT!' I cried out, my heart in my ass.

Rafael clutched his side, unreeling some kitchen roll from the countertop separating the living room from the kitchen. 'It's not too deep, I'll be all right.' He hasn't seen him.

'Look,' I said, as he followed my stare to the bedroom door. The boy stepped slowly into the living room. He wore ill-fitting jeans, white socks and a green jumper. I could not believe what I was seeing. My heart was thudding and I couldn't breathe. All I could think to say was:

'Who the fuck are you . . . ?'

'He calls me Luke. But my name's River.' He saw Mansur lying on the floor. 'Is he dead?' I nodded. 'You killed him?'

I nodded. 'We didn't know you were here.'

River looked at Raf. 'Did he hurt you?'

Raf shook his head, his eyes fixed on River. 'Why are you here? Who are you?'

The boy padded closer, thick white sports socks. Jeans that were too long. He started crying. And before I could stop him, he hugged me.

'I wanna go home.' He was shaking all over.

'How long have you been here?'

'I don't know. My name is River.'

'We gotta get out of here,' said Raf, heading for the door. 'Come on.'

'Did he kidnap you?' I asked the kid. He nodded. His hair smelled of French fries and the faintest hint of floral soap. 'When?'

'I don't know.'

'Jesus Christ.'

'Did he send you? Jesus? I asked him for help. He sent you, didn't he?'

'Jesus?' He nodded. 'We've got to go.' I turned to leave.

'Wait, don't leave me, please don't leave me here with him!'

'Uh . . . look, there's a coffee shop across the street . . . it's still open. Go in there, tell them to call the police. Call your parents. Go on. Go. Now.'

'They're gonna think I killed him.'

'No, they won't,' I said. 'Tell them someone broke in. All right?'

'Angels broke in, sent by God.' He smiled at me and then Raf.

And I smiled back. And that was the moment I knew – whatever happened now, after this moment, *that* was why I had been put on this earth. All the bad luck, anxiety, stress and trouble I'd been afforded over the last thirty years, *that* moment when I guided that boy down those stairs and watched him run out of that door, over to that coffee shop; that made it all worth it.

That was what I was put on this earth to do. Not fucking admin.

Wednesday, 13 October 2021 – early hours

1. *People who put nail varnish on their dogs' claws*
2. *That news guy who got caught sending nudes to kids on Insta – I wonder what will be first, comments turned off or Notes app apology?*
3. *Rebel Wilson*
4. *People who grab your phone to look at it closer when you show them a meme or an interesting Twitter thread – everyone in the family does this but only Nico has got as far as my album of Raf's nudes*
5. *Elliot Fucking Mansur*

'Why the fuck did you come here when you told me you weren't?!'

'Why the fuck did you follow me when you told me you were watching football?!'

'BECAUSE I KNEW YOU WERE LYING!'

'SO WHY DID YOU FUCKING GO THEN?'

'TO STOP YOU FROM FUCKING KILLING HIM!'

'SO *YOU* COULD FUCKING KILL HIM INSTEAD?'

'YES!'

'WHY?!'

'BECAUSE HE WAS MINE TO KILL, NOT YOURS.'

That stopped me in my tracks. 'You *wanted* to kill him?'

'No. But I didn't want you taking the rap for him. I told you about him – I realise now I shouldn't have done that – but it wasn't your responsibility to take him out. I couldn't let you take him. Not when I could.'

'I had it covered.'

'Did you? Did you really have everything covered?'

'Yes!'

'THEN WHO WAS THE KID?'

'I don't know. He wasn't supposed to be there. I did it for you, Raf.'

'Yeah. And I did that for *you*. Ugh, fuck my fucking life!' he roared, starting the car. 'We gotta go through every little detail about tonight and get our stories straight.'

It was all about minimising the consequences. We'd been wearing gloves and masks and it was dark out so we knew there was a good chance we hadn't been seen leaving the building. The only ones hanging around at that time were meth addicts and a shouty homeless woman who needed a sharp blast of Febreze up her skirt. Nobody else would have been in that area at that time of night so for once, the Tenderloin was the safest place to be.

In case of witnesses, Raf said it would be better to exchange the Mustang now at the Hertz rental three blocks away, with the excuse that it kept cutting out at traffic lights. The guy at the Hertz desk clearly wasn't paid enough to argue and gave us a Ford Focus for our return journey. It was gone midnight by the time we had thrown the flick knife into the harbour and made it back to the hotel and up to our suite.

I couldn't stop looking at him as he stripped off his T-shirt and set to doing some first aid on his stab wound.

'Are you sure you don't need the ER?' I asked him. I felt like Meg Ryan at the end of *Sleepless in Seattle* when all she can do is stare at Tom Hanks, hardly daring to believe he's real (even though the kid told him to meet her up the top of the Empire State but whatevs). I couldn't stop looking at my unbelievably sexy Clyde Barrow–esque husband who had killed a man with his bare hands and been stabbed in the process but was shrugging it off like it was just a big zit.

'It's fine.' Raf hit the mini bar and downed two small bottles of Jack Daniels in quick succession, spitting both lids across the carpet. He sat on the wide windowsill, dousing a bunched-up shirt with vodka and dabbing his side. After the blood had been cleaned up, he applied an extra-large bandage from the aid kit – the wound comparatively small so it wouldn't take long to scab over. He must have been in so much pain.

I walked over to him at the window and put my arms around him and he held me. I've never wanted him inside me more. But this wasn't the time. We had a lot to talk about. And, possibly, a quick getaway to make.

'Who was that kid?' he asked.

'I don't know,' I said, strapping my brace back on. The relief in my wrist was immediate. At least some of the pressure in my body had eased.

'You said he lived alone.'

'I thought he did.' Bloody Pfister. I'd kill him if he wasn't already dead. 'I knew there was no CCTV on that street—'

'—how?'

'I sent Pfister here a couple of weeks ago to scope the place out. I was blackmailing him for his phone.'

'Oh my God.'

'He was right about the CCTV – just not about the boy.'

'You realise we are in serious shit now, don't you?'

'Yeah well, I've been there before. What's new?'

I thought I would hate seeing Raf like that – all crotchety-eyebrows and thin-mouth. I'd never needed him to be angry like me – to be a killer like me – but now that he was and he is, and I had seen it happen with my own eyes, I'd never been so turned on in my life.

'I feel really close to you, all of a sudden,' I told him. 'Like we're . . . bonded. We just did something pretty astonishing.'

'We liberated a missing kid,' he said. 'We are gonna be on every news network in the country by morning.'

'No, the kid might but we won't. And it *is* morning.' I checked the time – five minutes after midnight. 'Anyway, he only saw me; he didn't really see you.'

'You *spoke* to him. He knows you're English. It's not gonna take long for people to start putting two and two together.'

'Right, well, we go home then.'

'*Today.*'

'Yes, today. We drop off the Focus at the Hertz in San Diego and we go home and pretend we were never here.'

'Yeah, all right. That's a start.'

'But if we hadn't gone there, Raf, he'd still be in there. River. God knows how long Mansur had him. Doing Christ knows what. And now Mansur's dead. And *we* killed him. Doesn't that make you feel proud?'

Raf looked at me and nodded. 'It felt good, killing him, yeah.'

'See?' I said, stroking his cheeks. 'Remember when we were in Rocas Calientes and you beat up those two guys who were making those lewd comments about me? *You* escalated that, not me. I was willing to walk on by. This fire that's in me to defend you – you've got it as well.'

Raf got up and went back to the mini bar, taking out a Snickers and tearing it open like he was going to war with it. 'So, what's next?' He sat down carefully at the dining table, holding his side and still chewing. 'Do we jump in the rental car and go back down the coast, kill a few more kiddy fiddlers along the way? Knock over a couple banks?'

'No. We go home.' I fished around in my hoodie pockets and pulled out our Calico Critters rabbit bride and groom from our wedding cake. 'I saved them from the Mustang.' I waved them in front of me like jazz hands. I placed them on the windowsill. 'We saved him, Raf. We're awesome.'

'God knows what's coming in the morning.'

'Should we leave tonight?'

'Too suspicious. We'll leave first thing.'

'You still love me?' I joined our hands so the broken hearts mended.

He nodded. 'It feels dangerous. It feels wrong, in a lot of ways. But yeah, I do. In fact, I don't think I've ever loved you more.'

We each had a shower to wash the events of the Tenderloin off our skins and spent a fractious night packing our stuff, changing Raf's bandages and emptying the mini bar of all remaining alcohol. Neither of us slept much. I wish I was exceptionally stupid. Stupid people don't have anxiety because they're not intelligent enough to worry about what comes next. They see no consequences to their own stupidity. Whereas my own stupidity comes with a conscience and what lay heaviest on my conscience was the thought that Rafael could go to prison for something that was my idea in the first place. I couldn't face losing him – I could face losing *myself* but not him.

We kept refreshing our phones for updates but there was nothing until Mike Targitt's breakfast bulletin on *Good Morning America*.

By then, it was everywhere.

NEWSFLASH – Missing Boy Found Alive After Three Years!

That stopped us both in our groggy tracks.

'*We go live to our correspondent Cress Fratburger who's live outside the apartment in San Francisco where the miraculous discovery was made late last night. Cress . . .*'

'Shit, turn it up,' Raf ordered, slinging his rucksack onto his shoulder where it had fallen off.

'*Yes, I'm outside the unassuming apartment on Filmore Street in the Cow Hollow district of San Francisco where last night an extraordinary story unfolded. This is as close as we can get as police clear the scene but a short while ago, we brought you these pictures of a body being brought out, that of fifty-two-year-old Elliot Mansur, who it is thought, had abducted and imprisoned missing River Dade Goffey these past three years.*'

Raf turned to me, like the kid in *The Exorcist*. 'River Dade Goffey? That kid was River Dade Goffey?!' He sprang up, pacing the floor.

'You know him?'

Mike Targitt couldn't get over it either. '*This is unbelievable, Cress, so has River, who would be eleven years old now,* killed *this guy?*'

Cress shook his head. '*No, witnesses in the coffee shop across the street here, are saying the boy ran in and screamed at someone to call the cops, saying two people had broken into the apartment and one of them was a woman. They told him to go and get help and meanwhile, the other assailant, a man, killed Mansur and the woman told him to go get help.*'

'*Could he recall any details about the man and woman who saved him?*'

'*He said she gave him a hug and she looked like "the angel he'd been praying for". That's all we know at this time.*'

Raf was still pacing. I couldn't take my eyes off the screen. They flashed up a picture of the boy from the apartment, three years younger, smiling on the school football field. It was taken days before he disappeared. He was small and scrawny with thick black glasses and a tooth missing at the front. He didn't have a tooth missing last night. He was fatter too.

'They didn't say I had a British accent, or that you're Mexican, so that's something,' I told him, trying to extricate a bright side from this clusterfuck.

Raf shook his head. 'We're not out of the woods. Why didn't you use your American accent anyway?'

'I panicked,' I snipped. 'I didn't expect him to be there, did I?'

Switch to Mike Targitt back in the studio. '*And is River in good health do we know?*'

Cress nodded emphatically – the Botox clearly hadn't affected his neck muscles yet, even if his eyebrows had stopped emoting years ago. '*Yes, though obviously he has been through a hell of a lot for a young boy but we understand he's in good health and being looked after by the San Francisco PD. Obviously, he is eager to be back with his folks who are flying in from Kansas later today. We'll bring you the latest on this as it unfolds.*'

Mike grinned. '*It's one of those days when you truly believe anything is possible. And there are two questions on America's lips this morning – who are these avenging angels who found River Goffey and where are they now?*'

Rafael turned round to stare at me, open-jawed, not for the first time.

'We gotta get out of here.'

Friday, 15 October 2021

1. *Joggers*
2. *People who do maternity photoshoots for their dog / cat/ferret*
3. *People whose voices are unnaturally loud – e.g., guy outside the vax hub who REALLY wants everyone to know he's got a Tesla*
4. *That rapper who replaced all his hair with gold chains*
5. *Seren. If you're not fucking dead now then you better be working on it.*

Turns out, River Dade Goffey was quite well known in the USA. He'd been missing for three years, presumed dead. At one time, there were posters of him everywhere, mainly around Wichita, Kansas, where he lived. He had the Amber alert, freeway signs, sniffer dogs, helicopters, volunteers combing through the countryside, the whole nine milk cartons. He was famous.

But as days missing turned into months missing then years, the hunt was scaled back; the trail went cold and slowly everyone began to forget about him. His family didn't, of course. They continued to appear on news bulletins or *60 Minutes*–type docus now and then, pleading with the police to keep looking for him. They formed their own search parties, printed thousands of flyers and renewed the appeal with candlelit vigils and updated posters of 'what he might look like now'. They crowdfunded for private detectives and sniffer dogs in areas where there had been sightings. They tied yellow ribbons around trees. His siblings grew up without him and all the time, in their minds, River was eight years old. He simply stopped growing. He had vanished, in a puff of engine smoke from a dirty black van.

Until one balmy Tuesday night in October 2021 when he'd run into a coffee shop in a San Francisco back street, socked-feet, three years older and one foot taller, and asked a green-haired barista to 'call his mom and dad'.

Since we've been back in San Diego, we've not spoken about it, although we've kept a close eye on the events unfolding in San Fran but by some miracle, we didn't seem to be on anyone's tongues. All anyone in America could talk about was the miraculous escape of the 'Wichita Wonderkid'.

Billy, the Irish sniffer dog that he was, clocked it straight away.

'It was you, wasn't it?' He grinned, swigging his pale ale and leaning on the doorframe as I watched the latest bulletin.

'What the hell are you doing here?' I said, irritated by the fact that not only had he named that tune in one but that he was at the house in the middle of the day when the only one around was me.

He gestured towards the laundry room. 'Bianca put a wash on for me before she went out vaccinating. I'm waiting for the dryer. It is though, isn't it? You did that. You freed that kid. Does Raf know? That's why you two have been acting weird since you got back; I knew something was up.'

'What do you want, another fucking medal?' I left the TV on and went to change the water in the dogs' bowls, not that it needed changing. I had to busy myself. Not look at him. Not engage with this at all.

'I'm not gonna tell, Rhiannon; I told you your secret was safe with me.'

'Don't call me Rhiannon in the house,' I said, through clenched teeth.

'Nobody's here. Bianca's down at the vax hub until twelve and Raf's at work. What are you worried about?'

I gestured towards the six little faces peering up at me beneath the food bowl I was carrying. They thought it was breakfast time again. It wasn't. I got them all a calcium bone from their tin instead. 'They heard you.'

'The dogs?' Billy laughed.

'Dogs know stuff.'

'Hey, I love dogs but I don't think they're about to spill your beans anytime soon. Talking of beans, did you see how many hits your YouTube video's up to? Over three hundred thousand since it hit TikTok.'

'Oh Christ, I forgot about that.'

'Don't worry, nobody's clocked it's you. You were masked up. And you don't look anything like all the pictures going round. But the comments are all good – they love you!'

'That's something at least.' I sighed, leaning on the countertop rubbing my eyes, not that they needed rubbing; I just wanted to hide for a bit. 'What are the comments saying?'

Billy brought over his phone to show me and I scrolled through the list of nice things people were saying.

You are a hero, Bean Qween!

Protect this gal at all costs.

Real heroes don't wear capes – they wear unicorn face masks!

Hope this woman gets the recognition she deserves.

I salute you, Bean Qween.

Where's the update? Who is this unicorn-masked wonder woman?

There was a warm glow in my chest. I didn't feel tired anymore. I felt like, dare I say it, a normal person who had a purpose now in this baffling world. Like I wasn't a freak. Like I wasn't as useless as the P in receipt. Like I hadn't just been born to have periods and write press releases. I'd been born for *this*.

When I looked up, Billy was leaning on the counter opposite.

'For what it's worth, *Ophelia*, I think you're astonishing. And if it *was* you who killed that bastard and freed that little boy, that's taken you to another level in my mind. Don't you dare be ashamed of it . . .'

'Don't be ashamed of it?' I echoed. 'We're going to have to leave the US, you do know that right? We're both going to go to prison for this if they identify us – if that kid starts talking about me, if he mentions I have a British accent or my height or weight, they are gonna be on us like stink on shit.'

'I doubt it. If the Bad Seeds are anything to go by, nobody will be looking for you. Your own fan club haven't recognised you yet, I doubt anyone else will. You're not gonna find many people who want justice for that cunt anyway. People *like* people who kill paedophiles. *They're* Public Enemy Number One, not you.'

'Tell that to the San Francisco Police Department.'

Billy swigged his ale as the dryer beeped to announce it had finished. 'That'll be me done.'

The story came up on the news again and I ran to the remote to turn it up. The glossy blonde on *Good Morning San Diego* called us 'River's avenging angels' and all the vox pops said we were 'heroes' though I got the impression they thought River was making it up. They kept talking about his 'love of comic books and superheroes' especially the Avengers, and the guy with the chin kept referring to me as Black Widow. I think it was him who started the rumour I'd been wearing spandex. Chinny prick.

'Finally this morning we bring you the miracle homecoming America's been waiting to see – the Wichita Wonderkid, River Dade Goffey, is back home in Kansas tonight and any second now, he will be reunited with his sisters. Marcie, is there any sign of him yet?'

'Oh shit, he's back!' I yelled.

Billy hurried out of the laundry room with an armful of clothes. 'He's home?'

'Thanks, Chuck, yeah I'm here outside the Goffeys' home in Matlock Heights where we're expecting the car any minute to come around that very bend. Inside the house here are River's two older siblings, Misty and Willow . . .'

You can barely hear the uptight newswoman, Marcie Fitzpatrick, for all the whooping and hollering from the crowds of people lined up and down the street. Someone's letting off fireworks, banners saying 'Welcome Home' and 'We Love You River', helium balloons batter and wobble in the breeze. There are satellite vans parked all the way up the street from news outlets all over the country, if not the world, and there's even a full brass band playing 'When the Saints Go Marching In' because his dad Greg is a member of the band. The camera fixes on the road, waiting for the car.

'Can't they leave the kid alone for five minutes; he's been through enough.' Billy sighed.

'It's hot news,' I said. 'Kids rarely come back alive. This is . . . special.'

Marcie Fitzpatrick adjusts one pearl earring, looks once off camera, and then straight down the lens, affixing her rock-hard journalist stare. She has a Texan drawl and a concrete blonde Rachel-cut and she's all over this.

'Greg and Jennifer Goffey have had three unendurable years of suffering, wondering what happened to their little boy who went out to play with his older sisters and disappeared. Willow remembers seeing a truck – "black with shiny tyres" but not the driver. By the time the girls got home to raise the alarm, River was already in the clutches of a predator: Elliot Mansur.

'Just this week, in a miraculous turn of events, they got a call from the San Francisco PD saying he had been found safe and well and living over a thousand miles away with convicted sex offender Elliot Mansur. Now the circumstances of River's release are still unconfirmed at present but what we do know is that Mansur is dead and that a person or persons liberated River from his imprisonment. What we don't know is who those people are . . .'

Billy looked at me. He'd heard something. Then I heard something too – at the front door. Bianca was back early. I switched off the TV and Billy walked back to the laundry room.

'¡Hola, mis angelitos! Is your washing all done, Billy?'

'Ah not quite but there's no hurry. The man who made time made plenty of it!'

'Well, when it's ready, I will fold it for you.'

'Ah it's no bother, really.'

But Bianca had already moved on to me – that was her way, tornadoing around the house finding something that needed doing or someone who needed help and seeing to it. 'Mi cielo, you are not wearing your brace again – you must wear it around the house or it will never get strong.'

'Yeah, I'll get it in a minute, it's upstairs.'

'Lemme help you with that,' said Billy, placing the laundry basket on the sofa to assist her with the Food Gnome shopping bags she'd brought in.

'Have you two had lunch? That terrible woman was at the store again, shouting at the top of her voice. I think she'd been drinking – Luiz and Manny had to carry her out. Have the dogs been fed, *Ophelia*?'

I nodded. 'Yeah, all done.'

'Thank you.' She beamed, bustling her way upstairs to change.

Billy picked up the remote and put the news back on quietly. River's car was just coming up the road to his parents' house. The screams and cheers had grown louder; balloons waving, yellow ribbons flapping on the breeze, and Marcie Fitzpatrick had become far shriller than before.

'*Oh my God here he is, here he is everyone, the Wichita Wonderkid, he's home!*' yells Marcie over the hubbub. '*And we can see his Gramma and Grandpa at the window with his two sisters, who would have been ten and twelve when*

River disappeared – Willow is now thirteen and Misty is fifteen . . .'

A woman gets out the back of the car – her frizzy mullet and burgundy skirt and block heels providing a stark contrast to Marcie's sleek do and Balenciaga hourglass coat. The frizzy woman wears a thin gold crucifix around her neck which glints in the camera flashes as she emerges.

'So *here's River's mom Jennifer right now. JENNIFER, HOW DOES IT FEEL TO HAVE YOUR BOY BACK HOME?'*

Jennifer smiles meekly at the camera, clearly startled by the flashing lights and noise from the surrounding well-wishers.

Then Greg gets out of the other side of the car – brown leather jacket, jeans, checked shirt, looking about twenty years older than the three-year-old family photo they keep flashing up of the family in happier times.

'And *here's Greg Goffey, River's dad,'* says Marcie, ducking and jumping over heads to try to get a peek at River who is being protected by his parents and a couple of cops as he is guided from the back of the car. The cops yell at people to 'get back' and 'let him through'.

Marcie continues to fill air time while River and his parents stop to be asked questions by another news crew – she is clearly seething and continues to fill the dead air with stuff the viewer already knows.

'. . . *he took him nearly four hundred miles away to Memphis at first, where they lived for a year and moved on several times since – first to Springfield, then on to Fort Worth, Albuquerque, Sacramento and finally, San Francisco. He was planning to move on again soon. They kept moving. Mansur was on probation. The police had him on their system but he knew when they were coming so he could hide River each time. When anyone in the neighbourhood asked who he was, he'd say he was his godson visiting. He dyed his hair and made him speak in a Southern accent to fool them . . . RIVER, HOW ARE YOU FEELING TO BE BACK HOME? RIVER? RIVER, HOW DOES IT FEEL TO BE BACK WITH YOUR FAMILY, HONEY?'*

River looks different to when we found him – he is wearing clothes that fit properly and he's been cleaned up with his hair brushed back away from his face. He clings to his mum's hand.

'*HAS RIVER SAID ANYTHING ABOUT WHAT HE HAS BEEN THROUGH?*' shouts Marcie as Greg Goffey throws her the briefest glare.

And there it is. *Give us the dirt, Goffeys. How did he, when did he, how many times.* Ugh. This is what people are thinking about. This is what gets the ratings up after all.

His sisters Misty and Willow run out of the house and the crowds part for them. The cameraman gets the shot he's waited all day for – River accosted by desperate, sobbing hugs. The grandmother falling to her knees to deliver an impromptu prayer at the boy's feet.

Marcie Fitzpatrick breaks through the throng of cameras and neighbours and family members to shove a microphone into River's face.

'*RIVER, HOW DOES IT FEEL TO BE HOME?*'

'*Really good, thanks,*' the boy says with a small smile.

'*CAN YOU RECALL ANYTHING ABOUT YOUR RESCUERS, RIVER?*'

'*It was a woman and a man. And she hugged me.*'

'*HOW DID THAT FEEL?*'

'*Really great. I knew I was safe when I saw her.*'

Another news crew tries to muscle in to interview his mum and dad as River continues to be pushed towards his front door.

'*DO YOU HAVE ANY MESSAGES FOR YOUR RESCUERS, RIVER? ANYTHING YOU WANT TO SAY TO THEM RIGHT NOW?*'

'*Thank you,*' he says. '*You're angels.*'

Marcie laughs, loud and forced. Jennifer butts in, craning her neck to the microphone. '*We're not putting pressure on him to tell us what happened – we're just glad he's back home. We're focusing on that.*'

Marcie nods, head on a sympathetic lean as the river of people suddenly stops. They've reached the front door – his sisters have not let go of his hands. They stand either side of him as his parents try to shield him. '*RIVER, DO YOU BELIEVE IN ANGELS THEN?*'

Greg Goffey butts in. '*We're a Christian family and River prayed while he was away from us. We believe his prayers were answered.*'

'*GREG, AS A GOD-FEARING MAN, DO YOU SANCTION MURDER?*'

Greg stops on his doorstep, ushering his three children inside the house, followed by his wife. He turns to the reporter who's barked the question at him. '*In the Bible it says, "Do not take revenge, but leave room for God's wrath, for it is written: 'It is mine to avenge; I will repay,' says the Lord." And I truly believe, that whoever liberated my boy were sent by God to repay that man for taking him. And I for one am mighty glad today. Mighty glad.*'

Marcie throws it back to the studio where the focus is on the promise of the '*world exclusive interview with River and his family in the coming weeks*'.

I switched off the TV.

'They're gonna interview him?' Billy asked.

'In the coming weeks, they said.'

'Even so.'

'Even so what?'

'If he puts two and two together in the meantime, he's gonna know exactly who you are. Have they identified that body in Vermont yet?'

'No.'

'But they're gonna dig, right?'

'Yeah.'

'And then they'll know you're still alive.'

'Yeah.'

'And that kid heard you talking in a British accent.'

'Yeah.'

'And he saw Rafael.'

'I won't let them get to Raf.'

'How the hell are you gonna stop them?'

Saturday, 16 October 2021

1. *People who make cereals, esp. muesli – stop being so mean with the raisins*
2. *Zookeepers who shoot animals that have escaped from zoos*
3. *Journalist Guy Majors – stop trying to make 'Ripperella' a thing*
4. *Hilarious Baldwin*
5. *Pandas – I don't respect any living creature who drops their kid at the sight of an apple.*

Billy had successfully put the fear of God in me about taking Rafael down with me should River spill my particular brand of crazy beans in his upcoming world exclusive interview. I spent a restless night staring at the ceiling and thinking through all my possible options.

1. Stay here and face the music, get arrested, get sent to death row – *not fucking likely.*
2. Tell Raf everything – *I'm not a complete bitch.*
3. Run away and start again somewhere else alone – *tried that before. I don't function well on my own.*

So where did that leave me? The third option was the most painless, for everyone else that is. Being chainsawed in half would be less painful for me but it was the only way I could keep Rafael out of this. If I left, he could have his life back. He could have his family back – Liv would come round again. Nico and Ariela and the kids. Bianca would have all her family back together and I would make a quiet exit stage left, pursued by flashing blue lights. I had no idea where I would go. But I had to get out before that kid googled 'female vigilante' and saw my old face plastered all over the internet.

So in the dead of night, while Raf was snoring soundly beside me, I silently made my plans to leave him. If you love someone, set them free and all that. It sent me straight back to the churning worming anxiety in my belly when I left Ivy in that incubator and fled the UK. Not right but right enough for her. And ultimately, I didn't care about me.

I always knew I wasn't good enough for him. I've always known that. But being with him has made me the best version of myself. I'd gone a considerable amount of time without killing anyone while I'd been here. Eight hundred and forty-one days. And do you know what made me kill again? What Edo did to Raf's sister. Up until then, I was happy to be Ophelia – 'OJ'. Mrs Rafael Arroyo-White. Liv and Nico's sister. I looked at the photo of the three kids and Mikey on the swings at Briercrest Park that we'd taken only last month. Their auntie. That's all I wanted to be. But my mind was made up.

And as soon as Raf left for work the next morning, I started packing.

A couple of the dogs, Diablo and Traumatised Bob came upstairs and scurried around my feet as I stuffed my rucksack;

the one that had only just been unpacked from San Fran. Every pair of knickers, every balled-up pair of socks that went into that bag felt like a lead weight. I did not want to do this. I did not want to go. But it was always going to end this way – me leaving. It was just a matter of when. And how.

What I hadn't expected was an audience.

'What are you doing?' came the voice behind me.

'The fuck?!' I said, whipping my head round to see Rafael in the doorway. I hadn't heard him come back in. 'Why aren't you at work?'

'Because something's wrong. You're acting weird again.'

'Well yeah, that much is obvious,' I said, moving to the wardrobe to carry on pulling things off hangers, though it was even harder now with him watching me. 'You're gonna be late.'

'Where are you going?'

'Nowhere,' I said weakly, even though my actions negated the word.

'You were tossing and turning all night, what's happened?'

'You *know* what's happened. River fucking Goffey, that's what happened. The second that kid opens his mouth, it's over for us. He'll recognise us. He'll mention my accent, your Mexicanness and that'll be it. Our photos will be beamed up on national television, probably *international* television, and then that's us done. And I'm not taking you with me. I'll take all of this. This isn't on you. It was my idea to go there. This is my problem.'

I couldn't look at him as I stuffed my make-up bag in the top of my rucksack.

'Well, you're not going anywhere without me,' he said, pulling his sports bag out of the bottom of the wardrobe and throwing it onto the bed, narrowly missing the two snoozing dogs. He'd already packed up the contents of his sock drawer when he spoke again. 'I called Salomé last night; asked her if we could stay with her for a while. There are a couple of flights we can get—'

'—*you're* not going anywhere,' I said, finally giving in to my own tears.

'What are you talking about, of course I am. If that kid identifies us, I'm in just as much shit as you are. We go down to Rocas for a couple weeks, just until this stuff blows over—'

'—what if it *doesn't* blow over? What if they study the CCTV at that Starbucks where I got the coffee? Or someone scrolls TikTok and sees the Bean Qween video, and identifies me? God, how stupid can one person be?'

'Who me?' he said.

'No, me. Once again, fucking ME. Another stupid boo-boo to add to the endless list. A grab-my-own-arm-thinking-it's-a-branch boo-boo.'

'This wasn't a boo-boo. We saved that kid. I don't regret that. And we wouldn't have gone there had you not had the idea in the first place. We did a good thing.' He held my arms and stopped me picking up my rucksack, not that I could carry it anyway, it was too heavy. 'We went there because you wanted to kill a guy who hurt me as a kid.'

'Yeah, stupid idea.'

He shook his head. 'No. It was the most fucking romantic thing anyone's ever done for me.'

'Romantic?'

'Yeah. Baby, I've never met anyone who's loved me like you. Every single day you prove it, even though you don't need to.

That Smith-Lansing woman at the store – if I hadn't pulled you back, you'd have torn her head off, all cos she yelled at me. The guy on the bus that time who spilled his beer on me, and you punched him in the throat?'

'He did that on purpose.'

'And those two guys on the beach in Rocas? You'd have stabbed them both to death with a broken bottle if I'd let you. That was . . . hot.'

'Don't sexualise my pain.'

'I'm sorry. But it is. It *was*. You didn't need to do any of that to prove how much you love me – I see it. I *feel* it.'

'Do you?' I said. 'I always hoped you knew how much I love you. But I wasn't ever sure if you did.' He nodded. 'You don't think I'm a freak?'

'A freak? God, you've got no idea, do you? You know why I followed you to Mansur's apartment that night, right? Because I was afraid of him hurting you. I knew you wouldn't be happy unless you came back with his scalp but your wrist would have stopped you. Then where would we be? I'd have lost you. And Mansur would have vanished and that kid with him.'

'I still shouldn't have gone.'

'Well, it's done now. And even though it's kinda tipped up the apple cart, I gotta admit, it was a hell of a rush.'

'Don't you start.'

He stroked my face. 'We're a team, princesa, right? That's what this means.' He brandished my own wedding ring finger in front of me.

'Your family hates me,' I said, sitting down on the edge of the bed. 'The way your sister looked at me. The way they *all* looked at me the other day, around the table. Ariela, Nico—'

'—Nico doesn't hate you; he's just too shit-scared of his wife to form his own opinions. And Liv'll come round – she knows what you did was for the greater good.'

It was easier not to believe it. 'They know what I am now.'

'What you *are*? What you are is my wife.'

I shook my head, strapping on my wrist brace. 'I'm a liability. And this doesn't help. It'll all come out before too long – River, Edo, Brad Pfister . . .'

'Oh, talking of which, did you see the latest?' he asked, scrolling his phone to find the report. 'I got an alert.' He held the screen before me.

The neighborhood of Julian in the north of the county has been rocked by the police announcement that a suspected serial killer had been using a remote hideaway as his kill site. The discovery of two bodies inside a burning house on Roadrunner Ridge last week began a police investigation during which one of the bodies was identified as that of missing 21-year-old Bradley Pfister. The medical examiner has yet to wrap up the autopsy on the other victim but investigators say they are not looking for a killer at large.

'They're not looking for anyone else,' he said, switching off his phone.

'Not *yet*,' I corrected as he opened more drawers and threw some boxers in his bag. 'When they discover that other corpse is Edo, that'll be it. All roads will point to me. You think Ariela or Liv are really going to keep quiet about me when all this comes to a head?'

'They will if I tell them to,' he said firmly.

I shook my head again. It was all I could do. 'You can't stop me going. I'm trying to save you from me!'

'Why do you think I *wanna* be saved?'

I couldn't look at him anymore. I reached into the top of the wardrobe and got down the two Nike boxes. There was $40,000 left – I threw half of it over to his side of the bed. 'There. I've divided our estate.' I shoved the rest into my bag. 'You're a free man.'

He stood in front of the chest of drawers, barring my way to Richard E. Grunt and the little woollen gatita Tenoch had given me.

'Can you move please? I want my pig and my cat. GIVE ME MY CAT!' I grabbed Dickie and the gatita and shoved them in my pocket. 'MOVE!'

Raf sat down on the bed and watched me.

'Go to the gym. Go and see Nico. I'll be gone by the time you get back.'

The wardrobe floor was clear where we had removed our bags – mine was half-full, his was half-empty. A sliver of brown paper poked out from underneath the carpet at the back. I pulled it out, revealing the Barnes & Noble bag with Freddie's book inside it. The receipt tucked into the centre where the pictures of me as a baby were. I glared at it – and finally, because of me being me, I chucked it onto the bed beside him.

Here. It. Comes.

'Maybe this'll do it.'

He reached across the bed for the bag and removed the book. I'd dreaded this moment for nearly two years. Feared he'd find it himself sometimes, then other times, wishing he *would* then at least he would know everything about me and

I wouldn't have to lie to that beautiful face anymore. Now there was nothing to be afraid of – the worst was happening. How much worse could it get?

THE SWEETPEA KILLER: The True Confessions of Rhiannon Lewis by Freddie Litton-Cheney

You wanna know how messed up my brain really is – I can't fart in front of my husband but telling him I'm a serial murderer comes surprisingly easy.

'I'm tired of pretending. Everything you need to know about me is in that book. If you google that name, you'll get the gore and the headlines. If you read the book, you'll get the why. And I owe you the why.'

He stared at my picture on the cover.

I pointed at his ribcage tattoo with the half-inch scab on it where he was stabbed. 'That right there is not my name. It's Rhiannon. Lewis. I'm Sweetpea.' I pulled out my mobile. 'Call the police. Tell them. Maybe *you* can have a headline: "Hubby Grasses on Monster Missus." Maybe they'll commend you; let you back in the army. It's the right thing to do. Go on. DO IT.'

'I don't wanna do it,' he replied, and chucked the book back down on the bed next to him.

'She is me. That story is *my* story.'

'I know,' he said, looking up at me. 'I've read it.'

I froze to the spot. I couldn't believe what I'd just heard. 'What?'

'I said I've read it. I found it about ten months ago. I was looking for hiding places for your birthday presents and I stumbled across it.'

He'd read it, cover to cover, but never told me a thing, just kept updating himself with the latest news, the police search, the burial of my 'remains' in Vermont. He allowed the news to process and went to his therapy sessions to talk it out. 'I get you. I get why you are the way you are.'

'How can you have read it and still . . . ?' I started. 'You know everything? *Everything* I've done?'

He nodded, but he didn't look at me the way I'd expected him to. He didn't look at me the way my mum would have or my teachers used to. He didn't smile, he didn't step away and he didn't leave. He simply sat there on the end of the bed and waited for me to sit next to him.

'I was waiting for you to tell me yourself. You started to tell me bits and pieces – the hammer attack. About Ivy. Your mom and dad. The guy who cheated on you – Creg?'

'Craig,' I corrected.

'Ivy's dad. As far as I'm concerned, you suffered a trauma few people can understand. Priory Gardens changed you fundamentally. That's what people who hurt kids do – they change us in ways we were never supposed to be changed. They kill the person we were meant to be and they replace them with something else. I think Elliot Mansur changed me in a small way. It's always there. That River kid will be changed too. We can't save him from *that*.'

'What are you saying?'

'I'm saying a lot of people don't even begin to heal from their childhood traumas until they're adults, and that's only if they get the right support. I'm saying I get it. I'm saying I'm all in. I'm saying I'm prepared to be fucking devastated by you, Rhiannon.'

It was like he'd punched me in the heart. 'You called me Rhiannon.'

'That's your name, isn't it?'

It was my turn to nod – it was all I had; I was too stunned to speak.

'I've been calling you that in my head. I think Ophelia suits you too though. They're both beautiful names. Rhiannon was a Welsh witch, right?'

I nodded. 'You knew and . . . you still wanted to marry me?' I looked down at his rib tattoo with the large Band-Aid over it. 'Why did you get that?'

'Fresh start. New beginnings. I figured I'd make a statement.'

'I hate it.'

He laughed; a golden laugh. 'I'll get it lasered.'

'You can't still want me after knowing all this. I'm rotten to the core. I'm a bad seed.'

'And that little seed ain't been given what she needs to grow until now, has she?'

'What?'

'I get why you are the way you are. Why you're angry. Even why you . . . used to do that stuff with . . . dead guys.'

My cheeks bloomed. 'It was only one dead guy. I don't tour graveyards and hump the mounds or anything. And I haven't wanted to do that since meeting you. Oh God I can't believe you know about that . . .'

Suddenly I got it – why Mum had shouted at me when I'd interrupted her scarf dancing. It was because I'd *seen* her, seen as she truly was. Free. Untethered. No act. And that embarrassed her, me walking in on her and seeing her truthful self. The one she showed nobody else, not even Dad. Now Raf was seeing mine. He'd read the book. He'd seen my own cringy-ass dance with scarves. And I was embarrassed too. My cheeks went all hot and I couldn't look at him. But Raf got it.

'The dead don't leave, right?'

I stared at him, feeling like the first time I was seeing him too.

'It's all about that rosebud moment,' he continued. 'When everything changed. So you took it back, bit by bit. All the control you didn't have. The book made me realise that. It said every person you've ever known has let you down or left you. But I *won't*. I read this book ten months ago and I'll admit, it shocked me. I thought about leaving.'

'You did?'

'Yeah. I thought this is too specialist for me to deal with. I'm not strong enough – I don't have what you need to look after you. But I love you. I can't help it – I just do. And you know what I realised? I *do* have what you need. I'm a trained fucking soldier. And one of the many things that teaches you is perseverance. Quitting is not in our nature. Every time you feel physical pain, you push through it. Even when your body is telling you to quit, you keep going. Staying, persevering, being challenged shapes you. I look at my parents' marriage and that's what I want. Tough times – you stay together. Through everything, you're a team. You work at it.'

'Neither of your parents was a serial killer though.' I sobbed. I couldn't pinch my arm hard enough – tears came anyway.

'No, but I love you. This person, right here, whatever her name is. Whoever this person is in front of me, with the scar on her wrist, and the scar on her head, and the wicked sense of humour, and the amazing ass . . .'

'Ah you ruined it.'

'Sorry.'

'You were doing so well.'

'OK, look – whatever and whoever you are, what you've given me the past two years, has rebuilt me. You've given me a purpose again. I've been working for a future. You're not too much for me – you know why? Because I can't get enough of you. You've made me remember why I like being alive.'

'But I'm a killer. I killed my own dad, Raf. How can you forgive that?'

'It's not for me to forgive. And your father was dying. He asked you to. If my dad had the strength to ask me when he was dying? I think maybe I'd have done the same.'

'And the taxi driver?'

'You were fucked up.'

'I still am. I would kill for all of you. I *have* to. Because there's always going to be someone in this world who wants to hurt you. And I won't let that happen, not when I can stop it.'

He took the little woollen cat from me. 'This is you, isn't it? The little cat who keeps bringing dead mice to the doorstep to impress her owners – gatita. You don't have to do that anymore. And *I* need to protect *you*. Remember when we met, at the airport? And you were all pissy because you'd bought a book in Spanish and I was all pissy because . . . well, I was thinking of killing myself . . .'

'What?'

'Around that time, every thought I had was a negative one. I'd been kicked out of my job; a job I'd devoted myself to since I was seventeen. My wife had dumped me for a guy I thought was my friend. And I couldn't see a reason to carry on. My whole family were around me, excited about the party we were going to, but I remember thinking one night I'm gonna walk into the ocean. I was planning how I was gonna do it. Whether I'd leave them all notes.'

'Why have you never told me this?'

'Same reason you never told me you were a serial killer. Shame.'

'It's not the same thing.'

'No, and it's not your responsibility to be my reason to live either.'

'You want me to kill you, is that it? Is this part of your death wish?'

'No. It's part of my *life* wish. I forced myself to talk to you that day. And it was so easy. You were so funny.'

I sniffed. 'I *am* pretty funny.'

He squeezed my hand. 'And you know what I thought? For a second, I imagined us sitting there, waiting for our flight to take us on our honeymoon.'

'You are kidding me.'

He shook his head. 'Pretty sad, right? I even took a sneak photo of you and sent it to Billy. I said, *What do you think of my Future Wife?*'

I wiped my nose on the sleeve of my hoodie. 'Raf, I left that airport calling you my Future Husband. I called you that in my head for ages!'

We laughed, a lot, for minutes. Both my hands gripped both of his.

He smiled. 'I found peace in your violence, as the song says. A lot of people feel the same. Did you know there's whole websites devoted to you? People write letters, asking for your advice. People who've been abused or bullied. They ask you to kill for them.'

'The Bad Seeds, yeah I know.'

'You give people hope they can kill their own monsters. And you killed mine. Without even knowing it.'

I got a golden surge in my chest. 'Really?' I said, pretending not to have scrolled those sites and watched those videos every day for the past two years. 'I haven't seen the letters.'

'Yeah. Dear Sweetpea, my ex is stalking me . . . Dear Sweetpea, this dude raped my mom. Dear Sweetpea, this man killed my child. They say you inspire them to take revenge. To fight back. You're a warrior.'

'It won't last,' I said. 'I'll be like that fly on Mike Pence's head. Worldwide stardom one minute, forgotten the next. Nothing lasts these days.'

I couldn't believe it. I *wouldn't* believe it. Because if what he was saying was true, then I had truly found my jewel in the desert. 'A fortune teller once told me I needed to be on my own. She said I'd have no one.'

'Then she was wrong.'

'My friend Caro, she once said I deserved to be loved.'

'Then she was right, Rhiannon.'

And suddenly everything felt better. The ache in my chest had melted away. The pain in my throat cleared. I hadn't lost him. He knew who I was, *all* of who I was, and he was still here with me, saying he loved me. I hadn't made a boo-boo this time. The avalanche had come down and it hadn't suffocated us. We'd stood on the mountainside as the deluge had washed down and we'd survived. And the sky beyond it had never looked so blue.

'You can still call me Ophelia if you want?' I said. 'If you're used to it.'

And then he kissed me, and hugged me and demanded I play with his ears. He knew who I was and we were still here, not suffocating under copious snow. We'd made it. I couldn't believe it.

'I just have to fart in front of you now and you've seen everything.'

'I heard you fart,' he said.

'What?'

'You do it in your sleep all the time.'

'Fucking hell.'

He laughed and kissed my head again, getting up off the bed, and reached in his pocket for his phone again. For a second, I thought he was about to call the cops – but he said:

'I've been looking at flights – there's one tomorrow night to Mexico City at 7.30 p.m. We can grab an internal one to Rocas from there.'

'What about the Food Gnome?'

'I'll quit – I'll finish my shift tomorrow and you can pick me up in an Uber. We can go straight to the airport.' He was genuinely excited. I hadn't seen him like this in a long time. Maybe I'd *never* seen him like this.

'What are we going to do for money?'

He shrugged. 'Work at Salomé's gallery, get a bar job, hotel jobs. I don't care. All I care about is you. We have the Tenoch cash; we can put what's left in a couple new bank accounts maybe.'

My eyebrows jumped. 'You're not so sniffy about that money now we're *both* murderers then?'

'Drop in the ocean now, isn't it?' He pulled open the bottom drawer and rummaged around under his jeans for a brown envelope. He walked back over to me, emptying the contents into my hands: two biometric passports.

'Got these a while ago. Thought we might need 'em someday, in case.'

'How?'

'Max,' he said. 'My army friend with the Slovakian connection, remember? We don't have to use them yet but, you know, if all else fails, we get our hair cut and assume these new identities.'

I read the names on each passport – a shiny, brand-new married couple from Slovakia with our faces but totally new names. All the right foil work, watermarks, fluorescence, intaglio-printed illustrations, dates, the lot; even the right font in the MRZ section under the photos. He'd used one of the machine photos of me I'd had taken when I'd had to apply for a driving licence. For forgeries, they were as good as, if not better than, my Ophelia passport.

'Max knows his stuff,' I remarked. 'I'll have to have my hair cut again. Get bangs. No, not bangs. I looked like Lord Farquaad.'

He laughed. 'I'll shave mine.'

'Your family won't like this.'

'If they love me, they'll come around.'

And he enveloped me in his warm arms again and held me so gently against him that I cried, harder than I'd cried all the time I'd been an adult. I even cried the two dogs out of the room – it was even too much for Traumatised Bob. I think it was a cry I'd been storing up since I was six and my dad walked into that hospital room, racked with guilt. And then I saw Mum, who couldn't look at me because my scarred bald head was 'so ugly'.

And I knew I *should* cry – I knew that was the thing to do at that moment when I was six and in the hospital and waiting for my parents' loving arms around me, but they didn't come. And I couldn't let it out. It was trapped under ice, waiting to thaw.

And now it had.

Sunday, 17 October 2021

Another missed call from Seren. And a text too. *Rhiannon call me. It's urgent.*

Tough shit. Call someone else's sister because I sure as shit don't have one anymore. Keep calling, go on. See if you like it, you ignorant anal flea. Whatever she had to say could wait, like I had to wait for her to show any interest in me. Like I had to make do with an answer phone message of her voice on my wedding day. So what if Géricault knew where I was – so what if they *all* knew? I was going now anyway – far away, possibly not to return. I'd spent weeks waiting to hear my sister's voice; weeks of having texts ignored and calls connecting to a non-existent number. Weeks of googling her to see if the internet could tell me what she couldn't but every time I reached a brick wall. I'd lost her like I'd lost all my family. Again.

All except Raf. He loved me. He stayed. He was all I needed now.

We were booked on the first flight leaving San Diego for Mexico City that evening. Business class, returning in a month's time. We'd sold it to Bianca that the honeymoon had 'made us realise that we wanted to be by ourselves for a bit'.

'But you can have your space here,' she argued. 'I'm out all day, most days. We can get an extension on the garage maybe if you wanted to.'

'It's not that,' said Raf. 'Mom, we need our own place.'

'But why now? You've only just got back. You have to go again?'

'Yes, Mom,' said Rafa. 'Salomé's given us a place to stay and stuff to do to help her out around the gallery. She's building a new wing. We won't be sitting idle.'

'But what about your job?'

'I'm quitting tomorrow.'

Bianca looked at me across the dinner table. 'I've already lost *my* job. And they gave me a payout. We'll be all right for money for a bit.'

She clocked our hands, gripped next to our plates on the tabletop, then looked down at her own half-empty plate and pushed it away. 'But what will you do for work? You must earn money, mi joya . . .'

'I know, but if Dad's death has taught me anything it's that life is too short to wait for retirement. We gotta grab the good times now. It doesn't make sense to work overtime in a job all day, every day, for our whole lives only to get, what, ten years of relaxation when we're in our seventies? Besides, I miss Ophelia.' He looked at me and I offered him my hand, which he kissed without further prompting.

Bianca shook her head. 'A whole month away? Just like that?'

'We'll be fine, Mom. We want to do this. Dad would have told us to go for it, wouldn't he?'

'It's not the cartel, is it? You're not being told to go somewhere or being threatened?'

'No,' said Raf firmly. 'We're not. It's just a holiday, Mom. That's all. We had one week to enjoy San Francisco and it wasn't long enough. We need a little longer. A proper break from everything.'

'From me, you mean,' Bianca harrumphed.

I gave up around this time – as soon as they start harrumphing it's like you had to carry two knapsacks up the hill cos one of you had completely given up but Raf soldiered on, the way only a soldier can, and managed to weave his magic and convince her all was well and that this was a good thing.

By morning, she returned from walking the dogs and set down their food, as happy as the proverbial Larry. Or at least, Larry's distant cousin.

'I'll be at the vax hub until five today – I said I would cover Emmanuel's shift so he can go and see his mother.'

'OK.' I yawned.

'Liv's coming over tonight with Mikey.' She looked at me across the kitchen island as I ate my Pop Tart, rearranging the contents of her handbag to incorporate her lunchbox. 'And Nico and Ariela are bringing takeout. Thought we'd get the fire pit lit in the garden and sit outside to eat. Maybe toast some smores like we did at Christmas. The kids loved that.'

'That'll be nice,' I said, my heart seeming to enlarge in my throat. I would have done almost anything to be there at that fire pit tonight.

Bianca had some kind of strange sixth sense, despite how much I smiled at her and pretended everything was normal.

'I will see you later then, mi cielo,' she said.

'Yeah,' I replied. 'See ya.' I wanted to hug her. I wanted to hold her so tightly, fearing it was the last hug from a mum

I would ever get, but to do so would have given the game away. She had to know nothing. Raf wanted it that way, for now at least.

As the front door closed, and the house was left in silence but for the soft mouthy noses the dogs made as they chomped greedily in their bowls, I said my silent goodbye to them too. I texted Billy.

Can you swing by and entertain the mutts for us at lunch? Got to go out.

Sure, he returned. *Be there at one.*

So Bianca was sorted. The dogs were sorted. All that was left to do now was wait for three o'clock and go and pick up Raf from the Food Gnome. And then we would be off. Away. Gone from here. I was fractious all morning.

It was just after lunchtime, as I was bringing all our stuff downstairs to the hallway and booking our taxi, that my phone blew up again with Seren's name and number. This time, she wouldn't stop calling, no matter how many times I declined – fifteen times in all. So eventually, I answered.

'Fucking WHAT? Suddenly it's urgent for YOU, right? YOU need to speak to ME. You ignore all my calls; I've sent you a million texts too but no, Rhiannon doesn't get an answer but when Seren rings—'

'—Rhiannon?' came the wobbly reply, followed by an unnerving delay.

'What is it? What's Géricault done now? Bugged your underpants so she can hear you piss? It better be something huge, Seren.'

'It is. It *is* huge.'

Her voice sounded funny – flat, like she was reading it from a script and was not a good actress. Like when Peter Andre tries to present TV programmes. 'Rhiannon, I don't know how to tell you this—'

Things suddenly felt a bit sinister, like the floor beneath my feet had shifted. Like the moment before a quake. Like the moment when Dad's doctor looked at me over his glasses and said, 'It's in his bones.'

I sat down on the bottom stair, holding the phone between my chin and shoulder so I could tighten the Velcro straps on my brace. 'What?' Black thoughts about Ivy had gathered, not so greyscale this time but looming and dangerous and heart-hurtingly close.

'I'm in the UK. With Claudia and Mitch.'

'How come you're in the UK?'

'Just. Listen, Rhiannon . . .'

Was she crying now? My chest cavity flooded with dread. I couldn't imagine what I was going to hear next. My first thought was Ivy; the second was Mitch.

'What's he done to her?'

'It's not Mitch . . .' There was a tremble in her voice. 'Oh God . . .' I gripped the stair rod with my weak hand. I couldn't grab it hard enough. 'Ivy's sick.'

Those two words – if an English person had said them, wouldn't matter so much but it was Seren saying them. An American. And *sick* here doesn't mean *sick* like it does in the UK – we use *sick* as in a Wetherspoons doorway on a Sunday morning. *Sick* in America means ill. *Sick* means dying.

'Claudia told me a couple weeks ago that she'd taken Ivy in for some tests because she was off her food and had spiking temperatures. She got this rash on the backs of her legs and the doctor kept fobbing Claudia off with viral conditions but she kept pestering them for more tests and made an emergency appointment when the rash spread to her neck. A blood test confirmed she had JMML. Juvenile myelomonocytic leukaemia.'

All I heard was blah blah blah blah blah — *leukaemia*.

'Leukaemia? That's cancer.'

'A rare form of blood cancer. It affects children under four. Abnormal cells start in the bone marrow and it's difficult to treat but if she has stem cell treatment the prognosis is good. So I flew over here, about a week ago, to see if I was a match, being her only living blood relative . . .'

'You've been in the UK for a *week*? And you've had a test? I can't get my head around all this. Are you a match? You must be . . .'

The delay on the other end was getting longer. 'I'm not, no. I just got my results back today. She needs a more direct relative. Like a parent.'

I'd spent so long worrying about Mitch hurting Ivy, I hadn't factored in the other major dementor that had blighted our family: cancer.

'So . . . I would be her only match?'

'Yes.'

'Jesus. So what are you saying? What happens now?'

'If she doesn't get a stem cell transplant, she'll die. Within weeks.'

Prior to that moment the worst pain I'd ever felt was heaving her into the world. But nothing could prepare me for hearing Seren say that about her. That that little pink jellybean in the incubator – that tiny smiley two-year-old who had my skin and my bones and my teeth – was going to die. Was going to leave this world without me. 'No, no, no, please, this is a lie. This is a dream. I'm going to wake up now . . .'

Seren carried on talking for me, like I was six and she was eleven again and we were in that rehab centre in Gloucester and she was guessing what toy I wanted to play with and relaying it to the adults. Always Sylvanians.

The middle of my body was a church of hot fear, and my stomach churned. I didn't know whether to puke or cry. My hand clenched, seeking a knife to stab with – but who to stab? I couldn't 'kill' cancer. I couldn't go after anyone – this was life; this was just something that happened. No one to blame. I couldn't even blame myself.

'Please tell me this is a joke. I'll fucking hate you but I'll get over it.'

'It's not a joke.' Seren sniffed down the phone. 'It's spreading – she's getting worse.'

'Why aren't you a match; you're as good as me? We've got the same blood, the same parents.'

'It needs to be *her* parent. I'm so sorry.'

'Why the hell has she got cancer, Seren?'

'I don't know. It's a crapshoot, isn't it? Cancer's cancer. Nothing caused this; it's just something that happens to some kids.'

I was up off the stair, pacing the hallway, although I couldn't feel my feet. 'It's punishment, isn't it? This is God, punishing *me* for what *I've* done. Keston said I'll reap what I sow. This is fucking it.

'Don't think like that.'

'He saves River, and he takes Ivy instead.'

'What river? Rhi, listen to me – you can't do anything—'

'Yes, I can. I'm her mother. She came out of *me*. Chances are I've got the exact cells she needs.' I looked at our collection of bags waiting to go with us to Mexico; to freedom and safety.

'You can't come here—'

'Of course, I can. Airspace is open again now. *You* got to England, so I can come to you.'

'I don't mean you literally can't fly; I mean . . . you can't come back *here*.'

'Why the bloody hell did you tell me if you don't want me to come over? What am I meant to do from here, pray? Send happy thoughts? Light a fucking candle? Did you expect me to hear this and do nothing? Where the hell else are they going to get a match for her?'

'There's a register and a waiting list—'

'How long would she have to wait?'

'Until a suitable match becomes available.'

'That could take months, *years*. She's a baby!'

'They'll arrest you the second you land.'

'No, they won't; everyone thinks I'm dead. And I look completely different now. I've got long hair and better lenses. *You* barely recognised me when you saw me again. And I have a new passport, new papers, new name. And everyone's still wearing masks there, right?'

'Even so—'

'—even better. Does Claudia know about me? Does she know anything?'

'She thinks you're dead, like the rest of the known world.'

'Except Géricault.' Seren was sobbing by this point. 'There are no winners here, are there?'

The road had finally run out, as suddenly and as unexpectedly as that. Everything I'd been worrying about was immaterial. Ivy was dying. All other bets were off.

'This is worth it, isn't it? If anything is worth getting caught for, it's this.'

'Oh God,' she sniffed. '*Don't come here, please.*' She said it so quietly I could barely hear it.

'We can't let my baby die.'

'No. We can't. You're right – you *have* to come. And even if you do get caught at the airport, just tell them . . . they'll get the tests fast-tracked I'm sure if it's life or death. Do you know when you might be able to get here?'

'No. A week? A month. I've no idea.'

'Well, which is it, a week? A month?'

'I don't know, Seren. Do you think Claudia would let me stay with her?' No answer. 'No, probably not seeing as I cut her nephew into six pieces and buried him in someone's garden. OK, text me her address anyway. I'll worry about it when I get there.'

'She's moved out of London now – she's in the Cotswolds.'

I flicked her over to speaker while I googled flights to London that left tonight, but as I was waiting for the Virgin Atlantic page to open, a thought occurred. This couldn't be a trap, could it?

'Last time you called me, you said Géricault had bugged your house.'

'Yes. She *was* bugging me. I heard that noise you told me about but I couldn't find it. She also put a tracker on my car and in the lining of my coat. I couldn't be sure when it was safe. That's why I've been ignoring your calls.'

'. . . and now I talk to you and find you've flown to England, staying with Claudia, and my daughter is suddenly "sick".'

'What are you saying? That I'm lying? I'm *here*, with her, right now. I'm in the same house! I've been going to the hospital appointments; I've had needles stuck in every part of me for the past week.'

'All right, all right.'

'You honestly think I'd lie about a child dying? Claudia's taking her to have her hair cut off next week, so she's not too traumatised when, you know, it falls out with the chemo.'

My chest pulsed painfully. Seren would lie about *me* being dead but she wouldn't risk Ivy, no way. She cared about her as much as I did. But Géricault – I didn't know much about her. I didn't know *what* she was capable of.

'Are you sure this isn't an elaborate ruse to get me back there? Something Géricault has cooked up with Claudia maybe and strung you along for the ride? You're stupid enough to fall for something like that.'

'No one in their right mind is going to pretend that little girl is ill when she's not.'

'I want to see her.'

'Claudia?'

'No, Ivy. I want to see a picture of her. I want to see the track marks on her arms from where they've taken blood. She'll have bruises too . . .' I swallowed – I thought I was going to be sick. 'Take a picture on your phone.'

'She's asleep. It's five in the morning here. Why do you think I'm whispering?' More delay. Scratching sounds.

'Because I don't believe you.'

Seren lost her temper. 'For God's sakes, I'll text you a photo of her when she wakes up, all right? Gimme a few hours at least.'

And the line went dead.

Sure enough, around four hours later, two texts pinged through, one after the other. A picture and then a message. The message said, *Happy now?* with a sad face emoji next to it. The picture was a fuzzy, badly lit photo of my baby girl, lying in her bed, and as white as a sheet, grey circles around her beautiful brown eyes. She was wrapped in a Winnie the Pooh blanket with a pink beanie tight on her head. She looked terrible.

OK, I text back. *Message received.*

Tell me when you're coming so I can look out for you. And one kiss. Seren never added a kiss, not to my texts.

Nothing else mattered. Killing wasn't what I lived for. The only thing I could think of was getting to the UK and saving my baby. I'd get stabbed with a thousand needles if that was going to keep her little heart beating in this world. Even if they caught me en route, so what? Some things mattered more than freedom. Raf's abuela once told him I would strengthen him. But ever since a doctor had told me Ivy existed, she had weakened me. Cos that's love, isn't it? Love means you'd give up everything for someone. Like Rafael was giving up everything for me. The problem was, he had weakened me too. I was on autopilot. I said goodbye to the dogs, fed the fish, kicked around the house with only my own broken brain to keep me company and tried to decide what to do but every thought brought me back to the obvious: I had to go.

'Uber for OJ White?'

I didn't look back at the house as the driver – Carl – helped me heave my bags into the trunk. I put Richard E. Grunt in my hoodie pocket and got in the back and kept my face forwards. Not daring to look back at Rafael's bags sitting there expectantly by the door.

Don't look. Just don't look.

I sat in the back of the car with that terrible song playing on the scratchy radio in the front – Evanescence, 'Bring Me to Life'. Carl was trying to rock out respectfully, mouthing all the words. We passed endless pavements thronging with families or workers on their lunchbreaks. I wasn't looking at them. Or at the happy couples; Latino husbands wearing Padres shirts or Lakers vests. Not looking at their happy wives. I was *not* staying in San Diego. I was going to England – alone – and then, when I'd done what I was put on this earth to do, I was going to jail.

There were so many Latino men about. So many reminders of him. Gorgeous, muscular, brown shining-eyed guilt trips everywhere I looked.

Get out of my way. Get away from me.

He needs you. Rafael needs you as much as you need him.

No, he doesn't. He will be fine. Ivy needs me more.

I tried to lose myself in my daily ten minutes of meditation; focusing on my breaths – trying to clear a space in the mess. Hold for seven, out for four. Release slowly. *I am here. I am breathing. I will save Ivy the same way I saved River. It's all on me.*

I leant my hot forehead against the window, trying to will myself to feel the peace that I eventually felt on that flight out of New York twenty-two months ago. Doing the right thing never felt right to me but I was definitely in right's vicinity now. Rafael *would* be better off without me. And when they catch me, which they will, I will keep his name out of it. Nobody needs a serial killer for a wife. The only person who needed me, at that moment, was Ivy.

'Don't look back,' I muttered as the car sat in traffic and the song changed – Beyoncé. 'Dangerously in Love'.

I stared at my broken heart tattoo, covering it with my sleeve.

I checked through my Ophelia passport. Stared at the picture Tenoch had taken against his office wall – the same wall all that money was hidden behind. Stared at the eagle emblem on the front. As I put it back, I noticed the pink rosebud from Carmel, all dry and crispy at the bottom of the bag. Reminders everywhere. He was in the sunshine and the sky. In the lingering kiss of lovers at a bus stop. In the faces of the young Latinos walking towards the skatepark with their boards. In the warm cinnamon dusting of a hastily bought cappuccino on the way – a cappuccino I drank while it was still roasting hot to feel the pain in my throat that I didn't want to feel in my heart.

'Forget him. Look forward, not back.'

Carl – who had dreads and a melee of empty candy wrappers on his passenger seat – gave me eyes in the rear-view mirror. 'Little pep talk?'

'Yeah.'

'I do the same. It's a good thing to do – to get your ass out the door. What is it, fear of flying? I had an uncle who was afraid. He had this neat trick for getting through it – you start by—'

'—how many stars do I have to give you *not* to talk to me?'

'Five.'

'Fine.'

He didn't say another word, leaving me to concentrate on what I had to do – get to the airport, get on a plane and leave.

We came to a stop at the lights on Marshall Street – the street the Food Gnome was on. The traffic was stupid-busy and horns blared in every lane.

Don't look at it, that's all.

But as much as I tried, I couldn't turn my head away. The building loomed into view; the broken sign proud on top of it. It had lost a few more letters since I'd last seen it. It was the 'Foo n me' now.

The car slowed down. The car stopped.

'Why are we stopping?'

Carl looked at me in the mirror. 'Am I allowed to say?'

'Yes!'

'Cos the traffic is making me?'

I looked ahead – a sea of red tail lights. The overhead matrix sign said 'Collision Ahead'.

'Ugh, fuck my fucking life!'

The pain was physical, in my throat and my chest and my head. My lungs felt too small for all the air I needed and there wasn't nearly enough in that car. . It was the same feeling as when I boarded the plane to come back here; when I *didn't* go to Ivy. This time I could stop this. The doors were openable. I needed to see him. I needed him to stop me going to *her*.

I needed him to hold me. Hold me back, please hold me back. I can't go, I *can't*. I have to. *I CAN'T!*

'Pull in here and let me out.'

'You wanna stop at the Food 'n' Home?'

'Yeah.'

'You got it.' Carl swung into the parking lot, helping me with my bags.

'I'm sorry I was rude,' I sniffed, holding back my tears as long as I could before one betrayed me. I handed him a $100 tip. 'Bad day.'

He tipped his cap. 'Thank you. I hope today goes your way.'

And he got back in the car and swung right out again.

So much for *head down, keep going*. I wheeled my bag into the store and marched straight up to the staff office. But I was collared en route.

'Hey, Phee, how you doing?' said Luiz, bright and breezy as ever despite his crummy wages as deputy store manager. The true store manager, Toby, was 'off sick with Covid'. A month ago, it'd been a leg injury following a car accident. Six weeks ago, a toothache. Nine weeks ago, a hangover.

'I'm OK, thanks,' I said, clearing my eyes and forcing myself to ask, 'How about you?'

'Yeah, good. Did Rafael tell you Natalia's working on our second bun? Yeah, Ángel's gonna be a big brother!'

'Ahh, congratulations, I'm so happy for you guys.' It was so much easier to fake enthusiasm when he was at our house for a cookout and I had copious amounts of alcohol in my system.

Once the rest of the staff in the office knew I was there, their faces brightened and they all came over to greet me, one by one, still in awe over my Bean Qween antics that some of them had witnessed first-hand.

> *She went down like a sack of*
> *shit, man!*

> *How did you do that?*
> *Were you a pro?*

> *Did Rafael tell you we sold*
> *out of beans that day?*

> *Yo, League of Their Own!*
> *Where d'you learn to pitch*
> *like that?*

> *You related to Blake Snell?*

Raf appeared from the staff bathroom. We locked eyes, then he saw my bag. 'Hey, you're early. I thought our Uber was coming at . . .' My face must have changed because so did his.

'We have to talk,' I said.

And one by one, everyone else 'had to get back to work'.

'What is it? What's happened?'

I felt a hand on my back. Luiz, sriracha blob on his tie, upper lip all sweaty. 'Guys, if you wanna talk, you can use Toby's office.'

'My lunch's finished, Lu,' said Rafael.

'Doesn't matter, go on. I mean it. Take as long as you need.'

Luiz practically pushed us both into Toby's dank little work-room with the piles of paper everywhere, badly stacked box files on wobbly shelves and the two used coffee mugs furring over on the windowsill, and shut the door. I sat down on the creaky swivel chair. Raf didn't move far beyond the door.

I couldn't speak – the words wouldn't come. All I wanted to do was hold him and cry.

'Baby?' He knelt down before me on the carpet and held onto my knees.

'What's going on? Our flight's not until seven, where are you going now?'

I shook my head. 'Change of plan. My sister called. She's in the UK. Ivy's sick. Leukaemia sick.'

His eyes widened. 'Oh my God.'

'Seren went over to see if she was a stem cell match but she isn't. I'm her only hope.' I opened my texts and showed him the screen but he was already turning his head away. 'I'm not lying.'

'I *know* you're not. Were you just gonna go?'

'The next flight to London is at six.'

'You were just gonna go, *on your own*?'

'I have to. I can't let my baby die.'

'What about me, huh? You were just gonna go over and leave me here?'

'What do you want me to do?'

He shook his head. 'I don't know. Are they sure it's cancer?'

'Seren wouldn't lie to me.'

'Wouldn't she?'

'No,' I said, with a wobble. I flicked open my phone again – Seren had sent through screenshots of a couple of forms – hospital admissions forms. Prescriptions for painkilling medication. 'Look at the photo of her. She's *grey*.'

'All of this could be fake. You said you and your sister haven't got on for years. She lied about shooting you dead; she informed on you to the cops in the first place. Isn't it reasonable to presume she's lying to you about this? To catch you out?

What's the one thing that would get your ass back to the UK under the jurisdiction of the British police?'

'Ivy,' I muttered. 'But what if she's *not* lying and I stay here and just let her die? I'd never forgive myself. I have to go. I don't want to; I don't want to leave you and yes, I love you more than I thought I could ever love anyone . . . but if she's dying . . . what would *you* do?'

He searched the carpet with his eyes and took a series of long, deep breaths. And when he eventually spoke, it was the most beautiful collection of words I'd ever heard. 'I'd go and save my little girl. And if I got there, and I found out they were lying, I'd kidnap her and I'd burn their fucking house down.'

It was my turn for the jaw drop.

'You with me?' he asked, his hand wavering in midair as it waited for mine, and though it was probably the boo-boo to end all boo-boos, and getting Ivy out of there was going to be nigh-on impossible, I reached out and took it.

And everything suddenly felt better. The ache in my chest melted away. The pain in my throat cleared. And the thorn in my side had vanished.

He held my head and kissed me once, right on the top where my scar was, and looked at me. 'Come on. Let's go get our little girl.'

I smiled at him and buried my face in his warm neck. And I knew, beyond any doubt, that he meant it.

'You haven't finished your shift,' I reminded him.

'I'll quit now.' He shrugged. 'We're not busy.'

'What if police are waiting for me at Heathrow?'

'Then I'll be with you.'

'What if they arrest you too?'

'We can cook up a story – I never knew your true identity.

You had surgery, you lied a lot. It's fine. I don't care. As long as we're together, right?'

'What if we *do* get through security?' I asked.

'Well, either we get there and it *is* all some hoax and somehow your sister's falsified Ivy's medical notes, or . . . we get there and it's legit. And she *is* dying. But you can save her life.'

'It's been worth it then. Hasn't it?'

'Yes. But I'll be with you the whole way. I'm not leaving you. I wouldn't.'

I bit the inside of my cheek. 'But it means. . .'

Neither of us wanted to say it. The words were too comfortable inside our mouths where they couldn't do any outside damage. We gripped our hands tighter so the hearts fused again.

As always, Raf was the brave one. 'You'll have to hand yourself in. And you'll go to jail. Not like we can find a surgeon to harvest your stem cells and have them Door Dashed to the hospital I guess, is it?'

'No,' I sniffed. 'There's no other way.'

'Say Rafael loves me. Say it back to me. I want you to believe it.'

'No.'

'Say "Rafael loves me."'

'No, that's weird.'

'No, it's not. I wanna hear you say that you know I love you.'

'You love me. Ha ha.'

'Say it again and *mean* it. No one's around; it's just us.'

'Rafael loves me.'

'Say it again . . .'

'Rafael loves me.'

'Again.'

'No.'

'SAY IT.'

'Because Rafael loves me.'

'Once more.'

'BECAUSE YOU FUCKING LOVE ME!'

'Damn right.' He hugged me and kissed my shoulder in our hug. 'Donde quiera que vayas, llevas mi corazón contigo, mi amor.'

Wherever you go, you take my heart with you. I couldn't speak.

One hand rested on the office door and with the other, he reached for mine. 'Wanna watch me hand in my notice?'

He draped an arm around my shoulder as we exited Toby's office. 'What do I call you now? I mean, you're still Ophelia on your current passport . . .'

'You can call me what you want in private. I've been called many things: Phoebe, Phee Phee, Felicity, Antonia. Rhianna.'

'Antonia?'

'Yeah. But I don't mind you calling me the wrong name. You're used to OJ or Phee. So call me OJ or Phee.'

'OK.' He smiled, rubbing his nose against mine.

We passed the Pop Tarts. I reached out for a box, remembering we were just out at home but then I remembered we were only going there to get his bags. Home wasn't home anymore. Home was wherever he was.

'It's gonna be all right.' He smiled, obviously sensing my discomfort. He kissed my temple. 'It's all gonna be OK.'

'HEY WETBACK TRASH!'

410

'You don't know that, Raf.'

'No, but we can kid ourselves for a while, can't we?'

> *'HEY, YOU THERE! SPIC*
> *LOVER!'*

'Billy's going to see to the dogs. Bianca won't forget to feed the fish, will she?'

'I'll text her from the airport.'

> *'I'VE BEEN WAITING*
> *FOR YOU!'*

'*SHE'S GOT A GUN!'*

'What's going on?'

'Oh fuck it's her . . .'

'*GET DOWN!'*
'*EVERYONE MOVE!'*

The words swirled around us. I turned around and she was right there, at the end of the aisle – Mama Fratelli. Andi Smith-Lansing. She was yelling and screaming and marching towards me, a small gun in her hand pointed straight at me. Unwavering. Dead eyes. Arm outstretched. Before I could blink, an enormous *BANG* rang out that seemed to split the warehouse roof in two. A second later, I hit the floor – left shoulder to cold hard marble.

'FUCKIN' PIECE OF
SHIT!'

'GRAB IT! GET HER,
MAN!'

Another shot rang out, and the *BANG!* reverberated again from the warehouse walls, and then another, before someone yelled—

'GET DOWN! HE'S BEEN HIT!'

Raf was on top of me. We lay there, surrounded by shouting and chaos and boxes of Pop Tarts falling from shelves and glass breaking and cans rolling, my back was pressed to the coldness. I looked over and the guy in the blue shirt – the deputy manager, Luiz, lay an arm's length away, not breaking his stare. The front of his blue shirt bloomed red. He was gone.

I turned my head, my face smothered by Raf's hair. He wasn't moving.

'Raf?' I couldn't say it again – I couldn't breathe; he was too heavy on top of me. Too still. I tried to push him off but he was dead weight. I tried to wake him up, pull his shirt, slap his face, but he wouldn't respond. Both my hands were covered in warm red wet.

I'd never been so scared of a dead man in my life.

Acknowledgments

Jenny Savill, Silé Edwards and all at Andrew Nurnberg Agency.

Editors Katie Seaman, Eldes Tran, Cat Camacho and all the team at HQ, inc. Hanako Peace for their support.

The Fam, especially Matthew Snead for always being my first reader.

Juliana Galvis and Paola Gómez for facilitating and executing the sensitivity read so brilliantly.

Bill and Ted for forcing me away from my desk now and again to go walkies so I know there's always more to life than tapping away at a keyboard.

All the bloggers, readers and reviewers who have waited so impatiently for these last two books. Without your constant nagging and enthusiasm, I'd have put my pen down long ago.

Can't get enough of everyone's favourite serial-killer-next-door, Rhiannon Lewis?

Don't miss the rest of the Sweetpea series

SWEETPEA

Although her childhood was haunted by a famous crime, Rhiannon's life is normal now that her celebrity has dwindled. By day her job as an editorial assistant is demeaning and unsatisfying. By evening she dutifully listens to her friend's plans for marriage and babies whilst secretly making a list.

A kill list.

From the man on the Lidl checkout who always mishandles her apples, to the driver who cuts her off on her way to work, to the people who have got it coming, Rhiannon's ready to get her revenge.

Because the girl everyone overlooks might be able to get away with murder…

IN BLOOM

Rhiannon's back and killing for two . . .

Rhiannon Lewis has successfully fooled the world and
framed her cheating fiancé Craig for the depraved and
bloody killing spree she committed. She should be ecstatic
that she's free.

Except for one small problem. She's pregnant with her
ex-lover's child. The ex-lover she only recently chopped up
and buried in her in-laws garden. And as much as Rhiannon
wants to continue making her way through her kill lists,
a small voice inside is trying to make her stop.

But can a killer's urges ever really be curbed?

Victim. Murderer. Serial Killer.
What next?

DEAD HEAD

Can a serial killer ever lose their taste for murder?

Since confessing to her bloody murder spree Rhiannon Lewis, the now-notorious Sweetpea killer, has been feeling out-of-sorts.

Having fled the UK on a cruise ship to start her new life, Rhiannon should be feeling happy. But it's hard to turn over a new leaf when she's stuck in an oversized floating tin can with the Gammonati and screaming kids. Especially when they remind her of Ivy – the baby she gave up for a life carrying on killing.

Rhiannon is all at sea. She's lost her taste for blood but is it really gone for good? Maybe Rhiannon is realising that there's more to life than death . . .

And don't miss the twisty standalone crime thriller that will keep you guessing

THE ALIBI GIRL

**JOANNE HAYNES HAS A SECRET.
THAT IS NOT HER REAL NAME.**

And there's more. Her flat isn't hers. Her cats aren't hers.
Even her hair isn't really hers.

Nor is she any of the other women she pretends to be. Not
the bestselling romance novelist who gets her morning snack
from the doughnut van on the seafront. Nor the pregnant
woman in the dental surgery. Nor the chemo patient in
the supermarket for whom the cashier feels ever so sorry.
They're all just alibis.

In fact, the only thing that's real about Joanne is that
nobody can know who she really is.

But someone has got too close. It looks like her alibis have
begun to run out . . .

Dear Reader,

We hope you enjoyed reading this book. If you did, we'd be so appreciative if you left a review. It really helps us and the author to bring more books like this to you.

Here at HQ Digital we are dedicated to publishing fiction that will keep you turning the pages into the early hours. Don't want to miss a thing? To find out more about our books, promotions, discover exclusive content and enter competitions you can keep in touch in the following ways:

JOIN OUR COMMUNITY:

Sign up to our new email newsletter: http://smarturl.it/SignUpHQ

Read our new blog www.hqstories.co.uk

𝕏 https://twitter.com/HQStories

🅕 www.facebook.com/HQStories

BUDDING WRITER?

We're also looking for authors to join the HQ Digital family!
Find out more here:

https://www.hqstories.co.uk/want-to-write-for-us/

Thanks for reading, from the HQ Digital team